Every Day Filled with Hope

A Weldon Novel
Book 2

ENDORSEMENTS

Every Day Filled with Hope by Shelia Stovall is just that—a story full of hope and second chances. Stovall knows little towns, and through her words you become an honorary citizen of Weldon, Kentucky. Her characters will grab your heart as you follow them along their story roads through adventures and challenges, all the way to Africa and back. You will love visiting Weldon and finding out what happens next.

—**Ann H. Gabhart**, bestselling author of *Along a Storied Trail*

Shelia Stovall has another hit with the second novel in her Weldon, Kentucky, series. *Every Day Filled with Hope* is a page-turner served up with those famous fried fruit pies, a taste of all things Southern, and a surfeit of hope. Mrs. Stovall delves more deeply into the lives of supporting characters introduced in Book One of the series. Each brings their own stories and trials to light. Mrs. Stovall proves she isn't afraid to tackle tough issues and handles them with grace. From Weldon to Africa and back to Weldon, the twists, turns, and relatable characters will leave you longing for Book Three.

—**Debra DuPree Williams**, award-winning author of *Grave Consequences, A Charlotte Graves Mystery.*

EVERY DAY FILLED WITH HOPE

SHELIA STOVALL

To Brenda,
"Hope never fails"
Romans 5:5
Shelia Stovall

ELK LAKE PUBLISHING INC
PUBLISHING THE POSITIVE
Plymouth, Massachusetts

Cover and Interior Design: Derinda Babcock, Deb Haggerty

Editor(s): Michele Chynoweth, Cristel Phelps, Deb Haggerty

Author Represented By: Credo Communications LLC

PUBLISHED BY: Elk Lake Publishing, Inc., 35 Dogwood Drive, Plymouth, MA 02360, 2022

Library Cataloging Data

Names: Stovall, Shelia (Shelia Stovall)

Every Day Filled with Hope / Shelia Stovall

392 p. 23cm × 15cm (9in × 6 in.)

ISBN-13: 978-1-64949-525-9 (paperback) | 978-1-64949-526-6 (trade paperback) | 978-1-64949-527-3 (e-book)

Key Words: small towns, missions trips, Africa, salvation message, relationships, cancer, romance

Library of Congress Control Number: 2022935856 Fiction

And how shall they preach unless they are sent? As it is written: How beautiful are the feet of them that preach the gospel of peace, and bring glad tidings of good things! (Romans 10:15, NKJV).

DEDICATION

In memory of Don Phillips. I'll never forget his friendship, his love for the Lord, and his ministry. Don invited me to join a short-term mission team to Niger, Africa, and then taught me how to be a witness for Jesus Christ. May the seeds Don sowed in my life continue to reap a harvest.

ACKNOWLEDGMENTS

Thank you to my talented editors, Jamie Clarke Chavez, Michele Chynoweth, Cristel Phelps, and Deb Haggerty. I consider you all a gift from God.

I am thankful for my agent Pete Ford, with Credo Communications. I appreciate his wisdom and guidance.

The fingerprints of my two critique partners, Kelly Liberto and Carrie Padgett, are all over this novel. Thank you, friends, for sharing your talent.

Much appreciation is extended to award-winning authors Ann H. Gabhart and Debra DuPree Williams for endorsing this novel. Your friendship and support are blessings.

This novel would not exist without Don and Janice Phillips's invitation to travel to Niger, Africa. Don Phillips has left us for heaven, but Janice Phillips continues to be my friend and mentor. I cannot disclose the name of the African missionaries with whom I've served as it might put their lives in danger, but I appreciate their patience and the many sacrifices they make to serve the Lord. I'll remind my readers this is a work of fiction, and I assure you my missionary friends took great care of our team members. I did not experience the same situations as my characters.

Thank you to Elk Lake Publishing for taking another chance on me. I am grateful to be among such a talented group of authors.

I am grateful for the members of the Weldon Fan Club and to the readers who bought my first novel, *Every Window Filled with Light*. Thank you to those who took the time to write a review. You will never know how much your words lift me up.

Finally, thank you to my husband. He is long-suffering, putting up with scorched meals and poor housekeeping while I escape to Weldon, Kentucky. I love our simple life on the farm.

Let the words of my mouth and the meditation of my heart Be acceptable in Your sight, O Lord, my strength and my Redeemer. (Psalm 19:14 NKJV)

It is all for him.

CHAPTER ONE—CASEY

The plain white envelope sat in a stack of Christmas cards on the kitchen island. Casey Bledsoe took in the unfamiliar address, the loopy script. The writing looked girlish. Like a teenager's.

Casey's legs weakened. Her lungs stopped working, and she slid to a counter stool.

Funny, the sensations that hit. The smell of the peppermint-chocolate fudge on the plate before her. "Santa Baby" playing low over the speakers. The coolness of the marble counter.

How many times had she imagined her daughter sitting here with her? Now, just one month after her baby girl would have turned the magic age of eighteen—this envelope. Looking like the one Casey had imagined and dreamed of and prayed for.

And prayed against.

Casey ran a hand through her hair, remembering the red fuzz on the baby's head. How the color had matched her own ...

She closed her eyes. *Get a grip. It's only a Christmas letter.*

With resolve, she pulled out a single piece of white-lined paper.

Even before she unfolded it, she knew.

> Dear Ms. Bledsoe,
>
> My name is Madison, and I've been told you are my birth mother.

Casey's breath caught. Tears stung her eyes, and the paper slipped from her grasp. She hunched over the counter, pulling in air until she could retrieve the letter with trembling fingers.

> Mom said you gave permission for me to learn your identity when I turned eighteen.

The terrible memories flooded back. Clutching the tiny baby for one last time, kissing her wrinkled hands. Eighteen years then had seemed like forever. Had seemed ... safe.

> I can't remember a time when I didn't know I'm adopted, and I've always wondered about you. Do you ever think about me?

Casey strangled a sob.

> I never would have guessed my biological mother used to model. Wow! You're famous and beautiful. I'm not like you at all other than we share the same shade of hair, but mine is wild and unmanageable.
>
> I'm athletic, a basketball player.
>
> I have many questions. I hope you're willing to answer them. Please understand—I don't need money. And I'm very happy. My parents are the best, and I love them. My mom will always be my mom.
>
> Will you write me back? I don't want to ruin your life or anything.
>
> I hope to hear from you soon.
>
> Madison Warren

Madison. Madison Warren. Casey stared at her daughter's name until the letters blurred. The kitchen clock's hands circled as Casey reread the letter, over and over. She'd never tell her about her father.

Casey covered her face with her hands as she remembered the horrible night. A river of memories poured from the secret chamber of her heart. She'd screamed, "No!" but the brute had ignored her pleas. A chill settled over her as she recalled his strength, his soulless gray eyes, and her innocence lost forever.

Casey's breath caught. *What if her daughter resembled ... the monster?*

Pain from her ankle called her back to reality. "Meow." Fats rubbed his pointy chin against her leg.

"Sorry, baby. Are you hungry?" Casey rubbed the place where Fats had clawed her and ran her sleeve across her cheek. The cat's ragged black ears were down, and he yowled.

After filling his bowl with kibble, Casey lifted the phone, then halted. *News this shocking should be shared in person.* It was past midnight, but she was sure Emma wouldn't mind being awakened for this.

Ten minutes later, she stood at the back door of her best friend's old Victorian, spying two pink bicycles leaning against the porch. Emma must have picked them up for Hallie and Callie, the twin girls she'd fostered a few weeks ago.

A dog barked. "Shhh. It's me." Casey scurried toward the two dog houses. Max and Buster licked her palms. The two rottweilers belonged to Harley, a thirteen-year-old girl Emma fostered last year. Emma had a gift for rescuing people and dogs.

Casey scratched the dogs' soft ears and whispered. "We don't want to wake up the neighborhood." Mr. McCullough, the self-appointed neighborhood security guard, lived next door. Casey held her breath as she stared at his dark windows. When no lights appeared, she exhaled.

She dug through her purse and found her phone. After four rings, light streamed from the downstairs bedroom window. "Casey! What's wrong?"

"I'm fine, but I have news."

"Did Daniel propose?" Emma's sleepy voice lifted.

A cloud extinguished the moonlight as a wave of sadness welled up inside of her. "No." Casey returned to the porch. "I'm at your back door."

"You're here?"

"Hurry. My feet are freezing."

"I'm on my way."

As Casey waited, her thoughts drifted to Daniel, and her stomach clenched. How would she ever find the words to tell him about her daughter? *Madison.* A surge of hope lifted her spirits, and she bounced on her heels. *My daughter's name is Madison.*

Emma swung the antique door open, and it banged the wall. Her shapeless terrycloth robe hung loose on her thin frame. "What's going on? You've been crying."

Casey stepped inside and gripped Emma's shoulders. "I got a letter today."

"Who sends letters anymore?"

"My daughter."

Emma's hand flew to her chest. "Whoa! Tell me everything before I stop breathing." Emma led her to the suede sofa. "How are you?"

"Almost hopeful."

"Almost?" Her best friend gave her an understanding smile.

"I'm afraid."

"Oh, hon. What does her letter say?" Emma pushed her shoulder-length brown hair behind her ear.

"She told me her parents are the best—"

"A prayer answered."

"Absolutely. Her name is Madison Warren."

"Madison," Emma whispered.

Casey knew her best friend had faithfully prayed for her daughter through the years too, though she'd never mentioned her. Instead, she'd loved Casey like a sister and pulled her to the light, time and again, as depression threatened to overtake her.

"It's time to stop being afraid." Emma curled her feet up under her.

"I want that—more than anything."

"You used to be fearless."

"Having five older brothers will do that for you." Casey placed her palm over the ache in her heart. "How can I explain this to my family?"

"They love you."

"Daniel might drop me like a hot skillet when he learns I gave away my baby."

"He'll understand when you tell him everything."

"I doubt it."

"You were traumatized and barely an adult."

"What if she'd ended up with awful parents?" Casey pulled at her hair.

"But now you know she's okay!"

Casey removed the envelope from her bag and gave it to Emma.

"Are you sure you want me to read it?"

"You're the only one who knows everything. I need someone to tell me what to do."

Emma removed the letter from the envelope and read with her mouth open. "She's curious."

"I can't tell her about her father." Casey chewed her manicured nail.

Emma pulled Casey's hand down without looking up. "She's probably anxious to hear from you. Are you happy she wrote?"

"Of course."

"Start there."

"Okay, but I want to meet her, to get to know her, and to do that, I have to tell everyone."

"Waiting won't make this easier, and who knows what will happen if the paparazzi get a whiff of this."

"No one cares about an ex-model."

"You were a super-model, and you're still famous."

"No, I'm not."

"Then why do women travel from all over the country to Weldon, Kentucky, to visit your boutique?" Emma fiddled with her robe. "I mean, your clothes are chic, but ..." She lifted a shoulder.

"You may have a point." *Everyone loves a scandal.*

"You'd better bless your biscuits she didn't show up in Weldon without warning instead of sending a letter."

Casey closed her eyes. "Her father ..." She couldn't bear to say his name. "... is still in the tabloids. What if someone links her to him?"

Emma gave her a stern look. "You need to tell your parents before you leave for Africa."

Casey's stomach lurched. The mission trip. *I'm the last person to be preaching to anyone.* "I'm not going. I never should have signed up."

"Daniel asked you to go—it's his dream."

"And my nightmare. The pictures of Niger look like a different universe. What was I thinking?"

Emma elbowed her. "That Dr. Sparky wants to play doctor with your boyfriend?"

Casey gave her a vinegar look. "I trust Daniel."

"Tell that to someone who doesn't know you. I've seen the way you scowl at Sparky."

"I overheard her say something ugly about me before I signed up for the mission team."

Emma narrowed her eyes. "What did she say?"

"It doesn't matter." Casey sighed. "I'm glad a doctor is going, even if she is cute. But perky does get old after a while."

Emma rolled her eyes. "Yeah, it would be more fun to travel with a sourpuss." She opened the letter again. "I wish she'd sent a picture."

"What if she has..." Casey gulped. "Jansen's eyes?" Saying his name made her shudder.

"It won't matter, and I can tell by her description, she's all you."

"I still have nightmares."

"Oh, Casey." Emma gave her a tender look. "Maybe we can look for Madison on social media?"

Casey shook her head. "No. I need to take her in slowly."

They sat in the stillness for a long time. When the antique grandfather clock chimed two bells, Emma yawned.

Casey sighed. "You need to get back to bed if you're going to open the library on time in the morning."

"I won't return to the library until after the school's Christmas break."

"Lucky you."

"Take the day off to tell your parents. It's your store."

"I can't leave Tricia to deal with disappointed customers who drove all the way to Weldon to meet Cassandra."

Emma pulled her up from the sofa. "Go home and get some rest."

"Okay." She hugged Emma again. "I have a daughter named Madison." Her heart lifted.

"Thank you, Lord," Emma said.

"And all the guardian angels from heaven."

Casey sat up the rest of the night, trying to write a response. When the pink haze of dawn brightened the horizon, she placed her head on the kitchen island's cool granite. A pile of crumpled false starts surrounded her. After gathering them up and tossing them into the trash, she trudged upstairs, defeated. The flying geese quilt featuring sapphire triangles against a snow-white background caught her eye as she passed the guest bedroom. She'd been too excited about her modeling contract and the ticket to New York to appreciate the parting gift from Granny. Words from the past floated back to her. *"If you ever need a hug, wrap up in this quilt, and you'll feel my arms around you."*

The token of love always comforted her. She lifted it, lay on the bed, and wished Granny were here to tell her what to do. Drained of energy, she closed her eyes. She'd told many lies to her family to keep her pregnancy a secret. She wouldn't make the same mistake twice. Nothing would keep her from getting to know her daughter—unless Madison changed her mind and chose not to have anything to do with her. A tear rolled down her cheek. Just knowing her name caused a seedling of hope to break through the wall she'd built around her heart.

Fats jumped up on the bed, purring as he nudged her hand with his nose.

"At least, you'll still love me."

She pictured her parents' stricken faces to learn they had a granddaughter. Nothing was more important to them than family. Her hands trembled as she stroked Fats. They might never forgive her.

After a long while, the rumbling in Fats's chest relaxed her. Casey's lids grew heavy as she imagined holding her daughter. Then, in the in-between heartbeat of consciousness and dreaming, she heard her granny's voice whisper in her ear. *"The truth will set you free. Don't be afraid."*

CHAPTER TWO—DANIEL

Daniel Sheppard fiddled with the top button of his shirt. "Are you saying the only choice is surgery?" Every muscle in his body tensed, and he held his breath.

The oncologist's snow-white hair seemed to glow under the bright fluorescent lighting. Bushy brows shadowed his hazel eyes, and his lips formed a tight line. Dr. Peterson leaned forward and rested his elbows on his knees, causing his lab coat to stretch across his stocky shoulders. "The MRI shows a deep brain tumor."

Hearing the words *brain tumor* made Daniel feel like he was in free fall, and he gulped, trying to dissolve the lump in his throat. "I hoped Sparky, um, Dr. Compton might be wrong."

"I agree with her diagnosis." Dr. Peterson sat up straight.

Daniel ran his hand over his short brown hair. How had a migraine turned into a brain tumor? All these months, it had been growing. Why hadn't he seen a doctor sooner?

Dr. Peterson adjusted his reading glasses over his bulbous nose. "The pattern of the tumor appears to be a meningioma, and they're usually benign, but we won't know for sure until the neurosurgeon takes a biopsy during your surgery."

A knock sounded on the door. "Come in." Dr. Peterson glanced up.

A heavyset young woman with short blonde hair dressed in blue scrubs stepped inside the room. "It will be the end of January before Dr. Bertrand can see Mr. Sheppard." She kept her eyes on the doctor.

"That's a long time to wait." Daniel polished his forehead with his hand. "I can't sit around waiting, knowing this thing is growing."

"With the holiday season, I'm surprised it's not longer." Dr. Peterson placed the chart on the counter.

"But tumor cells are multiplying in my brain." Daniel's throat constricted.

"Slow growth is typical in this sort of mass."

"Yeah, but I want it out now." Daniel's fist clenched.

"I understand." Dr. Peterson's kindly face softened. "And I'm sorry for the wait, but this surgery will require a very skilled surgical neurologist. Dr. Bertrand is the best, in my opinion, and worth the wait."

"Okay, I have the surgery, then what?" The room was spinning.

"It depends on the result of the biopsy. You may need further treatment."

"Like what?"

He looked him in the eye. "Radiation, chemo, or proton therapy."

Daniel blew out a long breath. The gravity of the situation began to sink in, and he realized he might die, or even worse, be helpless—on life support. Perspiration formed on his upper lip.

"Let's deal with one problem at a time." The doctor hunched over the computer and started typing.

Daniel cleared his throat. "I need to think about this." Only he couldn't think with the room spinning faster.

"Of course. I'll give you material to read before you leave."

Daniel took in a deep cleansing breath. He was a cop, trained to deal with crises. *Focus.* He squeezed his eyes shut and silently counted. When he opened his eyes, calmness washed over him. "Is there anything else I should know?"

"For the time being, I recommend you avoid driving or operating heavy equipment." Dr. Peterson's shaggy brows drew together. "The chance is slim, but you could experience a blackout."

"I'm a cop. Driving is a requirement."

"Perhaps you can work at a desk for a while."

The room started spinning again. Daniel gripped the arms of the chair and focused on breathing. The room settled again. "What about travel?"

"Air travel shouldn't be a problem. I'll give you a prescription for the headaches."

"So, there's nothing to do but wait?"

"That's right. It's a shock to hear news like this. Most patients think of questions later."

Daniel blew out a long breath and stared at the floor, numb all over. "Man, a brain tumor."

"Please call when you've had time to consider questions." Dr. Peterson tucked his reading glasses into his lab coat pocket. "My assistant is gathering a packet of information for you." The doc closed the computer. "Try not to worry." He stood, squeezed Daniel's shoulder and left him.

Daniel sat there, considering who to call. Pastor Bob, his longtime pastor, would come, but he'd just retired and was encouraging people to lean on the new guy, Luke Davis. He couldn't call him, though, since Luke was dating Emma, Casey's best friend. If Emma got wind of him being picked up at a doctor's office in Nashville, she'd tattle to Casey. His chest ached. *How do you tell someone you love you have a brain tumor?* A few minutes later, a knock startled him.

The same nurse in blue scrubs stuck her head in the door. "Here are some papers for you to read."

"Thanks."

"That's all for today." She held the door open and stared at the floor.

He lumbered to his truck and sat there. *Now what?* At last, he opened his phone and dialed Sol Gregory's Chevron station and asked for a tow. After giving Sol the address, he massaged his temple. People hurried down the street, people having a typical day, a normal life.

Daniel opened the truck's glove box, extracted a faded navy-blue velvet ring box, and opened it. His mother's art-deco platinum-and-diamond engagement ring sparkled in the sunlight. He rubbed his forearm across his damp cheek. No way would he ask Casey to commit herself to him when he might end up helpless.

He'd fallen for her that first night at Dot's Deluxe Diner—the 'Triple D' to the locals. When Dot had asked him to share a booth with Casey because of the crowd, he couldn't believe his luck. As she talked about the University of Kentucky's basketball team, he thought he must be crazy to think she was also flirting with him. All these months, he'd yearned to tell her he loved her, but he'd held back. He still found it hard to believe they were a couple. She'd probably been told by many men they loved her. He'd been saving those precious words for when he asked her to marry him. Now, that would likely never happen.

I'll have to cancel our trip to Africa. His spirits sank lower. He sat in the quiet and considered what to do. Maybe he could keep this a secret until after their mission trip. *I'll have to lie.* The weight on his shoulders doubled. He hated a liar. *But everyone sometimes lies, especially to protect someone they love, right?* This was for a good cause. Daniel rested his head on the steering wheel. *Keep telling yourself that, and maybe you'll be able to believe it ... someday.*

CHAPTER THREE—CASEY

Casey overslept and had little time to primp. With only a couple of hours of fitful sleep, she needed a fabulous outfit to draw attention away from the dark circles under her eyes. Everyone would be dressed in holiday colors, so she chose a fuzzy tangerine sweater with a suede miniskirt the color of eggplant and matching thigh-high boots. After adding a long amethyst beaded necklace, she scrutinized her reflection. Most people only noticed the jaw-dropping clothes and flawless makeup as she created the persona of Cassandra. Casey had hidden behind the mask for so long, it seemed impossible to remove it.

Almost three years ago, she'd retired from modeling and moved home when a student had stabbed and killed Emma's schoolteacher husband, Chris. Emma and Weldon had needed her.

Customers flocked to her store on the corner of Main and Chestnut Street because she kept the designer labels affordable and chic. Women didn't seem to mind the hour-long drive from Nashville if they could meet the famous ex-model, Cassandra. The day-shoppers boosted the sales of all the downtown businesses. It was good to be home, among friends, instead of strangers in the city.

It was almost time to close when Casey passed an emerald beaded dress to one of her favorite local clients, Arvazean Cothran, an aging, Dolly Parton look-alike.

Arvazean studied the long bell sleeves and frowned at the open shoulders. "This style might be too youthful for me."

"Trust me," Casey spoke with confidence. "Try it on, you'll see."

Casey waited next to a tall mirror framed in antique silver leaning against the whitewashed brick wall. The perfect lighting emanating from the charcoal dome light fixtures did nothing to conceal the worry lines in her reflection.

Moments later, Arvazean exited the dressing room, her sapphire eyes twinkling. "It makes me feel years younger."

"The peek-a-boo shoulders are sexy," Casey winked.

"It will be perfect for New Year's Eve."

A few minutes later, Arvazean stood at the checkout counter. "You look tuckered out, Hon. You should take the day off tomorrow."

"On a Saturday, before Christmas Eve?" Casey lifted a penciled brow.

Tricia, the assistant manager, pushed her long blond hair behind her shoulder. "There would be rioting in the streets." Tricia's red cashmere sweater and winter-white slacks blended in with the holiday shoppers.

Casey sighed. "Unless my body is on display at Johnson's funeral home, I'll be here tomorrow, but then I'm off for almost three weeks."

"And she's leaving me to deal with the masses who want to meet Cassandra," Tricia zipped up the hanging bag.

"When do you and Daniel leave on your trip?" Arvazean dug through her wallet.

"On Thursday, right after Christmas." Casey accepted the credit card.

Arvazean had a dreamy look. "To be in my thirties again and on a two-week holiday with someone as handsome as my young neighbor."

"He's thirty-seven," Casey said. "And there will be little chance for romance on the mission trip with Pastor Bob and Eleanor watching us like we're teenagers."

"The way he looks at you should be more than enough romance for anyone. You should snap him up, lickety-split."

"Hah! Says the woman with three widowers courting her." Casey's phone buzzed. "Excuse me, but it's Daniel."

"Don't keep him waitin'," Arvazean accepted the tote from Tricia. "Merry Christmas!"

"Merry Christmas." Casey hit the accept button and ambled to her office. "Hi, Daniel. Your timing is perfect. Our last customer just left."

"Great. My truck's at Sol's Chevron. Do you mind picking me up at the house?"

"No problem." Casey wanted to go home and fall into bed, but she knew he would be worried if she canceled their regular date. "I can be there by six-thirty."

"Thanks, sweetheart. I'll be ready."

She and Daniel had started dating over a year ago when Dot, the owner of the Triple D, had asked them to share a booth on a busy Friday night. They hadn't missed being together on a Friday night since that fateful evening unless the police chief scheduled Daniel to fill in for the night shift.

Casey wished she'd already told him about Madison. She should have done that the moment their relationship became serious. Emma was right. What if Madison had visited Weldon instead of writing a letter? She'd tell him, but first, she needed to reveal everything to her parents. Casey dialed her mom. *Just do it. Just ruin her Christmas. Ruin everything.* The tension in her shoulders increased with each ring of the phone.

Jolene answered on the fourth ring. "Hi, baby."

"I guess you're baking up a storm."

"More like a tornado."

"Why don't you let me treat you and Daddy to breakfast in the morning?"

"You have time for breakfast?"

"Everyone needs to eat. How about seven o'clock at my house?"

Casey held the phone from her ear as her mom yelled to Casey's dad.

"Sorry, baby. My to-do list is longer than Santa's, and your daddy says he's gonna be out of here and in the mall by seven o'clock." She lowered her voice. "I'll bet he hasn't bought one gift yet."

"Maybe we can have breakfast together Sunday morning."

"We'll see. I need to take a cake out of the oven. Gotta go."

And her mom hung up.

Sunday morning would be her last chance to be alone with her parents before family members arrived on Monday, Christmas Eve. That would give them a day to recover. Casey rubbed her palms over her face. She would shatter their hearts, and eternity didn't hold enough time to heal the damage.

A few minutes later, Casey and Tricia ambled to the city center's parking lot. Twinkling lights covered the limbs of the cherry trees surrounding the town square. It still seemed a dream to be home with family and friends. After being attacked by Jansen, she'd trusted no one in New York and lived a quiet, isolated life for many years behind the facade of the haughty Cassandra.

What would her Weldon friends think about her having an eighteen-year-old daughter? Her midsection began to ache again as she remembered her loneliness in the city. Everyone would soon learn she gave her baby away and would believe her to be the most selfish person on earth. She could almost hear the whispers, see the judgmental looks, feel the scorn. But no one could think less of her than she did herself.

Daniel held open the Triple D's green art-deco door for Casey, and she inhaled the heavy scent of fried food. "What's wrong with your truck?" She turned to him.

"Oh, nothing to worry about." Daniel's brown hair was mussed in the back, and she smoothed it. He caught her hand and kissed it, his blue eyes drinking her in.

Casey admired his broad shoulders. If only she could snuggle into his chest with his strong arms wrapped around her and hide away from it all. But not even Daniel would be able to shield her from the tabloids when the news broke.

Dot, the owner of the diner, escorted them to a green vinyl booth in the rear. She wore her standard old-fashioned waitress uniform.

When Daniel placed his palm on Casey's back to guide her, she leaned into his touch.

Plastic snowflakes adhered to each of the plate glass windows. Dot's growing collection of kitschy collectibles sat on tables throughout the restaurant. Casey and Daniel spoke to several diners as they made their way to the back booth.

Dot pulled a pen from her white beehive as they sat down. She looked over her onyx cat-eyed glasses. "Are y'all having the catfish tonight?"

"Yes, ma'am," Casey said. She had no appetite, but Daniel would worry if she didn't eat.

"I've been looking forward to it all week," Daniel grinned.

Dot removed an order pad from her pocket. "Sweet tea with lemon to drink?

"Yes, ma'am." Casey unfolded her napkin.

Dot looked her up and down. "Only you could get away with wearing that gosh-awful Tennessee orange and still look good."

"Why, thank you." She beamed her brightest smile.

"She looks good in anything, just like you." Daniel winked at Dot.

"You got that right, but I don't know about wearin' more boot than skirt." Dot crossed her arms. "And Casey looks plum worn out."

And I don't know about wearing the same Pepto-Bismol pink uniform for forty years. But she's right. I'm way past tired. Casey lifted her chin. "All I need is a day off. My holiday schedule is crammed, and I've been packing for our trip."

"Not that anyone's asked for my opinion, but I think you two need to forget Africa and stay home."

"It's the chance of a lifetime." Daniel drummed his fingers on the table.

"I won't get a minute's rest from worrying while y'all are gone. I'll be praying day and night." Dot's lips turned down.

A feeling of remorse for her unkind thoughts washed over Casey. Dot cared for everyone in Weldon. If only she could lose the *I know what's best for everyone* attitude, she'd have more customers. Casey stood, hugged Dot, and inhaled the faint scent of Cinnabar perfume. "Thank you, but there's no need to worry."

"I guess I'll have to trust the Lord to take care of you." She patted Casey's back. "I'll be right back with your tea."

Daniel traced his finger on her open palm, then his thumb caressed her wrist, and she melted like butter on hot cornbread. She never took for granted the attraction she felt for him. After Jansen, a man's touch made her skin crawl, but everything had changed with Daniel.

They'd dated for weeks, and she'd worried about what might happen in the bedroom. Then when he didn't press for intimacy, she'd fretted. The powerful attraction gave her courage because she'd waited years to experience a special tenderness for the right man. One night, she made a bold step and invited him to spend the night, but he'd cupped her face in his hands and asked her to pray with him. She'd thought he was kidding. What kind of man prays when a woman offers herself to him? But as he spoke to God, she realized his goodness, far better than she deserved. He'd poured out his heart as he spoke, and the intimate experience left her shaken.

Casey's muscles tensed. How would such an honorable man react when he learned she gave away her child?

Dot placed their drinks on the table and snapped Casey's attention to the present. "Be back in a sec with your food." She twirled and left them again.

Casey couldn't stifle a yawn. She must return a letter to Madison. The poor girl was probably checking the post box every day.

A few minutes later, Daniel tapped the table with his finger. "You didn't go to Africa without me, did you? You look worried."

Casey smiled without showing her teeth. *I should tell him I can't go to Africa.* She shrugged. "I was just thinking about Mom."

"Is she working herself into a frenzy?"

"Yes." The dark shadows under Daniel's eyes matched hers. "Are you feeling okay?"

Daniel turned his head and scanned the restaurant. "I had another headache last night."

Worry tickled up her spine. "Have the pills Sparky gave you helped?"

"Nope. And, by the way, she insists we call her Dr. Compton in the office."

"That's old news—and I can tell you're trying to change the subject. What else did she say?"

Daniel stared out the plate glass window.

He's keeping something from me. Casey squeezed his hand.

"I have an appointment to see a specialist when we return from our trip."

"Why wait?"

"That's the first opening on the doc's schedule."

"I'm concerned about you."

Daniel sipped from his glass. "Lots of people have migraines. My biggest problem now is figuring out how I'm gonna get around town for the next few days without my truck."

"Get a rental."

He shrugged. "I can get by without one if you don't mind giving me a lift to your parents on Christmas Eve."

"Of course," Casey gripped his hand. "Are you sure you're okay?"

"I'm fine."

Casey wished she could remove the sadness from his eyes.

Dot plopped a bowl of slaw in front of each of them, then added plates filled with fries and fried catfish. "Enjoy."

"Thank you," they said in unison. Daniel gripped her hand. "Let's pray." As he blessed the food, Casey lifted a silent petition. *Thank you for keeping my daughter safe.* Although she dreaded telling her family about Madison, her anxiety was slight compared to the burden of worry she'd carried for eighteen years. She might lose the respect and love of everyone important to her, but she was willing to risk it all if a relationship with Madison was the reward.

CHAPTER FOUR—DANIEL

The next day, Daniel dialed his partner, Scotty.

"What's up?" Scotty's voice was upbeat.

Daniel held his breath. Maybe he could navigate this conversation without lying. "My truck's at Sol's Chevron. Can you give me a lift?"

"Sure. Where are we going?"

"I need to meet with the chief."

Silence. "Okay."

"I need to ask for some time off."

"You're already off the schedule for three weeks. What's going on?"

Daniel pictured Scotty's blond head tilted. "The doc gave me some new pills for the migraines, but he said they might make me drowsy at first," the words tumbled from his lips. "He suggested I take a few days off to see how they affect me. That's why I need to see the chief today."

"Man. I hope they work. You looked like a dead man walking after your last round."

Daniel rubbed his temple. "Yeah. That's why I'm willing to try these, even with side effects."

"Why not just call him?"

"Because, as mentioned, I'm already off for three weeks. I'd rather speak with the chief in person."

"Okay. I get it. What time should I pick you up?"

"He's expecting me at ten o'clock."

"I'll get you there."

"Thanks, buddy." Daniel was grateful his partner didn't ask any more questions ... grateful for him in general. He needed a friend in his corner now more than ever.

After meeting with his boss and arranging to be off until after his trip to Africa, Daniel bought Scotty lunch at the Triple D. Scotty downed a Manhattan sandwich smothered in mashed potatoes and gravy and two fried peach pies with a side of vanilla ice cream. The kid would have a paunch soon if he continued to eat like a racehorse. When paying for their food, Daniel purchased a box of fried pies to share with Casey that evening. After dealing with holiday shoppers all day, he knew she'd be exhausted. When he phoned Casey to arrange dinner plans, she readily agreed to a foot massage and pizza at his home instead of going out.

That evening, Daniel watched Casey bite into a fried peach pie. She closed her eyes, and a look of sheer bliss crossed her face. A deep yearning stirred within him. If he kept watching her eat, he'd need to walk around the block in the cold.

"You have a crumb." And he leaned over and kissed her, tasting the sweet peach filling. "Now that's what I call dessert."

They moved to the sofa in front of the gas logs, and Daniel draped a wool throw across their laps. Casey snuggled under his arm and yawned. "Excuse me."

Her eyes looked trusting. Guilt pressed in on him, and he almost gave in to the urge to tell her about the tumor. But he knew she'd insist they cancel their trip, and he couldn't do that to Pastor Bob. Besides, this might be his only chance to see the real Casey Bledsoe. She needed to see that her fancy clothes and makeup weren't important to him. He loved the heart that had somehow been damaged. Would she ever tell him what had happened to cause her to be skittish? He guessed it was some rich city jerk who'd betrayed her.

When she'd first returned to Weldon, the paparazzi sometimes showed up looking for dirt. Still, the locals remained tight-lipped when anyone asked about Cassandra.

Lost in thought, he heard soft snoring and chuckled. Few had any idea what a simple lifestyle the former superstar model enjoyed. Curling up with a good book, walking along the riverbank, or a night watching the Hallmark movie channel were among her favorite things to do.

Instead of waking her, he sat staring at the fire, dreaming of what it would be like to spend the rest of his life enjoying simple evenings like this. If only he could have her in his arms all night long. A deep longing made his chest tighten, and he squeezed his eyes shut for a few seconds. *Savor this moment*. He sighed, and as he watched the flames burn, his muscles relaxed, and he, too, drifted to sleep.

The mantel clock chimed twelve bells, and he shifted, causing sharp prickles to course up his numb arm. "Sweetheart, I hate to wake you, but it's late." Daniel kissed the side of her neck.

Casey yawned and stretched. "Goodness." Her eyes widened. "Look at the time. You should have woken me."

"You were tired, and I was enjoying holding you, but then I fell asleep too."

He stood, stretched, rubbed his aching torso, and pulled her up into an embrace. "My neighbors will be gossiping about us."

Casey wrapped her arms around him. "Arvazean watches your house like an FBI agent on a stakeout, and believe me, she reports everything to the coffee club. But that's okay, she's rooting for us."

Daniel leaned down and kissed her while inhaling the sweet scent of something exotic. Her lips were soft and yielding, but he pulled away. It would be easy to lead her to the bedroom. *Ah ... me and my dumb idea of waiting. Still, it will be worth it.* He rested his chin on top of her head, and a long sigh escaped him. Waiting was still the right thing to do, especially now. "Let me walk you to the car."

"No. It's cold."

After one long, last kiss, he helped her into her coat. He stood on the front porch and shoved his hands in his pockets as she crept down the slick sidewalk to her Mustang. A heaviness settled over him. How many more days would he have with her? How much time did he have?

CHAPTER FIVE—CASEY

The cold air hit Casey in the face and cleared her foggy brain. She smiled to herself as she turned the key in the ignition, recalling how nice it was to fall asleep in Daniel's arms. But then as usual lately, she let worrying thoughts creep into her brain as she drove home. She couldn't stop thinking about the unwritten letter to Madison.

After brewing a cup of chamomile tea, she turned on music. Ella Fitzgerald's sultry voice filled the air as she sifted through the cubbies of her old desk to find more stationery. *Lord, I need help, and I need it now.* After taking a sip of tea, she squared her shoulders and began writing.

Dear Madison,

Thank you for contacting me. Your letter is a blessing and filled me with joy. It's the best Christmas gift ever. To know you are healthy and have loving parents lifts a burden and fills me with gratitude for answered prayers.

It makes me happy to learn we share the same hair. I understand the difficulties of dealing with thick curls. A good conditioner helps. I use the Gold Treatment and trust me, it's the best. I'll ship a bottle to your PO Box.

Another thing we share is a love of basketball. I'm named after Mike Casey, a famous University of Kentucky basketball star. In fact, my parents named all six of us kids after UK basketball stars.

If you write another letter, don't worry if you don't receive a reply right away. I'm leaving after Christmas for a two-week mission trip to Africa. No one would consider me the missionary type—it's a long story, too long for this first letter. I'm an ex-model for goodness' sake, and still trying to figure out what I can offer African people.

Your letter left me dazed, but it's filled me with joy and hope. I've struggled to find the words because there is much to tell. My best friend Emma said you are probably nervously waiting to hear from me. Hopefully, this letter will relieve any anxiety.

Ambitious and selfish sums up my teen years. I made many mistakes and had no idea of the treasure I was giving up. Worry for your well-being has been my constant companion since you left my arms.

Your mother is wise to recognize it might be a little awkward to meet without knowing a thing about each other. Please relay my thanks to her for sharing my contact information.

My family and friends call me Casey. Cassandra is an image created by my agent in New York. While some people may think me glamorous because of my modeling career, I'm a small-town girl and live a very simple life. Weldon is my favorite place in the world, and I hope that someday I can show you around my hometown.

If it's not too much trouble, please send a picture. Whenever I see a red-haired girl your age, I experience an extra heart palpitation, wondering if she's you.

It's brave of you to reach out to me. Please write again. I hope we will become good friends.

Casey paused. She wanted to write "Love, Casey." But she didn't deserve Madison's love. Instead, she closed the letter with "Warmly."

After addressing the envelope and sealing it, she sat in the stillness of her house. Billie Holiday's melancholy tune, "Good Morning Heartache," emanated from the Bose speaker.

Casey had learned to live with permanent heartache, but she hoped maybe now the hurt would lessen. She lay down on the sofa and remembered all those years ago. Her ambition and drive to be a model in New York. How silly and naïve she'd been. Fats jumped up and arranged himself on her stomach. Absently, she smoothed the cat's soft fur as she remembered the fateful day all those years ago that had changed the course of her life ….

Alexis, Casey's agent, slammed a folder on the desk. "A thousand girls would do anything to have a private dinner with Jansen Moore." Alexis looked like a Jennifer Aniston replica, but she lacked her girl-next-door appeal. Instead, Alexis possessed a hard steeliness that frightened Casey.

"He's a creep." Casey shuddered as she recalled his thick finger tracing her collarbone.

"His cosmetic company is looking for a new representative."

"But I've heard rumors." *And I ain't gonna sleep with him to get a contract.*

"There's always gossip about someone as wealthy as Jansen."

Casey scrunched her face in disgust. "The note he sent me with the roses is a recipe for vomit."

"Your naïveté is showing. Anyone successful in this business learns to work with difficult people."

"He's not difficult." Casey crossed her arms. "He's revolting. I'd rather have a slug slithering on my skin than his touch."

"We all endure his roving hands."

"He tried to unbutton my blouse after the photoshoot." Casey shuddered. "I won't do it."

"Listen closely. You will have dinner with Jansen, or you can find someone else to represent you."

Casey's pulse quickened. "You wouldn't."

"Don't test me, little girl. You may be the prettiest princess in your little village, but this is the Big Apple, and there are more beautiful faces than losing lottery tickets."

"But we have a contract."

"I only represent models who want to work."

"But I do want to work. You said the *Teen Town* shoot went great."

"It takes more than one lucky break to make a career."

"But I've done everything you've asked of me."

"Up until now." Alexis stood up. "Jansen is the one calling the shots. His car will pick you up at eight this evening."

Casey blinked back tears. "Okay," she said in a shaky voice.

"Stop by Belinda's desk and pick up the dress I selected for you."

"What's wrong with my clothes?"

"Jansen likes leather."

Casey slouched and chewed her manicured nail.

"Don't keep him waiting." Then Alexis yelled, "And stand up straight!"

Casey corrected her posture. "Yes, ma'am."

"Go." And she pointed at the door.

Casey blew out a long breath and hugged her stomach. *I should have pressed charges*. Thoughts of telling strangers the details of the terrifying and humiliating experience left her shaking her head. It wouldn't have changed anything. Alexis was right. *A thousand girls would have willingly fallen into Jansen's bed, and no one would have believed I didn't.*

Fats rubbed his chin against hers, and she ran her hands over him again. *If only I'd stood up to Alexis*. But then ... Madison wouldn't exist. She would never regret the decision to have Madison, but how could she tell her parents the reasons for the other choice she'd made?

On Sunday morning, Casey awoke with a stomach bug. After calling Daniel and her parents, she swallowed an anti-nausea pill and returned to bed. She wouldn't risk exposing others to a virus.

By Sunday evening, she managed to keep crackers and ginger ale down, and she slept through the night.

The phone woke her the following day, and Emma's name showed on the caller ID.

"Merry Christmas!" Emma's voice was cheerful.

"Merry Christmas, yourself." Casey yawned.

"How do you feel?"

She closed her eyes and fell on the pillow. "Better. Yesterday I felt like a pile of dog poo."

"I hoped you were playing 'possum."

"Why would I do that?"

"So, you don't have to face your parents."

"Thanks for having such a high opinion of me." She placed the back of her hand on her cheek. "I don't have a fever, and I feel hungry."

"Sounds like a twenty-four-hour bug," Emma slurped something from a straw.

"I guess."

"Hallie and Callie are dying to give you your Christmas gift, and Harley has something for you too."

"That's sweet."

"Do you feel up to it?"

"Yes, but I need a shower first."

"Okay. Maybe around lunchtime?"

"I can make grilled cheese sandwiches and tomato soup." Casey's stomach rumbled.

"Sounds good. That's Harley's favorite meal."

"And from what I've seen, the twins will eat anything that doesn't bite them back."

"True. By the way, you missed the congregation praying over the mission team. It was very moving."

"I know. Eleanor called and woke me yesterday afternoon. I hate that I missed it."

"Your Mom and Dad looked happy. I guess they're still clueless about Madison?"

"Oh, shut up."

"Don't talk ugly. I've threatened to wash Hallie's and Callie's mouth out with soap for saying that to each other, and I can do the same to you."

"You sound just like your mother."

"Stop trying to distract me. You need to tell them."

"This might give Daddy a heart attack, and on Christmas

Eve of all days, and Mama will have a hysterical fit, to be followed by an army of family descending on her."

"Your dad doesn't have heart problems, and your mom throws hissy fits anytime something doesn't go her way."

"Get off my back."

"I will when you stop acting like a jack—!"

Why was it Emma never talked ugly to anyone but her? Casey snickered. "Now who needs her mouth washed out with soap?"

"You need to listen to me. Please visit your parents and tell them everything."

"Stop meddling."

"Stop procrastinating. Eighteen years is long enough to suffer."

Casey closed her eyes. The hole in her heart would always be there. "No, hon, it's not." And she disconnected.

Emma walked through Casey's front door holding a twin in each hand, and Harley followed them, toting a stack of presents. Emma kept Callie's long red hair in a braid and Hallie's in a ponytail to help identify the identical pair. Casey's heart melted when Callie wrapped skinny arms around her hips and said, "Merry Christmas."

Casey smoothed her palm over Callie's braid. "Merry Christmas."

"We have a present for you." Hallie jumped up and down, her ponytail bouncing.

"And I have gifts for you too." Casey led them to her Christmas tree decorated with old-fashioned multicolored lights. She fished out two boxes wrapped in paper embellished with reindeer and passed one to each child.

As she watched the girls tear into the packages, a heaviness settled over her. *If only I hadn't ...*

"She looks just like me!" Callie removed a doll sporting a long red braid from the rectangle box.

"I got one too!" Hallie said, "And mine has a ponytail."

"Now, you each have your own identical baby."

"Twins for the twins," Emma crowed. "Terrific."

"Open your presents," Callie said.

"No. Harley next." Casey handed a long oblong box to Harley wrapped in Harry Potter gift wrap. In the last year, the thirteen-year-old had let her hair grow out, and recently, she'd started pulling her hair back in a ponytail that matched Emma's.

Harley caressed the package. "Thanks." She removed the paper with care. "I'm saving this."

"Go on. You're killing me." Casey bit her lip.

At last, Harley pulled the lid off the box. "Wicked." Nestled in tissue paper lay a phoenix floor lamp from Pottery Barn's Harry Potter collection. "Super wicked." Harley beamed a smile.

"You can exchange it if there's something else you prefer."

"No way." The dark-haired teenager grinned. "I can't wait to show Papaw."

"Now, it's your turn." Emma crossed her arms.

Each twin handed Casey a small square box.

Casey ripped through the paper and extracted a necklace made of macaroni noodles painted crimson from Callie. "I love it." And she delicately hung it around her neck. "It goes perfect with my emerald sweater."

"Open mine." Hallie bounced on her heels.

"Okay." Casey removed a matching macaroni bracelet with the added embellishment of bells. When she slipped it over her wrists, it jingled. "It's perfect for the holidays." She gave each child a hug.

Harley handed Casey a package wrapped in cartoon newsprint.

Casey's heart softened. "Thank you." Casey removed the paper and discovered a pocket-sized travel journal. "Just what I needed. How thoughtful!"

Harley stared at the floor. "I thought it might come in handy for your trip."

Casey hugged the coltish girl. "Thank you. Now it's Emma's turn." Casey handed her friend a green foil package.

Emma tore into the paper and whooped with joy as she realized she was holding a first edition of *To Kill a Mockingbird* signed by Harper Lee. "I'll treasure it forever." She hugged it to her chest. "Now, open your gift from me. I put it under your tree last week." Emma lifted a package from underneath the tree and handed it to Casey.

Casey shook the box. "It's a shoebox."

"You're impossible to buy for." Emma bit her lip.

Case ripped the paper and discovered a pair of purple zebra print Converse sneakers. "These are perfect for the trip!"

"I thought the same thing." Emma removed her phone from her pocket. "Let's take a snapshot." She took a photo of Casey showing off her macaroni jewelry with the girls holding their dolls. In the picture, each of the twins had a cheek pressed to hers. Harley stood behind them, holding her lamp. A few minutes later, the aching in Casey's midsection intensified as she studied the photo. "You girls are precious," she said over-brightly, sniffing, trying not to think of all she had given away.

CHAPTER SIX—DANIEL

Daniel bounced the basketball and shot another hoop.

"Three points!" Kevin, the director of the YMCA, shouted. Daniel had known him for years. "You're bouncing that ball like you have something against it. What's up?"

Daniel wiped sweat from his brow with his arm. "Nothing. When the kids left, I thought I'd take advantage of the empty court." He shot another basket and chased down the ball. "It seems strange for the place to be empty."

"Well, it is Christmas Eve."

"What time are you locking up?" Daniel dribbled the ball.

"As soon as I get a certain someone to check in his equipment."

"Sorry, man. You should have said something."

"I am."

"Let's go." Daniel threw the basketball at him.

Kevin tucked the ball under his left arm. "I'm not in that big a hurry. Let's sit down for a minute in my office. I need a favor." His friend, a former college basketball star, limped beside him. Kevin's old ankle injury always aggravated him when the temperature dropped. Kevin ran his hand across his thinning black hair.

Uh, oh. Daniel dropped into the plastic chair across from Kevin's scarred desk.

"You look like you could use this." Kevin tossed him a bottle of water and pushed up the sleeves of his gray sweatshirt.

"Thanks." Daniel unscrewed the top, emptied the bottle, and wiped his mouth with the crew neck of his T-shirt. "What's on your mind?"

"I have a favor to ask ... you don't have to do it if you don't want to." Kevin leaned forward and clasped his hands together.

"I've heard that line before," Daniel said sarcastically.

"Don't worry, this will be easy." Kevin held his big hands out, palms up. "I mean it."

"That's what you said when I took on coaching the seventh graders."

"I'm sorry I tricked you. Hear me out. I need a reference."

Daniel lifted a brow. "For what?"

"I'm applying for a position as the director of a large YMCA in Nashville and would love to use you as a reference."

"Take it from me, you don't want to leave Weldon and live in Nashville."

"It's all about M-O-N-E-Y." Kevin paused between each letter.

Daniel grimaced. *You'll learn money's not everything, buddy.*

"Give them your honest opinion." He sat up straight. "But maybe, don't mention me bamboozling you into taking on the seventh graders."

Daniel leaned back in his chair and rested his ankle on his knee. "I'll be glad to, but you need to let them know I'll be out of the country for two weeks."

"These things take time. You'll be home long before they sort through the first round of applicants."

"You've got my cell phone number. I'll start planning my speech."

"Thanks, buddy."

Daniel stood. "It's nothing. Let's go. I need a nap."

"What's going on with you? You look worn out."

Daniel held his breath. *It might help to tell someone.*

"I'm just tired. I haven't been sleeping well."

"When do you guys leave for Africa?"

"Thursday."

"I can't believe you talked your fancy girlfriend into going to a third-world country. Big mistake."

"She's more than a pretty face."

"You're right about that. She's several notches above pretty, which is why I can't understand her being with a boring guy like you." Kevin ducked as Daniel threw his empty water bottle at him, then grabbed his jacket. "Merry Christmas."

"Merry Christmas, Kevin."

Daniel walked the six blocks to his home. He needed to put on his game face for Casey's family's Christmas Eve get-together. If Kevin noticed something amiss, then Casey's mom Jolene would discern something wasn't right. That woman had an invisible radar that detected trouble. Guilt darkened his mood as he turned up his coat collar and hunched his shoulders against the wind. He hoped going to Africa wouldn't be his last opportunity to do something good in the world. Still, if it was, at least he'd be able to share the experience with the woman he loved.

CHAPTER SEVEN—CASEY

Casey and Daniel attended the Christmas Eve candlelight service at Loving Chapel. Casey was comforted by Luke Davis's closing prayer. Last Christmas, Luke was just filling in as an interim pastor, and it had been evident to all he was smitten with Emma. Casey suspected his interest in her best friend was why he'd applied for the head pastor position after Pastor Bob announced his retirement plans. Luke had left a prestigious position as an associate pastor for a large congregation in Bowling Green, Kentucky, to serve the smaller church in Weldon. Since then, he spent much of his free time with Emma and the girls.

After the service, Casey and Daniel stopped by her parents' home for a family gathering. All five of her older brothers managed to return to Weldon with their families for the holidays, plus a few stray aunts, cousins, and friends joined the mix. Upon their arrival, Casey's six-year-old niece Ada Mae wrapped her arms around Daniel's black wool slacks. Without missing a beat, he lifted her. "Give me some sugar." And Ada covered his cheeks with a smear of chocolate.

He's good with children. Casey's midsection fluttered. When Ada scampered away, Casey fingered Daniel's mint-green shirt collar. "It's smudged with chocolate. I have a stain stick in my purse."

Daniel kissed her cheek. "Don't worry about it." Then he maneuvered her to the mistletoe, wrapped his arms around her, and whispered in her ear, "Maybe you can cover it up with lipstick." And he stole a kiss.

Emma and Luke arrived with the twins, Harley, and the teenager's papaw, Rick West. Emma had thought her dream to build a family impossible after her husband Chris's death. With Harley's adoption, fostering the twins, and a serious romance with the new pastor, it looked like Emma had gotten a second chance for love and a family. And now, it seemed as if Casey might be getting a second chance for a happier future as well. If only she could summon the courage to tell everyone about Madison.

When the clock struck nine, the parents in the crowd started rounding up overstimulated kids. Finally, Casey and Daniel made their escape from the mayhem. Snowflakes drifted down as Daniel held Casey's car door open. "Do you want to drive?" Casey asked.

"No, thanks. I love having a beautiful chauffeur."

She fastened her seat belt. "Sol should have given you a loaner."

Daniel shrugged and closed her driver's side door.

Weldon began to take on a Christmas card appearance as lights glowed amid the drifting flakes. "The perfect Christmas snow." Casey turned on the ignition.

"Nothing is charming about slick roads."

"It looks like the road crews salted the streets."

"Be careful. There might be black ice. I wish we were in my truck." Daniel drummed his fingers on his thigh.

Lights hung from the homes on Daniel's street, and Arvazean's yard featured a manger scene.

When Casey parked the car, Daniel unfastened his seatbelt. "Don't get out." He leaned across the console. "My sidewalk will be slick."

The cedar and spice scent of his cologne filled the small space, and he caressed her cheek. When she leaned in, their lips met, and her ability to think coherently left her.

Daniel ended the kiss and whispered, "Merry Christmas."

His husky voice returned her to the present, and she rested her head on his shoulder but became aware of the console digging into her rib.

"Merry Christmas." She cupped his cheeks, savoring the feel of the soft stubble. "I'll pick you up about ten o'clock for brunch."

"I can't wait."

He gave her one last, long kiss and left her with a craving for more as she imagined what it would be like to spend the rest of her life wrapped in his arms. For months, she'd hoped he'd declare his love for her. She hoped he'd place his ring on her left hand. Why hadn't she already told him about Madison? If he offered her a ring tomorrow for Christmas, she'd have to tell him all her secrets before accepting.

As she waited for him to walk to his front door, shoulders hunched, he seemed to wear a coat of sadness. The light on the front porch highlighted his face, and when he turned to wave at her, she discerned a pained expression instead of the intense desire she was experiencing. *Maybe, it was another headache from too much noise and all her brothers speaking over each other.* After tooting the horn, she drove home dreaming of a future Christmas when she'd never again experience the aching loneliness that weighed on her chest. Maybe she was hoping for too much ... for a future with Daniel *and* her daughter.

On Christmas morning, Casey sat at the antique vanity for over an hour and used every makeup trick she knew to hide the dark circles under her eyes.

Earlier that morning, the sound of her screams had wakened her from the grip of a nightmare while she fought the tangle of covers. Rather than attempt to return to sleep, she'd risen and brewed a pot of coffee.

Casey tossed a cotton makeup pad into the trash as she considered what to do if Daniel proposed today. If only she'd followed Emma's advice and told her parents about Madison the night she opened her first letter, she'd be free to explain everything to him. It was only going to be the two of them for brunch. Maybe she should just tell him and let the snowflakes fall. They'd either survive the storm or not. It was the *or not* that kept her adding more concealer. If only she could get a decent night's sleep and her stomach would stop tormenting her.

Dressing with care, she slipped into a winter-white cashmere sweater with a cowl neck. A classic tartan blanket scarf woven of cranberry and black threads added holiday color. After debating skinny jeans or leggings, she decided the length of the sweater was perfect with her deep burgundy leggings. A pair of onyx suede ankle boots completed her outfit.

In the kitchen, she grabbed an apron and started cooking the Christmas brunch. Hash brown casserole, cheesy grits, country ham, and biscuits would take time. Her grandmother's antique china sat in place on top of a new crimson tablecloth with intricate cutwork.

With her eye on the clock, Casey shoved a tray of biscuits into the oven, set the timer, and adjusted a jaunty black French beret to protect her hair from the snow. Twenty minutes should be enough time to drive to Daniel's house and return before the biscuits burned.

As she drove with care, snowflakes drifted down. The front door opened as soon as she parked the car. Without hesitating, she rushed to Daniel and launched herself into his open arms for a Christmas hug, causing him to stagger against her impact.

"Whoa," he said. "Careful, or we'll both end up in the snow."

He hugged her and buried his face in her hair. "I love the fresh scent of your hair. It reminds me of spring."

The wool of his shearling coat rubbed against her cheek. "We have to hurry, or the biscuits will burn."

He didn't move. "Give me a minute." He squeezed her tighter. "I want to remember this moment forever." His voice sounded sad.

"What's wrong?" She pushed away from the embrace and cupped his cheeks with both hands.

He winced. "I visited the cemetery this morning."

Casey hugged him again. "This is your second Christmas without your parents."

"Even though I miss them, I wouldn't wish them back, not with Dad battling Parkinson's while watching Mom disappear into Alzheimer's."

Casey squeezed him tighter. "You should have called me. I would have taken you to the cemetery."

"I didn't plan to go, but as I took an early morning walk, somehow, I ended up standing over my parents' grave. It's hard to explain, but I miss them most during the holidays."

"I wish you'd phoned."

"I'm sorry, honey. I didn't mean to put a damper on your holiday spirit." He leaned down and kissed her, and her body hummed with electricity.

When she opened her eyes, the snowflakes floated around them, and it seemed they were inside their own private snow globe. Casey kissed him back, and for a few seconds, forgot her troubles.

When she withdrew from his lips, his eyes still held sorrow.

"Let me grab your gift." Daniel returned to the house.

Cardinals surrounded the birdfeeder in his neighbor's yard, and their scarlet coats glowed against the pristine landscape. Then she spotted Arvazean waving from her front window, and Casey lifted a hand. *There are probably more eyes on us than birds in the air.* When Daniel returned carrying a giant box brandishing an oversized scarlet bow, her heart sank. *Too big for a ring.* That's a good thing, she mentally scolded herself, but her traitorous heart hoped he'd hidden a small box inside the large one. But then what would she do?

They returned to her home, a white bungalow she'd inherited from her granny. It had sat empty for years until she'd decided to hire local craftsmen to update it. It was her safe haven. An evergreen wreath embellished with a massive red bow decorated each window, and her Christmas tree's multicolored lights twinkled from the front room.

"I love my little nest." She pulled Daniel up the front steps.

Daniel wrapped his arms around her. "Tell me more things you love."

She sniffed. "I love the scent of wood smoke, peppermint-chocolate fudge, fried peach pies, and shoe sales!"

"My ego can't take much more of this."

"And I love a man who appreciates me just as I am—a workaholic, short-tempered, jazz-loving, shoe-shopping clotheshorse."

He leaned down and kissed her again. When he lifted his head, she sighed. "I don't care if the biscuits burn. I can make more."

"Let's go." Daniel grabbed her hand.

The oven timer buzzed incessantly as they walked through the threshold.

"Maybe we're not too late." Casey rushed to the kitchen and removed the pan of toasty cathead biscuits. "I think they're okay."

He studied the buffet, placed his hands on his hips, and whistled. "Someone got up early. You've gone to a lot of effort for just the two of us."

"It's all for you—your reward for enduring the Bledsoe clan last night. I'm lucky you didn't head for Africa without me after putting up with my brothers and their tribes."

"They don't scare me."

He reached for her and gave her another hug. "Thank you for doing all this. Let's pray so we can eat."

After the prayer, Daniel filled his plate, put the first bite of the breakfast casserole into his mouth, and sighed. With his mouth full, he mumbled, "A woman who can cook as good as she looks." Daniel ate as if he hadn't had food for a week. He cleaned his plate and leaned back. "Next week at this time, we'll be in Africa. Who knows what we'll be eating?"

Casey fiddled with her necklace. "It's only for two weeks, but I've not taken a vacation since I opened the boutique."

"You deserve a break."

"What if something happens that Tricia can't handle?"

"She can call you, and even if she can't reach you, I don't think a fashion emergency qualifies as a crisis."

"You're right," Casey sipped coffee from her china cup.

Daniel rubbed his stomach and leaned back in his chair. "I need to walk away from the table."

"Me too."

"It might be a good time for me to give a certain someone her Christmas gift."

Casey jumped up, grabbed his hand, and pulled him up. "Now you're talking!"

They went to the living room, and Casey turned on music. Bing Crosby crooned in the background. Daniel walked to the tree and retrieved the big box. "You go first." He handed her the gift box. "Jane wrapped it for me at the station."

"How sweet of her. Remind me to thank her." Never being one to salvage wrapping paper, she ripped off the fancy trimmings. As she pulled a travel backpack out of the box, she looked inside to find mosquito repellant, hand-sanitizing wipes, water purification tablets, and various items she could use for their trip. When she searched each compartment, she finally discovered a jewelry box, and her spirits lifted, then fell. *Too big for a ring.* With effort, she kept an artificially large smile on her face while she opened the oblong box and discovered a heavy, intricately woven gold bracelet. Daniel pointed out the pattern of X's and O's hidden in the weave.

"It's beautiful! I can't wait to show Mama and Emma." Daniel hugged her, and she savored his embrace. *It's for the best,* and she swallowed the lump in her throat. "Now it's your turn." Casey retrieved his gift from under the tree.

Daniel unwrapped the box slowly, and Casey clenched her fists.

"You're killing me." She pounded his knee with her fist.

He raised his eyebrows. "What?"

"Stop torturing me."

He laughed, tore the red foil paper, and lifted the box top. He stared at the quilt, then gulped and stroked the golden starburst. "I recognize this material." His voice sounded husky.

Casey's words rushed out. "I know it's a strange gift to give a man."

"You must have worked for weeks." He lifted the quilt to his face and inhaled. "Lavender always reminds me of Mom."

The idea to make a remembrance quilt had percolated when she'd taken Daniel's parent's clothes to Goodwill for him. It took weeks to select and sew the bright colors from his mother's dresses into starbursts. Stitching the quilt on her sewing machine required hours of work, and she'd ruined some of the fabric by using the seam ripper one too many times. On the verge of giving up, her mother's quilting group rescued her and spent an afternoon helping. Then, Jolene used her quilting machine to finish it.

The lime green, orange, and yellow starbursts glowed against the navy background comprised of his dad's old police uniforms she'd had to scavenge from the dumpster behind Daniel's back.

"I used your mom's dresses for the starburst. Your dad's work shirts made the perfect background for the Night Sky pattern."

He looked up and met Casey's gaze with tear-filled eyes and swallowed her in a hug. "Thank you. I didn't know you could quilt."

Casey relaxed in his embrace. "I pieced most of it, but Mama's quilting club rescued me when time ran short, and Mama used her quilting machine to finish it. I don't have her skill."

"What a great way to remember my parents."

"The idea came from a gift quilt Granny gave to me when I left for New York."

"It's always good to have a token from home."

"You can't imagine the comfort it gave me—even though my roommates made fun of it."

"They were likely jealous of your success."

"I'd return to my cramped apartment, exhausted and homesick, but I'd wrap up in her quilt, and it seemed I could feel her arms around me."

"Do you miss modeling?"

"No. I worked long hours with people impossible to please, and someone was always trying to climb to the top by crushing someone else."

"I'm glad you came home." Daniel wrapped his arms around her.

"I learned to appreciate Weldon and the people who live here." Casey returned his hug.

"Me too. I liked being a detective in Nashville, but when I had to come home because Dad got sick, I remembered there's a lot to love about Weldon. Many people stepped in to help us."

She stroked his cheek. "Wrap up in this quilt, and I hope you'll remember those who loved you best."

"This gift will always remind me of my parents ... and you." He kissed her. "I love it."

But do you love me? She waited, hoping he would say the words. Instead, he snuggled under the quilt with her and studied the decorated Christmas tree.

Daniel started to doze, and her thoughts drifted to Madison. How could she find the words to tell him everything? When she'd learned she was pregnant, her new agent, Stacy, sat with her in the abortion clinic, but Casey had run out. After packing her bags, she'd called Emma, who encouraged her to return to Weldon. The shame of facing her parents kept her in New York, trying to decide what to do. She couldn't terminate the pregnancy, but the fear she wouldn't be able to love her baby kept her pacing in the small apartment.

The thought of giving up modeling made her feel more despondent. But then she decided that maybe she could return to the city and pick up her career in a few months. After all, she had an impressive portfolio. She'd then called the Eagle's Nest—a women's shelter her church helped support.

After a brief phone call, Casey developed a plan to 'disappear.' A chain of lies convinced her family she'd be working in Europe for six months. Then she boarded a plane bound for Atlanta, where a kindhearted woman met her at the airport and transported her to the shelter located in the mountains in Northern Georgia.

Six months later, when the nurse placed the tiny baby girl on her stomach, Casey instinctively cradled the infant but closed her eyes.

"Don't you want to see her, at least this one time? You need to be sure." The midwife's soft voice seemed to echo in the quiet room.

What if she looks like him? As the baby cuddled closer, Casey opened her eyes to see the child sucking her thumb while sleeping. An overwhelming love filled her being, confusing her, and she vowed the stain of Jansen's sin would never touch this innocent.

What would Jansen Moore do if he discovered she'd had his child? Of course, he'd probably want nothing to do with it, but what if he did? The baby must be protected from him. And she couldn't pick up her modeling career with a baby in tow. Her daughter would have a better life with two parents who would love her, wouldn't she?

But Casey hadn't realized her feelings for her daughter would intensify and that by handing her infant over to a stranger, she'd given up her ability to protect her. If only she'd known of the never-ending worry and intense love she'd experience for her daughter.

When she returned to New York, a darkness lingered, and her photos revealed a haunted look from which she couldn't escape. Stacy, her savvy new agent, recognized the change in Casey's demeanor and embraced it. She lined up photoshoots for magazines that featured the avant-garde, and Cassandra was born.

For years, Casey remained aloof, and no one in the fashion industry penetrated her professional barrier. The camera loved her hollow cheekbones and the emerald eyes that smoldered. Through the years, she lived a simple life in a tiny flat; she was anonymous among the packed streets of New York. Weldon was her safe haven when she visited, a place where she could almost be herself. Her parents were proud of her success, and she always dressed to impress in Weldon.

Would she ever free herself of the Cassandra image?

Casey's muscles tightened as she imagined Jansen's cold gray eyes. *Stop it!* Casey mentally scolded herself. *Don't think about the past. It won't matter if Madison looks like Jansen.*

Casey stood by the window and watched the falling snowflakes. Her mother was planning a special dinner for them tomorrow night before their departure to Africa. Maybe she could tell Daniel and her parents together. The timing was terrible, but there was never going to be a good time to break her parents' hearts, and like it or not, Daniel would be stuck with her for the next two weeks. Maybe that would give him time to get over the shock ... *or maybe not.*

CHAPTER EIGHT—DANIEL

Daniel was waiting for Casey when she arrived at his home. They planned to eat lunch at the drugstore counter before going to the church to organize their supplies. Casey wore faded jeans with a pair of turquoise cowboy boots sporting a double fringe. Her royal blue cashmere sweater hugged her curves. Daniel's mouth went dry as he held the drugstore door open for her.

When they approached the lunch counter, Alma Lee was wiping the faux marble with a towel. The drugstore's matron was as broad as she was tall, and she sometimes had a sharp tongue. Alma Lee had worked at the drugstore for more than forty years and rarely missed a day. She was more than a little critical about her boss, Dave, traveling to Africa with them.

"Hey, Alma Lee." Casey slid onto a red vinyl stool. "I'm starving for one of your chicken salad sandwiches."

"I'll have two of those." Daniel sat down next to Casey. "Those croissants are almost as good as Dot's fried pies."

Alma Lee sniffed. "Almost?" She ran her hand over her short white hair that had been permed.

"He's just teasing you." Casey winked and elbowed Daniel.

A few minutes later, they enjoyed their flaky croissants filled with chicken, grapes, and pecans.

Alma Lee watched them eat and crossed her arms. "I still can't believe Dave is leaving Weldon high and dry for two weeks."

"I'm sure he's leaving the pharmacy in good hands," Daniel mumbled with his mouth full.

"Hmph." Alma Lee methodically cleaned the counter with a white cloth. "You don't have to go all the way to Africa to tell people about Jesus. You should go to the trailer park with Randall and me some time to talk about Him."

Daniel swallowed and wiped his mouth with a napkin. "The community center you started at the AA Trailer Court is making a big difference for the families who live there, but I've had the dream to go to Africa since I was a little kid."

"But now you're an adult and know West Africa isn't a safe place for Americans, particularly for someone as pretty as Casey."

Daniel gave Alma Lee a serious look. "There is no safe place ... not even in Weldon." Chris, Emma's husband, had been killed in Weldon by one of his students. No place was safe.

After lunch, Casey and Daniel went to Loving Chapel to consolidate their luggage with the supplies. Eleanor, Pastor Bob's wife, had asked everyone on the mission team to be there.

As they walked down the church's dim hallway, they discovered Sparky, still wearing her lab coat, leaning against the wall.

"Finally." Sparky walked toward them. "I need to go."

"But Eleanor said it would take all afternoon to organize and load the supplies." Casey crossed her arms.

"The medical provisions are in those boxes." Sparky pointed to a stack of containers. "But I need a private word with Daniel before I return to the clinic." She looped her arm through his, led him into a conference room, and shut the door.

"Smooth," he said sarcastically, feeling his face flush.

Sparky planted her fists on her hips. "I can't believe you're still going." She spoke in a hushed tone.

"There's no reason to let Pastor Bob down." Daniel stood stubbornly, feet planted firmly on the floor.

"Did Dr. Peterson really give you permission to go?" Sparky narrowed her eyes.

"He said as long as I'm not driving, traveling is not a problem."

Sparky thumped him on the elbow. "You didn't tell him your travel plans include a trip to Africa, did you?"

He looked at the commercial-grade blue carpet and kept his mouth closed. A wave of guilt washed over him.

"Does Casey know?

"It's bad enough *I'm* losing sleep." Daniel lifted his chin.

"I thought you two are pretty serious."

"That's none of your business."

"I care about you. You're like a second big brother to me."

Daniel squeezed her shoulder. "Billy and I were pretty disappointed you were a girl." He had many fond memories of Sparky tagging along behind him and his childhood best friend, Billy.

"Stop trying to distract me with tales of my big brother. You can't keep something like this a secret from the team."

"The tumor's been growing for years, and the only restriction from Dr. Peterson is not to drive."

"You should stay here and rest."

"Not happening."

"At least tell your girlfriend. I've already given her plenty of reason to give me the cold shoulder."

"What'd you do?"

"I said something mean-spirited. It doesn't matter because I can't un-say it."

"Other women have been unkind to her too. Why is that?" Daniel's jaw hardened.

"Maybe because most of us feel like we've been whacked with the ugly stick when we stand next to her."

"If you took the time to get to know her, you'd realize she has a tender heart."

"I'm hoping she'll forgive me and that we can become friends on the trip."

Daniel hugged her. "That sounds more like it. Thanks for keeping my secret, Dr. Sparky."

She elbowed his ribs.

"Ow! Why'd you do that?"

"For calling me, Dr. Sparky. Do you know how hard it is for a woman to be taken seriously in this town? I'm Dr. Compton."

"You're gonna have to get over yourself, Gladys May."

"I don't know why Mama had to name me after my grannies," Sparky muttered. "Don't you dare let anyone else hear you say my given name."

"I'll keep your secret if you'll keep mine." Daniel rubbed his side.

Sparky glared at him as they walked down the hallway, where they found Casey leaning against a stack of trunks. "Are we ready to get to work?"

"Sorry, but duty calls." Sparky waved. "The boxes with the medical supplies are labeled."

"I thought you were here to help," Casey squared her shoulders.

"You thought wrong," Sparky said in a sing-song voice.

Daniel pecked Casey's cheek. "You're even prettier when your cheeks turn that color."

"Why did Sparky need to speak with you privately?"

Daniel lifted the lid of a trunk and peeked inside. "This thing is full of crayons."

"Answer the question." Casey's lips turned down.

"She's worried about the migraines."

"As am I."

"I feel great."

"What did Sparky say?"

"She asked me some more questions. I think she's nervous about the trip."

Casey's brows drew together, but she didn't have a chance to say any more as Eleanor walked in and turned on all the lights. She wore a chambray shirtwaist dress and a blue cardigan. She stopped in front of Casey and looked her up and down. "I hope you plan to wear more sensible shoes for our journey."

Casey held out her turquoise, double-fringed, cowboy boot. "What's wrong with these?"

Eleanor smoothed her gray hair, pulled back in a chignon. "The desert is no place for fancy shoes."

"I've packed two pairs of sturdy sandals, and they pass the ugly test."

"Good." Eleanor looked through her reading glasses at the clipboard. "I want to weigh each piece of luggage."

"Yes, ma'am." Daniel gave a mock salute.

"It can't be over fifty pounds," Eleanor dropped her chin.

"We know." Casey rolled her eyes.

Thank you, Lord, for Eleanor. Daniel weighed the first trunk.

"Where's the rest of the team?" Casey picked up a stack of folders.

"Bob is still visiting shut-ins."

"What about Tyler?" Casey rifled through a box and made room for the folders.

"He's spending the day with his girlfriend. The way she's carrying on, one might think he's never coming home from Africa." Eleanor smirked.

Casey sighed. "She'd better get used to this if he's planning to spend his life traveling the world with his clean water research."

"I thought the same thing," Eleanor gave a wry grin. "And Dave's afraid Alma Lee will throw a hissy fit if he leaves the drugstore, so it's just us. Let's get to work."

CHAPTER NINE—CASEY

It was dark by the time Pastor Bob arrived at the church. Casey was just recording the items in the last container. Daniel weighed it and added a label and purple tape for easy identification while Eleanor watched their every move.

They were scheduled to meet four additional volunteers tomorrow in Detroit. The two small groups would unite in the terminal, connect to Paris, and then to Niamey, Niger, where Raymond—Pastor Bob's missionary nephew—would meet them.

Daniel shoved the last trunk into the van, and Eleanor slammed the door. "That should do it."

"Any last words of advice before we meet in the morning?" Daniel brushed his hands together.

"Go to bed early." Pastor Bob rested his arm on Eleanor's shoulder.

"And have a good meal tonight." Eleanor patted Pastor Bob's hand.

Daniel rubbed his tummy. "Jolene is cooking a special dinner for us."

"Mom's fixing all our favorite dishes," Casey said.

"I'm not surprised." Brother Bob dropped his arm. "Maybe we should have a quick prayer before we head home." The group gathered hands while he prayed.

After he said, "Amen," Eleanor made a sweeping motion with her hands. "Now, shoo. There's nothing left to do but let go and let God."

If you only knew what I have to do next. Casey shoved her hands into her jacket pockets and fingered her keyring. "We'll see you in the morning."

Casey tossed her keys to Daniel. "Why don't you drive?"

Daniel snatched the keys from the air, but lifted her hand, placed the keys in her palm, and closed her fingers around them. "I like having a pretty girl drive me around." He kissed her knuckles.

On the short drive to her parent's home, she gripped the steering wheel as her heart thundered in her ears. *Tonight's the night.* Lights shone from every window in the red-brick ranch home, while icicle lights hanging from the roofline lit the night sky. Then she noticed her sister-in-law's minivan and her brother's pickup. Her stomach plummeted. "Looks like Connie and Kent will be joining us."

"Your family is great."

"Yeah." Casey drummed her fingers on the steering wheel. In the kitchen, pots simmered on every burner while her mother delivered orders like a sergeant in a mess hall to Casey's sister-in-law, Connie, and Casey's niece, Olivia. Jolene wore a stained apron, and strands of her auburn hair escaped from her chignon. She must have been working in the kitchen all afternoon.

"Surprise!" Connie stirred a pot on the stove.

"Looks like we'll have a great send-off," Daniel looked over Connie's shoulder.

A heaviness pressed down on Casey's shoulders. She couldn't tell her parents everything with Olivia in earshot. Her niece stretched to remove a stack of plates from the cupboard, revealing a new henna tattoo on her back.

Wandering a minefield with snowshoes would be more relaxing than spending time with Kent and his rebellious teen.

The girl's free spirit reminded her of herself at that age as she recalled the same arguments with her parents about curfews and clothes.

"Not those plates, use the best ones." Jolene adjusted a knob on the oven.

"But it's a weeknight," Olivia said, "and you won't let us use the dishwasher with your china."

Jolene pointed a wooden spoon at her granddaughter. "It's a special occasion."

Casey stepped up and hugged her mother. "The regular plates are fine."

Jolene turned and scowled at her daughter-in-law. "Don't take your eyes off the gravy. It will scorch in an instant if you stop stirring."

"I've made gravy before." Connie rolled her shoulders.

"And you've burned it too."

Connie stopped stirring, looked up at the ceiling, and silently mouthed something.

"Goodness, Mama, lighten up or you're liable to end up with a wooden spoon smacked over your head." Casey nudged Connie's shoulder.

"Nonsense, Connie would never do such a thing."

"I might," Connie muttered.

Jolene wiped her hands on a towel, twirled it, and popped it at Connie's behind and then at Casey. Both girls screamed, giggled, and jumped out of her reach.

"It's not nice to sass me in my kitchen." Jolene threw the towel on the counter and peered up at Daniel. "Do you have everything packed?"

"Yes, ma'am."

Casey grabbed a vintage bib apron from the kitchen drawer and watched Daniel pretend to scrape the icing off a double-decker dark chocolate cake with his finger.

"Maybe I should sample this to make sure it tastes okay."

Jolene swatted Daniel's hand with a wooden spoon. "You'd better join Frank and Kent in the den before you get into trouble. Casey, I'll put you to work creaming the potatoes." She peered over Connie's shoulder. "It looks like the gravy is ready to take up." She smoothed her hair. "I'll let you girls finish up while I freshen my makeup. The rolls are still browning. Keep an eye on them for me."

"Your makeup looks perfect," Connie said.

"It wouldn't hurt you to add some lipstick, Mom," Olivia looked her mother up and down.

Connie sighed. "You girls have something in your genetic code that's missing from mine."

When they sat down to eat, Daniel held Casey's hand while her father blessed the food. Casey didn't close her eyes and noticed that when her dad bowed his head, light from the dining room chandelier reflected on his bald head. Age spots covered his folded hands, and there were crow's feet around his eyes. Her Dad had always been athletic, and he never tired of playing basketball, but he'd grown a paunch since retiring from the post office. *When did he get older? And how could she give him news that would age him even more?*

After the prayer, Casey filled her plate with the tender pork roast, creamed potatoes, glazed carrots, and rolls, but she could hardly eat. The envelope in her purse consumed her thoughts.

Daniel placed his hand over hers. "Are you feeling okay? You aren't eating any of your favorite foods."

Casey gulped. "I seem to have lost my appetite."

"When I think about my baby being in West Africa, it terrifies me." Jolene sipped sweet tea from her glass. "But Eleanor promised to keep an eye on you two."

"What's Mrs. Eleanor gonna do if someone tries to kidnap Aunt Casey?" Olivia smirked.

Casey forced a smile. "No one is going to kidnap us."

"Call me every day." Jolene's blue eyes were huge. "I don't care about the expense."

"We may be in a remote village," Daniel speared a piece of salad.

"And Raymond warned us that the internet and electricity often go down. Don't worry if I don't call or send a text in reply." Casey dabbed at her mouth with her napkin.

"It's our job to worry," Frank said, looking at his daughter with his soft hazel eyes.

After the meal, Casey hugged all the members of her family. "Thank you, Mama, for making all my favorite dishes."

"You didn't eat a piece of the chocolate cake."

Casey held up a plastic bowl with a lid and said, "I have a piece for breakfast."

Her mother cupped her face and kissed each cheek. "You're still my little girl."

"Always, and thanks for taking care of Fats for me."

"I'll spoil him just like he's one of my grandkids." Jolene smiled through her tears.

Casey hugged her dad, and he held onto her for a few extra seconds. "I'll be all right, Daddy. We'll see you in the morning."

They waved to her parents, who stood on the back patio.

"They're worried, and I can tell you are too," Daniel said. "I felt your hands trembling at dinner."

Casey kept her eyes on the road and hoped he couldn't see her face in the dark car. "Niger is a long way from Weldon."

And two weeks is too long to keep Madison a secret. As she bit her lip, she considered turning the car around, but she kept driving.

Daniel placed his hand on her thigh. “Thank you for making this sacrifice for me.”

“It will be an adventure.” She swallowed hard.

“I wonder where we’ll be next week at this time.” Daniel sounded wistful.

“Lord only knows.” After dropping off Daniel, Casey sat in the drive for a long time. Should she return to her parents and tell them everything? At last, she left the car. She’d carried this burden for eighteen years. She’d gift her parents with two more weeks of ignorant bliss, and then, no matter what, she’d tell them everything.

CHAPTER TEN—DANIEL

Daniel pulled back the bedcovers as his phone vibrated on the bedside table. Sparky Compton's name lit up on the display. He ignored it. A minute later, the phone vibrated again. Daniel lay in bed with his hands clasped behind his head and let the call go to voice mail.

Five minutes later, his doorbell rang. Daniel sighed. He knew Sparky would be pounding on the door in a matter of seconds. He grabbed his jeans, and by the time he pulled a T-shirt over his head, the expected beating on the door started, but she was also yelling.

Daniel jogged down the hallway and jerked open the door. "Are you trying to wake up the entire neighborhood?" he asked, trying to keep his voice low.

Sparky glared at him. "I don't care. I'm not the one with something to hide."

"What do you need?" Daniel ushered her inside.

"I spoke to Dr. Peterson this evening." Sparky narrowed her eyes.

Daniel shrugged. "And."

"He's not any happier than I am about your plans to travel to Africa tomorrow."

"I'm going." Daniel crossed his arms.

"You owe it to Pastor Bob to tell him what's going on."

"Why?"

"If something happens to you on the mission trip, he'll feel responsible." Sparky stomped her foot. "I'll feel responsible."

"I'm an adult." Daniel drew in a deep breath. "Put yourself in my shoes. When I return home—"

"If you're able to return home."

"I'll visit the neurosurgeon, then maybe have brain surgery, which I might not survive, or even worse, end up helpless. During these final weeks, I'm going to spend my time doing what I want."

"If you get proper medical care, things might turn out okay."

"But you can't promise me that."

"I can't promise that to anyone." Sparky paced around the living room. "Niger doesn't have adequate medical facilities for an emergency surgery. If your condition worsens, you'll have to be evacuated to South Africa or Europe. You might not survive the journey."

"The tumor's been growing for years. Two weeks shouldn't make a difference."

"I've never known you to be selfish before." Sparky's voice cracked.

Daniel's chest tightened. "If wanting to spend the last two weeks of my life with the woman I love means I'm selfish, then I'm selfish."

"You can spend the next two weeks with Casey in Weldon. There's no way she'd go without you, and she's going to be upset when she learns you kept this from her."

Daniel rubbed the back of his neck. "She'll be upset no matter when she learns about the tumor."

Sparky paced back and forth. "As your doctor, my hands are tied, but as your friend," tears filled Sparky's eyes.

Daniel hugged her. "Don't worry, Sparky. Whatever happens, I'm the one responsible for the choices I'm making. Not you."

"But everyone in Weldon will blame me. Please cancel this trip."

Daniel swallowed the lump in his throat. "No."

The wall phone in the kitchen rang. Now what? Only telemarketers called on the landline. Daniel jerked up the receiver. "I'm not buying."

"Is everything okay?" It was Arvazean.

"Hey, Arvazean. I'm sorry. I thought a telemarketer was calling. What makes you think something is wrong?"

"I heard a woman yelling. It sounded like it was coming from your house."

Daniel ran his hand through his hair. "It was Sparky. I was already asleep and didn't answer the phone. She came over to make sure the travel doctor gave me the right immunizations." A wave of guilt washed over him at the quick lie.

"Oh, my. Did you get the right vaccine?"

"Yes, ma'am. I'm good to go."

"Okay then. I'll be praying for you."

The knot in his stomach twisted. "Thank you."

He disconnected and turned to face his friend. "That's just great. Everyone at the coffee club will hear about your pounding on my door in the middle of the night."

Sparky stuck her tongue out at him. "Serves you right, you big fibber."

He smirked. "I was trying to protect your reputation."

Sparky snatched open the front door. "Then stay home and follow your doctor's orders."

"I can't do that."

"Won't do it," Sparky yelled and stomped into the darkness to her car.

Daniel walked out onto his front porch. Arvazean had probably heard that too. It was a good thing he was leaving town in the morning. The last thing he wanted was for Casey to learn of Sparky's visit. He'd work hard to gain her trust. This might shatter it. This was a mess, but there was nothing he could do to fix it...*except to tell the truth.*

CHAPTER ELEVEN – CASEY

The Weldon mission team traveled to the Nashville airport and on to Detroit, where they joined another group from Louisville. It had been Raymond, Pastor Bob's missionary nephew, who suggested the Louisville church members merge with the Weldon team. Even though it was more challenging to organize logistics, most Americans felt more comfortable being in a larger group when visiting a third-world country. This was the first time they'd all met in person. Per Eleanor's request, everyone sported the same purple T-shirt imprinted with a creosote outline of Africa. Casey rested her chin in her palm. *You'd think we're first graders on our first field trip.*

Pastor Bob made notes when each person gave a brief introduction as they sat in chairs clustered together in the terminal. Margie and Ed, a banker and a homemaker in their early fifties, told the group how they were still learning to cope with an empty nest. Margie's brunette hair was cut at a sharp, sleek angle and her makeup was flawless. Ed's dark hair was thinning, but his arms were bulky. Casey guessed he lifted weights. The two held hands, which Casey thought was sweet.

Leslie and Jeff were former high school classmates of Raymond, Pastor Bob's missionary nephew. Leslie, an elementary schoolteacher, was thin and a head taller than her rotund husband. It tickled Casey to learn he was a PE teacher. Both had blond hair, and like Casey, they had ivory skin. They'd all sunburn unless they kept their skin covered.

Then Dave, the pharmacist in Weldon, said he'd joined the team at Sparky's request. Everyone in Weldon speculated Dave and Sparky might become a couple. Dave's quiet ways would be a good foil for Sparky's temper, and he had a boy-next-door appeal, with chestnut hair, freckles, and a ready smile. But she'd also been seen around town with a new guy, Carson Williams.

And finally, Tyler, a student conducting water research, let everyone know he'd begged Pastor Bob to allow him to join them when he learned they planned to visit Niger, a place where women spent the better part of their day collecting water. Tyler was tall and lean, his brown hair tied back with a leather strap. His knee bounced up and down impatiently as he sat on the edge of his seat.

The group of eleven had spent the last two hours of their layover getting to know each other better and discussing ways to organize the medical clinic and the Bible school for the children. When the airline steward announced it was time to board their plane to Paris, Casey looked at her watch and yawned.

"You look worn out, and we've barely started the journey." Sparky frowned.

Casey attempted to stifle another yawn but failed. "I didn't sleep well last night, and you've got dark circles under your eyes too."

Sparky dug through her purse and pulled out a small packet. "This is an over-the-counter sleep aid. Take it when we board the plane, and maybe you'll be able to rest on the next flight. I'm going to take one too."

"I don't like to take unnecessary pills."

"We need to be ready to hit the ground running when we land," Pastor Bob said.

Eleanor looked at her notebook. "Raymond organized a full schedule."

"Okay," Casey accepted the packet. "Relax, everyone. I'll take the medicine."

Almost an hour later, their plane sped down the runway. Within minutes, she fell asleep and drifted among a throng of people on a crowded New York sidewalk. In the distance, she spied the back of a tall girl with hair the same shade as a red fox. The girl's long ponytail swayed, and Casey tried to catch up to her, but she couldn't because too many people blocked her. She attempted to push ahead and reach the girl, but people kept appearing in her way. "Madison! Wait!"

The girl stopped, turned, and glared at her with cold gray eyes. Jansen's face stared at her, and his thick hand slapped her. Casey heard someone screaming as she awoke from the nightmare.

"Honey, you're having a bad dream," Daniel shook her shoulder.

"What?" Casey shook her head and placed her hand on her racing heart. "Thanks for waking me."

"Are you okay? You called out in your sleep, and then you started screaming."

Casey blinked and stuttered. "I had ... the craziest dream."

"You've been out for hours." Daniel looked at his watch. "We'll be landing in Paris in a few minutes."

"My head feels like it's filled with congealed oatmeal. Remind me not to take anything else Sparky gives me."

"I heard that." Sparky's girlish voice drifted over the headrest. "It might be your malaria medicine causing hallucinations."

Casey rubbed her eyes. What? Maybe it *was* the malaria medicine causing the terrifying dreams. As she thought about it, her shoulders drooped. She knew what was causing them and it wasn't the medicine.

The scent of coffee wafted in the cabin. "I need caffeine."

"Sorry," Daniel squeezed her hand. "The flight attendants are preparing the cabin for landing."

An hour later, Casey sat in an airport restaurant. She bit into a warm, buttery croissant, sipped dark, sweet coffee, and studied the stylish travelers in the Paris airport. "Look at her boots." Casey sighed with longing.

"Those zebra print Converses you're wearing make a statement too." Sparky gave a wry smile.

"Thanks."

"It wasn't a compliment." Sparky lifted a brow.

Daniel glowered at Sparky, and she raised her hands. "I'm kidding."

"That's okay." Casey focused on keeping her tone light. "I'm used to people commenting on my fashion choices."

"I'll bet," Sparky bit into her croissant.

Eleanor gave Sparky a fierce look.

"Sorry," Sparky mumbled with her mouth full. "I shouldn't tease when everyone's grouchy from lack of sleep." Her eyes twinkled.

"We'll be in Paris for three hours. I can't wait to check out the shops." Casey studied a listing of stores on the map posted next to their table. "Emporio, Armani, Hermès, Dior, Gucci, and Prada have shops in the airport mall. It's heaven."

"It is exciting to be in Paris," Leslie smoothed her hand over her blond hair. "I can't wait to show my pictures to the girls in my class."

"I'm going to take a nap while we wait for our next flight," Pastor Bob said.

Daniel rubbed his temple. "I'm getting a headache, so I think I'll do the same."

Sparky gave Daniel a serious look. "Let me see your hand."

He extended his palm.

"It's not trembling," Sparky and Daniel locked eyes.

"I'm just tired." Daniel leaned back and put his hands behind his head.

Casey studied the two and felt a growing tension. "What's going on?"

"Nothing," Daniel shrugged. "I'll take a pill."

Sparky smiled tightly. "Guess I'm overreacting."

He probably had a tension headache. Casey ran her finger along the edge of the envelope in her backpack, and she inhaled sharply. *I can buy something for Madison. Any girl would love a Gucci handbag.* Casey's heart filled with hope.

CHAPTER TWELVE—DANIEL

Daniel strode down the portable stairs attached to the plane and felt as if he were walking into a furnace as heat waves shimmered across the tarmac.

At the bottom of the stairs, Casey turned to him. "I remember saying, 'I love you, but I am not going to Africa.'"

Daniel squeezed her shoulder. "And yet, here you are." He winced. His headache had intensified about an hour ago.

Casey's brows furrowed as she followed Eleanor to the bus. "Does your head still hurt?"

"Yeah, let's get out of this heat," he said in a clipped tone.

She sniffed. "I smell wood smoke." An attendant motioned for her to get on the bus, but she paused. "The terminal's over there. Why don't we just walk?"

"Because he wants us to get on the bus." Sparky's eyes darted back and forth. "We're not in America."

"Plus, I can feel the cool air." Daniel placed his hand on Casey's back. "Let's enjoy it."

"And don't forget we've been warned not to take pictures of the airport," Eleanor reminded them all.

Pastor Bob followed them onto the bus. "It's a good way to lose your camera, and it might result in a visit to the police station."

Daniel relaxed into the comfortable seat and dug into his bag. "I need my sunglasses."

Casey looked at her reflection in the rearview mirror and scowled. "My hair is a mess." She searched through her bag and pulled out a purple silk scarf. In an instant, her skilled fingers adjusted the material around her head. "Maybe I can make a French braid tomorrow."

"You look beautiful." Daniel pecked her cheek.

"We're not required to have our hair covered in Niamey." Eleanor wiped her brow with a tissue. "Only when we go into the villages."

"Have you looked at my hair? I should cover it now." Casey tucked a strand of her red hair under the silk.

With the last seat filled, the driver departed for the terminal. It took all of thirty seconds to reach the doors.

"*Bonjour!*" The security clerk wore a blue uniform. He indicated for Daniel to place fingers from his right hand on a scanner. The clerk snapped a picture and stamped his passport. "*Merci.*" Then he did the same for each of them.

The clerk at the next station wore a dress that covered her from head to toe. The lime green fabric with blue triangles seemed to glow in the dim light. With a hesitant smile, the clerk pointed at Daniel's disembarkment card, stamped it, and said, "*Merci,*" then pointed toward the doorway.

When they crossed the threshold, a group of men in blue coveralls swarmed around them, shouting for their attention. Daniel squared his shoulder. Their instructions said to look for baggage clerk number two. A slight man with number two embroidered on his pocket pushed through and held up a sign with BOB JOHNSON printed in bold letters. Casey extended her hand, but he shook his head. Daniel leaned close to her and spoke over the din. "Remember, Muslim men do not touch women who are not their family members."

Casey bit her lip. "I'm sorry."

"Okay." The kindly man smiled at her, then shouted something to the other men still loitering around them. He then made a sweeping motion with his sign toward them. The baggage clerk made a gesture like a police officer stopping traffic and started gathering their luggage from the carousel.

It was a mystery to Daniel as to how he knew which bags were theirs, but then he surmised the purple masking tape Eleanor had added to each trunk made their bags easy to identify. Daniel and Tyler assisted the baggage handler with their luggage, and they moved through security.

Baggage clerk number two smiled and said, "Okay," then led them outside, pushing the overloaded luggage cart into the hot, dusty wind. Hawkers dressed in brilliant colors surrounded them, and children in rags held out their hands, shouting "*Cadeau*"—gift. The baggage clerk yelled at them, and the path cleared.

Brother Bob pointed. "There's Katie and Raymond."

A couple who looked to be in their late twenties started waving. Daniel recognized Katie and Raymond, their hosts, from the pictures Pastor Bob had shared when recruiting people to join the mission team. Katie's blond hair was pulled back in a ponytail, her height almost matched Casey's, and Raymond looked like a younger version of Pastor Bob, except he still had a head full of brown hair, although it was trimmed short. The couple reached the party, and Raymond hugged Eleanor. "You made it."

"Yes, we did." Eleanor squeezed him.

Red dust framed everything, and the air smelled of burning charcoal. A bald white man in dusty jeans approached their group, and Raymond placed his hand on his shoulder. "This is Sam Jones, another missionary on our team. He came to help us transport your luggage."

Sam stood with hunched shoulders, hands in his pockets. "Welcome to Niger." Sam gave a weary smile and placed his hand on the shoulder of a slight African man wearing a light-blue collared shirt tucked into jeans. "Let me introduce you to Hama, your bush taxi driver."

Hama nodded and looked down at his black sandals.

Daniel extended his hand. "*Fofo*—hello."

Hama smiled and gripped Daniel's forearm, then he turned and climbed to the top of the bush taxi. Raymond started passing trunks to him, and the men stepped in to assist. The bush taxi only had room for eight, so Raymond instructed the Louisville team, Margie and Ed, and Leslie and Jeff, to ride with Sam.

Daniel stared at the van's worn seat cushions.

Sparky spoke under her breath, "This is not exactly a luxury vehicle."

Eleanor swatted at a fly. "I'm sure it's reliable."

"This is a luxury vehicle compared to how most people in Africa travel," Katie leaned on the open door. "This van may seem rough compared to American standards, but it's never let us down."

"I'm sorry," Sparky looked down. "I didn't mean to sound critical. Please forgive me."

"That's okay," Katie squeezed Sparky's shoulder. "It's a culture shock. Watch for jagged pieces of metal on those seats. I've skinned my leg more than once."

"I like the vintage look." Casey climbed in and scooted across the cracked black vinyl seat to the open window. "The van's character adds to the sense of adventure."

Katie laughed. "You'll see vehicles like this crammed so tightly with people you couldn't wedge a shoehorn between them."

"Does our driver speak English?" Daniel stepped up into the van and sat next to Casey.

"I'm sure he understands more than we realize, but no," Katie shook her head.

"Is he Muslim?" Eleanor's blue eyes were wide.

"Yes. But he's a trusted friend." Katie patted Eleanor's knee.

"Everything looks just as I imagined." Daniel riffled in his backpack and found the prescription pill bottle.

"Are you okay?" Casey bit her lip.

Daniel's head throbbed at the base. "I'm fine." He swallowed the pill without water.

The traffic jumble made Daniel wince more than once as perspiration beaded on his forehead, and his damp T-shirt stuck to his skin. Hama beat the horn while he squeezed the bush taxi into a roundabout crammed with other honking vehicles. Motorcycles wove in and out through the ribbon of traffic. People walked along the dusty road, and most women carried a baby strapped to their backs while balancing baskets on their heads. Several donkey carts, cattle, goats, and loaded camels wandered along the busy highway. The air smelled of animals and charcoal.

When the van turned on Embassy Row, Katie pointed. "That's the American embassy's gate."

"I feel safer already." Eleanor looked back over her shoulder as they sped past.

A few blocks later, the van swerved right, then ambled through a maze of lanes. At last, Hama slammed on the brakes and stopped at a metal gate. The guard that protected it was tall and lean and wore a blue collared shirt that matched Hama's. "This is our compound." Katie waved at the guard. "Welcome to our mission complex."

The guard opened the gate and waved.

Casey dug her phone out of her backpack and started snapping pictures of the iron gate and wall. "This picture will make Mama feel better."

The group emptied from the bush taxi and examined their sanctuary. The garden looked lush but well-tended. A children's swing set and slide sat in the back corner of the lawn, and a blue parrot balanced on the top limb of a palm tree. In the distance, the Niger River reflected the light of the setting sun. The beauty of the landscape stunned Daniel. He hadn't expected this.

"May I walk down to the river in the morning?" Daniel stared at the vista. The intense orange of the horizon would be etched in his memory forever.

"Sure, but be careful, and remember there are crocodiles and hippos in the river." Raymond clapped him on the back.

"And watch for snakes." Katie shuddered. "A black cobra almost scared me to death last year."

"A cobra! Lord help us," Eleanor placed her hand over her heart. "You never mentioned that in your emails."

"Every worker in the compound grabbed a club or a machete and hunted it down," Raymond planted his fists on his hips.

"It terrified me." Katie's eyes were wide. "But when the men crushed the head of the snake, I remembered Romans 16:20: 'The God of peace will soon crush Satan under your feet.'"

Raymond placed his arm around Katie. "Most Americans have a false sense of security because their pantry is full, and they can call 9-1-1."

"You're right," Pastor Bob sighed.

"In Niger, we're always aware of our dependence on God." Katie's face was somber.

"Any other warnings?" Sparky rolled her shoulders.

"Don't be surprised if you hear people in the morning," Katie pointed. "Squatters are living outside the compound wall."

"What's a compound?" Casey asked.

"Many residences in Niger include a wall surrounding three to four buildings. Think of it as a fenced yard, but you can't see over the fence, and it's gated." Raymond pointed toward a brown building. "Our compound includes the two mission guest houses, our offices, and a playground. Let's go inside."

When they entered the foyer, Katie took off her shoes. "Leave your shoes here. It's impossible to keep the white tiles clean, but we do our best not to track in the sand."

Raymond assigned shelves to the team in the kitchen then led them to two refrigerators and opened a door. "We reserved the lower half for you."

Katie placed her hand on the water faucet. "It's critical you fill your water bottles from this tap."

Tyler examined the water filtration system. "Cool."

"There are other residents, so it's important to respect everyone's space." Raymond picked up a Sharpie. "Mark your water bottles with a permanent marker."

"Does the water comes right from the river?" Tyler turned the knob and water dribbled.

Raymond snatched a glass and placed it under the tap. "We have a water tank, but yes, it's filled from the river." He filled the glass and turned the lever. "Have a glass."

Tyler drank the water. "It's good. I don't taste anything unusual."

Katie removed a tray of sandwiches from the refrigerator. "I know you're exhausted, but it will be better to eat before you turn in."

The group sat at a long harvest table with benches. "Let us pray." Pastor Bob bowed his head.

With his eyes closed, Daniel struggled to stay awake through the long prayer as Pastor Bob thanked God for their safe travels, for being in Africa, and so on. At last, he ended with "Amen."

Daniel shook his head and started to eat. "Mm. The rolls remind me of the bread in Paris."

"Niger was once a French colony." Raymond pinched off a piece of bread. "You'll see the French influence throughout Niamey. But once you get to the villages, it's all Nigerian."

Leslie pushed a strand of her blond hair behind her ear. "I can't wait to visit the orphanage. Many of my third-grade students donated pencils and plastic sharpeners for the children.

"The orientation program is first on the schedule in the morning." Raymond crossed his arms. "To be followed by a shopping venture to the Grand Marché, then on Sunday afternoon, we'll visit the orphanage."

"We want to make the most of every minute." Pastor Bob pushed his glasses up on his nose.

"Will I have the opportunity to interview people and ask about their water source?" Tyler leaned forward.

Raymond slapped Tyler on the back. "Yes. Everywhere we go, women and children draw water from wells or the river. By all means, talk to them."

After everyone finished eating, the group cleared the table, and Casey washed the dishes while Daniel dried.

"I wish I'd packed paper plates." Casey sighed.

"Nonsense," Eleanor wiped the counter. "Dish duty won't hurt us."

Casey's examined her manicured hands. "This dish soap with bleach is killing my skin cells."

Eleanor elbowed her. "I can't wait to see what God has in store for you."

Casey lifted her chin. "I can handle bad hair days and ugly clothes, but I'm not sure about cobras and crocodiles."

Daniel pecked Casey's cheek. "You're a lot tougher than you think."

"Yes, she is." Eleanor's expression was grave. "If I thought otherwise, she wouldn't be here."

"Thanks ... I think." Casey dried her hands with a towel.

Once the kitchen was in order, Casey made a quick call home, then Daniel escorted her down the long hallway. When they stopped in front of her room, he wrapped his arms around her. His chest tightened. "I'm proud of you."

"Why? I haven't done anything." Casey tightened her arms around him.

Daniel inhaled a faint hint of her orange blossom perfume and savored it. "You came."

"So did you." Casey rested her head on his shoulder.

Yes, he'd come when he should have stayed home. Daniel swallowed the lump in his throat. The pain in his head had eased since he'd taken the pill, but his vision remained blurred. *Father, forgive me for deceiving everyone.* Daniel hoped Casey would forgive him when she learned the truth too. She might never trust him again.

CHAPTER THIRTEEN—CASEY

Casey awoke and listened to the sounds of strange birdcalls as a faint pink hue lit up the horizon outside the window. Her whole being craved a cup of coffee. Daniel had laughed when he noticed the instant coffee in her carry-on, but he wouldn't be the only one suffering headaches if she didn't get a daily dose of caffeine. She climbed from the bunk and slipped on a pair of shorts and flip-flops.

In the dim light, she crept to the kitchen, found a teakettle, and started filling it with water.

"Good morning." Daniel's deep voice rumbled in the dark.

Casey jumped and clutched her chest. "You almost gave me a heart attack."

"Sorry, I couldn't find the light switch."

Her pulse steadied. "Why are you up so early?"

"Same as you. I guess our internal clocks are still on Weldon time."

She smoothed her hair and wished she'd taken the time to run a comb through her tangles. And she didn't have on a drop of makeup. "This is the first time in my life I'm ahead of schedule."

Daniel hugged her, and she cuddled into him as he nuzzled her neck. "This is a bad idea," he whispered.

Casey rested her head on his shoulder. Nothing had ever felt as right as this.

Daniel pushed away from her with a heavy sigh. "Pastor Bob and Eleanor are in the next room."

"What's wrong with hugging?" Casey's arms felt bereft without him.

"Holding you in my arms with my face buried in your hair is a recipe for melting all my restraint."

"I like the sound of that." She stepped forward, but Daniel backed away and held out his arms. "Let's go outside and watch the sun come up."

"Chicken."

"No, ma'am. I'm all rooster." And he grabbed her hand.

They went outside, and something stung Casey's leg, then her arm. "We're breakfast for the mosquitos."

"I'll say." Daniel slapped his neck.

They went back inside and sprayed on Deet. Steam rose from the kettle. Casey made two cups of instant coffee, handed Daniel a mug, and followed him to the sweetheart's swing. Casey sipped her coffee. "Yuck. I must have gotten bug spray on my lips."

"Let me help you remove it." Daniel bent down and stole a kiss. "That'll have to do. Eleanor's probably watching from her bedroom window."

"It's a nice way to start the morning." Casey closed her eyes and listened to the birds. "It sounds like a Tarzan movie." The scent of hibiscus flowers and charcoal lingered in the air.

Movement on the other side of the wall made her curious. She raised a finger to her lips, pulled a chair to the mud fence, and peeked over the bricks that made up the compound barrier. In the dim light, a young woman with a baby tied to her back bent over a small charcoal fire. Behind her, a black tarp supported by pieces of wood was attached to the compound wall. Two children lay asleep on a mat with no mosquito netting to protect them.

The young woman turned away from her fire, and Casey ducked down, feeling like a criminal, and hoped she hadn't been seen. She tiptoed to Daniel. "There's a woman with two small children and a baby living right there."

"Katie told us about them."

"Yes, but they slept on the ground, and she's cooking. It's not a real shelter."

Daniel looked down into his coffee mug and sighed. "Pastor Bob warned us about the poverty."

Casey's stomach knotted. *Why am I here? What can I possibly offer?*

Daniel's face had a pained look.

Casey swallowed her coffee. "Do you still have a headache?"

He seemed to be holding his breath and grimaced. "A little."

At that moment, Sparky stepped outside and walked toward them. Casey jumped up and met her. "Daniel still has a headache."

Sparky gave him a hard stare. "How bad is it?"

"It's hardly anything."

"Let's go inside to my kit." Daniel dumped his coffee and handed Casey his mug. As Sparky and Daniel approached the door, he leaned down and spoke into Sparky's ear. Casey stood staring at their joined shadows and heat infused her body when Sparky placed her arm around Daniel's waist. Casey's fingers tightened around the mugs as she followed them into the mission house.

A slew of ugly words crossed her mind as she washed the cups. Thank goodness no one could hear her thoughts ... except the One who heard them all.

CHAPTER FOURTEEN—DANIEL

Sparky and Daniel entered his room.

"Lay down." I'm going to get my pack." Sparky turned.

Daniel sat on the small twin bed shoved against the wall and leaned his elbows on his knees. His skin felt clammy, and he fought back a wave of nausea.

A thin steam of light filtered in from the small window in the corner of the room. Sparky returned, hit the light switch, and closed the door.

Daniel winced when fluorescent light flooded the room.

A soft knock sounded. "That will be Casey." Sparky's lips formed a tight line. She stood and stuck her head out the door. "I'm sorry, but I need privacy with my patient." Sparky closed the door and turned the lock.

Daniel knew Casey well enough to know that she'd probably be pounding on the door in a minute. Sparky and Daniel stared at each other. Sparky seemed to be holding her breath, then her shoulders relaxed, and she spoke under her breath. "If looks could kill, I'd be dead."

Daniel rubbed his jaw. "We both might get a tongue lashing before this is over."

"Yep." Sparky's tone was resigned. "And we'd deserve it."

Daniel flinched when Sparky beamed a light in his eye. Sparky held his eyelids open, and the deep throbbing at the base of his skull intensified.

"You should tell the others." Sparky turned off the light.

Daniel blinked rapidly. "It will only add a burden of worry."

Sparky crossed her arms. "And you don't think they'll be worried when I tell them you're going to be spending the day in here?"

Daniel gripped the bedsheet. "Just give me a minute."

Sparky glared at him. "I should have my head examined for not putting my foot down and removing you from the team."

Daniel leaned against the headboard of the twin bed and closed his eyes, hoping the room would stop spinning. "I'll take a pill. I just need time for it—

"No." Her voice sounded harsh as she cut him off. "There's no way I'm allowing you to go out today. You're staying here, in the bed, either sleeping or staring at these four walls."

Daniel rubbed his jaw and sighed. "I guess I don't have a choice."

Sparky removed two pills from a bottle. "Take two."

"The tablets make me groggy."

"Good. Perhaps you'll get the rest you need." Sparky picked up the water bottle on the bedside table. "Take them."

Daniel swallowed the pills and closed his eyes. He had the feeling they'd be coming right back up.

Sparky placed her palm on his forehead. "You're clammy." She went to his bathroom and turned on the tap. A few seconds later, she placed a cool washcloth on his forehead.

"This isn't how I envisioned my first day in Africa." Daniel gave her what he hoped was a pleading look.

"It's not exactly a dream situation for me either. I feel like I'm the one being untruthful to everyone."

"Daniel sighed. "I haven't lied to anyone."

"You lied to Arvazean."

"That was just a little white lie."

"There's no such thing."

"I haven't lied to anyone on the mission team."

"Withholding the truth is the same."

"No. It's not."

"I'm not arguing about this. From here on out, you do as I say."

A heaviness pressed down on Daniel.

"I'll see you later."

"Okay." Daniel closed his eyes. "I'm sorry to put you in the middle of this mess."

"I'll be all right, unless Casey's laser looks blast me to kingdom come."

"Just ask her to forgive you for whatever you said. I'll be the one to deal with the fallout when she learns the truth."

"Let's hope she forgives both of us."

Sparky pulled down the window shade and hit the light switch as she left.

Daniel rubbed his forehead in the darkened room and remembered the flash of disappointment on Casey's face when she removed the bracelet from the gift box. The over-bright tone she'd used when exclaiming over the x's and o's in the weave hadn't fooled him.

He closed his eyes as the throbbing in his head lessened. The engagement ring would remain in his lockbox at the bank ... forever.

Who knew what he'd be facing when he returned home? Dr. Peterson had said that the tumor was deep, and it might be inoperable. *The mission team would be better off without me. I should have stayed home.*

Casey would be better off with him. Somehow, he had to find the courage to end it with her. He'd picked up on the idea that she seemed to be jealous of Sparky, which was ludicrous. Why would Casey be insecure around any woman? Couldn't she see he loved her? Still, if she was jealous, maybe he could use that to his advantage. If she broke it off with him, then there'd be no danger of her trying to tie herself to him forever. He could eliminate the risk of her wasting weeks or months by his bedside. A feeling of hopelessness washed over him. He would have to fight for his life—without the woman he loved by his side.

CHAPTER FIFTEEN—CASEY

From the kitchen, Casey watched Sparky tiptoe across the common room. Sparky stopped by the front door and slipped on her sandals.

"How's Daniel?" Casey hadn't meant to sound sharp.

Sparky jumped. "Goodness. You gave me a fright." Her eyes darted across the room.

Casey arched a brow. *She looks as guilty as Eve.*

Sparky gulped. "As you know, he has a headache. He's going to stay in his room and rest today."

Casey crossed her arms. "I didn't appreciate having the door shut in my face."

"Doctors and patients require privacy." Sparky lifted her chin.

Casey narrowed her eyes. "You two seemed very chummy walking in."

Sparky shrugged. "I grew up tagging after Daniel and my older brother Billy."

"I remember Billy, but funny, since I've returned to Weldon, I've not seen him and Daniel hanging out together."

"Billy is a high school principal, and he has three preschoolers. We only see him on the holidays."

"Is Daniel's okay?" Casey tilted her head, deciding to change the subject.

Sparky bit her lip. "Just to be on the safe side, I'm going to call the neurologist this afternoon. I'd call now but it's two o'clock in the morning at home."

"I guess you won't be sharing the specialist's opinion with me either?" Casey's jaw hardened.

Sparky gave her a sympathetic look. "You'll have to get that information from Daniel."

"I will." Casey turned on her heel and flounced to Daniel's room. She tapped on his door. When he didn't answer, she peeked her head inside. It was hard to see him in the dim light with the shades closed, but he snored softly on the bed.

Casey tiptoed in the room and placed her palm on his forehead. Daniel didn't have a fever. She leaned down and gently kissed him on the cheek. A wave of tenderness washed over her.

As she returned to the kitchen, the feeling that something wasn't right kept niggling at her. There was nothing she could do except brew another cup of coffee before she developed a headache. She'd had plenty of experience in New York dealing with deceitful people. She'd figure out what was going on. Sparky and Daniel were keeping something from her. Lies had a way of coming out. She only had to wait.

After a breakfast of oatmeal and cereal, everyone except Daniel spent the morning in an orientation program. Raymond explained greetings, eating customs, and the importance of reading from their Bible when teaching. They'd been practicing storytelling in simple words, easy to translate, but now they were here, Casey felt stupefied and couldn't concentrate.

Casey wondered if there was something about crossing time zones that made you lose maturity. Come to think of it, Pastor Bob looked twenty years younger, and even Eleanor seemed youthful, while Casey felt like an insecure teenager.

Who was she kidding? She'd never been this crazy with insecurity. The long skirts made her look like a light pole, but she didn't have a choice, and her makeup melted off the minute she stepped outside.

Sparky looked like a cute schoolgirl with her blond hair up in a high ponytail and a blue bandanna wrapped around it. Her skirt was made of a light floaty material that seemed to lift on the air when she walked. Casey knew she was just jealous, but she couldn't help herself.

Sam, the bald and lean missionary who'd help transport them from the airport, stood up as two Africans entered the room. Sam hugged the heavyset black woman who wore a traditional African skirt and hair wrap. The bright orange material with cobalt blue swirls brightened the dim room. Her large gold hoop earrings shined against her ebony skin.

The woman's companion was a tall, rail-thin black man. His grin revealed perfect teeth.

Sam shook the man's hand. "This is Isaaca, your translator." Sam turned toward the elegant ebony woman. "And his lovely wife Aissatou." Sam went around the room and introduced them. "Isaaca and Aissatou speak English and French, as well as seven African languages." Sam clapped Isaaca on the back.

"That's impressive." Casey placed her hand over her heart. She spoke a little French and Spanish but was only fluent in English.

Isaaca sat down in an empty chair and rested an ankle on the opposite knee. "It's not uncommon for Africans."

"He's being modest." Katie sat down next to Isaaca.

"The rest of the morning passed quickly, as Isaaca teased them and made jokes, while Aissatou looked down and placed her hand over her mouth, stifling giggles. Isaaca told them that eight years earlier, Sam and his wife, Lisa, had set up housekeeping in a remote village, and Sam had hired Isaaca to teach them Zarma. As the two men spent time together, Sam repeatedly shared Bible stories with the locals and Isaaca translated for him.

Isaaca stood. "I became the first man in the village to become a believer." He clasped his hands together. "Joy filled my heart, but then ..." His eyes held sorrow.

"What happened?" Pastor Bob sat up straight.

"Persecution ... And I became very ill, then a flood washed away our home."

"That's terrible." Eleanor gripped Pastor Bob's hand.

Isaaca looked at them gravely. "This is Satan's territory. He does not like anyone speaking the name of Jesus."

Sam's brows furrowed. "Often, mission team members or new believers will be struck by a sudden illness."

"We need to keep your sick team member in our prayers today." Isaaca folded his hands. "Satan truly is like a crouching lion seeking to destroy."

Katie's face softened. "Let's pray for each other and for our families as Satan will attempt to distract us."

Casey sat up straight. "Daniel started having migraines right after he signed up for the mission trip."

Sparky rolled her eyes. "Daniel's headaches aren't related to—" She stopped mid-sentence. "Never mind."

Margie fingered the red scarf on her head. She looked different with her chic hairstyle covered and no makeup. "Even though our children are adults, I hate being so far away from them. Yes. Let's pray for our families."

The group stood, and Sparky extended her hand to Casey. Casey hesitated but took it. While Pastor Bob prayed, Casey's thoughts drifted to Daniel. She stared at the new gold bracelet on her wrist. It was lovely, but not a token of love. And now she knew Sparky and Daniel had a history, and even with the seven-year age gap between the two, it wasn't impossible to believe they might be attracted to each other.

Pastor Bob said, "Amen," and Sparky dropped Casey's hand.

The group sat back down, and Raymond leaned forward in his chair. "In the morning, we'll be attending a church service." Raymond flipped through some papers checking his itinerary, then looked up at the group with an enthusiastic grin. "Afterward, we'll enjoy lunch with the pastor, and then visit an orphanage."

Casey's stomach ached at the thought of seeing the orphans.

"Our church members donated money to buy clothes for the children." Pastor Bob's broad smile sent wrinkles fanning out from the corners of his blue eyes.

"That's why we're visiting the Grand Marché this afternoon," Raymond rested his elbows on his knees. "Keeping a large party together will be difficult in the crowded market. I've decided the women will go with Isaaca and buy clothes for the children, and the men will go with me and search for school supplies."

"Don't forget I brought pencils and plastic sharpeners." Leslie sounded excited.

"I love shopping!" Casey clapped her hands together. *Finally, there's something on the agenda I know how to do.*

Margie rubbed her palms together. "I can't wait either."

Raymond raised his eyebrows. "The Grand Marché can be intimidating."

"You haven't seen the Big Apple Flea Market during the holidays." Casey fiddled with her gold bracelet. Her spirits lifted at the thought of buying gifts for the children, her family, and for Madison.

That afternoon, as the team emptied from the van, they divided into two groups. Casey wrinkled her nose as she stared at a skinned animal hanging from a tree nearby. Meat cooked on a grill, and smoke blew into her face. The mass of people stunned her, and children approached with extended hands, saying, "*Cadeau*—Gift, *cadeau*!" They'd been warned not to pass out anything because it might create a crush of desperate people.

"It is not safe to carry your backpack on your back, ma'am," Isaaca told Casey. "Might I suggest you carry it in front of you with your arms through each strap?"

Casey complied. "This seems awkward."

"But your belongings will be more secure," Isaaca said.

Heat radiated from her skin. She dabbed her forehead with a tissue and looked at the app on her phone to check the temperature. "It's one-hundred-ten degrees."

"Yes. A typical day." Isaaca shrugged. "Perhaps you should put the phone away."

"Watch out!" Sparky yelled.

A donkey brayed, and Isaaca yanked Casey backward. The rubber tire of a loaded cart grazed the edge of her sandal.

"He almost ran over me!" Casey's was indignant, her heart racing.

"Are you all right, ma'am?" Isaaca's eyes were wide.

"Yes." Casey placed her hand over her heart.

"I'll take that." Eleanor snatched Casey's phone.

"If you're injured, you won't want to visit our hospital," Raymond arched a brow.

Eleanor gave Casey a fierce look. "I promised your mother I'd keep you safe."

"You must pay attention." Isaaca's gentle voice made Casey feel remorseful. "Please, ladies, line up and follow me."

Eleanor fell in behind him, then Margie, Leslie, Sparky, and Casey trailed single file like baby ducklings.

They meandered through the tight maze of stalls. Strange fruits, dried herbs, pots, pans, and water jugs filled the tables. Everyone called to them. The air smelled of too many people, animals, and dust. Casey avoided animal waste under her feet and focused on keeping up with Sparky. The heat of the sun burned through the thin cotton material of her blouse, and she wondered how people lived in such a brutal environment.

When they found a stall selling soccer jerseys, Isaaca negotiated to buy all child-size shirts identical to those worn by Niger's national soccer team. They needed eighty-four of the orange and green tops. Still, they wanted to buy a few extra in case additional children had joined the orphanage since Raymond's last visit.

The vendor and Isaaca had an animated discussion, and the boy waved his hands. "He has twelve shirts," Isaaca said, "and he knows where he can get more." The market boy disappeared. The women waited until he returned a few minutes later with ten more jerseys and ran away again.

Casey fanned herself as she stood under a small tarp, hoping freckles weren't popping out all over her skin. The carnival atmosphere held her interest, but the heat wilted her enthusiasm for shopping.

The vendor reappeared from the crowd with ten more jerseys and took off running.

After opening her water bottle, Casey downed half of the contents and then wiped her face with a tissue. Two little girls stared at her. "*Fofo*"—Hello. Casey smiled, but they screamed and ran away.

"They fear you are a witch because of your unusual hair and green eyes," Isaaca's lips turned down. "Also, sometimes parents tell their children that white people will eat them."

"But why?"

"The Songhai are superstitious," Isaaca's dark eyes looked sad.

I'm melting like the wicked witch. Casey wiped her face again. *And how am I going to teach Bible school if the children believe I'm going to eat them?* They waited for the market boy to return. It seemed like each minute lasted ten in the oven-like heat.

At last, the young man returned with enough jerseys to complete the order, and he stood panting as Isaaca counted the shirts.

Isaaca touched the child's head and murmured something to him in Zarma. He explained to the women, "I've told him 'well done.'"

The boy's hand shook as Isaaca counted out the money. Other people circled as the bills were placed in his palm. Casey could hardly breathe as the crowd pushed in closer. The crush of people made her heart rate increase, and she tried to back out of the melee, but the people were too close.

"They are all counting to ensure that the proper amount has been paid," Isaaca unfolded more bills. "It's okay."

"I wished we'd waited and purchased our supplies here rather than lugging them all the way from Weldon." Casey fanned herself with a piece of paper.

Isaaca counted the last piece of currency for the third time.

A wave of compassion washed over Casey as she examined the market boy's ragged, dirty shirt. "Please tell him we appreciate his help gathering enough jerseys, and we want to reward him with a twenty-dollar tip."

"Are you sure? Twenty dollars American is almost a week's salary for a teacher in Niger."

"Absolutely." Casey's heart softened.

When Isaaca told the young man about the extra money, he looked up with eyes shining and said something to Casey. Isaaca interpreted. "He says, 'thank you, and if you ever need anything in the market, he will be happy to be your finder.'"

Casey beamed a bright smile and nodded her head.

Isaaca placed the extra money in the boy's trembling hand. Applause erupted from the crowd.

"This sale is likely the largest he'll ever make in his life. He'll never forget your generosity." Isaaca smiled.

"And I'll always remember his joy." Casey blinked back tears.

Casey and Sparky shared a look, and neither spoke. She considered the thousand euros she'd wanted to spend on a purse in Paris for Madison. Yet, a twenty-dollar tip seemed significant to this child who should have been in school rather than working.

As they made the return trip to the bush taxi, a stall of beautiful fabrics held Casey's attention, and she stopped for an instant to study the different patterns. They'd bought soccer jerseys for the boys, but didn't the girls need dresses or skirts? She knew her mother would appreciate these bold designs for her quilts. The keen vendor started pulling out bolts of fabric. Mesmerized by the bright colors, Casey fingered the stiff cotton. She looked up to get the attention of Isaaca, but she didn't see him or anyone from their party. It seemed the mass of shoppers had swallowed them. Casey didn't know which way to turn, and the crush of shoppers smothered her. She grabbed for her phone in her empty pocket. *Oh, no.*

Casey didn't recall hearing what to do if she became separated from the group. Two small girls looked at her with wide eyes, then screamed when she smiled at them. Ignoring the stares, she stayed put, having no idea which way to go.

People continued to stare and pass her, and many held out their hands and said, "*Cadeau.*"

She did her best to look respectful and confident but not too friendly. The last thing she wanted to do was to offend someone.

Her face burned in the brutal heat. Casey removed sunscreen from her bag and hoped the cream was powerful enough to protect her from the harsh rays and wondered again what to do—stay put or attempt to find her way to the van. After waiting for ten minutes, she decided to search for the van. Without a clue as to which direction to move, she shrugged and turned left.

Casey trod with care through the tight aisles, hugging her backpack. Everything looked the same. Two goats ran in front of her, and she stepped in dung. While she attempted to clean her sandals with a hand-sanitizing wipe, a donkey cart almost ran her down.

A young man broke through the crowd, grabbed her hand, and pulled forward. Another teen grabbed the other hand. Boys swarmed and started pushing her through the throng, yelling at each other. She felt helpless to do anything except move with the current of energy. She screamed. "Help!"

People looked up but didn't help. The boys pushed her through the maze of lanes. After a few minutes, Hama's bush taxi came into view.

Isaaca rushed forward. "Well done!" He clapped and passed out money to each boy as they let go and said, "*Aisabou*"—thank you.

Pastor Bob and Eleanor pushed through to Casey.

Eleanor hugged her. "Are you all right?" A strand of Eleanor's gray hair had slipped from her blue bandanna.

The thick dust and soot on her face didn't conceal the deep worry lines.

"Yes, just shaken."

"When we lost you, I offered a reward." Isaaca shoved his hands into his pockets. "There were young men all over the market looking for you."

Casey wiped her wet face with a tissue. "I stopped to consider a piece of fabric, and then I didn't see anyone from our group."

"I almost fainted when I realized we'd left you." Eleanor wrung her hands. "Then, Isaaca came up with a plan to find you."

Isaaca's brows were furrowed. "It's rare for white people to be in the market. I knew it wouldn't take long for the market boys to find you." Isaaca dropped his head. "I'm very sorry for your distress. Please forgive me."

"You warned me to pay attention. I'm sorry to have upset everyone." Casey placed her palm over her racing heart.

"I won't say the thoughts running through my mind." Eleanor started digging in her purse, then thrust the confiscated phone to Casey. "Keep this with you at all times."

She slipped the phone in her pocket and grimaced at being treated as a child. "Yes, ma'am."

One of the boys returned and spoke to Casey.

Isaaca translated, "This young man asks for your blessings. He believes you have a special magic because of your red hair. This is an opportunity to speak about Jesus."

Casey's hands shook, and she wondered what to say, what to do. For weeks they'd been practicing sharing the gospel, but she froze. The boy looked to her with curious eyes and she placed her hand on his shoulder. "I came to Africa to tell people about Jesus."

Isaaca spoke, the boy's eyes grew large, and he took off running. Sand flew in the air when he turned the corner.

Isaaca shrugged. "If they don't want to hear, we can't make them listen."

Casey's stomach plummeted as she watched the boy race away after hearing the mere mention of the name of Jesus. The realization he might never have another chance to learn about Christianity made her feel despondent. As she studied the crowded market, she saw countless opportunities to make a difference here. If only God had sent someone better equipped. Daniel was far better suited for this work than she, yet here she stood. She lifted her chin and told herself to straighten up. *You may not be the best missionary, but you're better than nothing.* She promised herself she'd do better the next time she had the opportunity to tell someone about Jesus.

CHAPTER SIXTEEN—DANIEL

Later that afternoon, Casey sat on the edge of Daniel's bed, and he winced as he sipped from the glass of water and took another pill.

Casey placed her palm on his cheek.

"Is there anything I can do to help?"

Daniel inhaled the scent of her sunscreen. "No. The pills ease the pain, but they put me to sleep."

Sparky knocked on the door and stepped in. "How's my patient?"

Daniel straightened his shoulders. "Better, thanks."

"Excuse me, Casey," Sparky shoved between them. "I want to examine Daniel's eyes." She pulled out her flashlight.

Casey stood up, and Sparky sat down where Casey had been sitting. Casey looked over Sparky's shoulder. "What are you looking for?"

"I'm looking for direct and indirect pupil response to light."

"But what does it tell you?" Casey frowned.

"I'm looking for damage to the cranial nerves."

"But why? He didn't hit his head."

Daniel couldn't see anything except for the beam of light.

"Is there something going on that I need to know about?" He could detect the anxiety in Casey's voice.

"I'm better." Daniel sat up straighter, and his head swam.

Sparky shut off the light. "I don't see any improvement. Hold out your hand."

Daniel blinked to clear his vision from the floating white orbs. "Just give me a minute. I was in a deep sleep when Casey came in." He held out his hand.

"They're steady. That's good."

Sparky stood and pointed her finger at him. "Stay in bed, and that's an order." Her voice sounded all-business. She turned on her heel and strode out of the room.

"Some bedside manner," Casey muttered as she removed the red headscarf and scowled at her reflection in the mirror. Dust covered her from head to toe.

"Sit back down and tell me about your day." Daniel reached for her hand.

"I need a shower." Casey grimaced. "And you need your rest."

"That's all I've been doing, and Sparky's likely beat you to the shower."

Casey sat on the edge of the bed. "I'm a mess."

"*Beautiful are the feet of those who preach the gospel of peace ...*" Daniel quoted the Scripture.

"That's not me." Casey's lips turned down. "The kids literally ran away from me screaming. Isaaca said they might believe I'm a witch."

Casey told him about becoming separated from the group and his chest tightened. A wave of guilt washed over him. "I should have been with you.

Casey squeezed his hand. "The men were with Raymond. You wouldn't have been able to save me."

"Isaaca should have been more careful."

"It was all my fault. He warned me more than once to pay attention, and believe me, from this day forward, I will."

Daniel pulled her close to him. "Thank the Lord you're safe." He nuzzled her neck.

A sharp tap on the door made Casey jump. She pushed away from the embrace and sprang up.

"Come in." Daniel sighed.

Pastor Bob stuck his bald head in. "How are you feeling?"

Daniel scratched at the stubble on his jawline. "Better."

Casey ran her hand over her French braid. "I'm headed for the shower," she said, and exited the room.

Pastor Bob closed the door behind him and pulled up a chair. "Let me pray for you."

"Thanks, I'd appreciate that." As Pastor Bob prayed, Daniel's heart constricted and a deep yearning for his father tugged at his heart. But his dad was gone. He should be thankful for Pastor Bob as a fill-in.

When Pastor Bob said, "Amen," he leaned forward and rested his elbow on his knees. "What's going on with you?" His blue eyes looked sympathetic.

"Just ... you know, these migraines."

"I was sitting in the garden, enjoying the view of the river a few minutes ago when I overhead Sparky talking to someone on the phone."

Daniel gulped. *Uh-oh.*

Pastor Bob squeezed his hand. "Sparky didn't notice me, but I was close enough to hear the conversation was about your medical condition."

Daniel rubbed the stubble on his jaw and gulped. "Last week, I learned the headaches I'm experiencing are the results of a deep brain tumor."

Pastor Bob nodded and kept his eyes on Daniel.

"It will be a couple of weeks before the neurosurgeon can meet with me. I figured ..." Daniel shrugged. "... why not go to Africa? It might be my last chance to do something good in the world."

Pastor Bob laced his fingers together. "I understand." He just sat there, staring at Daniel with a piercing gaze. Finally, he spoke. "Last year, while recovering in the ICU, I doubted I'd ever leave the hospital, so I understand feeling like your dreams are slipping away—to lose hope."

"Everyone was praying for you."

"And now, I'm in Africa." Pastor Bob gave a wry grin. "It sounds to me like you've been trying to handle this on your own. Does Casey know?"

"No. Only Sparky and the oncologist, Dr. Peterson, the guy she probably called on the phone."

"You've been carrying a heavy burden."

Daniel swallowed the lump in his throat. "I feel like God's abandoned me in this mess."

"Unrepented sin can make us feel like we're separated from God, but he is always with us, and he's available to help us in every situation." Pastor Bob gave him a long look. "This sort of deceit will damage your relationship with Casey."

"That might be a good thing."

Pastor Bob's brows furrowed. "What do you mean? Anyone who looks closely can tell that you love her."

Daniel swallowed the lump in his throat. "That's why I won't let her tie herself to me when I might end up helpless."

"You're underestimating Casey and her love for you."

"I'll tell her about the tumor as soon as we return to Weldon."

"I won't speak with anyone about this, but I advise you to tell everyone."

"Not yet."

"There's a better way."

"I'm just not ready to tell Casey, or anyone for that matter."

"I'm talking about taking this to the Lord. Let him handle it for you, and if you'd tell others, they would be lifting petitions for you too."

"I'm just not ready."

"Okay." Pastor Bob nodded. "Let me pray with you again before I go."

"Thank you. I'd appreciate that."

As Pastor Bob prayed, a sense of peace washed over Daniel. When Pastor Bob stood, Daniel swiped his forearm across his damp cheek. "Thank you."

"I'll continue to pray for your healing and for God to give you and your doctors wisdom." Pastor Bob squeezed his shoulder. "Your secret is safe with me."

Daniel lay on the bed and considered telling Casey. *No.* She'd insist they return to Weldon. At last, he gave in to the desire to close his heavy eyelids. *Father, forgive me.*

CHAPTER SEVENTEEN—CASEY

The next morning, Casey pulled out a chair, sat down across from Daniel, and crossed her arms. "I'm staying with you today."

Daniel reached for her hand. "It would be selfish of me to keep you here when Pastor Bob needs your help to minister to the children at the orphanage." He squeezed her hand.

"But—"

Daniel looked out the window. "The team is getting into the bush taxi. Please go. It will make me feel worse to know I'm keeping you from helping the team."

Casey stood and trudged toward the van, and Daniel followed.

"The children ran away from me screaming yesterday." Casey hated that her voice sounded whiny.

"But that was in a crowded market among strangers."

Casey gave Daniel a last hug while inhaling the comforting scent of Old Spice, then she climbed into the van.

Sparky sat in the front passenger seat looking cute with her perky blonde ponytail swaying in the breeze. Today she had on a red bandanna. Tyler and Dave filled the back bench. "There's room for you next to me." Eleanor slid over on the cracked black vinyl seat. "The Louisville folks crowded into Sam's Toyota."

"This is going to be a tight squeeze when Daniel joins us tomorrow." Casey stepped up into the van and battled with her long brown skirt.

Isaaca and Aissatou sat on the bench behind her. "You're in Africa," Isaaca leaned back in the seat. "This little van will hold many more. Watch as we drive down the road. You'll see."

They all waved at Daniel as the van pulled outside the compound gates.

Motorcycles and donkey carts, cars, trucks, and bicycles filled the narrow asphalt highway, and everything with a horn constantly honked. Hama wove the dilapidated vehicle through the heavy traffic of Niamey. Modern buildings sat next to mud-brick huts and concrete structures painted a variety of shades. A hand-painted sign advertising a hairdresser caught Casey's attention. Plastic-covered sofas were lined up in front of a furniture shop. Tiny stores had bars in their windows.

Casey gripped the seat in front of her when Hama hit a pothole. Little homes the size of a small bedroom in America lined the highway. Most were made of mud or concrete bricks and had corrugated tin roofs. A few looked to be made of twigs intertwined. In front of the homes, women cooked over charcoal fires and children of all ages, wearing rags or no shirts, waved to their passing bush taxi. At last, the traffic cleared as they exited the city. Casey closed her eyes and inhaled the ever-present scent of charcoal.

It seemed plastic bags clung to every scrub brush and thorn tree, and she wondered again how she'd managed to find herself in Africa when she should be home explaining to her parents about their granddaughter. Sparky snapped a picture of a camel ambling by loaded with woven grass mats.

The bush taxi turned off the highway onto what looked like a sand trail. As they bumped along, it reminded Casey of an amusement park ride. Every bone in her body jarred as Hama hit a hole and then swerved onto what looked like a footpath. Dust swirled behind them, and the landscape looked uninhabitable.

The burnt-orange sand extended for miles, then straw huts, mud-brick buildings and fences started appearing. Hama slowed the van and parked on a village street.

Casey exited the vehicle and followed Isaaca into a compound protected by a large iron gate. He pointed to a mudbrick building with a corrugated tin gabled roof. A large wooden cross had been attached at the top of the gable. "This is the only church for miles. The pastor's home is over there." Isaaca pointed to a tiny mudbrick home similar to those they passed on the highway.

The group of eleven crammed into the interior of the small church already filled with Africans. The only light in the room came from the four windows on each side. It took a few seconds for Casey's eyes to adjust. Many sat on crude wooden benches, others stood in the back, and a few sat on woven mats. The front row bench remained empty.

Isaaca directed them to a man wearing a white shirt that seemed to glow in the dim light. "It's my great honor to introduce you to Pastor Djibo."

After Raymond made formal introductions, Pastor Djibo indicated for them to sit front and center.

As the service started, Isaaca interpreted every sentence Pastor Djibo spoke. The preacher stood in front of what looked like an oil barrel covered with a white linen cloth embroidered with red flowers along the edges. Casey and the others had practiced African hymns in preparation for the trip, and Pastor Djibo asked them to start the singing. After the first few words, the congregation joined them in praising God. A man in the front to the left of the pastor beat on a large drum, and two teens played smaller drums. The African congregation swayed to the beat of the music. Tears rolled down the cheeks of a tall thin woman to Casey's right. Casey looked over her shoulder and saw many of the dark faces looked joyous as they lifted their hands toward heaven. For the first time since they'd arrived, Casey felt blessed to be in Africa and wondered if this would be like heaven, with people of all races and languages worshipping together.

Her thoughts drifted to Loving Chapel, where many of the members stood with dour faces. Oh, how she wished everyone could be here to experience worshipping with the Africans. *Maybe we'd all learn to appreciate how God has blessed us.*

In yesterday's orientation program, they'd learned the Christians in Niger faced persecution, even abandonment by their families when they accepted Christ. There were no "attenders" or "pretenders" here. Their joyous worship lifted Casey's spirit. No organ, no air conditioning, no plush seats, no stained-glass windows, and yet the Holy Spirit flowed through this simple building and washed over her.

Pastor Djibo spoke of the need for each of them to shine the light of Jesus, to turn the other cheek, to love those who persecuted them, and to forgive them. He looked upon his flock with compassion and concluded, quoting the gospel of Matthew, Chapter 18, verses 21 and 22: "Then Peter came up and said to him, 'Lord, how often will my brother sin against me, and I forgive him? As many as seven times?' Jesus said to him, 'I do not say to you seven times, but seventy times seven.'"

For a brief instant, Casey's heart lifted. *Maybe my family will forgive me.* But the hope turned to an ache as she considered forgiving Jansen. *I can't do it.*

Pastor Djibo asked them to form groups of three or four and to pray for each other in their own languages. As Casey listened to the prayers in English and Zarma, she knew it was a divine moment. Tears poured down the face of the woman whose dark fingers clutched Casey's hand. Her callused palms were tough but sturdy. A wave of love permeated the air as Casey lifted a silent prayer for God to bless this woman and her family. It seemed God Himself entered the area and pushed out everything except love.

As she lifted a prayer for Daniel, compassion flowed through her, but then shame flooded her thoughts as she remembered her jealousy of Sparky. She thought of Madison's letter in her bag and focused on prayer. *Thank you for protecting her. Help me to learn to forgive and to stop being afraid.* A burden seemed to shift, and joy filled her being. *Wow. What just happened?* Her pulse quickened, and for an instant, she felt nothing but happiness. But then, her traitorous mind pictured Jansen, and her pulse raced as she asked herself for the hundredth time. *What if she looks like him?*

Pastor Djibo invited the mission team to be his honored guests for lunch. Casey considered the pot suspended over the open fire and remembered the skinned animal hanging from the tree in the market with flies swarming around it. She had a protein bar in her backpack, and there would be time to eat it in the van on the return trip to Niamey.

Katie indicated they should sit on the mat rolled out for them. They all slipped off their shoes and formed a circle.

The simple, mud-walled compound boasted one large palm tree. A water filtration system made of sand sat in the center of the courtyard. Pastor Djibo's wife, Sakina, placed a dish filled with macaroni noodles, tomatoes, spices, and meat in the center of the mat.

"I can't eat this," Casey whispered to Sparky.

Sparky spoke under her breath. "It's safe. The pot was boiling. We're not going to dishonor their hospitality."

Raymond led the blessing, and everyone said, "Amen."

"Remember," Katie pointed at the large round dish. "It's customary for everyone to eat with the right hand and to imagine the tray divided like a pizza. Each person will eat from their section of the platter."

The others started dipping their hand into the dish. Eleanor elbowed Casey, so she pinched a noodle and lifted the first bite to her mouth. At that instant, she felt a sharp jab on her ankle and dropped the food. A chicken pecked at the food on the dirt floor.

"Don't waste it." Sparky hissed to Casey.

Casey held her palms out. "I'm sorry."

"It's all right," Pastor Djibo brushed his hands. "The chickens need to eat too."

"I work at a pharmacy." Dave swiped at his auburn bangs. "And I brought some medical supplies, but the needs are overwhelming. I wonder if we can make a difference with our limited resources."

"You can't fix poor." Pastor Djibo's face was somber. "You will never be able to bring enough food to feed all the hungry or enough medicine for the sick. But what did Peter offer to the man at the temple gate?"

"The name of Jesus." Margie beamed and squeezed her husband's hand.

"Exactly," Raymond said. "That's why we're here."

"You're looking at material possessions and think Nigerians are poor," Katie pinched a piece of meat. "They might feel Americans have a deprived life."

"In the States, few take the time to visit family and friends." Raymond looked around the group. "Everyone seems to be working or rushing to the next event."

"I feel like I'm running all the time." Casey fingered her skirt.

"The quality of life here is rich in a way most Americans wouldn't understand," Katie sipped from her water bottle. "They stop to visit, enjoy a cup of tea, and they share everything with each other."

"No one knows from one day to the next if they'll have food. The Africans share with their neighbors because tomorrow they might be the one in need," Raymond and Katie exchanged a look.

Casey thought of her hectic life at home. It was rare to have time to enjoy a cup of coffee with Emma since she'd started fostering children.

Sakina, Pastor Djibo's wife, had built a fire and cooked over an open flame in this heat, and yet she still beamed a smile and watched them eat.

Casey smiled back. "How do you say thank you?"

"*Aisabou*," Aissatou said.

Casey nodded at Sakina. "*Aisabou*—thank you."

Sakina placed her palms together and bowed her head.

"It's just the second day, and I can already feel God removing scales from my eyes." Eleanor lifted her face to the sky.

"Me too." Sparky blew out a long stream of air. "We thought we were coming to change lives, but maybe we need to be changed first."

"I think you may be on to something," Casey's heart softened toward Sparky.

The group finished the meal and thanked the couple for their hospitality. A treadle sewing machine sat under a covering made of twigs with a tin roof next to the house. Casey asked Aissatou to ask Sakina if she sewed.

Aissatou spoke to the pastor's wife. She led the women inside the house and opened a plastic storage box filled with bolts of beautiful fabrics, each more splendid than the last.

"She teaches a sewing class," Aissatou clasped her hands together. "Girls come here to learn the trade two mornings a week."

"Could I hire her to make dresses for the little girls at the orphanage? And I'd like to order several long-wrap skirts, like the one you're wearing, to take back home as gifts." Casey felt hopeful.

Aissatou asked Sakina, and her eyes were bright as she nodded yes.

"Choose the material you like, and she'll have them ready by the time we return next Sunday for the church service." Aissatou's beautiful smile split her face.

"Wonderful," Casey turned to Raymond. "Will you exchange some of my American cash for Niger currency?"

"Instead of dollars, we use CFAs in Niger." Raymond grinned. "And I'll be happy to."

"How much will I owe her?"

Aissatou spoke to Sakina, who chewed her lip and looked down before answering.

"Is six dollars American for each skirt satisfactory?" Aissatou asked.

"I'll pay more. Negotiate for me to pay more," Casey's heart lifted.

"We'll worry about that later." Raymond brushed his hands.

Sparky, Eleanor, and Margie ordered wrap skirts for family and friends too, and Sakina wrote down the details.

Sakina spoke again, and Aissatou translated. "She said, 'All her students will be happy to help.'"

"This sale will help feed their family." Katie's voice was gleeful. "With food scarce, their hospitality is a sacrifice."

"I'm glad I saw the sewing machine," Casey said.

"Is there anything else we can do to help without offending them?" Eleanor looked around the compound.

"Add Pastor Djibo's family to your prayer list," Raymond's face softened.

"Of course," Pastor Bob swallowed hard.

"It's time to go to the orphanage." Raymond wiped his hands on his jeans. "We'll return next Sunday to pick up the skirts."

Sakina beamed a smile and nodded.

The group started loading into the bush taxi. "I'll take the back seat." Casey lifted her long skirt and weaved through the narrow aisle to the rear. "I'm getting the hang of it."

She missed Daniel, and a constant niggle of worry stayed with her, just as she fretted about him at home because of his job. The temperature in the van wilted her enthusiasm, and her muscles tensed as she considered their next stop. These children were orphaned because of severe poverty or the death of their parents. Had her reasoning for giving up Madison truly been to protect her from her father and his shame? As she considered the questions, she knew the answer. Fear of Jansen had played a part in the decision to let her baby go, but she also knew worry about the gossips in Weldon had bothered her. At last, she admitted that she hadn't wanted to give up her career. That knowledge weighed heaviest on her now. Oh, how she wished she could turn back the clock.

Hama drove down a sandy trail, and Casey wondered how he knew where to turn with no street signs. Small mud buildings crowded both sides of the path, and they passed many people living under plastic tarps. Children in ragged clothes chased the van. It appeared as though all the women of Niger had two things in common—work and babies. It seemed a woman had a baby tied to her back at each shelter while she cooked over a charcoal fire.

Aissatou pointed her finger. "We are here. See the gate?" The van stopped, Hama honked the horn, and tall wooden doors swung open wide. Casey steeled herself. *You can do this.* It seemed a dream to see a clean, wide-open play area and modern buildings. Children wearing clean clothing flooded from the doors.

She stepped from the back of the van and a little girl, who looked to be about four years old, clutched her hand. Another child snatched her free fingers, and both girls spoke with animated faces. Her shoulders relaxed when the girls didn't scream and run away.

Children of various sizes circled the team members and led them inside a building, where ceiling fans churned the hot air. A pristine white tile floor lay before them, but red sand dusted the squares as they filed in. The children talked nonstop, and bright eyes danced with laughter. Eleanor sat in a chair, lifted a toddler to her lap, and others sat at her feet. Casey found a stool, and a little girl climbed into her lap. A child wearing a tattered dress stood in the corner alone. She sucked her thumb, then covered her face with her hands when Casey made eye contact with her.

Raymond spoke to a man who seemed to be in charge of the orphanage. He wore a long cobalt blue tunic with white linen pants. A matching round kufi cap embroidered in mustard yellow sat atop his head. The cap could double as a bowl if turned upside down. He adjusted his gold wire-rimmed glasses and clapped his hands. The child in Eleanor's lap jumped up and ran to the front of the room. The children arranged themselves for a presentation.

The tall ebony man spoke in English with a French accent. "Welcome, friends. I am Thomas Dubois. When God sent me here ten years ago to build this orphanage, the task seemed impossible. It still is, but God is faithful to meet our every need. Even when I lack faith, he provides. We've been praying for school supplies, and it is my understanding you have delivered such gifts. Praise God."

He turned his back to them, faced the children, and raised his arms. Every child's eyes were on him. With a nod from Monsieur Dubois, the children started singing one of the simplest songs Casey knew. "*Fofo, Baba Iroquois, fofo*"—Thank you, Father God, thank you.

As Casey watched, the little girl in the frayed dress who had been in the corner stepped closer to her. When Casey extended her hand, the child walked into her embrace. She lifted her to her lap and felt the girl's damp tears on her neck. Casey wondered why the child was crying. As she rocked the girl back and forth, she listened to the other children sing. Joy beamed from their faces as they sang. Casey's spirits lifted as she discerned the hope in this place.

Aissatou sat down next to Casey and spoke to the crying girl in a quiet voice. The child looked up at her, whispered something to Aissatou, and tears filled Aissatou's dark eyes as she placed her palm on the child's head and prayed. Casey had no idea what Aissatou said, but it seemed to comfort the girl.

Aissatou removed her hand from the child's head and spoke softly to Casey in English. "This is Fatima. Her mama died, and there are too many children for the papa to feed. He kept her brothers but left her here yesterday."

Casey gasped. "Poor thing. Tell her I will pray for them to all be together again, someday."

Aissatou spoke, but the child hid her face in Casey's neck.

She continued to rock her as the other children serenaded them. After five boys, Casey's parents had treated her like a special gift, but here little Fatima's family abandoned her. She wondered how anyone could desert such a fragile thing. Guilt assaulted her as she remembered holding her newborn infant. *I did the same thing as this girl's father*, she realized. Her reasons had been different, but still ... Casey hugged the girl tighter.

The children finished singing, and Monsieur Dubois lined up them by size. The men from the mission team carried in boxes that contained backpacks filled with school supplies and clothes. Casey held Fatima while the others distributed the gifts. At the end of the line, the older orphans clutched their hands together and hopped from one foot to the other. The smaller children at the front of the line unzipped the bags and squealed.

Raymond knelt before Fatima and held out a backpack, but she hid her face again.

Casey stroked her back. "She arrived yesterday and is afraid."

Fatima peeked out as Casey accepted the gift from Raymond.

Monsieur Dubois clapped his hands again. "Children, please give our visitors a tour of your dormitory."

When she stood, Fatima clung to her waist as another girl pulled on Casey's free hand and led them through the schoolyard to a brown building. Inside, tattered books sat on a crooked bookshelf and bunk beds lined every wall. A few contained soiled mattresses, but most had plywood for the base. Girls huddled around her when she sat on the tile floor, yet Fatima pushed into her lap and pressed her face into Casey's shoulder. As she held Fatima, she silently prayed for each smiling face and vowed to do something to help these children.

Casey read the sign hanging over the doorway written in French and English: "In You the Orphan Finds Mercy.—Hosea 14:3."

Children's laughter drifted in. Outside the window, Dave and Tyler played a game of freeze tag with the boys. All the youngsters were wearing their new soccer jerseys. Even though the kids varied in size, the shirts seemed to be a perfect fit for everyone.

Two hours later, Raymond announced, "It's time to go." The sun dropped, and the others waited as Casey gently pried Fatima's fingers from her hand. She cupped the little girl's face with both hands, kissed her forehead, and prayed for the child to discover mercy in her new home.

She couldn't help but question why God had blessed her with wealth. Her granny's voice quoting Scripture floated through the flotsam of her memories— *"But from those who are given much, much is expected."* Granny's constant habit of applying Bible verses to daily life had made Casey roll her eyes when she was young. But now she understood Granny had been sowing God's word into her heart, and some of those seeds remained.

CHAPTER EIGHTEEN—DANIEL

Daniel sat in the sweethearts' swing in the shade waiting for the group to return. When the gate opened, he strode to the van. Everyone on the team was covered in dust from head to toe. Sparky made a beeline for him.

"The headache's gone." Daniel grinned.

"What a relief. "Sparky hugged him.

Daniel noticed Casey, and he stepped out of the embrace. "Here's a girl who needs a hug too."

Casey shrugged away from him. "I'm a hot mess."

"You look beautiful!"

"Apparently, the headache affected your vision."

"Nope, but I think the heat's turned up your sassiness. He grabbed her hand and led her to the swing.

They sat down. "Tell me everything," Daniel said.

Casey removed the scarf from her hair and wiped her face. "I don't know if I have the words." She gazed toward the river. "Today I experienced a multitude of emotions—wonder, joy, peace, shock, sadness, desperation, and hope."

"Tell me about the church service." He gripped her hand.

"Several of the men were dressed in tunics, just like I imagine Jesus wore. The mingled prayers created a holy atmosphere. I'll never forget it." Casey's face looked sympathetic. "I'm sorry you missed it."

Daniel sighed. "There's always tomorrow."

"And Pastor Djibo's wife, Sakina, is going to make dresses for the girls at the orphanage and skirts for me to take home as gifts."

"Trust you to find an opportunity to shop." Daniel winked at her.

"It's a way for us to assist them without giving charity. Pastor Djibo's wife teaches girls to sew."

He traced the line on her palm with his index finger. "I'm teasing you. I'm glad you discovered a way to help."

"Oh, and I wish you could have seen the children at the orphanage. They sang for us."

"I wish I'd been there. I'll bet that was something."

"One little girl in particular broke my heart."

"Only one?"

"The other children seemed happy and healthy, but she'd been left there yesterday by her father because his wife died."

"Poor thing." A wave of sadness washed over him.

"He kept her brothers but abandoned her."

Daniel wrapped his arm around her and kissed her temple.

"Her ragged little dress broke my heart. I held her for a long time, and she hid her face and cried."

"I'm sure the time she spent in your arms helped." Daniel wished he had the words to make Casey feel better.

"I had to pry her fingers from mine while the others waited. I'll never forget her clinging to me."

Daniel tightened his embrace and held her.

"What can we do to help her?" Casey asked.

"We can't save everyone," Daniel kissed the top of her head.

"Then why are we here?" Casey sounded frustrated.

"I've been listening to the family of squatters living next to the wall, and I want to do something for them too, but Raymond says the compound will be stormed by needy people if we start passing out food and medical supplies."

"We have to do something." Casey dabbed at her damp cheek with a tissue.

"Giving out aid has to be done in an organized manner, in a place away from the mission house." A sense of helplessness washed over him.

"But we can't ignore them."

"Raymond and Sam have to determine those most in need, but even then, they have to hire guards to keep the crowds controlled."

"We're like an ant trying to push a tank."

"You helped the young man in the market when you bought jerseys, and don't forget about the dresses for the girls and the skirts you ordered from the pastor's wife."

"I guess." Casey sighed.

"Every little bit helps."

They sat in silence, gently swinging. Sparky approached and passed her cell phone to Daniel. "Dr. Peterson wants to speak with you."

Daniel took the phone, and Sparky grabbed Casey's arm. "Let's give Daniel some privacy."

Daniel walked away, but he couldn't help but hear Casey and Sparky arguing. Then Eleanor stepped between them.

"Hi, Dr. Peterson. It's Daniel Sheppard." Daniel did his best to sound upbeat.

After answering a long list of questions, Daniel disconnected and returned to the mission house. He removed his shoes and walked to the kitchen.

Casey slammed a coke bottle on the counter. "Who's Dr. Peterson and what did he say?"

"I told you about the specialist I'm going to see. He asked me to stay in for one more day." Daniel rubbed the back of his neck.

Raymond tilted his head and narrowed his eyes. "I know it's disappointing, but I agree."

"I'm a little weak, that's all."

"Tomorrow, we have a three-hour drive across challenging roads and a ferry. Anyone who is not one hundred percent well should not go." Raymond crossed his arms.

Daniel pulled out a kitchen chair that scraped the floor, and he sat down with a thump.

"We have clear cell phone reception here." Raymond pushed up from the chair. "But we never know in the villages."

"I guess you're right," Daniel grimaced. "That will mean three wasted days."

"But we still have over a week in Africa." Casey wrapped her arms around his shoulders.

Pastor Bob walked in, fresh from a shower, his face glowing.

"It looks like Africa suits you." Casey looked him up and down.

"Wasn't today something?" Then Pastor Bob's glance fell on Daniel. "Oh, I'm sorry you missed it." He squeezed Daniel's shoulder. "How are you feeling?"

"Great." Daniel spoke loudly.

Pastor Bob opened his mouth and closed it. His lips formed a tight line.

Daniel held his gaze, his cop mask firmly in place. This was not the time to back down. He'd tell Casey everything when they returned to Weldon.

Pastor Bob gave him a sympathetic look, and a wave of remorse washed over Daniel. "I really am feeling better."

"An answered prayer," Pastor Bob said. "Thank you, Jesus."

"I guess," Daniel lowered his gaze as his frustration grew. He should have stayed home. But he was here. So much for his last chance to do something good in the world. He sighed heavily. *Father, forgive me.*

CHAPTER NINETEEN—CASEY

The group prepared to leave at dawn the following day. Daniel helped Casey lift her backpack.

"It's New Year's Eve," Daniel whispered in her ear. "We'll celebrate tonight."

"I completely forgot." Casey adjusted the straps. "Why is my pack heavy?"

"I added my two water bottles as well as yours. They're frozen, wrapped in dish towels."

"Do you think I'll need all this?"

"It's going to be over a hundred degrees today—don't forget to take the pill to protect you from malaria at lunch."

Casey rubbed sunblock on her nose. Maybe it wasn't too late to feign an illness. Outside the window, Eleanor organized the Bible school supplies, and Casey knew she couldn't let her down. "I'm sorry to leave you behind."

"Don't worry about me." He adjusted the scarf on her head and kissed her forehead. "Please don't get separated from the group."

"Sparky and I are partners." Casey resisted the urge to roll her eyes. "We'll watch out for each other."

Sparky, Pastor Bob, and Eleanor climbed into the air-conditioned Toyota Land Cruiser with Raymond and Katie. The others piled into the bush taxi. Casey waved to Daniel as they drove away. His slumped posture saddened her. She was sorry his dream to be on the mission field wasn't working out. And here she was, the most unlikely person ever to be in such a place, going off into the desert.

By the time they reached the ferry to cross the Niger River, the sun was heating up the day. It no longer surprised her to see women washing clothes in the river and gathering water, but it still made her feel sorrowful.

Hama parked in the growing line of vehicles for the ferry behind Raymond's Land Cruiser. Raymond poked his head in the van window and said, "The ferry is on its way back. It will be here in about fifteen minutes. Feel free to get out and stretch your legs."

Casey moved slowly, careful not to get her long skirt caught on the jagged edges of metal in the bush van. It felt good to get out of the cramped space.

Strange scents and sights surrounded her at the dock. The long line of transportation vehicles that led to the dock included bush taxies, trucks, motorcycles, and donkey carts. A van with at least twenty mattresses strapped to the roof parked behind their vehicle. It reminded Casey of the fairytale about the princess and the pea. People started exiting from that vehicle, and she counted ten, eleven, twelve. How had they all fit in the compact space?

Smells of fried foods filled the air as a wrinkled old woman cooked what looked to be minnows. Hawkers called out, but no one approached her.

"The dock is almost like a small village." Raymond said.

Casey inched closer to Eleanor and Brother Bob.

"It reminds me of a carnival." Eleanor shielded her eyes with her hand and scanned the horizon.

"This is the only ferry," Katie said. "We are lucky to arrive just in time. If you miss it, it's at least an hour before it makes the return trip."

As they waited, Casey watched a small child, about two or maybe three years old, squat and pee. No one seemed to notice or be concerned about the roaming toddler.

Raymond handed each of them a ticket. "We're not allowed to stay in the vehicle on the ferry."

"Why?" Casey asked.

Raymond shrugged. "If the ferry starts to sink, we can all swim to safety."

"Is it that risky?" Eleanor's eyes widened.

"I've heard stories," Raymond shrugged. "We don't have another option for the van, but if you don't trust the ferry, I can hire a fishing boat to take you across.

"I think we'll stick with the ferry." Eleanor gripped Pastor Bob's hand.

Casey remembered her backpack in the van with her passport and water. "Let me get my bag."

"Hama will lock the van." Raymond glanced around the area.

"I'm thirsty, and I don't want to be separated from my passport."

"Okay but be quick. We can't hold up traffic."

Casey scrambled to the backseat and lifted the heavy bag. As she exited the van, Hama assisted her.

"*Aisabou*—Thank you." Casey grabbed his forearm.

"Okay." Hama looked down.

A camel loaded with burlap bags stood on the side of the road. Casey sniffed, covered her nose with her arm, and rushed to Eleanor, who gripped Pastor Bob's hand.

They walked onto the ferry and the fumes of diesel floated on the breeze. The expanse of the river was as wide as the Mississippi.

"Why are people wearing coats in this heat?" Casey wiped her brow with a tissue.

"It's only about ninety degrees," Raymond grinned. "This is Niger's winter."

"But it's hot." Sparky fanned herself.

"Not to them." Sam brushed his hands on his jeans. "Last night the temperature dropped to about seventy-five. That's cold to Nigerians."

Casey removed her phone and snapped a picture of the river. "It's beautiful."

"Put your phone away," Sam said under his breath. "See the posts painted red and white? That means this is a no-photo zone. You might be arrested."

Casey crammed it into her bag. "Sorry."

"Now that we've left the city, it's important to keep your hair covered." Katie adjusted the scarf on her head.

"And don't be surprised if kids run from us." Sam covered his bald head with a cap. "It will be the first time for many to see a white person."

"How long will it take us to get to our destination?" Eleanor looked at her watch.

"About another hour." Raymond looked across the river. "We should arrive by ten o'clock, but we need to leave by two this afternoon. We don't want to miss the return ferry."

"What happens if we don't get to the boat in time?" Pastor Bob looked through a pair of binoculars.

"We'll have to wait for the next ferry, and by the time it returns, it will be impossible to return to the mission compound before dark. It's very dangerous to travel on the roads at night." Sam smiled tightly.

"Why is it treacherous at night?" Casey adjusted her grip on her backpack.

"There are too many things on the road we might hit." Sam pointed at the road. "You've seen what we've passed—donkey carts, herds of goats, cattle, and even people."

"But we have lights," Sparky frowned.

"Don't forget the potholes. Hitting one at full speed could cause a blowout or an accident." Raymond's face looked concerned.

"If we miss the three o'clock ferry, we'll have to drive very slowly or spend the night in the bush taxi," Katie said.

"Look at all these people." Pastor Bob spread his arms excitedly. "And most have never heard about Jesus."

"Yes, see Isaaca and Aissatou?" Raymond pointed. "I may be mistaken, but I believe Isaaca is sharing the gospel with that group."

Casey shielded her eyes with her hand and looked to where Raymond pointed. Isaaca read something from his Bible to a small circle of men.

"People in Niger have a culture of oral history and stories," Raymond said. "In fact, the Songhai don't have a written language. Almost everyone in Niger is a Muslim. However, many have never read the Koran."

"But we see them stopping to pray," Dave, the pharmacist, leaned on the rail.

"Yes, the men do," Raymond explained. "They have memorized prayers in Arabic. Most don't know what they are repeating. They are going through the ritual of doing what they've been taught to do to get to heaven."

"Why don't the women pray?" Casey asked.

"Most have too much work to do to stop and pray." Katie's lips turned down.

"I've noticed," Sparky said. "If the women don't go to the mosque and can't read the Koran, are they Muslim?"

"Ponder this." Raymond lifted his chin. "America is considered a Christian nation. Is everyone in America a Christian?"

"Of course not," Eleanor said.

"And just because a person is born in a Muslim country doesn't mean he understands the religion." Raymond crossed his arms.

"In the States, the majority have the opportunity to learn about Jesus, but here, most are still waiting to hear his name." Sam squinted. "And sometimes they accept and believe immediately."

"It can't be that easy," Casey crossed her arms.

"Not always, but sometimes it is," Raymond said. "God prepares the way. I can't tell you how many times I've visited a remote village, and someone tells me they had a dream about Jesus, and they have been waiting for someone to come. Some of these people said they expected us."

"That's hard to believe." Casey cocked her head.

"If I hadn't experienced it, I'd be skeptical too." Raymond lifted a shoulder.

"And it still amazes me too." Sam held his palms out. "Don't forget that when a person in Niger becomes a Christian, they risk being cut off from their families and villages. Everyone here depends on each other. Those who accept Christ must learn to rely on God."

Casey wanted to escape as the significance of their task began to sink in.

A foghorn blared. Raymond lifted his chin. "That means we can get off the ferry. We need to be quick."

Casey walked with the crowd and trudged through the sand to where Hama stood waving at them. She lifted her long skirt and climbed into the back of the bush taxi and wished she'd been the one to end up in the air-conditioned front of the vehicle, but she resigned herself to be happy in the back of the van. She rested her chin on her backpack, and her thoughts wandered to Madison, who should have received her letter by now. Would she send another note with a picture? Worry for Madison's response and Daniel's health made her anxious to return to Weldon.

She dug out her phone. The device had one bar, so she decided to give it a try and check on Daniel.

Daniel's deep voice answered on the first ring. "Hello?"

"How are you feeling?"

"Great. I'm having tea with the guard at the gate."

"Don't drink the tea."

"It's scalding hot. I'm sure it's safe."

"You're supposed to be resting."

"I decided to stretch my legs, and he invited me to sit down. I have no idea what he and his friends are talking about, but they made me feel welcome."

"You seem to be enjoying yourself."

"I am. How's your day going?"

"We just crossed the Niger River on a ferry. Raymond said it will be another hour before we reach the village."

"I may offer to help the gardener. Sitting here with nothing to do is killing me."

"I wish you were with us."

"Me too. Be care—And ..." Daniel's words were unintelligible.

"You're breaking up," Casey said.

Daniel didn't respond, and she looked at the blank screen. The van passed a donkey cart being driven by two boys who looked to be the age of kindergartners. There were no electric lines, and the landscape looked desolate. Casey marveled at anyone being able to thrive in such a challenging environment. Thorn trees and thistles seemed to be the common crop. Outside the back window, a trail of red dust followed. A feeling of inadequacy washed over her. What was it Raymond had said? "It's in Africa we feel our complete dependence on God." Casey lifted a silent prayer. *Help!*

When the van drove through the village, it looked uninhabited. Hama maneuvered through narrow lanes, then parked in front of a walled compound.

Dave turned around and looked back from the front of the van. "Looks like this is it."

A heavy metal door opened, and a thin African man shouted greetings to Raymond and Isaaca.

Raymond gripped the man's forearm. "This is Musa. He's opening his compound to use for Bible school."

"*Fofo! Mate game?* Hello! How are you?" Musa said.

"*Somay.* I am well," Casey said.

After formal introductions and greetings, Isaaca clapped his hands. "Who wants to gather children for Bible school?"

Casey took a step back. "I'll help unpack supplies."

"If we bounce a ball, children will come. It will be fun," Raymond bounced a rubber tennis ball and caught it.

Casey shook her head.

Sparky stepped forward. "I'll go."

Dave and Tyler also joined Isaaca.

"We'll go." Margie gripped Ed's hand. He wiped his broad face with a handkerchief with the other.

"Aissatou, I'm putting you in charge of keeping Sparky safe," Eleanor crossed her arms. "Please don't lose her."

Sparky giggled. "Don't worry. I've got more sense than to lose sight of Aissatou."

Casey thought it impossible to feel any hotter, but Sparky's snarky comment made her face burn.

"It is a small village." Aissatou fanned herself. "It's not possible to lose a white person here."

Isaaca pointed. "The men will take the street to the right."

"There's a well. Let's start there," Tyler pointed.

"Gather the children first." Eleanor dropped her chin.

"After each team gathers twenty children, you can go do your water survey."

"Yes, ma'am." Tyler looked longingly toward the well.

"We can handle up to fifty, maybe more," Eleanor instructed. "Now, get busy. Casey and I will work with Hama to get the mats off the top of the van."

The teams left bouncing tennis balls.

Casey helped Eleanor spread the mats under the one lone thorn tree in the compound. Eleanor opened the plastic storage bin and talked while she organized. "I've allocated fifteen minutes for each activity. We'll start with singing, then Bible stories, coloring pages, and games."

"They've never gone to a Bible school," Casey said. "I don't think we'll need such a rigorous schedule."

"But we need a plan."

Casey helped stack the crayons on a card table in the shade. "I hope these don't melt." Hama unloaded a box and placed it next to Casey. She opened it and discovered plastic folders. "What are these for?"

"I spent hours copying and preparing each folder." Eleanor brushed red dust from her hands. "Raymond warned me the wind might be a problem.

"It looks like you thought of everything," Casey stacked the folders on a mat.

A group of children accompanied the men down the street, laughing and jumping to catch tennis balls. Four children held onto Pastor Bob. A tall boy bounced a tennis ball in front of Isaaca, and children also surrounded Dave. Tyler carried a toddler on his shoulder and held the hands of another. Sparky, Aissatou, Margie, and Leslie came from the other direction with a group of children. Adults trailed the throng.

Casey bent down on one knee and greeted a small girl holding the hand of a toddler. Dried snot covered their faces, and she pulled out hand-sanitizing wipes and started cleaning the toddler's face. The little girl closed her eyes, smiled, and leaned into her touch.

"That's perhaps the softest cloth she's ever had on her face," Raymond said.

Other children crowded around Casey on the mat and waited for their turn. Even the older boys sat still with their faces lifted.

"Do we have enough wipes to clean all the children's faces?" Sparky asked.

"Yes, thanks to Daniel." Casey pulled out a clean wipe. "I have several packages in my backpack."

Casey held another child in her lap and cleaned her face.

Eleanor snapped a picture. "Your mama is gonna love this." She focused the camera again. "I remember teaching you in Bible school when you were no bigger than she is, and now, here we are in Africa. I never imagined this."

"Me neither. I don't know why I worried. Who would have thought cleaning a child's face could be such a blessing?"

Eleanor frowned at her watch. "There goes my schedule, but we still have time for a song or two. She clapped her hands. "Let's make a joyful noise to the Lord." She started singing, "*Fofo, Baba Iroquois, fofo* ... Thank you, Father God, thank you."

Casey read the first Bible story of creation. The children crowded in close on the mats, and adults huddled next to the compound fence. Each child sat still and listened intently as Casey read a sentence from her Bible, and Aissatou translated. When Leslie and Margie distributed the folders with coloring pages and crayons, they demonstrated how to hold them. The children didn't jostle or argue. Brows were drawn together in concentration as they worked, and some of the women moved in closer.

"I think they want to color, too, if you have enough supplies," Aissatou said.

"We have plenty," Eleanor opened another box.

Casey sat in the middle of a crowd of children with a toddler in her lap, with two girls wedged in on each side. All the team members had children in their laps, clustered close.

After a few minutes, Eleanor clapped her hands, again. "Raymond, you and the men can pull out the parachute. I'm sure the children will love playing with that."

A cry of delight rose from the crowd as the men pulled out the large rainbow parachute and started waving it up and down. Raymond demonstrated by running under it to the other side before it landed on his head. Isaaca called out instructions, and the children left their coloring.

Some of the smaller girls ran away from the parachute, and Casey sat them under the thorn tree in the shade. While playing pat-a-cake, an idea popped into her head when she noticed their small, dirty hands. Her fingers searched through her pack until she felt a familiar shape and withdrew a bottle of pink fingernail polish. "Will it be all right if I paint their fingernails?"

Aissatou asked one of the mothers standing in the background, and she nodded. "Yes. It is good," Aissatou nodded.

Casey shook the bottle and held a child's finger. After the first nail, she realized that the polish wouldn't stick because of the dried dirt. She took a hand wipe and did her best to clean the child's fingernails. Then she painted them. The polish dried quickly in the heat, and Casey moved on to the next child. Others joined and crowded in, and some of the women moved closer too.

"Do you have enough polish to paint the women's nails?" Aissatou's brows furrowed.

"Yes! Maybe God can use my talents after all."

Aissatou smiled. "He can use anything we have to offer."

"I can't quote scripture like Eleanor, and I don't have medical expertise, but I can paint fingernails and clean a face." Casey laughed out loud with joy.

After the games, the children gathered for another story.

"I've never experienced children listening with such intensity," Casey said.

"With no written language, they are trained to listen to stories from their elders." Isaaca grinned at the kids.

A crowd gathered on the tall wall surrounding the compound. They might have jumped down, but they stayed on the barrier. "Shouldn't we invite those people to join us too?" Casey shielded her eyes from the sun.

"No." Isaaca held his hand up with his palm out. "We invited everyone, but they chose not to join us. If we opened the gates now, when we start passing out snacks, we might be mobbed."

"But this makes me feel terrible."

"All sitting on the wall will still hear the message."

"I suppose." Casey wiped her face with a tissue.

"It's a hard lesson, but there's never enough supplies for everyone. But remember, we can share the name of Jesus with all who will listen."

After the games, the children gathered on the mat for another story, and they sang one last song.

Isaaca circled and spoke to the crowd on the wall. "We are about to open the door. If anyone has questions about how to receive eternal life in heaven, please come in. We have no money to give you, nor food to eat. But those who want to learn more about Jesus, please come talk with us."

At Raymond's head nod, Hama opened the door.

"Bible school is over," Aissatou brushed sand from her hands.

The children ran out of the compound and disappeared into the crowd, clutching their coloring pages and bags of rice.

The mission team waited, but none of the adults came inside to ask questions.

"I suppose it's too much to expect someone would hear the message once and believe," Pastor Bob watched the crowd disperse.

Isaaca shrugged. "Only God knows if someone believed."

Their host, Musa, pointed to a tall man in the crowd wearing a yellow tunic and spoke to Isaaca.

"Musa says that's the chief and his son," Isaaca said. "The boy is telling his father about Noah."

"And a little child will lead them," Eleanor whispered.

It felt like an oven inside the van, but it sheltered the team from the searing sun. Casey leaned her forearm against the wall, then jerked it back. "Shoot fire!" She blew on her seared skin.

Isaaca pointed out the window. "We'll travel a little way down the road, find a big tree and eat lunch."

Casey looked at her phone but had no service. Sighing, she returned it to her bag. A glimpse in the rearview mirror revealed freckles, pink cheeks, and damp strands of hair escaping from her red scarf. As she smoothed sunscreen over the burn on her forearm, she felt dizzy and surmised that she must be dehydrated. As she drank, the cool liquid had a faint metallic taste, but she guzzled it.

Hama parked the bush taxi as Casey returned the empty bottle to her bag.

Dave reached out to help her. "Why don't you let me and Tyler climb to the back on the way home?"

"I don't mind," Casey said. "I'm smaller and it's more difficult for you two to climb to the back."

The Toyota Land Cruiser pulled up behind them and unloaded. "The air conditioning is just what I needed," Sparky exited the truck looking as fresh as she had when they'd left this morning.

Hama rolled out a mat for them under the tree and motioned for her to sit down.

Casey plopped down, pulled out her hand-sanitizing wipes and started passing them around.

"How many of those things did you pack?" Sparky laughed.

"I don't know. Daniel added extra supplies this morning."

"It's a good thing," Dave said. "Cleaning children's faces seemed to break the ice."

Isaaca grinned. "One of the mothers asked me, 'Why do these white people love our children?' When you painted their fingernails, I think you made a good impression."

"I wish the folks back home could see you," Eleanor told Casey. "I've seen a whole new side of you, young lady, and it's refreshing."

Casey looked down at the chipped polish on her nail. *You'd think I'd never had my hands dirty*. She adjusted the scarf on her head. *Maybe I do worry too much about how I look.*

They ate their sandwiches, and Casey opened her third bottle of water. In the distance, a lone donkey cart ambled down a desolate trail.

"I hate to ask, but where's the closest restroom?" Casey cleaned her hands.

Raymond waved his hand. "Just walk until you find a tree or bush."

Casey rolled her eyes. "I guess I'll wait."

"It's a three-hour journey." Sparky pointed in the distance. "There are some bushes just over that hill."

"I'll be fine." Casey started gathering leftovers and trash.

Sam helped her. "Leave the plastic containers from your fruit cocktail. The children in the village will pick them up. It will be like a treasure hunt for them."

Sparky kneeled and started rolling up the mat. "You were great with the kids."

"Thanks," Casey bent down and helped her. "It's going better than I thought it would, but there's something that bothers me."

"What?"

"Perhaps, I'm imagining things, but it seems something is going on between you and Daniel."

Sparky eyes widened, and then she dropped her shoulders. "You'll need to ask Daniel about it."

"About what?"

"I can't talk to you about his secret."

Casey planted her fist on her hips. *Her boyfriend and another woman had a secret.* Her temper ignited. "My granny always said, if another woman steals your man, she'll get exactly what she deserves."

Sparky's eyes widened. "You're barking up the wrong tree."

"I'm not the dog in this story."

Sparky gasped. "I've done nothing wrong. You need to speak to Daniel."

She narrowed her eyes. "I will."

"Listen, I'm sorry, but—"

"What are you sorry about if you've done nothing wrong?"

"I knew this would turn into a mess. You'll have to wait and see for yourself."

Casey fought back tears.

Sparky gave her a sad look. "It's a long drive back. Why don't you take a turn riding in the Land Cruiser with the air conditioning? I'll take the back seat in the van."

Casey didn't trust herself to speak. Instead, she turned on her heel, snagged the overstuffed backpack, and headed for a bush in the distance. When she reached the bramble, she dropped to her knees and mentally scolded herself for following a man to Africa. There was no one to blame but herself for the disappointment. She'd told him over and over that she loved him, yet Daniel hadn't mentioned love or commitment.

When she had no more tears to shed, she blew her nose and realized the others must be waiting. After relieving herself, she cleaned her hands and started the long walk back to the thorn tree, berating herself with every step. *This is what comes of chasing a man. You end up in the middle of nowhere, hiding behind a bush to use the bathroom.* If her customers could see her now, they'd have a laugh.

She squared her shoulders and trudged to the top of the dune, but to her dismay, no vehicles sat under the tree. The bush taxi and Land Cruiser were gone. With her hand over her brow, she squinted, caught sight of a trailing cloud of dust, and her heart raced.

"Stop! Wait!" she yelled. With a thump, her bag hit the sand, and she ran, but the vehicles disappeared behind the cloud of dust, and she dropped to her knees in stunned disbelief.

The burning sun on her back brought her back to reality. *Now what? Should I return to the village? No. I only know a few phrases. What am I going to do?*

When she reached the thorn tree, she felt as insignificant as the ants cleaning up the crumbs of the picnic. With her hand shielding her eyes, she looked into the distance. *I hope they remember where they left me.* Casey dropped onto the dirt. *Then again, it might be better if they don't. Eleanor is likely to kill me.*

CHAPTER TWENTY—DANIEL

Daniel sat on the sweethearts' swing as the sun lowered and sighed. With all remnants of his headache gone, he kept his eyes on the compound entrance. When a horn blared, he stood. The guard opened the metal gate, and the dusty van entered. As team members exited in slow motion, he searched for Casey's face. Everyone wore a film of dust. *She must be riding with Raymond.* The group stood around him, mute, and Isaaca's head drooped.

"What's wrong?" Daniel asked.

Sam stepped forward and rubbed his jaw. "After we stopped for lunch, we had a mix-up because Casey and Sparky traded vehicles. When Hama counted heads in the bush taxi, he had the right number."

Daniel's jaw dropped.

Sparky yanked the bandanna off her head and twisted the fabric. "I told Raymond I was moving to the bush taxi, when I should have said, 'Casey and I are trading seats.'"

"Raymond, Katie, Pastor Bob, and Eleanor returned to the village for her. They'll spend the night there." Sam stared at the ground.

"You left her!" Daniel shouted.

Sparky looked down. "We had an argument, separated, and I forgot my responsibility."

"Raymond bought tickets at the ferry, distributed them, and had an extra," Sam took off his ball cap and he rubbed his bald head.

"That's when we realized we didn't have Casey with us." Sparky swallowed hard.

Daniel pounded his fist on his thigh. "I can't believe no one noticed her missing from the van."

"It's my fault," Sparky cried. "She's upset with me because ..." Her posture slouched. "It's not important, but I thought she might cool off if I gave her my seat in the air-conditioned vehicle."

Daniel's hands fisted, and he stomped away to keep from yelling or throwing something. His gut wrenched at the thought of his sweetheart alone in the desert. This was his fault. He should have stayed home, then she'd be safe.

"I'm sorry, Daniel," Sam squeezed Daniel's shoulder. "I'm sure she'll be fine. The others will find her quickly, and the people in the village are honored we visited. They'll be kind."

"I hope you're right."

"Let's gather around and say a prayer for Casey and the others." Sam held his hand out and Daniel wanted to punch him, but instead, he drew in a deep breath, exhaled, and took the missionary's hand.

A white pigeon landed on a branch above Sam as he bowed his head. "Thank you, Father, for loving us. Thank you for being our burden bearer. Our hearts are heavy with worry for Casey. We know you know exactly where she is. Please, Father, protect her and meet her every need. Also, Father, please guide Pastor Bob, Eleanor, Katie and Raymond and we pray for their protection as they travel to find her. Search our hearts for any anxiety, frustration, anger, impatience, anything that is displeasing to you and replace it with your love, joy, peace, patience, kindness, goodness, faithfulness, gentleness and self-control. Thank you, Father, for all that you have done, and all that you will do. In the all-powerful name of Jesus, I ask these things. Amen."

Sparky spoke next. "Father, forgive me for failing you and for failing Casey. I pray for all the hurting hearts in this circle, and I pray for all the kind people we met today. Please lead good people to Casey. May you bless the hearts and hands that help her. In Jesus's name, I pray, Amen."

As each person prayed aloud, the tight muscles in Daniels's shoulders relaxed a bit. When it was his turn, he cleared his throat. "Father, there's nothing I can add to what's been said other than to please forgive me for letting you down. Help me to forgive, as you have forgiven me. In Jesus's name, I ask these things, Amen."

They remained in a circle as the fiery sun dipped toward the horizon. The bright orange ball disappeared in an instant. Crickets and cicadas began serenading them, and the security light buzzed as it turned on.

At last, Sam spoke. "Let's go inside. The mosquitos will start swarming soon."

Sparky slapped her neck. "They already are."

After a few seconds, Margie and Bill held hands and led the way to the door. They removed their shoes at the entry, and the others followed.

Daniel paced around the courtyard and gazed toward the river where the moon reflected on its surface. *This is what comes of telling lies. You hurt the ones you love the most.*

CHAPTER TWENTY-ONE—CASEY

Casey cried until she had no more tears, then leaned back against a tree and closed her eyes. She knew they would eventually return. If she could kick herself in the butt, she would. How many times did someone have to tell her to pay attention? She bet Raymond never considered two members of a mission team having a catfight over a man. Her cheeks burned.

A glance at her watch revealed the time to be five o'clock, which meant they wouldn't have time to return to the compound before dark. Casey wondered if they might spend the night in the village or sleep in the bush taxi. Wherever she slept, she knew it would be a long night, and Daniel would be worried sick. *Let him worry.*

Another hour passed with no sign of anyone. As the sun lowered, her anxiety increased. They should have been here by now.

Casey shook the almost empty bottle. She was down to one canister of water. As she inventoried her bag, she discovered a lighter, and she hoped a fire would keep wild animals away. The village lay about a mile from her, but she didn't know if she could find Musa's compound, and Olivia's comments about kidnapping came to mind. Even though the people in the village appeared friendly, the television newscasts painted West Africa as a hostile environment. Indecision as to what to do plagued her.

It took a few minutes for her to gather all the twigs under the tree. The pile of sticks looked puny. It would never last the night. The sun dropped quickly behind a dune, and fear gripped her as the last orange hues dissipated. She worried about snakes coming out at night. Then, she recalled Isaaca's story about a pack of wild dogs. The lighter flickered as she ignited a piece of paper underneath the sticks. The darker the shadows grew, the faster her pulse raced.

In the distance, other campfires glowed, but she didn't know whether that was a good or bad sign. Don't all people have goodness? But what if bad people discovered her and saw an opportunity to collect a ransom?

She placed her head on the backpack and looked up into the sky. To calm herself, she started counting stars. A carpet of constellations revealed themselves, and her insignificance magnified. The sky seemed more extensive and light-filled than anything she'd ever witnessed.

Thoughts of the confrontation with Sparky made her miserable. Daniel wasn't the man she'd thought him to be. A wave of guilt pressed down on her. And she was not the woman she'd pretended to be. Tears flowed again, and she rubbed her forearm across her cheeks.

The air cooled as her thoughts rambled. Whatever Daniel's secrets, he was a good man. He probably couldn't help but be attracted to Sparky, a nice girl. After all, she'd signed up for this trip for the right reasons.

Casey studied the sky and imagined a future without Daniel and sniffed. Never in her life had she experienced jealousy. How could she, when no man except Daniel had been patient enough to coax her into a relationship?

Goats bleated in the distance while a galaxy of stars unfolded before her. All her life, she'd read, "God is with you." But was he? The fire faded, and she had no more wood.

If God was with her, he must be disappointed. Casey pictured little Fatima's face, her frail, thin body, and clinging hands. The seed of an idea sprouted. She could adopt the abandoned child. With or without Daniel, she was a woman of means. It was time to invest in something other than herself. If there was one thing she'd learned from Africa, it was that she was spoiled—spoiled rotten.

A dog howled in the distance, and she clutched her hand to her chest. The family of squatters who lived by the mission compound slept outside every night, and they survived. But they were in the city. As the embers from the fire faded, more stars lit up the sky.

Sitting up, Casey dug through her bag for mosquito repellant. *At least Daniel provided me with everything I need to survive in the bush.* A sense of helplessness washed over her, and she fingered the gold bracelet.

She turned to the words that always comforted when all else failed. "Our Father who art in heaven." The litany rolled from her tongue and gave solace as she stared at the sky. Then she continued with the habit she'd practiced all her life when anxious, a ritual that had sustained her during her darkest days of depression—she started counting her blessings, then she prayed for her loved ones, including Daniel. Her bruised heart ached as she ended with Madison's name. A fleeting thought crossed her mind.

Without Jansen, Madison wouldn't exist. Her biggest dream, to meet her daughter, was the result of his evil deed. Maybe Pastor Bob was right. God really could turn everything to his good.

The theme from Pastor Djibo's sermon drifted across her thoughts. *"Forgive."* Her heart hardened. Would forgiving Jansen free her of the fear? A shooting star spread across the sky. "Happy New Year," she whispered to the stars, but her voice sounded as sad as her heart felt. What would her New Year's resolution be? She pondered the question and then knew what would make the best improvement in her life. If Daniel didn't love her, she'd just have to learn to love herself, but to do that she'd have to forgive herself for her selfishness, forgive herself for being a coward, and, most difficult of all, she must forgive Jansen for his brutal assault. *Impossible.*

One of her granny's favorite Bible quotes bubbled up from her memories: "With God, all things are possible."

The leaves of the thorn tree rustled overhead while she cleared her mind, meditated, and lifted a wordless petition from her heart. Time seemed as endless as her tears. At last, she felt her brokenness yield, and she whispered with desperation, "I forgive it all." In the stillness of the desolate landscape when she should have been terrified, a wave of peace blanketed her. Her mouth opened in stunned disbelief as she stared in wonder at the stars. "I forgive it all." Her voice sounded stronger and sure. That's when she realized it was more than words. Something miraculous had just happened, as joy bubbled up, and she laughed aloud. *And I am forgiven.* More meteors showered down, and she hugged her knees, marveling at what God had done. Then she wiped her damp cheeks and bowed her head. *Wow! Thank you, Jesus.*

Casey lay back down and for hours, full of wonder, stared into the endless galaxy. At last, she closed her eyes and felt no fear as she drifted into slumber. Her last thought was, *Thank you.*

CHAPTER TWENTY-TWO—DANIEL

That evening, Sparky and Daniel sat at the kitchen table, and she beamed a flashlight into his eyes. As soon as she switched the light off, Daniel stood and almost knocked over the table. "The headache's gone." His tone sounded cold.

"I'm sorry. It was an accident." Sparky had tears in her eyes.

"I trusted you."

"If you'd told Casey the truth in the first place, then she'd know there's no reason to be jealous of me."

Daniel plopped into the chair and dropped his head in his hands. "How can she doubt that I love her?"

"It might have something to do with you keeping secrets from her," Sparky snapped.

"But I want to protect her!" Daniel slapped the table.

"Men are stupid."

"Is it wrong to want to shield her from this worry?"

"Do you love her?"

"Yes."

"Then tell her the truth and ask her to forgive you."

Daniel ran his hand through his hair. It had taken months to melt her invisible barrier, and he feared he'd never break through it again. Something had happened to her. Someone had hurt her and caused her to be distrustful. And now, his lies would result in her distrusting him too. It killed him to know she was alone and aching because of his lies. "She's going to be upset."

"And she has every right to be. I hope she'll forgive me. I feel awful."

"Can you think of anything that might help us get to her quicker?"

"We need to stay in place in case Raymond calls. The roads are dangerous at night due to potholes, and goats and people are wandering everywhere."

"Do you think the villagers will protect her?"

"The people we met were kind. I'm more worried about someone protecting her from Eleanor."

"Eleanor's the sweetest woman I know."

"Man! The stress of this trip is making her downright mean though. Her tongue scalded me, and then she started in on Raymond."

"I'm with Eleanor." Daniel stood. "I'm going outside."

"Don't forget mosquito repellant."

"I'm covered with the stuff."

He followed the path in the dim moonlight to the swing. It felt unbalanced to sit in it without Casey by his side. When he looked up into the sky, he wondered if she had shelter, something to eat and if she too might be looking up into the infinity of stars. Fear and frustration were familiar companions when Alzheimer's stole his mother's mind while his Dad succumbed to Parkinson's. After their funerals, he'd missed them more than ever and felt utterly alone, just like now. He'd thought those horrible days were behind him. *Why has God abandoned me?*

CHAPTER TWENTY-THREE—CASEY

The sound of bleating awoke Casey. The pink hues of dawn lit the horizon and she pushed up from the sand. Her neck pinched, and her hips ached. A herd of goats surrounded her, Casey rubbed her eyes, and made eye contact with a boy who stood at the edge of the flock. There were two of them. The tallest of the shepherds wore a brown quilted jacket, and his younger companion had on a stained red coat with sleeves much too long.

"*Fofo!*" Casey stood and brushed the sand from her long skirt.

The eldest child spoke to her, but she couldn't understand a word he said other than, "*Fofo*."

"Where's my cheat sheet?" Casey rambled through her bag, removed the folded paper, and scanned the list for something appropriate. "*Ai sii ma Zarma*"—I don't speak Zarma." Casey hoped she had pronounced the words correctly.

The boy in the brown jacket motioned for her to follow and started walking into the bush. After two steps, she stopped as she considered the others might return and would have no idea where to find her.

The smaller youth approached and spoke, waving his arms in the oversized sleeves, but Casey shrugged her shoulders and held her palms out.

He returned to his partner, and they led the goats away.

A few minutes later, she could make out the boy wearing the red jacket returning, accompanied by a tall woman. As the pair drew closer, Casey recognized the lady as one of the mothers who pounded millet during yesterday's Bible school. Her cobalt blue skirt featured a pattern of lime green diamonds.

Bracing herself on the tree, Casey stood and nodded. "*Fofo, mate gaham?*" Hello, how is your health?

"*Baani somay*," the woman said. Very well.

"*Mate fu?*" Casey said. How is your family?

"*Somay*"—Fine.

"*Mate zonkey?*" Casey asked. How are your children?

"*Somay, ay g'Irkoy Saabu*"—Fine, I thank God.

With the formal greetings completed, Casey smiled and shrugged. *Now what?*

The woman took Casey's elbow and pulled her to follow her.

"Wait!" Casey removed her arm.

The woman's brows furrowed, and she spoke rapidly. Of course, she didn't understand English any better than Casey understood Zarma. Casey held her index finger up in the air and then dropped it. She'd been warned not to point at people. They might think she was cursing them. She hastily gathered a few nearby rocks and formed them into the shape of an arrow pointing toward the distant village. After painting a bright orange dot of fingernail polish on each stone, she put on her backpack, returned to the woman, looped her arm through hers and smiled.

They walked about ten minutes, with the little boy following them. A single compound came into view and the elegant woman unlatched the gate and held it open for Casey. When she passed the threshold, Casey counted three huts. The woman left her, returned with a mat, unrolled it under a tree and indicated for Casey to sit down.

After slipping off her sandals, she complied.

The woman filled a small teapot with water, stirred the charcoal fire, and placed the kettle over it. While she waited, two other women approached. Casey stood up and gave formal greetings to each, and they responded.

They all sat together on the mat and Casey read from her sheet. "*Ay ma ga ti Casey*"—My name is Casey.

Their faces lit up. The woman who had escorted her to the compound nodded her head and said, "*Ay ma ga ti Wasilla*"—My name is Wasilla.

The woman to her left said, "*Ay ma ga ti Miriama*"—My name is Miriama.

And the third woman said, "*Ay ma ga ti Helima*"—My name is Helima.

Casey smiled and repeated their names as she nodded and made eye contact with each woman. "Wasilla, Miriama, Helima."

They clapped and started talking among themselves, chuckling and staring at Casey. The kettle began to boil, and Wasilla filled a tin cup and passed it to Casey. The dark liquid looked ominous, but she knew she couldn't insult them. Her hand trembled as she lifted the tin cup and sipped. *Please Lord, protect me*. The strong tea scalded her tongue.

Casey opened her bag and withdrew a packet of hand wipes and a granola bar. She passed a clean cloth to each woman, and they watched her clean her hands. "*Aisabou*,"

Wasilla said. Thank you. Each woman wiped her hands and face, then Casey broke off pieces of the granola bar and distributed a sampling to each woman. They watched her and slipped the granola into their mouths, smiled, and nodded their heads.

Wasilla rose and disappeared inside the hut, and within a few seconds, she returned carrying a bowl of rice. Flies buzzed around the dish.

Oh, no!

The African woman passed the bowl to Casey, and she pinched a few grains of rice, smiled, and said, "*Aisabou.*"

The other women also fingered rice from the bowl and returned the dish to Casey. Miriama brewed more tea. When the last grain of rice disappeared and the final drop of tea was consumed, Miriama and Helima stood and walked away. Both women had babies tied on their backs. The infants had been sleeping.

When they returned with water jugs on their heads, Helima motioned for her to follow. Casey felt clumsy as she trudged through the sand. When they reached the river, each woman filled their containers with muddy water. Casey shielded her eyes and looked across the vast river. Behind her, the heat shimmered across the sand. After downing the remaining half liter of clean water, Casey refilled her bottles and added a water tablet. How long should she wait before drinking it? She wished she'd listened to Tyler's ramblings about solar purification. Had he said six hours in the sun made the water safe?

When they returned to the walled compound, Casey placed her four murky bottles in the sun, hoping the water would be safe to drink soon. While she rifled through her bag for a tissue, she touched her phone and remembered several people at the ferry had a phone. Maybe it was only her service that didn't work here. After checking for a signal, she pointed at the screen.

"Do you have a cell phone?"

The women looked at each other, then back at her and shrugged. Feeling defeated, she returned the device to her bag.

The morning passed quickly as the women laughed, pounded millet, cooked, and cared for the children. Casey wondered about the men. There were children, so there must be husbands. What would they think about their wives sharing their food?

As she looked up at the noonday sun, she decided to return to the thorn tree in case the others returned. After retrieving her water bottles from the sun, she pointed toward the thorn tree and waved goodbye to the trio. "*Aisabou, aisabou*!"

By the time she reached her campsite, she felt dizzy and decided she must drink the water. After collapsing in the shade, she unscrewed the top and drank. It had a faint chemical taste, but she felt better after drinking most of the bottle. When she examined the sediment at the bottom, she shuddered. With her thirst quenched, she rummaged through her bag and decided to eat a handful of almonds.

Wasilla's generous gesture to share rice touched her. When the others returned, she'd find a way to repay the African woman's kindness. *Where could the others be?* The stifling heat drained her of energy, and she leaned against the tree and closed her eyes. Hours later, she awoke to discover the setting sun. The team should have been here by now. Something must have gone wrong. Casey rubbed her eyes, drank another bottle of water and paced. Her skirt caught on a thorn, and she yanked it free, ripping the material. In her frustration, she picked up a rock and threw it. Then she hugged herself as the sun lowered. She didn't want to spend another night alone in the desert. If she didn't go now, it would be too late. After drinking more water, she put on her backpack and followed her tracks in the sand to the compound. Maybe they'd take her in.

As she approached the gate, the boys herding the goats ran toward her.

"*Fofo*," Casey called out to them.

The taller of the boys waved. "*Fofo*."

Miriama greeted her and led her to a small group of men sitting on a mat, drinking tea. Miriama said something to the oldest man, and he stood and nodded at Casey.

One of the men opened his jacket and pulled out the folder of coloring pages.

Casey nodded. Oh, how she wished she'd studied the language sheets.

Miriama took her by the arm and led her to another hut, rolled out a mat, and motioned for Casey to sit. The last rays of sunlight disappeared, and the only light came from the charcoal fire where Miriama prepared tea. After sharing tea and rice with her, Miriama left Casey alone in the dark. With nothing else to do, she prayed. Through the long night, she tossed and turned on the mat. Her imagination ran wild with possibilities. It seemed she'd just closed her eyes for a few minutes when the sound of a rooster crowing and goats bleating woke her. As she rubbed her eyes, she noticed Wasilla stirring a fire in front of her.

"Good morning," Casey said. "Umm ... *Fofo*."

Casey opened her pack and cleaned her hands with a disposable wipe. Dark eyes watched, and Casey offered her a fresh cloth. Wasilla took it and sighed as she washed her face. Then she poured a cup of tea and passed it to Casey.

This time, Casey waited for the hot liquid to cool. They sat in silence and finished the tea while her new friend nursed her baby. A toddler came out of the hut, and Wasilla guided the child away from the fire. Casey reached for the girl, cuddled her in her lap, and cleaned the child's face.

It was peaceful here, and even though their lives seemed difficult to her, they appeared happy and content. Much more so than most of the people she knew.

When the baby finished nursing, Wasilla wrapped the infant and secured it on her back in one quick motion. After balancing a water jug on her head, she called out to the others. Helima exited from her hut, greeted them, lifted a ceramic pot, and balanced it on her head as they walked toward the gate. Casey stood, settled the baby on her hip, and followed the graceful gait of the African women. They never rushed but constantly moved—gathering water, pounding millet, nursing a child, preparing tea, cooking. These were the routines of the women of Africa, Casey realized, but what of the men?

They returned to the compound and shared a bowl of rice. Again, Casey marveled at their generosity and realized she hardly noticed the flies swarming anymore. After eating, the women talked among themselves then stood, and Helima beckoned with her hand for Casey to follow.

They traveled a sandy path, and Casey's damp blouse stuck to her back. At last, the village came into sight. As the sun heated her skin, she rubbed more sunscreen on her arms and face.

When they entered the settlement, it didn't look the same as on Monday. People swarmed the streets, as well as cattle, goats, donkey carts, and sheep. The lively atmosphere stunned her, and she figured it must be market day. With a hopeful outlook, she scanned the crowd for anyone using a cell phone. She listened to conversations, anxious to hear someone speak English. When she noticed several people unloading from a bush taxi, Casey touched Wasilla's elbow and pointed. "Niamey?" Casey said.

Wasilla shook her head.

Casey sighed and stayed close to her new friends, vowing to pay attention and not get lost again. Compared to the Grand Marché she'd visited in Niamey, this market was small, but a similar energy pulsed through the lanes. Where had all these people come from?

As they walked through the stalls, she felt the stares of the crowd. Miriam must have sensed it, too, because she put her arm through Casey's as they strolled through the crowd. They stopped in front of a table with spices of every color, and she recognized cardamom and whole cloves, but many were a mystery. Women sat on mats with peppers and onions piled high in front of them. Wasilla purchased a root that looked like ginger for a coin.

When the group paused in front of a vendor selling rice, Casey dug through her bag, gripped her flashlight, and demonstrated it to the vendor. He reached for the flashlight, unscrewed the end, and emptied the batteries. "Ah, American," he said.

He put the batteries into his shirt pocket and handed Casey a small bag of rice.

Casey smiled and lifted her purchase, but Wasilla gripped her forearm and started speaking heatedly to the merchant, pointed at his shirt pocket, and held her palm out. He threw his hands up in the air, then shoved another larger bag of rice to Casey.

Her new friend stood with her back ramrod straight and gave the merchant a look of condemnation. The women walked to a covered portico and sat on a bench. They had been sitting for over an hour when Wasilla sprang up and called out to a man. All the women stood and offered a formal greeting.

The African woman started talking very fast, flailing her hands and pointing to Casey.

The man looked with a frown, then he nodded his head.

He said something, and Wasilla indicated for Casey to go with him.

She hesitated. The thought of leaving with a stranger gave her the jitters.

"Niamey," the man said. He pointed toward the road.

Casey nodded.

He led her to a dilapidated truck, unlatched the tailgate, and Wasilla made a motion with her hands that reminded Casey of her granny shooing her chickens. *Maybe I should go back to the tree and wait,* she thought. *No. A herd of turtles could have returned by now. Something's happened.*

A clatter sounded, and Casey jumped. The owner of the truck had dropped a stack of aluminum pots into the truck bed.

Wasilla clasped Casey's elbow and tugged.

Okay. She searched her bag for the fingernail polish. When she found it, she handed it to Wasilla with the two bags of rice.

"*Aisabou,*" Wasilla said.

Each of her new friends gave Casey a hug, then she climbed into the back of the truck as she struggled with her long skirt.

Her friends waved and strolled toward their compound. After a few minutes, the man returned with two African couples carrying pots of various sizes. All the vendors started packing goods. Her driver arranged the odd array of aluminum cooking pots. Wondering if she should move, she scooted to the corner. The man in charge indicated for her to stay. The others stared at her as he secured the items. Once the merchandise had been tied down, the women climbed into the back of the truck with Casey. She smiled and gave the formal greetings. The men opened the truck door and sat in the front with the driver.

The little truck roared to life, and the smell of diesel fuel filled the air. It moved forward with a jolt. Dust swirled around Casey, and she gripped her headscarf. The bush taxi journey had been a carpet ride compared to the jarring in the back of the truck. As they passed donkey carts, she appreciated the speed of the vehicle.

The skin on her arm radiated heat, and the women watched her every move. When the truck stopped in line at the ferry to cross the river, Casey sighed with relief to know her location. The women exited from the truck bed. When last here, Casey had a cellphone signal. She dug through her bag for her phone and—*Yes!* A squeal of delight erupted, and she shouted, "I have a signal." She dialed Daniel.

He answered on the first ring, "Hello!"

"Daniel, it's Casey."

"Thank God!"

She couldn't speak. The comfort of hearing his voice drained her of energy, and her knees weakened.

Daniel was shouting. "Are you all right?"

"I'm okay," she said in a shaky voice.

"Where are you?"

"I'm at the ferry crossing. What's happened? Why didn't the team return for me?"

"They just called us. The fuel pump in Raymond's truck went out."

"Well, doesn't that just figure? Why didn't someone else come?" Casey's stomach churned.

"We expected them to return with you yesterday. When they didn't, Isaaca and I left with Hama and attempted to reach you, but we couldn't cross the river because the motor on the ferry needed repairs."

"This whole trip is a disaster."

"Raymond's truck is fixed, and he's on the way back to the village. If you're not with him, how did you get to the ferry?"

"One of the village women arranged a ride for me to Niamey."

"Raymond should be at the village by now."

"We must have passed each other on the road."

"They'll be worried when they don't find you."

"I arranged rocks in the shape of an arrow under the thorn tree, pointing toward the home where I stayed. Wasilla will send them back to Niamey. My biggest problem is that I don't know how to communicate with my driver."

"Isaaca is with me. He'll know what to do."

Casey relaxed when she heard Isaaca's bright voice. "I am glad to hear from you, Madam. Are you safe?"

"Yes, it's been an adventure and, I need a shower, but I'm okay, thanks to a sweet group of ladies who took me in."

"It is the custom of the Songhai to show hospitality to strangers. When you cross the river, there is an enormous tree to your left. Wait there."

"I won't move."

"Please, may I speak with your driver?"

Casey jumped down from the truck bed and approached the man sitting behind the steering wheel. His brow furrowed as he held the phone to his ear and Casey held her breath. Then he beamed a smile and said, "Okay," and returned her phone.

"He'll wait with you and make sure you are safe," Isaaca told her.

"Are you sure he won't mind?"

"You have been placed in his care. He's honored to be your protector. We'll pay him for his trouble when we arrive."

"That's wonderful." She disconnected the phone, and her shoulders relaxed.

The ferry arrived, and the long line of people, vehicles, and carts boarded. In two hours, she'd be with the others. Then she remembered Daniel and Sparky had been together for the past two days while she'd been left in the wilderness. Maybe she'd overreacted, but Sparky had told her that she needed to speak to Daniel. It hurt her to know that he shared a secret with another woman. Was there any hope for them?

She caught sight of her face in a side mirror of a bush taxi and hardly recognized herself. The French braid under her scarf remained secure, but she appeared changed. The tan on her previously pale skin looked unusual. Then she realized it was dust from riding in the back of the truck. As she studied her green eyes in the mirror, she lifted her chin with new confidence. It was looking pretty that had caused most of her troubles. Daniel Sheppard was about to meet her without her mask, and if he didn't love her as she was, too bad for him. She was tired of hiding her true self and worn out worrying about what others might think. *We'll have to learn to accept each other the way we are, or there's no hope for a happily-ever-after. Lord, help us.*

As the ferry chugged across the river, vehicles that had disembarked left a cloud of dust. Casey yearned to return to the village and repay the women for their hospitality. Such generosity astounded her. If an African Muslim stood abandoned on the side of the road in America, would someone stop and help? A heaviness settled over her as she searched her mind for a way to repay their kindness. And then she knew what she had to do. She'd return and share with them the most precious thing she had—hope for a better future—Jesus.

CHAPTER TWENTY-FOUR – DANIEL

Daniel leaned forward in his seat in the bush taxi. It had been almost two hours since he'd disconnected from Casey's call. Hama stopped the van next to an enormous tree, where people sat on a mat drinking tea.

He could see Casey standing and starting to put on her sandals. Daniel jerked open the door and sprinted to her, lifting her in a hug. "I'm never letting you out of my sight again." Relief flooded through him.

A film of red dust covered her from head to toe. Casey tightened her grip and buried her face in his shoulder.

Sam, Isaaca, Aissatou, and Sparky circled them, and everyone hugged Casey.

"I couldn't eat, or sleep for worrying about you." Daniel gripped her hand.

"A good night's sleep sounds good to me too." Her voice sounded croaky.

"Good news." Isaaca stuck his thumb in the air. "Raymond called, and they are waiting for the ferry on the other side of the river."

Daniel handed Casey a cold bottle of water and a bag of nuts.

"Thank you." Casey opened the bag and shared it with the women who sat on the mat in front of her and then ate the rest.

Isaaca spoke to Casey's driver, then turned to her. "This man's name is Ibrahim. He's the uncle of the woman who cared for you."

Casey nodded. "*Ay ma ga ti Casey*"—My name is Casey.

Daniel gripped the man's forearm. "*Aisabou*," —Thank you.

Wasilla's Uncle Ibrahim's eyes sparkled, and he spoke to Isaaca, who translated to the group. "Years ago, white men visited his village and told him stories about Jesus. He wanted to learn more, but the strangers left."

"Do we have time for you to preach?" Daniel felt a surge of excitement.

"Americans always worry about time. This man has waited years to hear the good news," Isaaca spoked directly to Casey. "Perhaps God prepared the way for the two of you to meet. It is your responsibility to share the gospel with this crowd."

"I don't know how." Casey held her hands out, palms up.

"Sam's the trained missionary." Daniel jerked his chin toward Sam.

"But Casey is the one who has spent time with them." Sam smiled.

"You can do it." Daniel squeezed Casey's hand.

Casey's hands shook as she searched her bag. She pulled out her Bible. "Okay."

Daniel prayed. *Father, give her the words that will save.*

Casey gulped. Her emerald eyes widened as she studied the somber faces. All eyes were on her. She shared the story of her own salvation. Daniel didn't think she'd ever looked more beautiful. Then she explained the parable of Jesus as the good shepherd. "His sheep hear his voice. He is the good shepherd who gave his life for us. We can never do enough good to earn our way into heaven. To accept his gift of grace, we simply believe that Jesus is the son of God, repent, and ask him to forgive us from our sins."

After explaining that baptism is a way to demonstrate to others their old sinful life is behind them, Casey sat down as twenty strangers stared with blank expressions.

Daniel whispered in her ear. "I'll never forget that. I'm proud of you."

Isaaca stood and started preaching to the gathered crowd, and then Ibrahim, Wasilla's uncle, stood, spoke, then gave a shout. "Ya Ya Ya Ya Ya!" Isaaca led him to the water.

Daniel cleared his throat and shoved his hands in his pockets. "Do you think he really believes?"

"Yes." Sam lifted his chin. "Don't forget, many might persecute him because he's proclaimed belief in Jesus."

The ferry landed, and people and vehicles started to disembark. Raymond's Land Cruiser exited the ship last. Eleanor reached Casey first and squeezed her.

"I can't breathe." Casey gushed.

Eleanor pushed back from the embrace but kept her hands on Casey's shoulders. "I feel like I should spank you."

"I'm sorry." Casey dropped her head.

"We all should have been keeping better track of each other." Pastor Bob squeezed Eleanor's elbow.

Casey's face softened. "Gracious women took me in and cared for me. And now their uncle is being baptized."

"While the mechanic repaired our fuel pump, we shared the gospel with a crowd," Pastor Bob's sunburned face seemed to glow.

Eleanor's eyes sparkled. "Two men were keen to learn more."

"We didn't plan to stop in that village, but God arranged it," Raymond clapped Pastor Bob on the shoulder.

"Is it possible to rearrange our schedule so I can return to Wasilla's compound?" Casey clasped her hands together. "They were very kind to me."

"We'll see." Raymond shrugged.

Sam looked at his watch. "Not today. It's time for us to say goodbye and get on the road."

Casey sank into the broken seat of the van. "This is plush compared to the back of the truck."

"I can't believe you traveled with a group of strangers." Daniel draped his arm across her shoulder.

"I can't describe it, but for some reason, I trusted Wasilla completely."

"She was an answer to my prayers," Daniel sighed. *Thank you, Lord, for Wasilla.* He savored having his Casey next to him.

Sparky turned and gave him a sad smile from the front seat, and he felt Casey tense under his arm. With each passing mile, a feeling of dread intensified. It was time to have a talk with Casey. *Father, help me.*

Daniel sat on the sofa, waiting for Casey to return from her shower. He leaned forward and rested his elbow on his knees. *Father, give me the words.*

Casey entered the room wearing a pink T-shirt and khaki capri pants. Daniel stood. "You look beautiful."

"The hot water felt luxurious, and after wrestling a skirt for three days, these capri pants feel like butter on my skin."

Daniel kissed her pink cheek free of makeup. "Let's go for a walk."

Casey smoothed her damp hair. "Okay."

They strolled in the moonlight on the path and Daniel stopped in front of the sweetheart's swing. "Let's rest here."

They sat on the swing, and he placed his arm around her shoulder. "There's something I need to tell you."

Casey's shoulders tensed under his arm. "I need to share something important with you too."

Daniel blew out a long stream of air. "I'm tired of hiding the truth." He cleared his throat. "There's nothing between Sparky and me—at least, nothing romantic."

"Then what's the secret you share?" Casey's voice was just above a whisper.

He looked up into the inky star-filled sky and wished things could be different. "I have a brain tumor."

Casey's gasped and clutched her chest. She sat there gaping at him.

Daniel leaned forward with his elbows on his knees. "I'm sorry, hon."

In the moonlight her eyes glistened. "How ... How bad is it?" she whispered. "Is it malignant?"

"The oncologist doesn't think so, but I'm scheduled to meet a neurosurgeon when we get home."

Casey stood and paced, biting her nail. "You need brain surgery?"

"Yes. Sparky found the tumor and sent me to an oncologist, who said it appears to be a slow-growing meningioma."

Casey stopped in front of him. "Why didn't you cancel the trip?"

"I thought I'd be okay and that maybe I didn't have to give up all my dreams."

She placed her palm on his cheek. "Oh, Daniel. When did you find out?"

"Just before Christmas."

"Christmas!" Casey wailed.

Daniel looked away into the darkness.

He ran his arm across his cheek.

Casey dropped to her knees in front of him. "Why didn't you say something?"

"Parkinson's slowly killed Dad, and the hand tremors reminded me of his disease."

"Oh, hon." She laid her head on his knee.

"I didn't want to face it, but I had to get a physical for work, and I needed the vaccinations for the trip. I couldn't put it off. That's why I took an additional week of vacation before we left Weldon. I didn't pass the physical."

Casey lifted her head. "Does the chief know?"

"No. All he knows is I didn't pass the physical."

"Lord, have mercy," Casey whispered. "When is your appointment with the neurosurgeon?"

"On the Friday after we return to Weldon.

"I can't believe you've carried this burden alone. Don't you know that I love you?"

"Yeah, but ..." He remained mute for several seconds. He would not say the sacred words and break her heart even more.

"You must think me pretty shallow." Casey looked into the distance.

Daniel rubbed the dirt with the toe of his boot. "I didn't want you to worry."

Casey pulled herself up, sat by Daniel's side, and gripped his hand. "Let's just hold onto each other."

He folded his arms around her. "You got it, darlin'." Daniel savored the embrace.

They sat in the swing for a long time then Daniel slapped his neck. "The mosquitos have found us." And he pulled her up and led her inside the mission house. After removing their shoes, he hugged her tightly, and whispered in her ear. "Do you forgive me?"

"Of course." She clung to him. "I don't want to leave you."

"I'll be right across the hall. Don't worry, I'm not going to lose you again." *At least, not until we return home.*

CHAPTER TWENTY-FIVE—CASEY

On numb limbs, Casey walked into the bedroom. The shock of learning about Daniel's tumor made her forget to tell him her secret. *Maybe I should tell him now*. Instead, she changed into a sleep shirt without turning on the light and climbed up to the top bed.

Sparky's girlish voiced drifted up. "Are you okay?"

Casey sniffed. "I'll be all right. It's Daniel who needs help."

"I begged him to tell you."

"He told me."

"Keeping this from the team made me feel terrible, but he swore me to secrecy."

"I owe you an apology. I'm sorry."

"And I'm sorry for making fun of you when you joined the mission team. I was jealous of your beauty and your success."

Casey sighed. "Don't worry about it. It's forgiven. The other models in New York said much worse things about me and to me. My skin is pretty thick."

"I'll bet they were mean as alley cats." Sparky mumbled.

"They were, but you're not. You just made a bad joke. It happens. I'm glad you've been looking out for Daniel. You were in a tough spot."

"Do you think it might be possible for us to become friends?" Sparky's voice lifted.

"We are friends." Casey pulled her hands behind her head on her pillow. Her hip bones ached from sleeping on the hard ground. Even though she was exhausted, Casey couldn't sleep. The peace she experienced alone in the wilderness had vanished. Casey focused on imagining scenarios in which the doctors declared Daniel healthy. But she knew it was wishful thinking. And what about telling him about Madison? His burden was so heavy. Maybe, she should wait. No. She wouldn't. Now, she knew what it felt like to be shut out. But how? When? What was she going to do?

At last, she slept, only to be awakened drenched in sweat with Sparky shaking her.

"You're safe. It's a nightmare." Sparky gripped her shoulder.

Casey sat up, panting. Her damp skin felt chilled in the air-conditioned room. "I'm ... I'm okay."

"You were screaming 'Help!'"

"I'm sorry. I guess ... the stress of the last few days got to me." The last words tumbled out.

The dim light shielded Sparky's face, but her voice sounded skeptical. "Are you sure you're okay?"

"I'm fine." Casey placed her palm on her pounding chest and squeezed her eyes shut, trying to forget the brutal hands choking her in her dream.

"I'm sorry I didn't look out for you."

"The nightmare is an old one." Casey brushed her hair from her face. "And I'm as much to blame as you for being left behind. Everything is forgiven."

As she said the words, she knew in her heart she forgave Sparky and the same peace that she'd experienced in the desert washed over her again. *We're not alone. God can do anything.*

Sleep remained elusive, so she climbed down from the bunk. *I need coffee.* With bleary eyes, she tiptoed to the kitchen, where she discovered Daniel staring into space.

"How do you feel?" She placed her palm on his cheek.

"Great, now that I'm not carrying a secret." He leaned into her touch.

"I wish we could go home today."

"No way. I'm actually going to do something other than worry."

Daniel stood and wrapped his arms around her. "Let's enjoy the moment."

She closed her eyes and tried to relax, but the oppression of her burden caused her to stiffen. *Tell him!*

"Oh, honey. You're tense. Try not to worry," he said.

"I have a secret too." Casey gulped.

He pulled his head back and looked into her eyes. "It can't be that bad."

After taking a deep breath and slowly releasing the air, she said, "I have an eighteen-year-old daughter."

He pushed away from the embrace and stared. "What?"

Her heart pounded. "She sent me a letter right before Christmas."

Daniel's face drained of color, and he dropped to a chair. He sat there, frozen, "You ... have a daughter?"

"I gave her up for adoption."

He sat there, blinking, with his mouth hanging open.

"I was raped," Casey blurted. "I didn't think I could love her, but I was wrong."

His face darkened. "Did the cops catch the guy? Is he behind bars?"

"No." Casey swallowed the lump in her throat. "I didn't report it."

"He's still out there?" Daniel shouted as he pounded his fist on the table.

"Shhhh. You're going to wake the others. I can't talk about it."

Casey turned her back on him, lifted the teakettle, and spilled water on the countertop as she made two cups of instant coffee.

"I'm sorry, hon. I didn't mean to yell." He rubbed his jaw. "I need a minute to process this."

Raymond hurried into the kitchen. "Is everything okay? I heard someone shout."

"Everything's fine." Casey's voice came out an octave too high, and she wiped her palms on her thighs.

Daniel's jaw clenched.

Raymond rubbed his neck, and his brows furrowed.

"Coffee?" Casey held up the kettle.

Raymond looked from one to the other, then inched toward the table. "Sure. I like it black, thanks."

Casey poured water into another mug. "I'm sorry we woke you."

"You didn't. I was thinking about our schedule."

"My carelessness destroyed your plans. I'm sorry."

"Flexibility is important with mission work. I think I'll separate the group and send Sam and Isaaca with Sparky, Dave, and the Louisville team to the Awontoo village for the medical clinic. Then I'll drive the two of you, Uncle Bob, and Aunt Eleanor back to the village."

Casey handed Raymond a mug. "Thanks for organizing the return visit."

Raymond blew across his cup. "I'm surprised you want to return. You must have been terrified."

"At first, yes. I'm not sure if I have the words to explain it, but I could feel God's presence."

Raymond smiled. "It's in the desert I feel closest to him.

Daniel stared out the dark window and didn't touch his coffee.

Casey started filling her water bottles from the tap with the filter and thought about her encounter with God. It hadn't been a dream, and she longed for the peace that had enveloped her to return.

Her glance fell to Daniel's hard profile. *What's he thinking?* The thought of losing him made her blink back tears. *Lord, help him to understand and forgive me.*

After a breakfast of oatmeal, the medical team started loading supplies into the bush taxi and left.

Casey packed crayons and coloring pages, her Bible, and extra lotions for the ladies. "I'm ready."

Raymond looked toward the rising sun. "It's time to roll. There's a lot of ground to cover."

"I wish we could stay longer," Casey grabbed her bag.

"Perhaps you can return next year," Raymond said.

"I don't know. Maybe. I keep thinking about Fatima and the other orphans, Pastor Djibo and Sakina, and the market boys."

"The needs of Africa can be overwhelming," Raymond's face looked sad.

"I'm also worried about Daniel, and some other things going on in my life."

"I have the feeling I interrupted something important this morning."

"Maybe it's best you did. It will give us time to think."

"I'll keep you both in prayer."

"Thank you," Casey crossed her arms. "My life is a mess."

"God can take a mess and turn it into a miracle.

"You sound like your uncle." And then she thought of Madison, her miracle, and smiled.

When the Land Cruiser passed the lone thorn tree, Casey closed her eyes. It seemed her night with only the stars and God for company was a dream. They parked in front of her rescuers' compound, and she exited the vehicle, calling, "*Fofo!*" The scent of charcoal drifted on the air, and the steady beat of someone pounding millet sounded from behind the wall.

Wasilla opened the gate, and her face brightened with a smile. Her skirt was bright yellow with green flowers. Her head was wrapped in the same material.

After the formal Songhai greetings had been completed, she introduced the group.

Wasilla beckoned everyone inside the walled area, where Helima and Miriama stopped pounding millet and waved. "*Fofo*!" Both women wore matching orange skirts with lime green squares.

Casey embraced each friend and reiterated the formal greetings.

Helima unrolled a mat under a shade tree, and they all sat down together.

Once everyone settled themselves, Casey spoke, and Raymond interpreted. "I came back to thank you for rescuing me."

Wasilla nodded, looked at the ground, and mumbled something.

"You honored her by being her guest," Raymond said.

"Because of your generosity and kindness, God placed a desire in my heart to return," Casey smiled. "You were generous to share your food with me—I want to offer you the most important thing I have. I want to tell you about Jesus."

A jumble of words fell from Raymond's lips.

Casey watched as Wasilla spoke to Raymond.

"She says they know about Jesus. He is a prophet," Raymond shrugged.

"I believe he is more than a prophet," Casey clasped her hands together. "He is the son of God."

After Raymond spoke, the women looked at each other, and Wasilla touched an amulet at her neck.

"Her necklace is something the witch doctor gave her for protection," Raymond's lips turned down.

Casey felt the tension. "We are not here to argue, only to share what we believe. Will you listen?"

Raymond spoke again to the women in Zarma, then they all nodded.

"It is their custom to respect guests. You may speak," Raymond said.

"This will take forever," Eleanor said. "You're the trained missionary, Raymond, and know the language. Why don't you speak and forget interpreting?"

"They know Casey." Raymond crossed his arms. "Men treat women as second-class citizens here. They need to see her read from the Bible and that we, as men, respect her."

Casey bit her lip, and a heaviness settled upon her. *I can't do it.* "Raymond. This is too important. I'll make a mess of it."

Pastor Bob chuckled. "Don't worry. If you make a mistake, I'm sure Raymond will correct it."

"I'm trusting you," Casey looked pleadingly at Raymond.

"And these women seem to trust you." Raymond smiled.

They sat in a circle on the mat while two toddlers spooned sand into a plastic bowl, and Casey cleared her throat. "What do you think will happen when you die?"

Wasilla answered, then Raymond responded. "They hope to go to heaven, but no one knows if the good they've done outweighs the bad things."

Casey smiled. "I have good news for you. I came to tell you that everyone can be assured of spending eternity in heaven, thanks to Jesus Christ." She lifted her Bible. "This is God's holy Word." She read in short sentences so Raymond could interpret. It took time, but she shared the story of creation. As she talked, the women listened without commenting. After she had spoken of Christ's crucifixion and resurrection, she closed with John 3:16. "Do you want to know more about how to be forgiven of your sins and how you can be assured of your future in heaven?"

All three women looked down, and Wasilla spoke. "No."

"That's all we can do," Raymond said. "You must remember, if they become Christians, they risk being thrown out of the compound. It is a big decision."

"Aisabou," Casey said. Thank you.

Wasilla spoke.

"She asks that you bless her children," Raymond said.

Casey turned in her Bible to the book of Numbers and read from Chapter 6: "May the Lord bless you and keep you; May the Lord make his face to shine upon you and be gracious to you; May the Lord lift up his countenance upon you and give you peace."

Raymond repeated the prayer in Zarma to Wasilla, and she smiled and said, "*Aisabou.*"

An idea struck Casey like a bolt of lightning, and she wondered if it might make a difference. "Is it possible for me to have a small basin of water?"

Raymond relayed her request, and Wasilla filled a bowl.

"Jesus washed the feet of his disciples," Casey said. "He did this to show them that to serve others is more important than being served. Please tell Wasilla it will honor me if she allows me to do this for her."

Wasilla fingered her amulet but nodded.

Casey removed a washcloth with soap from her backpack, lathered it in the water, and rubbed Wasilla's callused feet. As she worked, she told the Last Supper story, then she added lotion and massaged each foot. For her final treatment, she polished Wasilla's toenails with a bright crimson polish. "Christ's blood wiped away my sins. When you look at this red polish, I hope you will remember what Christ suffered for you and for me. His blood paid the price for our sins."

After she finished the task, she did the same for Helima and Miriama, talking all the while.

After finishing, she thanked them for listening.

Wasilla removed several beaded bracelets from her arm, placed them on Casey's wrist and said something.

Raymond said, "She wants you to keep the bracelets and hopes that when you wear them, you'll remember her family and say a prayer for them."

"*Aisabou*," Casey said. "Tell her I'll never forget their kindness, and I will keep her and those she loves in my prayers."

Raymond looked at his watch. "It's getting late. I'm sorry, but we need to return to the city."

After giving each of the women a final hug, they returned to the Land Cruiser. Daniel took her hand. "I'm proud of you."

"But I failed," Casey wailed.

"We don't know that," Raymond said. "Only God and the women know if they believe."

"And you returned." Eleanor patted her knee. "If I'd been the one left for two nights, I don't think I'd return for anything."

"Because of our mistake," Raymond started the vehicle, "we were able to start a relationship with the women, and we have an open invitation to visit again."

"God arranged it all," Pastor Bob lifted his eyes to the sky.

Had they accomplished anything in Africa? Casey wiped her brow with a tissue. They'd spent a fortune on airline tickets and wandered around in the desert like the Israelites. Electricity tingled up her spine. *I've wandered for eighteen years in the wilderness. Maybe God brought me here to change me. After all, he created the universe and doesn't need me to accomplish his work.*

CHAPTER TWENTY-SIX—DANIEL

That evening, Daniel read the letter from Casey's daughter, Madison. Casey sat across from him at the kitchen table, her knee jiggling all the while. Daniel focused on keeping his professional mask in place as he read the words. He stared at the letter for a long time, then looked out the kitchen window as moths fluttered around the light. "Tell me everything." His tone held no emotion.

Casey closed her eyes. "Alexis, my agent, arranged for me to have dinner with Jansen Moore. I knew better than to go, but my ambition spurred me forward. I'm ashamed to say the dream of being the new face of his cosmetics company tempted me. When he pushed for intimacy, I said no. But Jansen didn't take no for an answer."

"How did you hide your pregnancy from your family?" Daniel leaned back in his chair and rested his ankle on his knee.

"I told a chain of lies to Mama and Daddy. They think I spent six months modeling in Europe."

"Where did you go?" Daniel crossed his arms.

"I knew about the Eagle's Nest shelter because our church had supported it for years. I called, and they welcomed me."

"But why didn't you go home ... with her?" He leaned forward and gripped her hand.

Casey looked at the floor. "Fear that I couldn't love her was one of the reasons. Even now, I worry about how I'll handle it if she looks like her father."

Daniel swallowed the lump in his throat. He fought back tears but failed. He sniffed and rubbed his forearm across his damp cheek.

"There's more." Casey swallowed hard. "And ... a part of me didn't want to give up modeling. I couldn't go back to New York with a baby, and I worried about what Jansen might do if he discovered he had a daughter. No way could I allow him to be anywhere near her."

Daniel clenched a fist.

"I didn't realize, when I gave her away, that I'd be haunted with worry and filled with regret." Casey's lips were turned down and her tears dripped on the table.

Fury filled Daniel. "But he's still out there," Daniel enunciated each word. "He needs to be behind bars."

"No. He's rich and powerful. As far I know, he doesn't have children, and he might want an heir. There's no telling what sort of lies he might spin to get his way. Or even worse, what if he tried to harm Madison, to get rid of the evidence of his crime?"

Daniel pounded his thigh. "The thought of him hurting you!" He blinked back tears.

Casey placed her palm over his hand. "I'm okay."

"No. You can't let him get away with this."

"I'm trusting you to keep this to yourself."

"But–" Daniel's chest tightened, and his temple throbbed.

"I'll tell Mama and Daddy about Madison first thing when I get home. Then I'll share the news about her with the rest of my family. I'll never deny my daughter again, but I'm not going to allow her to discover anything about Jansen."

Daniel shook his head from side to side. "No." His voice came out too loud.

"Shhhh." Casey looked over her shoulder, then leaned forward and whispered. "No one would have believed me then or now."

"But what about the other victims?"

Casey stood up and hugged herself. "What other victims?"

"If he's that powerful, that rich, there are others. The first thing I'm going to do when we get home is look into this."

"No." Casey's lips formed a tight line.

"You need to file a report. I'll go with you."

"The only place you're going when we get home is to visit the neurosurgeon. It's too late anyway. It happened more than eighteen years ago."

"There's not a statute of limitations for rape in New York. I looked it up on the internet when we returned to the mission house this afternoon."

"I'm not going to do anything that might put Madison at risk."

He stood and wrapped his arms around her. "I'm sorry, hon, but the thought of this guy getting away with it ..."

"Focus on forgiving him. That's what I'm trying to do."

Daniel sighed heavily. "I don't know if I can do that. I'm a cop."

Casey rested her head on his shoulder and clung to him. "I've struggled with this for years, and forgiving him is the only thing that's given me peace."

"I'll have no peace while that guy is out there. Think of the other victims."

Casey shuddered. “There’s no way to protect Madison and go after Jansen at the same time.”

Daniel hugged her. *Somehow, he’d find a way to put this guy behind bars.*

CHAPTER TWENTY-SEVEN—CASEY

The next morning, the group agreed to return to the orphanage. "It won't take a master craftsman to build a bunk bed." Dave placed a toolbox in the back of the van.

"I've learned a little about woodworking while remodeling my home." Daniel held up a box of long screws. "Too bad I didn't pack my drill."

Raymond grinned. "A screwdriver will work just fine."

"We can read Bible stories to the children while you work." Eleanor put a canvas bag full of books into the trunk next to the tools and lumber.

Casey thought of Fatima, and she pulled Raymond aside. "I'd like to find out how I might go about adopting a little girl I noticed at the orphanage. Her name is Fatima."

"Whoa," Raymond said. "You can't do something like that without a lot of prayer, and it's almost impossible for an American to adopt children in Niger."

"Why?"

"There are stringent laws concerning adoption. In this culture, family members are expected to care for children if the parents die. The government imposes these rules to prevent child trafficking."

"What if I hire a lawyer?"

He shook his head. “A lawyer will take your money, but you’d have to prove the child has no family.”

“Her father left her at the orphanage. What if we can find him, and he signs a release?”

“The authorities would accuse you of paying him for the child.”

Her heart ached as she remembered prying Fatima’s fingers from hers.

“I’m sorry,” Raymond’s eyes looked sad. “If you are serious about adopting a child, I’d suggest looking elsewhere. Please pray about this and be very careful.”

“Thank you.” Sweat trickled down her back as she made her way to the swing. Listening to the family of squatters across the wall, she wondered how she could help.

As they traveled to the orphanage, Daniel waved at the children playing in the trash-filled streets. When the gates swung open, kids spilled out of a building and Casey searched for Fatima’s sweet face.

Isaaca raised his hand and calmed the youngsters. “The men will work on your bedrooms today, but we have no candy or other gifts. While the men work on your bunk beds, the women will read stories to you.”

The orphans clapped, and Casey studied the teeming crowd. Most wore the bright orange soccer jerseys they’d received the previous week. As she examined each smiling face, little Fatima’s didn’t appear.

Casey saw the director. “Excuse me, Monsieur Dubois.”

“Yes, mademoiselle?” He wore the same cobalt blue tunic and the embroidered round bread-bowl-like hat.

“I’m looking for a little girl I met when we first visited. Her name is Fatima.”

The director adjusted his wire-rimmed glasses and smiled. “The papa’s heart suffered, and he collected her yesterday. A cousin will help him. God answered your prayer."

"What?"

Monsieur Dubois said, "Fatima told me you prayed with her and asked God to reunite her family."

"Yes. I remember."

"She thinks you have a special relationship with God."

Casey attempted to smile and blinked back tears. "May I leave some money for her family?"

Monsieur Dubois shook his head and turned down his lips. "It will be difficult. There is too much poverty surrounding us. To help one and not another would seem cruel."

"I see."

"The needs are too great. Fatima's family would tell others, and they would come to me."

"Your job seems impossible."

"It is. But with God, anything is possible."

"I wish I had your faith."

"It's there for everyone. Trust in the Lord."

How could he say that when they were surrounded by so much need? As Casey helped Eleanor distribute coloring pages, she forced a smile to her face. They told stories, played games and sang songs while the men worked inside the buildings. Sparky and Dave tended to the children who needed medical attention.

While Casey played with the toddlers, a little more of her heart broke, and she couldn't help but think this was God's punishment for giving away her child.

These children needed a mother or father, someone, anyone to love them, and she could do that. *How can I help these children?* But her mind remained blank.

As Monsieur Dubois led the group in a song, she witnessed the joy on his face. She realized the children had Monsieur Dubois's love and that of the women he hired to help him, and they had Jesus, which was much more than most of the people in Niger. When it was time to leave, Daniel slipped a handful of CFAs to Monsieur Dubois. "Thank you for your sacrifice."

"I am blessed, every day," Monsieur Dubois said. He lined up the youngsters. "We have a small gift for you." The children started singing in English, "Jesus Loves the Little Children."

Casey wiped away tears as she listened, falling more in love with each sweet voice. *I have to do something, but what?*

CHAPTER TWENTY-EIGHT—DANIEL

On Sunday, the team returned to Pastor Djibo's church. As the minister stood in front of his small flock, using the oil barrel covered with the beautifully embroidered cloth as a lectern, peace washed over Casey. He read from the book of Philippians and closed the service with "Rejoice in the Lord always. I will say it again: Rejoice! Let your gentleness be evident to all. The Lord is near. Do not be anxious about anything, but in everything, by prayer and petition, with thanksgiving, present your request to God. And the peace of God, which transcends all understanding, will guard your hearts and your mind in Christ Jesus."

He asked if anyone in the congregation had prayer concerns. One woman had a sick child, another was going to have a new baby in a few months, a young boy needed work. As Daniel listened, he gained an understanding that their concerns were the same as those of Americans.

A heaviness pressed down on Daniel. He stood, scraped his boot against the dirt floor, and spoke softly to the crowd. "Before I came on this trip, my doctor informed me that I have a brain tumor. I'd like the other members of our mission team to forgive me for withholding this information."

Someone on the front row gasped, but Sparky looked relieved.

"All those with prayer needs, please come forward," Pastor Djibo said.

Daniel walked forward and knelt next to the young man seeking work. Others joined them on their knees.

"Please surround our brothers and sister as we pray for them."

The congregation gathered around the five of them kneeling, and the mingled voices of prayers sounded musical to Daniel. A tenderness touched his spirit as he listened. Wet tears rolled down his cheeks. To the left of him, Casey held a toddler. His love for her grew each moment, and he wanted to brand this memory in his mind forever, to savor the holy atmosphere in this small, mud-brick building, praying for those willing to humble themselves. Holiness infused the atmosphere.

Daniel closed his eyes and prayed. *Thank you, Father, for loving me. Thank you for forgiving me.* Several minutes later, when he opened his eyes, Casey was gone.

Sunlight blinded him as he stepped out of the church building. Dizziness caused him to weave as he stumbled. His heart raced, then he saw her. She was sitting under a small shelter on the ground. Her knees were pulled to her chest, and her head was down. He jogged to her. "Are you okay?"

Casey looked up and wiped tears from her face. "I was holding the little girl and couldn't help but wonder what Madison looked like at that age. I just had to get out of there."

He helped her stand and hugged her. "My heart just about stopped beating when I opened my eyes to see your empty seat."

"I'm sorry. I didn't mean to worry you. How are you feeling?"

"Until a few minutes ago, better than I've felt in months. You were right about hearing the prayers in different languages. When you described it to me last week, I knew it must be something special."

"It's almost mystical, isn't it? No, that's not the right word."

"Holy," Daniel said.

"You're right. But how do we tell people at home about it?" Casey stared into the distance with brows furrowed.

"It's not possible. They'll have to come and experience it for themselves," Daniel let go of Casey as Pastor Djibo approached them.

Today, he wore a gray suit with a white shirt and a bright blue tie. "My wife has prepared a meal, and she is very excited to show you the dresses and skirts her students designed for you."

Casey beamed her famous smile. "Wonderful. I can't wait to see their handiwork."

After a meal of chicken and rice, the group gathered in Sakina's workroom, where she displayed her students' creations and held up each item. Casey examined the perfect stitching of the brightly patterned material. "*Aisabou*—Thank you. It seems months ago, instead of days, since I last stood here."

"A lot has happened this week." Daniel squeezed her shoulder.

Raymond paid Sakina, her face lit up, and her eyes shined.

"Finally, I've been able to help someone," Casey said. "Somehow, I'll figure out a way to do more."

"I don't doubt that you will." Daniel sighed. *Too bad, I probably won't be around to see it.*

On Monday morning, the group prepared to visit one last village before returning to Weldon.

"You'll be the first team to visit this place." Raymond squared his shoulders. "Isaaca and I talked for a long time with the chief two weeks ago, and he invited us to return to speak with the elders. They'll be the ones to decide whether we can visit with the people."

"What will we do if they say no?" Pastor Bob asked.

"We'll pray, drive down the road to the next village, and see what happens," Raymond shrugged.

The trip to Manto took less than an hour, and as they exited the van, children circled, but the adults hardly noticed them. A long cord extending from a home was connected to a blaring TV sitting on a rickety table with men gathered around it. *At least there's electricity here.* Daniel looked at his phone. And he had cell phone service.

Raymond directed them to a compound and pointed toward a grouping of chairs. "Please, sit down. This is where we'll meet the elders."

Daniel squatted and examined the wobbly chair. "Are you sure? I might break it."

"The guests are expected to take the best seats," Raymond's face looked grim. "To reject it is to refuse a gift they are offering. Please sit."

Daniel was careful as he sat on the handmade furniture. A line of men filed in looking somber. The elders rested on a long, carved tree trunk that looked ancient. The now-familiar sound of a woman pounding millet beat in the background, and the familiar scent of charcoal permeated the air.

Raymond and Isaaca went through the string of formal greetings with each elder.

Aissatou leaned toward Daniel and whispered in his ear. "We need to pray."

The group of men sat across from them, straight as a ruler, and glared at the mission team in silence.

Casey whispered to Daniel. "What are we waiting for?"

He shrugged. "Perhaps for the chief to arrive, but I'm not sure. Aissatou said we need to pray."

"That's what I've been doing, because they don't seem happy we're here." Casey clutched her skirt.

A towering man stepped from behind the wall, and Isaaca and Raymond stood. Raymond said, "This is the chief."

Everyone stood, and the tall man spoke to a woman standing by the fence. She was tall and wore a bright blue dress with a pattern of red handprints.

After Raymond finished the formal greetings, the woman returned with a wooden bowl filled with water. She bowed her head and gave it to the chief, who bowed his head and extended the container to Raymond. He sipped the water and passed the awkward dish to Pastor Bob and whispered to him.

Oh, no! We can't drink the water. Daniel gulped. The tension in the air was palpable as the elders watched them.

Pastor Bob sipped, handed the vessel to Eleanor, and she copied his actions.

Aissatou whispered. "You don't have to drink. Just pretend to swallow." Daniel felt the stares as he lifted the basin to his lips.

As the wooden bowl moved from one to the other, each appeared to drink.

Lord, have mercy, Daniel prayed.

"It is a good sign when the chief offers water," Aissatou whispered.

The chief cleared his throat, spoke, and Isaaca interpreted. "The elders will listen to your message."

Raymond started speaking in Zarma, and the others watched. "He is sharing the creation story," Aissatou said. "We should pray as he speaks."

But Daniel couldn't concentrate and kept his eyes on the glaring men. When one of the elders jumped up and yelled at Raymond, Casey gripped Daniel's hand.

"He is saying Jesus is not the son of God," Aissatou said.

They watched the exchange, and Raymond continued to speak in a calm voice. Another man stood and shouted at Raymond.

Sweat beaded on Daniel's forehead. *Now what?*

The chief stood, and the two angry men sat down with nostrils flared, but the chief held up his hand as he talked.

Isaaca smiled. "He says it is good to hear what visitors have to say."

Raymond spoke a mishmash of words.

"He is saying we did not come to argue," Aissatou lifted her chin. "We only want to share what we believe and what is written in the Holy Bible."

The chief spoke to the mission team and smiled. "He thanked us for coming," Aissatou's face lacked its normal smile.

Casey watched the tall, elegant man sit down. As they waited, Casey whispered, "Now what's happening?"

"We are waiting for the elders to ask questions." Aissatou sat ramrod straight.

After two minutes, which felt like twenty to Daniel, Raymond and Isaaca stood, clasped the forearm of the chief, and did the same with each elder.

"It's time to prayer walk," Raymond grinned. "The women will go down the path on the left, and the men will take the trail on the right. We'll return to the van in two hours."

Daniel didn't want to be separated from Casey again, but he didn't have a choice. He squared his shoulders. This is why he'd traveled here.

As the women walked down the alley, sweat trickled down Casey's back, and she looked over her shoulder at him and waved. He started to return the wave, but two little boys ran up to him and grabbed his hands. They giggled and talked across him to each other. He had no idea what they said, but other children joined them.

A group of men were sitting on a mat under a tree having tea. They beckoned for them to join them. As Raymond and Isaaca talked, Daniel could see curiosity in the African men's eyes as they listened to the missionaries tell the gospel from creation to Jesus as one all-encompassing story. They spent about half an hour talking, then waited to see if the men wanted to know more. Sadly, no one expressed interest.

Two hours passed quickly, and they trudged to the bush taxi. "I guess it's a wasted trip," Daniel sighed.

"Over sixty men heard the name of Jesus for the first time today," Isaaca's eyes sparkled. "We planted the first seed. Soon, I'll return with other teams, and God will see to the harvest."

"I'll pray for them every day for the rest of my life," Pastor Bob's face was joyous.

"And someday, when we get to heaven, we may meet one of these men again," Raymond grinned. "All because we came to this remote village."

They waited by the van for the women to return. Daniel glanced at his watch. They were late. He heard Casey's voice before he saw her. "There's so many." Her voice sounded sad. "It's overwhelming. We are only a handful in a sea of millions." He surmised they were on the other side of the mud-brick wall.

"That's why we need to convince others to come," Sparky's voice was upbeat.

"True. If I can do it, anyone can," Casey said.

"I didn't know how you would fare on this trip," Sparky said, "but you've been a trooper. And you never complained, even when we left you in the desert."

"I came for all the wrong reasons," Casey said, "but God used me anyway."

"I'll have to admit, it surprised me when you signed up," Eleanor said with a lilt. "Why did you come?"

Casey sounded remorseful. "Jealousy of Sparky."

Eleanor hooted. "Hon, Daniel Sheppard doesn't have eyes for anyone but you."

"I know that now."

The women rounded the corner and Daniel strode to them. Even though he'd heard Casey's confession, it was hard to believe she could be jealous of anyone.

"We're all back, safe and sound," Eleanor sounded happy.

Daniel gripped Casey's hand and whispered in her ear. "Today, was everything I imagined. Thank you for coming."

Casey's cheeks were flushed. "I guess you heard us talking."

Daniel shrugged. "I couldn't help but hear Eleanor. I guess it's obvious to everyone." He gulped. "I think you're pretty special." He wished he could tell her how much he loved her.

When they returned to the compound, dusty and tired, they started packing. Raymond insisted they rest all day the next day before the long journey home as their flight to Paris departed at midnight.

Daniel walked to the riverbank and watched the sun paint the horizon a deep pink. It was time to somehow distance himself from Casey. It was time to let her go.

CHAPTER TWENTY-NINE—CASEY

The grueling and uneventful trip home left everyone exhausted. Jolene and Frank Bledsoe met them at the airport, full of questions, but Casey fell asleep in the car during the drive home from Nashville. When someone shook her shoulder, she opened her eyes and discovered the vehicle parked in her parents' drive.

"I have vegetable beef stew in the Crock-Pot," Jolene said.

"Thanks, Mom, but I'm not hungry, just sleepy."

"You need to eat," Frank said.

Daniel squeezed her shoulder. "Let's try to eat a bite."

She yawned. "Okay."

They trooped into her parents' home, and Casey walked to the kitchen faucet and filled a glass. "I'll never take clear, clean water for granted again." And she drank a full glass without stopping. As she savored the first bite of vegetable beef stew, her mother stared at her.

"It's wonderful." Casey filled her spoon again.

"Thank you. Now tell us everything."

"It's too much to cover in one sitting, but I promise after a good night's sleep, I'll show you our pictures and answer your questions." Casey covered her mouth as she yawned.

When she swallowed the last spoonful of soup, she touched a napkin to her lips." If you're satisfied, Mama, I need sleep."

"All right." Jolene's shoulders drooped.

Daniel stood. "Thank you for giving me a ride and for the meal."

Frank clapped him on the shoulder. "It's our pleasure. Thanks for getting our girl home in one piece."

The Bledsoes dropped Daniel off first. When Casey's cozy, white bungalow came into view, her shoulders relaxed. *I'm home.*

She unlocked her front door and walked into the foyer with her father following closely with her bags. "Just leave them here. I'm going to bed."

"Okay, hon." He hugged her. "I'm proud of you."

She felt every muscle tense at his words. *You won't be after I tell you about your granddaughter.* Fats howled and rubbed against her leg, and she picked him up. The deep rumbling in his chest relaxed her.

"That's the first time the ghost cat's come out of hiding. Your mama worried herself silly over him."

"He doesn't trust anyone but me."

The oversized black cat's chest vibrated, and he started drooling.

"Your mail is on the kitchen counter." Frank pecked her cheek. "We'll see you tomorrow. Get some rest."

The minute she saw the car back out of her driveway, she started searching through the pile of envelopes and magazines. When she recognized Madison's familiar scrawl, she sat on a stool at the island and held it to her chest. Fear gripped her. *I wonder if she sent a picture. Lord, help me.*

With trembling hands, she opened the envelope, and as she unfolded the stationary, a photo fell to her lap. Her breath caught as she looked at the beautiful red-haired girl. Madison wore a basketball uniform, and she had Jansen's gray eyes. They were full of warmth that shone even through the photo. Instead of the expected fear, love overflowed through the cracks of Casey's broken heart. "Thank you, Jesus," she whispered. After staring at the smiling face for a long time, she wiped her cheek with her sleeve and read the letter.

> Dear Ms. Bledsoe:
>
> It thrilled me to receive your letter. I can't believe you're going to Africa. Very cool! I've never traveled except for basketball tournaments. I'm not the best basketball player, but I earned a college scholarship to Middle Tennessee State University. I've always played sports, and basketball seemed to be a natural fit since I'm tall. I also love softball.
>
> Are you married? You might not want anyone to know you have a daughter. Mom said she's sure it's all right since you answered my letter.
>
> I'd like to hear about your trip to Africa. You said it's a long story. I like long stories. In fact, reading is my favorite hobby other than basketball, but practice leaves little time for anything except homework. What are your hobbies?
>
> Everyone at home is always asking me about my major. I don't know yet. I'm trying to decide whether I want to be a social worker or maybe a lawyer. At the same time, I can't imagine life without basketball. I'd also like to coach. Mom and Dad won't give me any advice on this other than to listen to my heart. How did you know you wanted to be a model?
>
> I hope you will write me again.
>
> Sincerely,
>
> Madison

Casey reread the letter and studied the picture. Her daughter must have a sweet spirit to consider being a social worker. Madison's parents had given her excellent advice. Gratitude for the knowledge her daughter had landed with good people filled her being again. *Thank you, Jesus, and all the guardian angels from heaven.*

Her heart lifted, but her stomach ached. Without hesitating, she dialed Emma, who answered on the second ring. "You're home!"

"Mom and Dad just dropped me off."

"Tell me everything!"

"I'm too tired."

"I want details."

Casey sighed. "Madison sent me another letter and a picture. She's beautiful."

"Oh, honey. Of course, she is. How could she be anything but gorgeous, being your daughter?"

"Her eyes are gray, but I didn't freak out."

"Of course you didn't. When are you going to stop allowing fear to make you stupid?"

"As soon as you start sugar-coating words."

"So sad for you then, cause that's not going to happen. Did you tell Daniel?"

"Yes."

"What'd he say? Is he okay?"

"I guess. But all he can seem to think about is going after Jansen."

"It makes sense, hon. He's a cop."

"He wants me to press charges."

"The same thought crossed my mind about a zillion times."

"No way. If I did, it would make the papers. She might run across it and figure out what happened."

"I understand."

"And there's more news. Are you sitting down?"

"Daniel asked you to marry him?"

Casey rolled her eyes. "You are worse than Mama. No. There are more important things in the world than me getting married."

"Like what?"

She paused as her chest swelled with indignation. "Daniel's sick. Those migraines are really a brain tumor."

"What? Whoa. Oh, no. Is it malignant?"

Casey filled Emma in on the details.

"I can't believe he didn't cancel the trip," Emma said.

"I know."

"Dang. I don't know what to say."

"That's a first. And that reminds me. I'm going to tell Mom and Dad about Madison tomorrow."

"It's about time. I'm going to sound like Eleanor quoting Scripture, but she would say, 'The truth will set you free.'"

"I had that same thought."

"It's about time you started thinking."

"I should have told them the first night I received Madison's letter."

"Wrong. Change that to eighteen years ago."

"Okay, I give up. You win. You're always right."

"Said so, Bledsoe."

"No one likes a smarty pants."

"I can't help it. I'm a librarian, but librarians are the best at keeping secrets too."

"True. I know I can trust you to keep my secrets."

"You've got that right."

"I need sleep. I'm beat."

"I can't wait to see Madison's picture."

"She's beautiful."

"Close your eyes and dream of her. I'll see you tomorrow."

After a long shower and marveling at the blessing of hot, clean water flowing from the tap without worrying about amoebas, Casey crawled under the coverlet. Before turning out her bedside light, she viewed the picture again and drifted to sleep smiling, dreaming of meeting Madison.

At three a.m. on Thursday morning, Casey stared at the bedside clock and her stomach rumbled. It would take days for her internal clock to adjust. Thank goodness no one expected her to work until Monday. With a sigh, she slipped on her robe and stared at the clothes hanging in her walk-in closet. When she considered all she had compared to the women with whom she'd spent time in Africa, it shamed her.

After breakfast, the first thing she planned to do was make a trip to Savoir Faire Diva, a high-end consignment shop in Nashville. She'd send the funds from the sale of her excessive wardrobe to the Eagle's Nest Shelter for women. No one needed this much stuff.

She meandered to the kitchen. The offerings in her pantry seemed paltry, but as she compared the food in her kitchen to Wasilla's bag of rice, she reconsidered.

A box of pancake mix that only required water seemed to be the answer, and then she discovered a package of frozen pre-cooked sausages in her freezer. *A feast.*

Every time she'd awakened early in Africa, she'd discovered Daniel in the kitchen, and she wondered if he too was wide awake and hungry. After a moment's hesitation, she dialed his number, and he answered on the first ring. "Is everything okay?"

"Of course. Were you awake?"

She heard him sigh. "Yes, but I'm worn out."

"Me, too, and I'm starving. Are you hungry?"

"Always."

"I'm cooking pancakes and sausages. Can you be ready in five minutes?"

"Yes, ma'am."

"I'll be right there."

Casey hit the start button on the coffee maker and abandoned her cooking supplies on the kitchen counter. The sight of her blue robe under her leather coat made her giggle. Who cares? And she slipped on her loafers and left.

Minutes later, the couple returned to the kitchen. Casey turned on the griddle, exchanged her coat for an apron, and started stirring the pancake batter. It didn't take long to warm the sausages and build a stack of pancakes. She poured Daniel a cup of coffee, and he kissed her cheek before taking the mug.

Daniel placed the brew under his nose and inhaled deeply. "Mm, heaven."

"My thoughts exactly. Why don't you say the blessing? I don't ever want to eat again without thanking God for food."

He hastily prayed and immediately started pouring maple syrup over his pancakes.

Casey sipped her coffee. "The tumor hasn't affected your appetite."

"Only when I have a headache."

"What time is your appointment tomorrow morning?"

Daniel swallowed. "Ten o'clock."

"You'll need a driver?"

"I'm sure your schedule is full."

"I'm going to stop by the shop today and sign some checks, but I'm not scheduled to be in the store until Monday."

"Hmph, I'll bet there are women lined up, waiting to see you."

"If there are, they can wait. I need to be with you." Casey put her hand in the pocket of her robe and felt the image of Madison. "I have something to show you." She placed the photo on the table.

Daniel swallowed and stared at the picture. His face flooded with tenderness. "Wow."

The shrill phone cut through the silence.

Casey stood. "Who can that be?" She snatched the receiver. "Hello."

"Thank the Lord! I didn't know you were home."

Casey held the phone away from her ear as she recognized the voice of her neighbor, Voletta Wright. "Yes, ma'am. Daddy picked us up at the airport last night."

"I've been keeping my eye on your house."

"Thank you," Casey said. "I'm sorry my light woke you."

"Oh, honey. At my age, it's necessary to get up more than once in the middle of the night. I thought someone might be robbing you."

"No, ma'am. I'm fine, but thanks again."

"You're welcome. And welcome home."

Casey replaced the receiver. "Nothing goes unnoticed in Weldon."

Daniel stood and wrapped his arms around her. "That's for sure."

She hugged him back. "I'm going to see Mama and Daddy after lunch."

"Do you want me to go with you?"

"No. I think it will be better if it's just us."

She rested her chin on his shoulder and stared at the dark window, seeing only her bleak reflection. *He has a brain tumor.*

Casey wrapped her knuckle on the back door of her parent's home and walked into the mudroom. After sleeping most of the afternoon away, she summoned her courage to face them. It seemed wasps battled inside her stomach. After hanging her jacket on the coat rack, she squared her shoulders despite the burden.

Jolene beckoned from the kitchen. "Is that you, Casey?"

"Yep."

"It's just me, you, and Daddy tonight."

Thank you, Lord. The last thing Casey wanted was to face an army of Bledsoes. She'd possibly end up in front of a firing squad.

"You can tell your brothers and everyone else about your adventures this weekend. They're all coming to the church service Sunday evening when you share your experience with the congregation."

Casey chewed her thumbnail. *They're going to get an earful.* Her mom faced the stove, and Casey looked over her shoulder. "I hope we're having the leftover stew. We practically slept as we ate last night."

"Your Daddy finished that at lunch today. We're having chicken tenders, green beans, mashed potatoes, and rolls."

"And pecan pie." Casey eyed the dish on the counter.

"I'm trying out a new recipe for the Garden Club next week. We're meeting on Martin Luther King Day. I called the library, and Emma looked up Dr. King's favorite dessert. Jolene narrowed her eyes. "You're chewing your nails. What's wrong?"

Casey crossed her arms and crammed her fists into her armpits.

Frank walked in and leaned down to kiss his daughter's cheek. "The prodigal daughter has returned."

"Oh, Frank, she's not a spendthrift nor wasteful."

He sat down at the kitchen table and shook out the newspaper. "She traveled afar against her father's wishes."

"Oh, for goodness sakes." Jolene smoothed her auburn hair.

"And I've never been prouder of her in my life." Frank looked over the top of the paper.

Not for long. Casey's mouth felt dry.

They sat in their usual places at the kitchen table, and Frank laid his paper aside. "Let us pray."

As he blessed the food, Casey chewed her lip. *Emma's right. There's no easy way to do this. Just spit it out.*

Her parents filled their plates, and the weight grew heavier with each second. *It's time.* Casey closed her eyes and blurted. "I have something to tell you."

"We know about Daniel's tumor," Jolene said in a hushed tone.

Her dad placed his hand over hers, and his eyes looked sorrowful. "We've been praying."

"What? How do you know about that?"

"Adelaide Stone let it slip at the knitter's club last week." Jolene's lips turned down.

"Sparky will have a fit when she discovers her clerk is blabbing confidential patient information." Casey's cheeks burned.

Frank squeezed her hand. "She said a neurosurgeon will remove the tumor if he can get to it."

Casey pulled her hand away from her dad's and covered her face with her palms. "There's something else I need to explain." With a jolt, she stood and paced around the room.

"Sit down." Jolene wrung her napkin. "You're making me nervous."

Casey removed Madison's picture from her sweater pocket, placed it on the table between her parents, and then sat down.

Frank removed his reading glasses from his pocket and lifted the picture. "Who is this girl?"

Jolene stood and lifted her glasses that hung on a chain around her neck, and she looked over Frank's shoulder. "She reminds me of you."

Casey gulped. "She's my daughter." The words were almost a whisper.

The blood drained from her mother's face, and she sat down quickly, almost missing her chair.

Frank leaned forward, his eyes narrowed. "How can that be?"

"You thought I went to Europe on a photo shoot, but I hid out in a shelter and had a baby girl." The truth tumbled out, and she closed her eyes. *Tell them all of it*. She sat back down at the table and gripped her hands together. "I was raped."

Jolene gasped and clutched her hand to her throat.

Tears streamed down Casey's face, and she wiped them with her sleeve. "I was traumatized, and I couldn't think straight."

Jolene came behind the chair and wrapped her arms around Casey's shoulders, and she could feel her mom sobbing.

Frank stood and started pacing around the table, muttering a string of incoherent threats. "Who did it? What's his name?" He spoke slowly and quietly. "I'll beat him till he looks like roadkill."

"You warned me to be careful, but I didn't listen."

Frank rubbed his hands over his purple face. "I should have put my foot down and said no to New York!" he roared.

"Oh, Daddy, no one could have stopped me." Casey shrugged. "I'd been warned by another girl." She covered her face. "He tempted me with a big contract, and I almost gave in, but in the end, I said no."

“I trusted Alexis to look out for you,” Jolene said.

Casey grabbed a tissue and blew her nose. “She threatened to stop representing me if I didn’t go.”

“I remember all those weeks you didn’t call.” Jolene stared into space.

“I pretended to be busy with photoshoots. More lies.”

“Where were you?” Jolene looked Casey in the eye.

“I hid out at the Eagle’s Nest shelter.”

No one made a sound. Her dad sat down with a thud, and she studied her parents’ stricken faces.

“Why did you give her away?” Jolene picked up a napkin and wiped her cheek. “Why didn’t you come home? We love you, and a baby is always a blessing.”

“I thought she’d remind me of the man who hurt me, and I wanted to protect her ...” Casey couldn’t speak further for the lump in her throat.

Jolene started fanning herself with a dishtowel. “I need some air. I can’t breathe.” She held her hand to her chest.

Frank studied his wife, rubbed his jaw, and went to the kitchen drawer. After rumbling through the contents, he pulled out a paper bag and expanded it by blowing air into it. “Breath into this. You’re just hyperventilating.”

She scurried to her mother’s side. “Maybe we should take Mama to the hospital.”

“No, we’ve seen her like this before. Just give her a minute.” He spoke in a soft voice to his wife. “Hold your finger over one nostril, just like Dr. Singer taught you.”

“I’m sorry.” Casey wrung her hands.

“Anytime one of you kids gets hurt, this is your mama’s reaction.”

After a few minutes of fanning his wife, Frank sat down. “I think she’s better.”

“I am.” Jolene grabbed a glass of iced tea and swallowed, then picked up the picture.

Casey blew her nose. "I just didn't think I could love her. I still have nightmares about that night."

Jolene closed her eyes. "Why didn't you tell us?"

"Oh, Mama. You were so proud. Practically the whole town came to my going-away party. They all but had a parade in my honor."

"Because they love you. Just like we do."

Casey looked away and sighed. "And a part of me didn't want to give up the dream of being a top model. I thought I could return to New York, like nothing happened."

Frank's face held a deep sadness. "When you came home with those dark circles under your eyes, I knew something more than depression beat you down."

"I'm sorry I lied," Casey said. "But I didn't want her father's shame to touch her."

"Honey, that don't make a lick of sense," Frank said. "That man's shame can't touch nobody but him. You should have come home. We could have helped you raise her."

Jolene sniffed. "Hush, honey." She touched his cheek. "Shoulda, coulda, woulda won't change a thing."

"Please, forgive me," Casey covered her face with her hands.

"Let's not think about what we lost, but what we have," Jolene sniffed. "We have a granddaughter." And she gave a weak smile.

"How did you get this picture?" Frank held it up, and his face held wonder. "She's a basketball player?"

Casey nodded. "Her name is Madison, and she sent me a letter right before Christmas."

Jolene studied the picture. "How did she find you?"

"I've always kept my address up to date with the adoption agency, hoping she'd want to connect with me."

"When are we going to meet her?" Frank asked.

"I don't know. We're just getting to know each other through letters."

They all sat staring into space, the food on the table forgotten, but Casey felt as if a mudslide had been bulldozed from her chest.

Jolene seemed to pull herself out of the fog. "Does Daniel know?"

Casey nodded. "I told him in Africa."

"He'll help me track the lowlife down," Frank said.

"We're not going to do that," Casey said. "I mean it."

"Who's going to stop me?" Frank glared at her.

"He's rich and powerful, Daddy. The last thing we want is for him to discover he has a daughter, and we don't want Madison to learn how she came to be in this world."

Frank pounded his fist on the table. "I'm not going to let him get away with it."

"Why do men always want someone to pay?" Casey wrung her hands.

"Casey's right," Jolene said. "Our granddaughter is the most important thing. Let God take care of the vengeance."

A voice of reason. Casey wiped her damp cheek with a napkin.

"But if I ever see Alexis again," Jolene's voice sounded menacing, "I'll snatch her bald-headed."

It's over. It's finally over. Why didn't I do this years ago? Casey's spirits lifted. *Maybe I'm finally free.*

Dear Madison,

Thank you for your letter and the picture. It thrilled me to discover it in my mail when I returned from Africa. First, I'll answer your questions.

I'm not married, and you have no brothers or sisters. There is a special man in my life, Daniel Sheppard. He's a police officer, and I signed up for the mission trip to Africa because he joined the mission team. Only time will tell if we are to be together forever. He knows I love him. But marriage requires more than love. It requires trust. I think he sees my love for him as too shallow to survive some health issues he's facing.

Telling people about you is healing. Since receiving your letter, I've shared everything with my parents. They were shocked, but my dad seemed relieved to know the reason for my clinical depression. Your letter did more to help me heal than years of counseling. My heart is still mending, but every day is filled with hope.

I'm happy to know one of your favorite hobbies is reading. My best friend, Emma, is a librarian. What's your favorite book? What are you reading now? I've just finished a book by Alexander McCall Smith. Emma recommended it to me because the setting is in Africa.

As for hobbies, I love fashion and go through clothes faster than popcorn pops. If I learned anything in Africa, it's that I have too much stuff, and I need to simplify my life.

Your parents' advice to follow your heart when considering your education is perfect. Listen to your heart, and you'll make good choices.

In Africa, the heat wilted me, and poverty surrounded us. The environment was brutal. If I didn't have the pictures, I'd almost be able to convince myself I dreamed it. Generous and kind people blessed me. I thought I was going to help people in Africa and change what they believe about God. But the Africans rescued me, and I am the one God changed! I experienced grace in Africa. Perhaps it all started with receiving your letter before I left. Maybe being alone in the desert for a time is when my outlook changed. I see the world differently since I visited Africa.

> I hope someday we can meet and become friends, and I'd love to meet your mother and thank her for being what I couldn't be.
>
> Please keep writing. I want to know about you, your family, and things that are important to you. You and your family are in my prayers.
>
> Sincerely,
>
> Casey
>
> P.S. How's your basketball team doing? My Dad is thrilled to know you are playing college-level basketball.

Casey sealed the envelope, and her spirits lifted as she visualized meeting her daughter one day. At least she had hope, and that was something she'd almost lost eighteen years ago.

CHAPTER THIRTY—DANIEL

Daniel stared at Jansen Moore's face on the computer screen. Memories of Casey experiencing something akin to a panic attack during a passionate kiss on his sofa came to mind. He was trained to recognize and deal with victims. How had he missed the signs?

On more than one occasion, he'd seen her face change from a smile to sadness when watching a child, and he'd thought it was because she longed for one of her own. When she'd shared that she'd battled depression for years, he believed it was due to a chemical imbalance. How had she kept this hidden from her close-knit family? No wonder she'd needed counseling.

If he wasn't careful, he'd need a shrink himself. *Think!* He closed his eyes. *There's a solution to every problem. What can I do to get this guy off the street?* And then he knew.

Daniel glared at Jansen Moore's face on his computer screen, and his gut wrenched. No way was this guy going to keep walking the streets. *I'll stop you if it's the last thing I do.*

His jaw clenched as he rifled through his desk for his leather address book and looked up the private number of his old boss, the former Metro-Nashville police chief. The chief hailed from New Jersey, and Daniel felt confident his mentor could help.

Joe answered. "Well, if it isn't my old buddy, Sheriff Andy Taylor!"

"That's not even close to funny, wise guy," Daniel said.

After they spent a few minutes catching up and insulting each other, Daniel cleared his throat. "I need your help."

"I figured that out five minutes ago. What do you need?"

Daniel relayed everything he knew about Casey's case.

"Man. Eighteen years ago. And she's not willing to file a report?"

"No. He's some kind of big shot in the fashion world. Supposedly untouchable."

"My favorite kind of criminal. I'll make some calls?"

"Thanks, I appreciate that, but first, I want to hire a PI. I'll bet my life savings there are other victims."

"I'm with you."

"Who do you trust?"

"Hmm. Let me think about it."

"Don't take too long–I have some other things going on."

"Like what?"

Daniel sighed. "I may be facing surgery in a few days."

"Is it serious?"

"Yeah." He told him the rest of his story.

Neither spoke for a few seconds.

"Man." Joe cleared his throat.

"I know."

"I'll get to work on the list of investigators. What's your email? I'll send a list of people I trust."

"Thanks, I'll owe you one," Daniel said.

"That's the way I like it."

Daniel twisted a paperclip. "I need one more favor."

"Sure."

"If I don't come through the surgery okay, I need someone to finish the job. Will you do that for me?"

"You got it, buddy."

"Thanks. Now get back to your paperwork and kissing up to the movers and shakers."

"Yeah, right." Joe's voice was heavy with sarcasm.

"Take care of yourself, and don't forget I'll owe you one.

"Just the way I like it." Joe sighed and lowered his voice. "Good luck, Daniel. I'll be checking in on you."

The two disconnected, and Daniel stared into space. *I should tell Casey I'm investigating this guy.* He typed in a few notes on the file he'd started on Jansen Moore. It had been easy to find the multimillionaire on the internet. A beautiful young woman always seemed to be on his arm. Bile rose in Daniel's throat as he stared at the photo. If only he could be the one to give him what he deserved. Then he sighed, knowing his malicious thoughts were the devil's snare, making him no better than the man he hunted. *Lord, forgive me.* Even though he thought the words, his anger burned hotter.

This guy is going to be locked up for a very long time.

Daniel and Casey sat in the doctor's waiting room for over two hours and then another hour in the examination room before Dr. Bertrand, the neurosurgeon, walked in. He barely looked up at them as he studied the chart in his hand. His dark hair was slicked back with gel. His white lab coat covered his dark suit, and a vibrant blue silk tie was knotted at his throat. Daniel guessed his alligator leather oxfords cost more than what a cop made in a month. Hopefully these were signs he was good at his job, even if he didn't have any bedside manner.

Finally, Dr. Bertrand spoke. "I've been on the phone with Dr. Peterson."

Daniel held his breath.

"I've been studying your lab results and the MRI pattern, and I agree with Dr. Peterson's speculation that the tumor appears to be a meningioma, but a biopsy will be required to confirm."

Daniel nodded. *Just breathe. Breathe in. Breathe out.*

"Dr. Peterson and I also agree you are a candidate for a surgical technique called an awake craniotomy."

Daniel's chest constricted. "How can I be awake while you're operating on my brain? Won't that hurt?"

"No, the brain is not a pain-sensitive organ."

Daniel rubbed his jaw. "I don't know about this." He placed his hand over his pounding heart.

"It sounds unbelievable, but you won't feel a thing. You'll be put to sleep, I'll remove the skin and the skull, and then the anesthesiologist will wake you up."

Casey gripped Daniel's hand as nausea threatened to overtake him.

"I don't like the sound of it," Daniel gulped.

"You'll be awake but groggy as I operate. I'll ask you to do simple things such as making a fist or holding up two fingers during the surgery. This helps me ensure the tissue I'm removing isn't affecting your ability to function."

"Isn't there another alternative?" His skin felt clammy.

"Your tumor lies adjacent to an area of the brain that controls sensitive motor skills." Dr. Bertrand pointed to an image on the wall. "A tumor is like a weed. The bad cells are growing next to the good."

Casey wiped her free palm on her slacks. “How will you know which cells to remove?”

“Sometimes I don’t. With this technique, I’ll ask Mr. Sheppard questions and to do something simple like moving his little finger.”

“Will I be able to do that with part of my skull removed?” Daniel shuddered.

“Yes. As I remove the tumor, I want to avoid extracting critical cells.”

“What happens if you make a mistake?” Daniel’s hand trembled.

“I’m most concerned with the tumor affecting the left side of your body. You could lose motor skills, but the chance of that happening is minimized with this technique.”

“It sounds like this is experimental,” Casey’s emerald eyes were wide.

“No, but Mr. Sheppard’s tumor is deep. It’s going to require extreme caution. In fact, his case will be reviewed by the tumor board.” Dr. Bertrand removed his reading glasses and looked down at Daniel. “They’ll be the ones to decide whether you are a candidate for this technique.”

“I don’t like someone else deciding my future.” Daniel sat up straight.

“It’s good to have the best doctors available reviewing your case. It takes a skilled team to perform this procedure.”

“What if they say no?” Daniel narrowed his eyes.

“Let’s wait and hear from the council before we consider other options.”

“I take it the alternative choices aren’t good.” Daniel ran his hand through his hair.

“We might consider chemotherapy or proton therapy. We’ll need to consult with your oncologists. In the meantime, I have two videos I want you to watch,” Dr. Bertrand stood.

"Is there going to be blood?" Daniel asked. "Casey's sort of squeamish."

"She might want to return to the waiting room. One video is of an awake craniotomy. The second film explains the advantages of proton therapy compared to other treatment options."

"I'm staying." Casey gripped his hand.

"Dr. Peterson and I believe you're a good candidate for the awake craniotomy. Of course, you might want another opinion," Dr. Bertrand gave a tight smile.

"I'd like to watch the video first, then decide," Daniel said.

Dr. Bertrand handed Daniel a notepad. "Good idea. I'll return in a few minutes to answer questions. Write down your questions as you watch the video."

The doctor left the room, and a minute later, a nurse walked in and placed a laptop on the counter. "The first movie will last about thirty minutes. You'll see the whole procedure and a follow-up interview with the patient. I'll return in a few minutes and start the second film."

"How long does the procedure take?" Daniel looked at the nurse.

"I'm sorry, I'm not qualified to answer questions, but Dr. Bertrand will return shortly."

When the film finished playing, Daniel and Casey sat and looked at each other. Casey's knee jiggled up and down.

The nurse then keyed up the video touting the advantages of proton therapy. Daniel felt as if he were watching an infomercial. The video ended and they waited in silence.

A knock sounded, and Dr. Bertrand entered. "Good. I see you've finished the videos. Do you have any questions?"

Daniel lifted his chin. "How long will we have to wait for approval from the tumor board?"

"They meet on Tuesday. Keep your schedule open because if they give approval, I'll want to operate right away."

"Do I have a choice?" Daniel crossed his arms.

"I believe this procedure is your best chance for a full recovery."

"How long will it take me to heal?"

"I can't answer that question, but some patients return home from the hospital in as little as two days. It depends on how well the surgery goes."

"When can I return to work?"

"We'll know more after the procedure, maybe several weeks or a few months ... or never. There are the risks of infection, hemorrhaging, seizures, stroke, and ... death." Daniel closed his eyes and focused on breathing in and out. "I guess we'll wait and see if I qualify for the surgery."

"Call or email me if you have other questions."

"Any other instructions?" Daniel asked.

"Have a nice, leisurely lunch, enjoy the afternoon and the next few days."

Casey squeezed Daniel's hand. "That's the best advice I've heard today."

Dr. Bertrand left them, and they sat for a minute in silence.

With a sigh, Daniel stood, lifted Casey's hand and kissed her knuckles. They ambled to her Mustang in silence. While she dug her keys from her purse, Daniel put on his sunglasses. He couldn't let Casey see him cry like a baby.

They both fastened their seat belts, but instead of starting the car, Casey stared at him.

"What are you waiting for?"

Casey reached across the console and grabbed his hand. "Will you marry me?"

Daniel closed his eyes as his heart broke into a thousand tiny pieces. When he thought he might be able to speak, he gently removed her hand. "You know I can't. You watched the video."

"And the doctor released the patient after two days."

"Do you think they'd show us the story of a person who died, or worse, the poor soul hooked up to machines forever?" He swiped at his damp cheek.

"But if something goes wrong, I won't have any rights. They might not even let me be with you."

"I'll make sure you aren't blocked."

"I wish you'd trust me to love you."

"I do. That's what worries me the most."

"What do you mean?" Casey removed his sunglasses, but Daniel looked away from her.

"I worry you'll waste the rest of your life trying to take care of me. I don't want that."

"But that's what I want to do."

Daniel shook his head. "I gave up everything to care for my parents. I'm not going to let you do the same."

"Do you regret it?"

"No. But I felt trapped, frustrated."

"I love you."

"I won't let you tie yourself down to me."

Casey's cheeks turned red. "What if I say it's now or never?"

Daniel swallowed the lump in his throat. "Then it's never." He was proud that his voice held none of the desperation he felt.

"Oh. This makes me mad." Casey's face had paled in the doctor's office, but now her cheeks flamed.

"I've had a lot more time to get used to the idea. You've only known for a few days. You're going to think differently I'll bet once it all sinks in."

"I wish I could do something to make this easier for you." Casey wailed.

"There is."

"What?"

"Let's follow Dr. Bertrand's orders," Daniel kissed her cheek. "I think this calls for lunch at the Cascades restaurant. Please don't stay mad. Let's just enjoy the day."

Casey gave a sad smile. "I've always wanted to eat there."

"What better place to enjoy a January afternoon than the Atrium at Opryland Hotel?" Daniel kissed her wrist. "Let's make the most of it."

"I'll try," Casey sounded mournful.

Daniel squeezed her knee.

"Let's go then." By the look on her face, one would think they were going to enjoy their last meal. Daniel gulped. *It might just be.*

CHAPTER THIRTY-ONE—CASEY

On Sunday evening, the African mission team sat in chairs in front of the congregation. The lectern had been removed to make room for everyone. As the sanctuary filled with a larger than usual crowd for a Sunday night service, Casey studied each of her brothers from oldest to youngest. Frank Jr., Tom, Kent, Scott, and Cliff. Casey's heart felt heavy. They appeared to be the perfect, big, happy family.

Under scrutiny, one could see the dark circles under Frankie's eyes. He worked long hours and hardly knew what his two boys were doing while his wife, Naomi, filled her days shopping. They'd almost lost their home twice due to credit card debt until he'd asked her for help.

Tom drummed his fingers on his kneecap. With two divorces under his belt, he only saw his two girls from different marriages every other weekend. He must have already returned his daughters before the service.

Kent and Connie were happier since returning to Weldon, but their daughter, Olivia, ran with the wrong crowd. They'd caught her sneaking out in the middle of the night, and she'd come home more than once smelling of beer.

Scott had battled alcoholism since his early twenties. Thank God he'd discovered AA.

And Cliff changed girlfriends as often as most people replaced cheap light bulbs. Each new woman looked younger than the previous one. Casey wondered if he'd ever grow up.

They'd all been baptized and raised in the church, and yet, each of them struggled with sin in their personal lives.

Earlier today, they'd gathered at her parents' home for lunch. Afterward, she'd shared the news about Madison with her brothers, but she hadn't mentioned Jansen. It surprised her they had come tonight because they'd barely spoken to her when she left her parents' home this afternoon.

Her brothers sat on the family pew and Kent glared at her. *This must be what it feels like to face a jury*, she'd thought ... No way could she tell them about Jansen. They'd likely go after him. It had been hard enough to convince her dad and Daniel to leave him be.

Her mother's makeup couldn't hide the dark circles under her eyes, and her daddy's eyes had lost their twinkle. Instead of giving her a hug, he'd dropped to the pew and looked defeated. Emma sat on the row behind them with the two little redheads on each side. Hallie—or was it Callie?—waved. They both sported a ponytail tonight. Emma gave her a thumbs-up. At least she'd always have Emma in her corner. She'd focus on being thankful for that.

Casey wondered what would happen if she stood up and told *everyone* she had a daughter. Connie, her sister-in-law, knew. It would only be a matter of time before the news spread.

Luke opened the service with a prayer. Casey had a hard time thinking of him as her pastor. It was apparent he was smitten with Emma. Casey's heart lifted as she thought of how much Emma had overcome and how maybe, now, they all had a second chance at love.

Luke turned the program over to Pastor Bob. As each member of the mission team took a turn sharing their experiences in Africa, she waited to be last. The heat from the spotlight was almost too much, and perspiration soaked her blouse.

When Sparky handed her the microphone, she froze. Someone coughed, a baby whimpered, and everyone waited while she attempted to gather her thoughts.

Casey stared at Pastor Bob, and he gave her an encouraging nod.

She stood. "A few months ago, I overheard a conversation, 'Casey Bledsoe a missionary? Give me a break. What's she's going to do? Teach the women how to strike a pose?'" Casey winked at Sparky. A couple in the congregation laughed, several smiled.

Casey lifted her chin. "Most of you know I used to model, and my training in fashion and style are tools I've used for years to create an illusion. Africa forced me to remove my mask. I've sung 'Amazing Grace' hundreds of times, but I never reflected on the words or their meaning. When I found myself alone in the desert, I experienced grace and forgiveness." Casey paused.

Just tell the truth. "I'm good at lying, and the lies I've told burned a hole in my soul that only God could mend."

Her eyes met her mother's, and Jolene dabbed at her cheek with a tissue.

"We're not the type of church where people confess their sins, and I can tell by the looks on your faces, I'm making some of you uncomfortable. I'm sorry."

She stared at the ceiling. "I had a baby when I was eighteen, and I gave her up for adoption." There were gasps and murmurings from the audience. Her brother Frankie leaned forward and put his face down on the pew in front of him, while Kent looked like he was wishing for somewhere to hide, but her daddy nodded his head, then wiped his cheek.

"I've hidden for years behind fancy hairstyles, designer clothes, and makeup artistry to camouflage my brokenness. I've finally asked God and my family to forgive me, and I'm asking the same of you. I suppose the big questions is, will you?"

Then she handed the microphone to Pastor Bob, sat down, and stared at the carpet.

No one moved. When Casey looked up, several of the women in the audience squirmed. Daniel stood and pulled her up into an embrace. Her team members circled for a group hug, and others from the congregation came forward, including her family. After a few minutes, Luke spoke into the microphone.

"We'll close tonight with the hymn Casey mentioned. While we're singing, if there's someone else in the audience who is carrying a heavy burden and would like to experience God's grace and forgiveness, please come forward."

As the pianist played the first notes of "Amazing Grace," Casey thought, *I'm free.*

On Monday night, Casey knocked on Emma's back door and walked in. It was half-past eight, but she needed to talk.

Emma jolted up from the sofa, grabbed her in a hug, and didn't let go. "How did you know I needed you?"

"What's wrong?"

Emma sniffed in her ear.

"What's going on?"

"Carol Carter with Children's Services just called, and she's picking up the girls tomorrow."

Casey pushed back from the embrace. "Tomorrow! What happened?"

"Their mother was released from prison last month, and she's convinced her aunt to let them move in with her."

"Oh, honey. Why didn't the aunt help with the girls before this?"

"I have no idea." Emma sighed heavily. "Their mom is working, and the caseworker says she deserves a second chance." Then Emma broke down crying.

Casey's eyes filled with tears seeing her best friend suffer, and she held on. At last, they sat on the sofa. A sense of déjà vu made her ache. When Emma had lost her husband, they'd been through these same motions, and again, Casey could do nothing to ease the pain.

"I kept telling myself not to get attached." Emma blew her nose.

Casey squeezed Emma's knee. "Who could resist those little munchkins?"

"I probably won't ever see them again."

"Where are they now?"

"Upstairs. I've just put them to bed, but it's routine for me to pop in at least once to settle them again." Emma wiped her eyes. "I'm going to wait until the morning to tell them because they'll be too excited to sleep."

"They've missed their mama." She smoothed Emma's hair.

A resounding thump sounded from the ceiling. They both looked up.

"Go. I'll wait here."

Emma sniffed and dabbed at her eyes. "Thanks."

The hands of the clock seemed to move in slow motion as she waited. At last, Emma returned.

Casey stood and opened her arms, and her best friend leaned into the embrace.

"Maybe their mom can stay sober." Emma sniffed.

"And what if she doesn't?"

"Children's Services will be checking on them."

"I'm sorry." As she held her sobbing best friend, her stomach ached.

Hours later, she backed her car out from the drive and studied the dark windows. When Emma had opened her home to the girls, the old Victorian seemed to come alive and Emma, too, experienced rejuvenation. Casey had admired her best friend for her courage to build a family after she'd lost her husband. A part of the journey included heartbreak, but Emma claimed love made it worth the suffering.

When Casey sat down at her own kitchen table, silence surrounded her. She felt compelled to write a note to Madison's mother. Casey struggled with what to say. At last, she put pen to paper.

> Dear Madison's Mom,
>
> Thank you for being what I couldn't be—Madison's mother. I am thankful you are confident enough in her love to give her my contact information, and I will be forever grateful to you for all you've done. The burden of worry for Madison crippled me for years, but her letter freed me of this encumbrance. Her letters reveal a happy, healthy young woman, and I am left with the hope that perhaps I made the right choice by releasing her for adoption.
>
> At the time of her birth, I was very young, emotionally damaged, terrified, and confused. God has been faithful to answer my prayers. Perhaps Madison is an answer to your prayers.
>
> My best friend is a foster parent and is suffering tonight because the two little girls left in her care are returning to

their mother tomorrow. I know it's not the same situation. Still, after seeing Emma's heartache tonight, I felt the need to write you and let you know I would never want you to be hurt by my actions. If I ever overstep or do something that makes you uncomfortable, please tell me. The last thing in the world I'd want is to hurt Madison or her family.

I have prayed for you, your husband, and Madison since she left my arms. May God bless you all the days of your life and then throughout eternity.

Sincerely,

Casey

Casey added a stamp to the envelope and sealed it. She owed this woman, and she wondered if they'd ever meet. *Does she have a clue how much of my heart I gave to her?* Casey dropped her head in her hands. *And I'll bet she gave Madison every bit of her heart too. And for that, I'll be forever grateful.*

On Tuesday, Casey paced around her office at the back of the shop and looked at her phone for the umpteenth time as she waited for Daniel to call. With a thud, she dropped into her desk chair and her elbow knocked over her Diet Dr. Pepper. A light knock sounded on the door.

"Come in."

Tricia poked her blond head in and whispered. "There's a client in dressing room number two who's tried on almost everything we have. I think she's stalling to meet Cassandra."

Casey mopped up the dark liquid with a tissue. "I'll be right out."

An hour later, the picky customer was oscillating between two outfits Casey had put together.

"Why not take them both?" Tricia pushed her long blond hair behind her shoulder.

"Two are over my budget," the customer said. She was a thirty-something wearing black yoga pants.

Casey's phone beeped. *It's Daniel.* "I'll give you 25 percent off if you take both."

"Really?" The customer blinked rapidly.

"Yes. Please excuse me, but I need to take this." And she left Tricia to deal with the customer.

"What did Dr. Bertrand say?"

"The tumor board approved my surgery. I'm checking in tomorrow afternoon, and the surgery is scheduled for Thursday morning."

"So soon?"

"The doc warned me to be ready."

"I know, but—"

"I'm relieved. I feel like a ticking time bomb."

"I wish I could give you a hug."

"I'll take you up on that offer later."

"I'm leaving in a few minutes because I need to stop by Emma's to tell the girls goodbye."

"Take all the time you need."

"Maybe we can all go to the Triple D for comfort food?"

"That sounds good, but if Emma needs you, stay with her. I'll be fine."

"You're both hurting, and there's nothing I can do."

Tricia was busy straightening up the racks nearby. Casey turned her back to Tricia and lowered her voice.

"Are you sure you're okay?"

"Yeah. Go to Em's. She needs your support."

As soon as she hung up, Casey spoke to Tricia. "I'm going to have to be off for the next two weeks."

Tricia stopped hanging up clothes and bit her painted red lower lip. "Is Daniel's going into the hospital to have brain surgery?"

Casey narrowed her eyes. "Who told you about Daniel's condition?"

"Your mom might have mentioned something." Tricia brushed at her skirt and stared at the floor. "And I can't help but hear you on the phone sometimes."

Casey ran her fingers through her hair. "News of his condition is spreading like a virus."

Tricia hugged her, her thin arms wrapping around Casey's waist. "I'll keep you and Daniel in my prayers."

"Thank you, and please add Emma to your list."

"What's going on with her?"

"The girls are leaving this afternoon. They're going home to their mother, and I need to go tell them goodbye."

"Poor Emma. Go. We'll take care of everything around here."

When Casey opened Emma's back door, she discovered her sitting on the back staircase with two suitcases and a plastic trunk in front of her.

"How are you?" Casey's midsection ached.

"Awful."

"Where are the girls?"

"I sent them upstairs to go to the bathroom. It might be a long car ride."

Casey sat and wrapped her arms around Emma.

Emma blew her nose. "This is what's supposed to happen. This is a happy day. This is a day to celebrate."

"Nobody is *that* good an actress." Casey rolled her eyes.

"You are." Emma gave her a teary smile. "Before Sunday night, everyone thought you had the world by the tail. You're the best actress I know."

"Gee, thanks."

Harley stood in the corner of the room, her arms crossed.

"Hey, Harley." Casey wanted to give Harley a hug, but she knew the surly girl would shrug away from her.

Harley remained mute.

Luke rushed through the back door. Emma jumped up and walked into his embrace.

Luke closed his eyes. "I'm sorry."

"Don't be. This is a good thing."

Harley said an ugly word and stomped outside.

Emma pushed away from his embrace and started after her.

Luke grabbed her elbow. "Let's give Harley a minute."

Emma's mother, Virginia Willoughby, the mayor of Weldon, pushed the back door open without knocking. "Have I missed them?"

Emma straightened her shoulders. "No. They're in the bathroom."

Virginia wore a charcoal suit with heels, and she stood straight as a pencil. "The city council meeting went on forever. I swear, Arnold Alexander drags the sessions out just because he knows it irritates me."

"Same old Arnold," Casey said.

Emma's housekeeper, Minnie, walked in from the kitchen, and her ebony face brightened. "I'm glad those little girls will have a good send-off. Will they have time to eat before they go?"

"Carol won't mind waiting." Emma said, standing up straight.

"I'll pack a snack for the car ride." Minnie turned on her heel and retreated to the kitchen, her broad back nearly filling the doorway.

Emma looked at Casey. "I might be receiving another little girl who's come from a difficult situation."

"But your heart is being broken." Casey gulped.

"Taking in the children is helping me glue the pieces of my broken life back together. I'll still love Hallie and Callie, and someday their love will return them to me."

Footsteps sounded on the stairs, and she looked up to see the twins hopping down.

"Careful." Emma stood, smiling at them.

"Is it a party?" Callie looked at Emma, Luke, Virginia and Casey lined up at the foot of the stairs.

"No, everyone just stopped by to see you before you go." Emma gulped.

"Is Mrs. Carter here yet?" Hallie jumped down the last step.

The front doorbell rang. "That will be her," Emma said in a sing-song voice.

"You sit here, Emma," Virginia said. "I'll get the door."

Casey noticed her squeezing Emma's shoulder when she passed her.

Minnie placed a tray of pimento cheese pinwheels on the coffee table, and Pepper, Emma's schnauzer, snatched one and streaked upstairs.

"That little ragamuffin!" Minnie planted her fists on her hips.

"But I don't want a sandwich," Hallie said. "I want chocolate chip cookies."

"What makes you think we have chocolate chip cookies?" Minnie brushed crumbs from her apron.

"We smelled them baking," Callie lifted her nose in the air.

Minnie smiled. "I've packed those for you to take with you. You can share them with your mama."

"I want one now." Callie crossed her arms in front of her.

"The last thing you two need is sugar before a long car trip," Minnie patted each little head.

Carol Carter from Children's Services followed Virginia into the room. The social worker's dark mink-colored hair was cut in a short pageboy style. "I see you've got everything ready."

"Yes, the girls are just eating a snack for the trip," Emma said. "Would you like a sandwich?"

"Thanks." Mrs. Carter reached for a pinwheel. "We have about an hour's drive. This is perfect."

"I'll take the trunk and put it in Mrs. Carter's car," Luke stood.

Casey jumped up. "I'll get the suitcases."

"I'll go too." Minnie held the door open for Luke, toting the trunk, and Casey followed with a small suitcase in each hand. They placed the luggage next to Carol's white government-issued sedan.

Harley came out of hiding, picked up a stick, and broke it over her knee. "This makes me sick."

Minnie placed her arm around Harley's shoulder. "You know how they've missed their mama."

"Yeah, but ..." Her voice trailed off.

Minnie looked to Casey. "I heard your young man is sick. How are you two holding up?"

"I don't know. He seems to be okay, but it's brain surgery."

Luke dusted off his hands. "I'll give him a call tonight."

Casey smiled tightly. "Thanks. I'm sure he'd appreciate it."

"The Lord has a good plan for both of you. Don't forget that." Minnie offered a tender smile.

"It's hard to see any good when someone you love is suffering. And what about these two little ones, going back to their mother who can't even care for herself?" Casey's voice trembled.

"We don't know that. It's admirable she's willing to try, and she has a family to help her."

"Do you ever think bad thoughts about anyone, Minnie?"

"Oh, that ol' devil pokes at me all the time, but I say, 'Jesus help me,' and he does." Minnie gently pinched Casey's cheek and grinned.

Hallie and Callie skipped to the car wearing their Hello Kitty coats that Emma had given them. Each girl clutched their twin baby doll.

With their possessions loaded into the trunk, the girls gave everyone a final hug.

Casey inhaled the fragrance of Callie's hair and recognized the green apple scent of the shampoo she'd given the little girl.

Hallie gave her a hug too. "Will you come to see us with Emma?"

Casey caught Carol's eye over the girls' heads—she was shaking her head no.

"We'll be right here in Weldon. You can always visit us. Don't forget us." Casey pecked each child's cheek.

"We won't forget," Callie hugged Luke's knees, and he lifted her and hugged her, then he did the same to Hallie.

Harley dropped to one knee and hugged both girls. Tears filled Harley's eyes. "Tell me our address."

Hallie rattled it off.

Callie elbowed her sister. "I know the phone number." And she said it.

Harley gulped. "Good job. You call if you need anything."

Emma helped the girls into the car, fastened the seat belts for each little girl in their booster seats, and gave them a kiss. They all smiled brightly and waved as the car backed out of the drive. As the taillights disappeared, Emma turned into Luke's arms.

"They know where to find us." Virginia caressed her back.

"But they're just six years old." Emma sniffed.

Minnie dabbed at her cheek with a tissue. "They won't forget my cookies or your hugs."

"Try not to worry," Virginia said. "I've made arrangements for Luther to check in on them."

"Mother, you shouldn't have hired a private detective to check on them."

"It's my money, and I can do whatever I choose with it. Children's Services has too many children to monitor. We only have two. Besides, Luther loves doing me favors."

Casey arched a brow. "I guess having a private detective for a boyfriend comes in handy."

Virginia stood ramrod straight as her cheeks turned pink. "Women my age do not have boyfriends." She sniffed. "He's a friend."

Luke winked at Virginia. "I, for one, am glad he's your friend."

Casey felt her shoulders relax. "How does he know where they're going?"

"He has his ways," Virginia lifted her chin.

"Let's go in and have something warm to drink," Minnie said. "My church ladies are praying for them. There is no doubt in my mind they are surrounded by angels."

"They'll need angels because their mama sounds exactly like my mom. Evil." Harley's face turned a deeper shade of scarlet.

When they went inside the house, Harley bolted upstairs.

They sat around the coffee table with the sandwiches, motionless. At last, Casey broke the silence. "Daniel checks into the hospital tomorrow."

"Why didn't you say something?" Emma said.

"And add more celebration to this party?"

Emma dropped her head. "I'm sorry. I knew Daniel expected to hear from the doctor today. I don't know how I forgot."

"A lot is going on today. Don't worry about it. He'll have the craniotomy on Thursday morning."

"How is he feeling?" Virginia asked.

"I don't know. He thankful it's not Parkinson's disease, like his dad."

"I'll sit with you during the surgery," Emma said. "We can ride together."

"Thanks, but I don't plan on leaving the hospital until Daniel is released, so I'll need my car. But I'd appreciate the company."

Emma looked at her watch. "I'm sure he's waiting for you."

"He knows where I am and why and doesn't mind waiting."

"What I need more than anything is to take a run." Emma stood up.

Virginia rose. "I'll go up and check on Harley and see if I can convince her to enjoy a pizza with me."

Emma gave a wry smile. "You in your suit and Harley dressed in her favorite grunge outfit in Pete's Pizzeria will give everyone in Weldon something to talk about."

Virginia's lips turned up. "There's always someone talking about me in Weldon. It will be good to be seen in one of the more casual eateries in town."

Emma made a sweeping gesture with her hands. “Shoo, all of you. I appreciate the support, but I know you have places to be, and I need to go for a run.”

Casey gave Emma a last hug. You and the girls are in my prayers.”

“And you and Daniel are in mine.”

After Luke backed his truck out of the drive, Casey started her Mustang and tooted the horn at Emma as she stretched in the yard. Casey tried to think of something to help but felt as useless as the hairdryer she’d carried to Africa.

CHAPTER THIRTY-TWO—DANIEL

Daniel settled himself inside the car, and Casey placed her hand on top of his. "How are you?"

He sighed. "I'm fine, but what about Emma?"

"Better than I would be. She was going on a run."

"That seemed to help her after Chris died. What about the girls?"

"They're excited about seeing their mom. I don't think they understand they might never see us again."

"None of us know what tomorrow might bring, but we can always hope."

Casey squeezed his hand. "I'm glad we have tonight. We're going to have lots of nights."

"I wish this were behind us." Daniel ran his hand over his short hair. Soon, he'd be bald. "If all goes well, there will be no more headaches."

"The thought of your suffering kills me." Casey swallowed hard.

Maybe, this story will help her. "When I was a kid, my mom kept putting off a simple surgery to prevent ear infections because she feared my being put to sleep. When she finally gave in to the doctor, I suffered very little compared to the earaches I'd endured. I'm hoping for a rerun of that scenario."

"You've lost both your parents and now this. How do you stay so positive?" Casey's eyes were sad.

Daniel sighed. "Dad taught me that every day you choose to wallow in misery is a day you cheated yourself out of being happy. He'd say, 'Every day is filled with hope.'"

"Wise words."

"It's simply the truth. And there's much for which to be thankful. I haven't had a headache since Africa." He sighed. "I'll never forget being surrounded by the Africans while they prayed for me. It was such a holy moment."

"Maybe their prayers are the reason you haven't suffered another headache." Casey gazed at him, and he saw love and compassion in her eyes.

He touched her cheek. "I can face this."

Casey bit her lip. "I wish you'd shared your worries with me sooner. I'm sorry you had to carry that burden alone."

He nodded his head. "I'm not good at sharing troubles, and I don't like to ask for help any more than you do."

"We all need a shoulder to lean on."

"I know. That's why I arranged today for a team of caretakers to provide me with assistance when I get home."

"But I can help you. From the video we watched, you might need very little assistance."

"Or I might need skilled nursing care. I've made provisions for that, too, if it comes down to it."

"I feel like you're shutting me out."

"I'm trying to make this easier for you."

She sighed and looked at the clock on her dash. "It's past seven. You must be starved."

"I am. Let's see what Dot has on the menu."

Empty seats lined the wall. Dot yelled in the pass-through window when she saw them. "Ray, I'm taking a break. Tell Lynnette to cover my tables."

Dot passed empty booths and led them to the back.

Casey sat down.

Dot nudged Casey's shoulder. "Scoot over."

Casey slid to the right, and Dot sat down next to her and looked at Daniel over the top of her vintage cat-eye glasses. "I hear you're taking a little break from the force."

"Yes, ma'am." *This must be what a moth feels like when pinned to a board.*

"What's going on? It's bad enough when someone gets sick, and then the gossips have to add their two cents' worth to make it interesting. Tell me flat out. What are we dealing with?"

Daniel stared into her piercing brown eyes, fanned with wrinkles. "It's a brain tumor. I'm checking into the hospital tomorrow for surgery on Thursday."

Dot looked fierce. "I hoped people were exaggerating. Why in the world would Sparky let you take off to Africa with a brain tumor?"

Daniel smiled and dropped his chin. "I made that decision, and I didn't tell the team, so don't start fussing."

"But—"

"The neurosurgeon couldn't see me until last week." Daniel shrugged. "I thought, why not go?"

"Do they know if it's malignant?"

"We don't know, but they'll do a biopsy during the surgery."

Dot studied Daniel's face like a high school principal interrogating a delinquent student. "Is that all?"

"Yes, ma'am."

She crossed her arms. "We'll be praying for you."

"I appreciate that."

"And when you're feeling up to it, I want a phone call from you. I want to hear from you myself that you're all right."

"Yes, ma'am. I'll be glad to let you know."

She looked at Casey. "And I expect a phone call from you, young lady, right after the surgery is over. Don't leave me waiting."

"Yes, ma'am." Casey's face looked somber.

Dot pulled out her order pad.

"What'll it be tonight?"

"I'll just have the chef salad and iced tea." Casey fiddled with a napkin.

"I'll have the Manhattan with extra gravy on my mashed potatoes." Daniel rubbed his tummy.

Dot peered over her glasses at him. "I fixed blackberry fried pies this afternoon."

"I'll have two with vanilla ice cream."

Dot pushed herself up and handed both Daniel and Casey a piece of paper. "That's my cell phone number. Do not give it to anyone."

"Yes, ma'am," they said in unison.

That woman. Daniel crossed his arms. *All of Weldon is probably abuzz about Casey and me. At least Dot never spreads rumors, unlike most of her regulars.*

When Dot delivered their order, Casey stared at Daniel's plate, piled high with roast beef and mashed potatoes. "If you eat all that, I don't know how you'll have room for two fried blackberry pies."

"It will be a challenge, but I think I'm up to it."

He ate with gusto, while Casey looked like she could hardly swallow.

After dinner, they returned to Daniel's home. As they sat on his sofa in front of the gas logs, Casey closed her eyes and laid her head on his shoulder. Daniel treasured the feeling of holding her close. *If only we could enjoy a life this simple, To have dinner, sit and enjoy the fire and each other's company. When will we have the blessing of another ordinary day?*

He yawned. "After a meal like that, I'm about to pass out. We've got a big day in front of us tomorrow."

"Just a little longer ... Maybe I should stay tonight?"

Daniel kissed the side of her face. *Tempting. It might be my last chance. But no.* "I don't want you to go either, but we've waited this long. I'll not have my neighbors gossiping about you."

"People already talk about us."

"That's their problem. Everything's going to be fine. He stretched and yawned again. "Sorry, hon. That meal just about did me in." He kissed her cheek.

"What time should I pick you up in the morning?"

"Ten o'clock. Oh, I forgot. I have a favor to ask."

"Anything."

"Do you think you can help me shave my head in the morning? I'd rather you tackle that chore than a hospital orderly."

"I guess I can try."

"I still have Mom's old clippers." Daniel squeezed her hand.

"I watched my mom give my brothers summer haircuts, all five of them like an assembly line—I'm sure I can handle it."

"We need to be at the hospital by noon. There's a whole team of people I'm scheduled to meet tomorrow afternoon." Daniel stood and pulled Casey up from the sofa and embraced her. "Don't be sad."

"This isn't exactly the time for a happy dance." Casey rested her head on his shoulder.

"It could always be worse."

"How so?"

"Hmm. Maybe an earthquake?"

"Don't even say that out loud." Casey gave him one last kiss and hug.

Daniel pushed back and swatted her backside. "Now go. We have a big day tomorrow."

He watched as Casey trudged to her car in slow motion, and he yearned to call out to her. Daniel returned to the sofa and stared at the gas logs. This might be his last night in his home. Two months ago, he'd thought they'd be celebrating at an engagement party upon their return to Weldon from Africa. At least he'd been able to share Africa with Casey, but it seemed paltry compared to sharing his life with her. He'd been able to fool Casey tonight, but oh, how he wished his Dad were here to help him stay positive. But he wasn't. Aching loneliness filled his chest. Had Dad felt this alone when battling Parkinson's? No, he hadn't. Daniel was sure of it. But his dad had something Daniel lacked, and it was trust. His Dad trusted in the Lord, no matter what. Daniel wished he had his dad's faith. But he didn't. *Father, help me to trust you.*

CHAPTER THIRTY-THREE—CASEY

On the drive home, Casey dialed her mother. She'd tried several times during the afternoon, but Jolene didn't answer the home phone or her cellphone. Frank didn't answer his phone, either, which didn't surprise her. But her mom usually answered hers. Casey drummed her fingers on the steering wheel. *Something's up.* Goodness, she didn't even want to think what else might go wrong. She redialed her mother's cell phone.

After six rings, Jolene answered. "Hi, honey."

"Where are you?"

Her mother babbled. "I'm sorry I didn't call you back, but the noise made it impossible to hear."

Something in Jolene's voice made the muscles in Casey's shoulders tighten. "Something's wrong."

"I'm with your father. We're on our way home." Her voice was half an octave too high.

"Where have you been? I've worried all evening."

"Your father got this silly idea."

"What kind of idea?"

"We went to a basketball game."

"Did you go all the way to Lexington to see the Cats play? Wait, they're not playing tonight."

"No. They're not."

"What other team does Dad care about?"

"The Blue Raiders ... Madison's team."

Casey swerved and almost hit a mailbox. She immediately pulled her car to the side of the road and slammed it into park. "Hot dynamite. You didn't!" Casey yelled.

"We did."

"I can't believe you two! You always think you know what's best. You never think things through. I might never get to meet her if you two scare her off."

"We were very discreet."

"You don't even know the meaning of the word *discreet*. Daddy undoubtedly yelled his head off and made a spectacle."

"He cheered for the team, but he never mentioned Madison by name."

"Lord, have mercy." Casey pounded the steering wheel and silently counted to ten. "How did you find her?" Casey's voice was shaky.

"On her picture, the jersey said, "Middle Tennessee," and your daddy looked up her team on the internet. The website's banner listed tonight's game, and we decided to go."

Casey's heart pounded, and her hands shook. "You didn't say anything to her, did you?

"No. We'd never do that. She is beautiful. I snapped several pictures with the phone's camera, but I couldn't figure out how to use the zoom lens."

"You and Daddy can't be stalking her."

"We bought Blue Raiders sweatshirts. I have one for you too."

Casey rubbed her temple. "We have to wait until she decides whether she wants to meet us."

"I know. No one noticed a couple of old people at a basketball game."

"You'd better hope and pray you're right."

Jolene sighed heavily. "I've been praying all day. How's Daniel?"

Casey immediately felt remorseful for her angry outburst. "He goes into the hospital tomorrow, and the surgery is Thursday morning."

"My goodness, that happened fast. It must be serious."

Casey rolled her eyes. "It's a brain tumor." She winced. Her sarcastic tone reminded her of her niece, Olivia.

"I know, but how *is* he?"

"He's acting all macho like this is nothing."

"That's a man for you."

"I guess."

"I'll call you tomorrow, sweetheart. It's late. Try to get some sleep. I'll sit with you Thursday at the hospital. Is there anything I can do?"

"Just feed Fats for me while Daniel's in the hospital."

"It's already on my list."

"Thanks, Mama."

"You didn't ask what Madison looks like."

"I have her picture."

"She's tall and graceful. Frank said she has real talent. I wished I'd been smart enough to figure out how to video her with my phone."

"You can't do that."

"And who's going to stop me?"

"I can't believe you two."

"I'll send you pictures from my phone."

Casey sighed. "I'd love to see them."

"We love you, and we love Madison." Then Jolene hung up.

Casey's heart still pounded as she thought about her parents tracking down Madison. As she parked her car in the drive, her phone pinged. The messaging app displayed a photo of a tall, coltish girl concentrating at the foul-shot line. Tenderness flooded every cell in her body. As she zoomed the picture larger, she studied those gray eyes inherited from Jansen and marveled they didn't cause angst or anxiety. How was it possible to feel such love for those eyes? *Love must have magical healing properties.*

CHAPTER THIRTY-FOUR—DANIEL

Daniel concentrated on smiling while Casey massaged the aftershave into his scalp.

"You look like a tough guy." Her voice sounded over-bright. "Very macho."

"Exactly what every cop wants to hear," Daniel ran his fingers over his slick head.

She wrapped her arms around his shoulders. "By this time next week, you'll be trying to decide whether or not to keep shaving your head or to let your hair grow."

"Let's hope so." Daniel cleared his throat. "Let me help you clean this up, then we can drink a cup of coffee before we go."

It took only a minute to clear the mess, then they sat at the table, both cradling their mugs of coffee but neither drinking. Daniel ran his hand over his head. "It feels different."

Casey placed her palm on his cheek. "It's a different look, but you're still the man I love."

Not for long. Daniel removed a folded piece of paper from his khakis. "Before we go, I need to tell you something, in case I can't, after the surgery."

She grabbed his hand. "Don't think that way."

"It's important. I called a friend of mine from New Jersey, and he gave me the name of a PI in New York."

He watched her lush red lips part and hang open in surprise.

"He claims Jansen Moore has been reported ten times for sexually assaulting women, but he's never been charged because of lack of evidence." Daniel slid the piece of paper across the table.

Casey picked up the paper and her eyes filled with tears.

"The PI wants you to file a report."

Casey's voice quavered. "You hired a PI." Her face flamed. "How dare you?"

Daniel pushed back from the table. "I can't go into the hospital without doing something to stop this guy."

"I trusted you." Casey narrowed her eyes.

"I'm a cop. You reported a crime."

"I told my boyfriend I'm a rape victim."

Daniel looked away, then faced her with his professional mask in place. "Your statement and Madison's DNA might be enough evidence for the DA to make the charges against Jansen Moore stick. You're Cassandra Bledsoe, for crying out loud. They'll take you seriously."

"What?"

"Plus, you're the only victim with evidence."

Casey slammed the paper down and flew up from the table. "I will *never* sacrifice her."

"Doesn't the thought of other victims bother you?" Daniel stood and planted his feet apart.

Casey squeezed her eyes shut.

"You need to file a report." Daniel crossed his arms.

Casey turned to him, her emerald eyes blazing. "No. I'm not going to let his shame taint Madison's life."

Daniel dropped his arms and his voice softened. "But he's hurt others."

The silence in the house magnified the tension, and Daniel focused on not backing down.

She turned away and ran her sleeve across her cheek. "I can't do it."

"Won't do it." His voice sounded harsh to his ears.

"I'm a rape victim. You have no idea what you're asking of me."

Daniel weakened, went to her and tried to hug her, but she shoved him away. "Get away from me." She stomped into the living room and paced in circles, mumbling. "Don't think. Don't think."

Daniel snatched up the paper with the photos of the victims. "You have to think about it." He crammed the piece of paper into her bag.

Casey shouted. "I can't deal with this today." She pulled at her long red hair. "Not today." She looked at the clock and her hands fisted. "Oh ..." She stomped her foot. "We need to go if we're going to get you to the hospital on time." Casey marched out the front door, her shoulders stiff.

Daniel returned to his bedroom for his bag. *At least that went as planned. Now, she'll probably hate me forever. Way to go, buddy.* He ran his hand over his aching heart. *It was for the best. Casey will be better off without me.*

The tension in the car increased with each mile during the silent drive to Nashville. When they arrived at the hospital, orderlies wheeled Daniel in and out of the room. After dinner, Dr. Bertrand and a line of medical students hovered around his bed. When they left, Casey returned to his bedside and looked at the clock. "I guess I'll head home. Is there anything I can get for you?" Her voice sounded cold.

"I have everything I need." Daniel picked up the television remote.

"I'll be here early in the morning."

He looked her in the eye. "I'm sorry."

Casey's eyes narrowed. "No, you're not." She turned on her heel and left the room without saying another word.

Daniel placed both palms on the back of his smooth head and pushed his chin to his chest. He'd wanted to put distance between them, and it looked like he'd succeeded. He should be pleased with himself, but he couldn't think of a time in his life when he'd felt more like a jerk. He sighed heavily. This might be his last night on earth. He closed his eyes. *Father, I feel so alone.* He sat there for a long time and watched the sun set. Outside the window, the sky turned to a bright pink, reminding him of Africa. It seemed like years had passed since then, instead of days.

A knock sounded, and Scotty's blond head poked in. "Hey, buddy."

"Hey, yourself. What are you doing here?"

Scotty walked in and shrugged. "I was just sitting at home and decided to check on you." His partner cocked his head. "Man, if you don't get to return to the force, you can be a stand-in for The Rock."

Daniel flexed his bicep. "Nah. I don't have Dwayne Johnson's guns."

After a few minutes of basketball talk and gossip about the force, someone knocked on the door. "Dinner is served." A woman with short gray hair wearing blue scrubs entered with a covered dinner tray. "Enjoy." She left at a fast pace.

Daniel lifted the cover to discover Salisbury steak smothered in congealed gravy.

Scotty wrinkled his nose. "There's a Panera Bread down the street. Why don't I go pick up something for you?"

"No. That's okay. I'm not that hungry."

"I'll go then, so you can eat while it's hot, but before I do, let's say a quick prayer."

Daniel smiled. "I'd appreciate that."

After Scotty prayed, he leaned in and gave Daniel a brief hug. "I'm working tomorrow, but I'll be praying for you."

"I'm counting on it."

After Scotty left, Daniel returned the lid to the dish and pushed his tray away. He reached across the bedrail and opened the top drawer of the cabinet next to his bed. As he suspected, a Gideon Bible was inside. He rifled through the pages to Psalm 23 and read. "The Lord is my shepherd; I shall not want ..."

CHAPTER THIRTY-FIVE—CASEY

When Casey passed the city limits sign on the outskirts of Weldon, she decided to stop in and tell Emma the newest developments. Her best friend met her at the back door with a much-needed hug.

"How are you?" Casey asked.

Emma sighed. "I'm okay. The girls are with their mom. That's where they need to be, and now I have room for another little girl who needs me."

"You amaze me."

"Each child is another blessing." She sighed, "But it hurts a little to let them go."

"Only a little?"

Emma sighed. "Okay, a lot, but enough about me. How's Daniel?"

"Let's sit down." Casey flopped down on the sofa.

"Have you eaten?"

"No, but I'm not hungry.

"I'd be nervous too."

"Daniel hired a PI to investigate Jansen."

Emma gasped. "Wow! That's a doozy of a step to take."

"I could shake him."

"The thought of someone hurting you is likely eating him alive. Lord knows it's chewed my insides for years."

Casey rubbed her hands over her eyes. "I've never thought about how much you've suffered while comforting me all these years."

"And you've walked over hot coals for me too. That's what best friends do."

Casey laid her head on Emma's shoulder. "The PI said there are ten women who've filed police reports for sexual assault against Jansen, but he wasn't charged due to lack of evidence.

"Ten." Emma ranted a slew of ugly words Casey bet no other librarian ever uttered.

"Whoa. I think you're channeling your ole granddaddy, and it's pretty scary."

Her best friend stared at the ceiling and blew out a long breath. "Ten women."

"I feel so guilty. What if I could have prevented someone else from being brutalized?"

"I doubt it would have made a difference. Stop beating yourself up."

"Daniel says Madison's DNA might be the evidence to make the charges stick."

"Oh, wow. That's—"

"I won't sacrifice her."

Emma squeezed Casey's knee.

"I'm furious with Daniel for putting me in this situation."

"Honey, he cares about you."

"And I love him, but ..." Casey dropped her head in her hands. "I didn't even kiss him when I left the hospital."

"Well, he did cross the line, but he's a cop. Let it rest for now and focus on getting through tomorrow."

Casey leaned back on the sofa. "You're right. By the way, look at this." She pulled out her phone and showed Emma the new pictures of Madison.

Tenderness softened Emma's face. "She's stunning. Did she send these to you?"

"No. Mom and Dad turned into internet sleuths and discovered her basketball team had a game in Murfreesboro last night."

Emma gasped. "Did they say anything to her?

"Mama said they didn't say a word, but I hope no one saw her taking all those pictures."

"Your dad must be thrilled."

"You think? Let's hope she didn't notice them."

Emma pulled her up from the sofa. "Follow me." She went to the kitchen and started pulling containers out of the refrigerator. After filling a plate, Emma placed it in the microwave.

A few minutes later, Emma put the plate on the table. "Eat!"

"I'll try."

After sampling the leftover chicken casserole, Casey realized she needed food and finished the green beans and potatoes. "Any word from the social worker about the girls?"

"No. I doubt she'd tell me anything."

"I'm sorry."

"Don't be. You know how much they missed their mama, and they have each other."

Casey hugged her. "And I have you. You're the best friend ever."

"Right back at you."

Emma talked nonstop about the new child arriving on Saturday while she cleared the table and washed the dishes. Then she stopped talking mid-sentence. "You look worse than the flowers Luke gave me last week. Go home and get some rest for tomorrow."

Casey yawned. "Thanks for everything."

On the drive home, she listened to an old song, "I'm Sorry," by Brenda Lee and felt terrible for how she'd left things with Daniel. The tune kept playing in her mind as she removed a bottle of water from her refrigerator. After sitting down at her kitchen table, she sent an MP3 file of the song to Daniel. *Maybe he'll listen to it before he goes to sleep.* Then she sent him another file with Ella Fitzgerald singing "Dream a Little Dream." Perhaps, he'd accept her apology in the morning. She realized she'd been selfish to leave him without even a hug and kiss on the eve of his surgery. She texted, *I'm so sorry.*

Casey bit her lip as she wondered again how many others had suffered from Jansen's hands. Might Daniel be right? But how could she offer up her daughter? What sort of lies might Jansen spin in his web of deceit?

CHAPTER THIRTY-SIX—DANIEL

Daniel tried to focus on the basketball game on the television lying in his hospital bed but he couldn't concentrate. His phone beeped, indicating a message, and he opened the attachment to hear a sad voice singing about regret. The singer's mournful voice made his gut wrench. Then he played the second file, and Ella Fitzgerald's sultry voice filled the air. As the last note faded away, his thoughts drifted. He'd never thought he'd feel as low again as when he'd stood alone watching the undertaker place the last scoop of dirt on his father's grave. But he'd been wrong. He'd hurt Casey this morning. He'd betrayed the woman he loved. He'd made a mess.

The thought of someone holding her down, violating her, hurting her, made him furious all over again. And the others on the list—how many women had this man attacked? *I can't let him get away with it.*

The nurse came in to take his blood pressure, and he concentrated on calming down. His emotions were a maelstrom. One minute he'd feel contrite, and then his anger raged again. He wanted to smash something.

"Your blood pressure is high," the nurse said.

Daniel concentrated on his breathing and tried to clear his mind.

"The doctor left an order for a sleeping pill if you need it."

"I'd rather not."

"I'll come back in an hour to see if you've changed your mind."

"I won't."

"You can't have anything to eat or drink after midnight. We'll see how you feel in an hour."

Daniel sighed heavily. "I'll be fine."

After the nurse left, his thoughts returned to Casey. He listened to the sad song and read her message again. He sent a text. *I'm sorry too.*

Whatever happened tomorrow, he knew Joe wouldn't let it rest. And Casey would do the right thing when she had time to think about it. At least, he hoped she would.

Since the visit from Scotty, reading the Psalms, and the apologies he and Casey had texted to each other, he hoped he might just get some sleep tonight.

His dad had always said the prayer that never fails is, "Thy will be done." But Daniel just couldn't bring himself to lift those four words. He could take dying because he had the hope of heaven, thanks to Jesus. Daniel considered the Scripture, "But if you do not forgive others their sins, your father will not forgive your sins." He rolled his shoulders. *Forgive.* Heaven might not be waiting for him after all, he thought. He gripped the bedsheet, then slowly loosened his hold. Daniel gulped. *Father, I come to you a sinner, and I ask for your forgiveness. You tell us we must forgive to be forgiven. Help me to forgive the man who hurt Casey. I can't do it without your help.* Daniel inhaled deeply and pictured Casey. *You know how much I love her, Father, but I've learned only you can protect her. I've made a mess of things. Forgive me for trying to handle things on my own. Please bless and protect Casey all the days of her life.*

And Father, please don't let me become a helpless invalid. Just take me if it comes to that. You are my only hope. I place my trust in you.

CHAPTER THIRTY-SEVEN—CASEY

Casey couldn't sit still. First, she cleaned out her kitchen junk drawer, then sorted the linen closet. After a cup of chamomile tea failed to settle her nerves, she wandered around touching odd mementos, and her fingers traced the stitching of the old quilt on the rack. With care, she unfolded it, wrapped the treasure around her shoulders and dropped into her grandmother's rocker. Next to the chair, Granny's Bible lay on the small table, and she opened it randomly. Her eyes fell on the Scripture in the book of John: "For everyone who does evil hates the Light and does not come to the Light for fear that his deeds will be exposed. But he who practices the truth comes to the Light, so that his deeds may be manifested as having been wrought in God."

She closed the pages and considered exposing Jansen's sin, but she shook her head. Sacrificing her daughter was too much to ask. And there was something more pressing she had to do before this night passed—forgive Daniel. There was no way she could let him go into the surgery with this heartache between them.

After crying for what seemed to be hours, she lay on the bed, exhausted and spent. *I forgive him.* Sleep came in an instant, and she slept wrapped in her grandmother's quilt with Fats purring in her arms.

Casey awoke to Fats pawing her chest, then he rubbed his whiskers against her cheek. Her neck ached as she bolted up. The clock on the bedside table displayed 5:30 a.m. *What? Oh, no. If I leave this very minute, I might get to see Daniel before he goes into surgery.* She pushed Fats away, and he yowled when she jumped off the bed, slipped on the first shoes she could find, her zebra print Converses, and raced out the door, pulling on her coat.

On the drive to Nashville, she cursed the stop-and-go traffic. The parking garage levels seemed endless, and she passed filled spaces. On level nine, she inched into a tight space, then jammed her gearshift into park.

As she paced in front of the elevator doors, she decided to call Daniel, but then she remembered placing her phone on the charger last night and stomped her foot. When she reached his room, she pushed the door open and saw him. "Thank God," she said and wiped her eyes. "I thought I might have missed you."

"Are you all right?" Daniel asked, smiling groggily up at her.

She hugged him. "I'm sorry. I cried myself to sleep and overslept this morning. I must look a sight."

"You look beautiful. I told you in Africa I like seeing you without your makeup."

"I guess I cried off all my mascara. When I started to call you, I realized I left my phone at home."

Daniel smoothed her hair and kissed her cheek. "You can use mine." He touched her cheek. "No more tears."

"I love you more than anything in the world." She cupped his face in her hands and saw a well of sadness in his eyes.

He whispered, "I'm sorry I hurt you."

She rested her forehead on his. “It’s forgiven.” Casey prayed silently. *Please Lord, let him be okay.*

A knock sounded on the door, and a tall young man with spiked black hair wearing green scrubs walked in, followed by a short, older woman with perm-frizzed hair. “Who’s ready for surgery? “The woman’s cheer grated on Casey’s nerves.

Daniel sighed. “Let’s get this show started.”

The woman’s tight gray curls bounced as she walked around the bed. “You’re in great hands. By this time tomorrow, you’ll be sitting up in bed eating eggs that taste like cardboard.”

“There’s the silver lining I missed. If I lose my sense of taste, my home cooking will be a lot easier to swallow.”

Casey tried to smile, but instead, her eyes filled with tears as she squeezed his hand.

The orderly winked at her. “We’ll take good care of him.”

“The surgery and time in the recovery room are going to take about six hours,” Daniel said. “And who knows how long it will take to get me ready. Why don’t you try to get something to eat?”

Casey nodded, but she knew she couldn’t swallow a bite. “Don’t worry about me.”

“And I’ll be dreaming a little dream of you while I sleep.”

She smiled. “Did you listen to the songs I sent last night?”

“I listened to Ella Fitzgerald over and over until I fell asleep and dreamed of you.”

Casey looked into his eyes and felt hopeful. Perhaps they might have a future together after all.

The nurse looked at his chart and smiled. “Looks like you’re going to be transferred to the VIP suite after your surgery.” She looked at Casey. “Can you gather his personal belongings and go to the ICU waiting room on the seventh floor? The surgeon will call you there after the procedure."

"My bag is packed." Daniel squeezed Casey's hand. "I'll pray for you, and you pray for me."

"You've got a deal." Casey let go of him.

They rolled him out of the room with the orderly talking all the while.

"I'll just check the bathroom and make sure we have everything," Casey said.

"No problem. Take your time." The nurse left the room.

Casey caught a glimpse of herself in the bathroom mirror and shuddered. What happened to the woman who never left her home without her mask? With a sigh, she washed her face in the bathroom sink, returned to Daniel's bedside dresser, and checked the drawers for any stray belongings. She took the nurse at her word and sat in the chair next to the window in Daniel's hospital room. There would be hours in the ICU waiting room, and she needed a few minutes of quiet time. As she sat in the silent space, she placed her palms together and let her heartache do all the talking.

At nine o'clock, Emma entered the ICU waiting room. "I'm sorry I couldn't get here earlier, but the traffic was terrible.

Casey stood up, stretched, and hugged her best friend, "Thanks for coming. This time alone is exactly what I needed."

Emma pushed back from the hug. "Why are you still wearing the clothes you had on last night?"

"I fell asleep in them, and I barely made it here before they took Daniel back."

"Do you want me to get you some things?"

She looked down at her camel slacks and smoothed her black sweater. The zebra print shoes made her grimace. "No, thanks. I'll have a shower when this is behind us."

Casey's parents walked in carrying a takeout bag from McDonald's. Pastor Bob and Luke followed them in. "We met in the parking garage," Pastor Bob said.

"Thank goodness." Jolene frowned at Casey. "I've called your phone a hundred times this morning."

"I left it on the charger at home."

"We might have wandered all over this building if it hadn't been for running into these two preachers." Frank gave a grateful nod to Bob and Luke.

"Are you all right, honey?" Jolene smoothed her hand across the back of Casey's hair.

"I'm fine."

"Did you spend the night here?" Frank asked.

"No."

Jolene looked her up and down. "You look like you slept in those clothes."

"I did."

Her mother dug through her purse. "Maybe a little lipstick?"

Casey rolled her eyes. "If that's an extra coffee Daddy's holding, I'll take it."

Frank held out the cup to her. "I like seeing my little girl without paint all over her face." He leaned down and gave her a kiss on the cheek.

"I've been praying for him and for you," Luke squeezed her shoulder.

"Thank you. That explains why I feel peaceful." Casey sipped the coffee.

They all settled themselves in chairs.

"I'm sorry about Sunday night," Casey bit her lip. "I didn't plan to shock everyone."

Luke shrugged. "That's okay. Our congregation needed a little wake-up call."

"There were a lot of people who looked uncomfortable." Casey sipped her coffee.

Pastor Bob leaned forward. "Probably because they were thinking about their own pasts."

"That's right," Jolene rubbed her thumb on Casey's cheek. "No one's perfect, not even me."

Emma looked at Casey and rolled her eyes.

"I'm proud of you," Pastor Bob said. "Carrying a secret like this must have been torturous."

"You've always said God can take our mess and make a miracle."

Pastor Bob winked at her. "He's good at that. I'm glad you remembered."

Hours later, Casey wanted to walk the halls to release her pent-up energy, but she didn't dare stray from the waiting room's telephone. The harried receptionist finally announced, "Casey Bledsoe," and she sprang up. The receptionist smiled and handed her the receiver.

"This is Casey Bledsoe."

"I'd know your voice anywhere," Daniel sounded groggy. "Dr. Bertrand thought you might like to hear my voice instead of his."

"Is it over?"

"Yes, but I'll be in the recovery room for a while."

"Are you in pain?"

"No, but I'm tired." He slurred his words.

"I'll be up to see you soon." Casey gripped the receiver. "I love you."

"I love you too," Daniel said, and her heart skipped a beat. Had he really just said that?

She handed the phone to the receptionist, then collapsed in her chair. "It's over. He's awake, and he talked to me on the phone. Dr. Bertrand will stop by in a bit."

"Thank you, Lord!" Pastor Bob grinned.

"What about the tumor?" Jolene wrung her hands. "Did they remove it all? Was it malignant?"

"I don't know. He didn't say, and I didn't think to ask."

Jolene bit her lip. "We're not out of the fire yet."

"Let's pray," Luke reached for Casey's hand.

After another two hours of waiting, the receptionist called Casey to the desk.

"Mr. Sheppard is in room 702 in the ICU. You can go back with one person to see Dr. Bertrand."

Casey looked at her family. "Daddy is always the calm one. Let's go."

When they entered Daniel's room, he was sleeping, and Casey felt her shoulders relax. A bandage circled his head.

Dr. Bertrand stood typing on a laptop attached to the wall. The green scrubs were a far cry from the designer suit he'd sported in his office. When he noticed Casey and her dad, he smiled and extended his hand to Frank. "I'm Dr. Bertrand, and this is Sandi, Daniel's nurse."

Frank and Casey spoke in unison, "Nice to meet you."

"The pleasure is mine." Sandi smiled. "Our patient is going to be sleeping for a while."

"Let's sit down," Dr. Bertrand said and extended his arm toward a small sofa in the corner. He pulled up a chair and sat down in front of them.

"This looks like a luxury hotel suite compared to most hospital rooms I've seen," Frank looked around the room.

"It's important for seriously ill patients to have family members nearby," Dr. Bertrand gave a tight smile. "The hospital allows two people to stay in the room with the patient these days."

"Is the tumor malignant?" Casey blurted.

"No. The pathologist confirmed it to be a benign meningioma."

Casey exhaled. "What a relief."

Dr. Bertrand grimaced. "That's not all."

Casey held her breath.

"We'll do a spinal tap to ensure the tumor didn't spread, but I want to make you aware that when we were performing the surgery, I made a difficult choice. As I removed tissues, Daniel's left hand became weak, but I thought it important to remove all the tumor. We don't want it to return."

Casey nodded her head. "I understand."

"He doesn't have use of his left hand at this time. Of course, he may recover—it will just take time."

"But it's not life-threatening?" Casey scooted forward.

"No. But it may affect his career."

She chewed her nail as she considered Daniel's possible reaction to the news. "Does he know?"

"No. He was awake during the surgery but not really fully conscious."

"Okay, what else?" Casey asked.

"We are still monitoring for bleeding. Sandi will be observing his condition constantly. Overall, I consider the surgery a success. He'll sleep for the next several hours. Do you have any questions before I leave?"

She gulped. "Is he going to be okay?"

"I can't make a promise for a full recovery, but he's young and strong." Dr. Bertrand squeezed her shoulder. "Sandi will beep me if Daniel needs me, and I'll be checking in regularly." He stood.

Casey jumped up and grabbed Dr. Bertrand's hand, then impulsively hugged him. "Thank you."

"You're ... welcome." He stiffened in her embrace.

The doctor left, and Casey noticed Daniel's nurse through the glass window, typing.

"It's in God's hands now," Frank squeezed her shoulder.

"Why don't you let Mom and the others know what the doctor said. I'm not leaving him."

"Let me get you something to eat." Her dad rubbed his tummy. "I'm about to starve."

Casey shook her head. "I'm not hungry. Daniel's suitcase is with Emma. Can you get it for me in case he wakes up and needs something?"

Her dad kissed her cheek. "He's going to be okay."

"Let's hope so." She gave her father a hug, and he removed his handkerchief and wiped the tears from her cheeks.

After her dad left, she stared at the pale face of the man she loved. His coloring seemed more gray than white against the starched sheets. She leaned in close and softly kissed his cheek and inhaled the scent of antiseptic.

When she looked up, her mother and Pastor Bob were entering the room. Pastor Bob carried Daniel's bag.

She tiptoed to them. "I'm sorry, but there's only supposed to be two people back here."

Pastor Bob placed his hand over Casey's. "Luke was kind enough to stay in the waiting room to let the old pastor have the honor of praying for you and Daniel. I'll just stay long enough to say a few words."

Casey sighed. "I'd appreciate that."

The preacher closed his hand around Casey's fingers. Lost in her worry, she missed his prayer as she kept her eyes on Daniel.

Jolene tugged her other hand. "Casey, are you listening?"

"I'm sorry, Mom. What did you say?"

"Your daddy and I are going to Weldon to pack a bag for you. If Daniel wakes up, it might scare him to see you like this."

"That's too much trouble."

"Nonsense. I'll send Emma back to keep you company until we return."

"I'll be okay. He's seen me look much worse than this."

"I'm your mama, and I know what's best. You may be here for several days."

"Go then. I can tell there's no stopping you."

Jolene kissed her cheek. "We'll be back soon."

When she unpacked Daniel's bag, Casey gasped as she discovered the quilt she'd given him. As she unfolded it and placed it across his bed, she felt hopeful for the future. A faint knock sounded at the door, and Emma tentatively stepped inside the room and whispered, "I don't want to wake him."

"He slept through Dr. Bertrand's overview of the surgery and Pastor Bob's prayer."

"The worst is behind him," Emma wrapped her arm around Casey.

"A lot can still go wrong. There could be bleeding, a stroke, or an aneurysm."

Emma hissed. "Stop being negative. It's those blues you hear all day long in your shop."

"I don't always play the blues. Jazz covers a broad spectrum."

"Yes, but you seem to lean toward the blues."

Casey rubbed her eyes. "Maybe you're right."

"I'm going to send you some new music that will lift your spirits to replace the sad songs you're normally playing."

"Thanks, but all I want is a normal day."

Emma smiled. "What's normal? I've never experienced that phenomenon."

"My vision of a blessedly normal day is I oversleep and run behind all day. I always seem to have coffee grounds in the bottom of my cup. Then I have a cold shower because the heating element in the water heater went out ... again. Customers are waiting to see me when I get to the boutique late, and I hop around like a wild rabbit trying to satisfy everyone. Around four o'clock, Mom calls to complain about my brothers never calling. Lastly, Daniel meets me for dinner and listens to me complain about all the things that went wrong, and he reminds me of all the things that went right. The perfect day ends with him kissing me good night. That's my vision of a normal day."

"That sounds pretty nice. It's when you're sitting in a hospital room like this, or in my case, at the funeral home staring at your husband lying in a coffin, you realize a normal, crazy day is a blessing."

Casey squeezed her hand. "And mentioning crazy days and schedules, it's time for you to head home. You've been with me all day."

"Mother's taking Harley to Triple D tonight. There's no one home waiting for me."

"But you need to get ready for your new ward."

"If I go home, I'll just fret about the twins."

"I'm worried about them too," Casey said. "It's adding wrinkles to my face every day."

Emma touched her cheek. "Wrinkles are the price of old age. Let's just hope we earn more by laughter than sorrow."

"I'll second that." Casey sighed.

The last rays of the evening sun disappeared as Casey watched the sky from the tiny hospital window with Emma by her side.

"Knock, knock!"

She jumped as Jolene walked in with her fuchsia cross-body purse slung over her shoulder. "We've checked into a room at the hospital's reprieve lodge next door."

"There's only supposed to be two visitors back here," Casey whispered. "Now there are four." She looked at her father standing sheepishly in the doorway.

Jolene waived her hand. "I'm sending you to get a shower and something to eat with your daddy."

"I'm not hungry."

"At least put on something fresh. I packed a bag for you, but it was a challenge. Where are all your clothes? Your closet is almost empty."

"I got rid of everything when we returned home from Africa, and I haven't had time to shop. As long as it's clean, I don't care what I wear."

"Who are you and what have you done with my best friend?" Emma teased Casey.

"She got lost in Africa."

"Come on." Emma lowered her voice. "Your mom will keep nurse Sandi from checking out Daniel's private jewels."

Casey's cheek grew warm. "I can't believe you'd say such a thing."

"I'm trying to shock you out of your stupor. Come on."

"Go." Jolene pointed her index finger at the door. "I'll call you if he wakes up." And she gently elbowed Emma. "You can sit with Casey tomorrow. Oh, and I forgot to feed her ghost cat. Do you mind stopping by to see about him?"

"I'll be glad to." Emma looped her arm through Casey's. "Let's go get you prettied up, pussy cat."

Casey allowed herself to be pulled through the hospital by her father and friend. Emma gave her a final hug at the exit door to the parking garage. "It's going to be okay. Take care, sweet friend."

"I will. You do the same."

Frank placed his palm on Casey's back. "The reprieve lodge is this way."

When they stood in front of room 118, Frank unlocked the door. "This is it." He held it open for her and Casey walked in. The bare-bones room included a double bed, a small table with two chairs, and a tiny bathroom.

"I'll go get us something to eat while you take a shower. Your mom left your rolling bag in the closet."

"Thanks, Daddy. A shower sounds wonderful."

She relaxed as the hot water streamed over her. It irritated her to admit it, but her mother had been right. As she dried her hair in the tiny bathroom, the scent of hamburgers wafted on the air, and her stomach rumbled. After pulling on jeans, a simple aqua turtleneck sweater, and her favorite turquoise double-fringed cowboy boots, she left the bathroom. "I smell food."

"It's just burgers and fries," Frank said, "but it's making my mouth water. I've already prayed. The Lord's probably tired of hearing from me today. Let's eat."

The first bite of the thick cheeseburger made every muscle in her body loosen. "Mm. This is fabulous."

"What do you think Daniel might do if he can't be on the police force?" Frank asked.

"It's too soon to think about the worst-case scenario."

"No, it's not. It might help Daniel if we have some ideas."

"Oh, Daddy. There are lots of things Daniel can do if he can't be a cop."

"Like what? And we all know his parents' medical bills left him flat broke."

"I'm not going to worry about that now. I've got more than enough money to take care of everyone I love. Let's be thankful the tumor is removed and benign."

"Like he'd take a penny from you. It's hard for a man to lose his work."

"Granny always said, 'When you have your health, the rest of your problems will work themselves out.'"

"That's right, but it doesn't mean working through those problems is easy."

A sigh escaped, and she wiped her mouth with a napkin. "It seems nothing in life is easy." She reached down, searched her purse until she discovered the crumpled ball of paper, then she smoothed it flat on the small surface. "Daniel contacted a PI to investigate the man who ..." It seemed all the air left the room. "Madison's father."

Her dad's chin lifted—his eyes were hard. "Good. I'm ashamed I didn't think of doing it first."

"But it all happened a long time ago."

"Doesn't matter."

Casey wilted. "The man Daniel hired sent this email. Read it."

Frank took his reading glasses out of his pocket, and his face turned a dark hue. "You are going to file a report." His voice sounded uncharacteristically harsh.

Casey flinched. "I can't. The press will vomit the scandal on the front page of every gossip magazine in the country, and the last thing I want is for Madison to discover her father's a rapist."

He rubbed the back of his neck.

"I'd like to beat the livin' tar out of this guy." His voice sounded menacing.

"Then you'd be no better than he is."

Frank stood quickly and almost turned over the table and paced around the room. Casey steadied it. "I don't know what to tell you. Protecting my granddaughter is important, but ..." His eyes glistened.

She stood and wrapped her arms around him. "I'm sorry, Daddy."

"We'll figure out what to do."

Her burden seemed lighter, but her dad's shoulders drooped.

She kissed him on the cheek. "I'm going back to Daniel's room."

"That's where you need to be."

"Thanks for staying."

Casey left him and followed the signs through the maze of hallways to the hospital, worrying. *I hope Daddy doesn't do something crazy like tracking down Jansen the way he did Madison. Surely, he's wouldn't ... but he might.*

CHAPTER THIRTY-EIGHT—DANIEL

On Monday morning, Dr. Bertrand beamed light into Daniel's eyes while a group of students surrounded the bed. "Our patient is alert and well enough to return home." He shut off the light and looked over the top of his glasses at his patient. "I'll see you in my office in two weeks."

"Dr. Peterson stopped by this morning too," Daniel said.

"Yes. He'll take over your care soon and recommend further treatment options."

Casey had also stopped in to visit and was sitting nearby. Daniel noticed her chewing her nail, and he cleared his throat. "Casey, would you mind giving me a few minutes alone with the doctor?" He'd been enough of a worry to her. It was time to start pushing her away again.

Her brow furrowed. "Um ... Of course."

When the door closed, Daniel looked Dr. Bertrand in the eye. "Give it to me straight. Is my hand going to get better?"

"I don't know."

"Then guess."

"I'm not in the habit of dashing hopes or raising expectations too high. Let's see if the physical therapy has good results."

"But I can't even crook my finger. It's useless."

"You must be patient and let your body heal."

Daniel rubbed his jaw with his right hand.

"The human body is a marvelous creation, and its ability to heal still astounds me."

"I hate—not knowing."

"Everyone does. You are luckier than many."

"But—"

"You have a future and a lovely young woman by your side."

He forced a smile and nodded.

"I'm prescribing rest and physical therapy. If you follow my advice, maybe there will be good news when we meet again. All is not lost." Dr. Bertrand shook Daniel's right hand and turned.

Left alone with his musings, the ache in his chest intensified. *All I love is lost. Without my hand, I lose my job. I will not be a burden to anyone.*

Daniel remained silent on the long drive to Weldon following his release from the hospital.

"Have I done something to upset you?" Casey turned on the car's blinker when they passed the Weldon exit sign.

"What makes you think that?" Daniel drummed his fingers on his thigh.

"You've hardly spoken a word since we left the hospital. Did Dr. Bertrand say something to upset you?"

"No."

They remained silent until Casey parked in his drive.

Daniel exited the car and lifted his face to the sun. "When we left, I didn't know if I'd ever see this place again. It may not look like much to most, but it's my home."

"I love your sweet house, and others can see you love it too by the care you give it."

A minute later, Daniel struggled with the key at the old door.

Casey adjusted the strap of his bag.

When he pushed it open, the scent of delicious food filled the air. "I'd recognize your mom's chicken and dumplings anywhere."

"She asked me about a spare key, and I told her to look under the planter on the patio."

Daniel put his keys in his pocket. "Your mom's slow cooker is on the kitchen counter. Your parents have been great."

"They care about you."

He walked to the patio door. "The bird feeders are empty. I should have asked Mr. Raybold to keep an eye on them." Daniel strode to the utility room, opened the closet, and attempted to pull a new twenty-five-pound bag of birdseed out.

Casey stepped in to help him.

"You're going to have to buy this in smaller bags," Casey said. "Let me fill the feeder for you."

"No. I've missed the birds." His tone was curt.

"Let me help."

A bead of sweat formed on his brow as he struggled to fill the container.

"You're overdoing it." Casey took the pitcher and strode toward the feeder, but before she reached it, Daniel snatched the plastic handle, dumped the seeds on the ground, and flung the pitcher across the yard.

Casey stood with her mouth open.

"There!" He stomped back to the house. He couldn't even take care of the birds. How could he take care of himself?

Daniel dropped to the sofa, placed his good elbow on his knee, and rested his forehead in his palm.

"I'll set the table," Casey's voice was just above a whisper. She started pulling plates from the cabinet, but then the doorbell rang. "Who could that be?" She rushed to the front of the house before Daniel could stand. His neighbor, Arvazean, stood holding a triple-layer chocolate cake.

"I saw you arrive a few minutes ago and couldn't wait to see how my favorite neighbor is doing," Her eyebrows arched as she looked around Casey.

Daniel strode to the door. "Come in." He licked his lips. "Is this for me?"

"Yes, siree! I know how you love my chocolate cake. I saw Jolene's car over here earlier and called."

As she extended the cake to Daniel, he slid his right hand under the platter. The weight of the heavy cake tilted the plate as he struggled to balance it. Casey grabbed for it but missed. The cake shifted to the right, and the platter and cake toppled to the floor.

"Oh, my!" Arvazean exclaimed.

Daniel said a word he thought he'd removed from his vocabulary when his mother had washed his mouth out with soap.

Casey's voice sounded upbeat. "I believe this is a case where the three-second rule applies." She sounded like a morning talk-show host.

"Absolutely," Arvazean said. "We'll just scrape it up. It will still taste the same."

Casey went to the kitchen and retrieved two spatulas. She and Arvazean salvaged what they could as Daniel resisted the urge to grab the ruined cake from them and dump it in the trash.

"I'll put this in the kitchen," Casey said. "We're going to have some of Mom's chicken and dumplings in a minute. Will you join us?"

"Oh, no, sweetheart. I'm not going to stay." She walked over to Daniel. "But I'm not leaving without a hug from this young man."

He leaned down and wrapped his good arm around his kindhearted neighbor, who always treated him like a beloved nephew.

"I'm still not a hundred percent. I guess you noticed my left hand doesn't work."

Arvazean smiled. "Just wait until you get older. Lots of my body parts don't work like they used to. It's the price you pay for old age." She placed her weathered hands on his cheeks. "I'm happy to see you home." Tears filled her blue eyes.

"I'm sorry I ruined your cake."

"Pshaw. You didn't hurt my cake. Let me know how it tastes. Now, it's time for me to skedaddle. I'm keeping you from the table."

Casey received a hug from Arvazean, who spoke under her breath. "Take good care of him."

"I will, if he'll let me," Casey rolled her eyes.

Arvazean waved. "Winona Williams will be bringing by supper for you."

Casey spoke to the closing door. "Thank you for the cake!"

Daniel scratched his chin. "Looks like I'm on the comfort meal committee's list."

"You are in for some good food."

"There are others who need help more than me."

"It's how they show their love."

"It's how they keep their noses in everyone's business." His voice sounded biting.

Casey's nostrils flared. "I'll set the table."

Casey ate like she'd been stranded in the desert again, but Daniel could hardly swallow for the maelstrom of emotions that burned through him. One minute he'd feel sorry for himself, and then he'd be angry, and his spirits spiraled down.

When Casey folded her napkin, Daniel stood. "I can load the dishwasher."

"Aren't you going to sample Arvazean's cake?"

"Maybe later."

"Why don't you lie down? I can take care of the dishes."

Daniel pinched the bridge of his nose with his right hand. "I just need some time alone."

Casey's eyes flashed. "Fine. I'm going to check my mail."

"Sounds like a good idea. I need to do the same and check email. The PI might have some more information."

Casey froze and gave him a pleading look. "Please. I'm begging you. Stop."

"I can't do that," he said.

"I'm not one of your cases. I don't want anyone prying into my private business." Her hands trembled as she grabbed her purse and searched for her car key.

Daniel knew what he needed to do next. He had to let her go once and for all. He sighed. He just didn't have the energy to do it today. He dropped to the sofa. "You know the way out."

CHAPTER THIRTY-NINE—CASEY

Casey gripped the steering wheel. How dare Daniel Sheppard open closets I want locked? And why was *he* angry with *her*? He was the one acting like a jerk. How could a man who claimed to love her a few days ago treat her callously? Casey sighed. Had he really said those words when he was groggy from the anesthesia, or had she imagined it?

When she arrived home, she checked her mailbox and found it stuffed full. She crammed everything into her hobo purse.

Fats greeted her with a yowl when she unlocked the front door and lugged her suitcase inside. "Maybe a cup of tea will settle my nerves," she said to the cat.

As the kettle sounded, Casey removed it from the burner and then started sorting mail over the trashcan while the tea steeped. "Bill, junk, junk, bill, bill." The pile of bills grew. When she recognized Madison's handwriting, she paused. "Finally."

> Dear Ms. Bledsoe,
>
> I searched for pictures of you on Facebook and ran across Dr. Compton's Facebook page. She tagged you in several pictures in the album she posted of her recent trip to Africa. My favorite is one of you with a little girl in your lap at the orphanage. You look very different with your

hair covered and no makeup. I could see that we look a little bit similar. I looked up Niger. 110°. It must have been like working in a furnace.

Mom told me about the letter you wrote her. I almost, sort of, understand why you gave me up. My mom and I found a copy of an old *Teen Town* magazine from 1984 with you on the cover on eBay. How did a teenager from rural Kentucky end up modeling in New York? You must have had big dreams.

When I think about how much I love basketball, how hard I've worked, and my dream to play in the WNBA, I can understand setting all other things aside. My parents call it obsessive behavior, and they don't like it. Mom tells me this all the time, "This too shall pass." She worries about how I will adjust when basketball is no longer a part of my world. I keep telling her that basketball will always be a part of my world.

Sallie Jones suffered a serious injury last year, and after two surgeries, she still doesn't know if she'll be able to play again. What if that happened to me? I'd be devastated. Or what if I found out I was pregnant and had to give up everything for the baby? It would be a difficult decision, and I'd be lying if I said otherwise. No one can say what they'd do in a situation like that until they've lived it.

I am a little disappointed to hear you don't have kids. I've always wanted a sister, but maybe my biological father has kids. You haven't mentioned him. It's nice getting to know you through letters. I might do the same thing with him. Do you have his current address? Of course, the internet makes it easier to find lost relatives today. What's his name?

Casey stopped breathing. *Oh, no.* She gulped and continued reading.

Mom asked me to tell you love multiplies and that I have plenty. Your letter made her all teary-eyed as she read

> it to me, and she said that it is very kind of you to be worried about her.
>
> She also mentioned you're perhaps wondering if I have a boyfriend. I think this is mom's hint that I need to tell you something important about me. I'm gay. I've always been a tomboy, and last year, I decided to tell my parents that I think I'm different.
>
> Mom asked our pastor to counsel me. (Poor guy). I dreaded it, but he made me feel okay. He said everyone has a sin problem that only Jesus can fix. Just between you and me, I think they all believe they'll be able to pray me straight. Ha. Ha. Maybe they will.
>
> My parents tell me there is nothing I can do to make them stop loving me. I hope this news doesn't upset you too much, but you need to know, I'm far from perfect.
>
> I've got to go, or I'll be late for practice. Keep writing.
>
> Sincerely,
>
> Madison

Casey read the letter repeatedly, then sipped her tea, but it had gone cold. After folding the stationery, she returned it to the envelope, leaned her elbows on the table and dropped her face into her open palms.

Her brain felt like it was filled with mush. *My daughter is gay, and she's asking about her father. Lord, help me.* The reality settled over her like a heavy, wet coat, and she felt terrible. Why did she feel such angst? After all, she had gay friends, and she loved them. It shouldn't matter to anyone whom she loves. Her granny's voice taunted her with Scriptures about turning from sin. With her heart hurting, she sat staring into space. Fats rubbed against her ankle, and she picked him up and cuddled him against his chest. "It wouldn't matter to you, would it?"

As she trudged upstairs, she considered calling Daniel but shook her head. She needed to get over being angry with him first. Plus, she wanted a shower more than a shoulder to cry on.

After a long hot shower, she went to the bedroom for a nap and wrapped herself in her granny's quilt. She hoped Daniel loved her more than being a cop because she didn't think she'd be able to forgive him if he hurt Madison. What a mess. How could they build a life together if they couldn't trust each other? *Don't think. That's what kept you sane all these years.*

Fats rubbed against her and curled up next to her stomach. Fingering the different textures of fabric, she listened to his soft purr. In the in-between seconds of drifting from consciousness to slumber, she imagined Granny kissing her temple, and she relaxed completely. Then her grandmother whispered in her ear, "The right thing to do is always the right thing to do."

Casey awoke from her nap and felt her stomach rumble. The instinct to call Daniel and make arrangements for dinner made her twitchy, but when she thought about the investigation he'd started, she decided to leave him be. He'd likely bring up filing charges again, and the last thing she wanted was another confrontation. The ladies from the church would feed him, and his neighbors watched him like mother hens.

After rereading Madison's letter, Casey sighed. How might her parents react when they learned their granddaughter was gay? The dread of telling them made her feel despondent, then she paused. She wouldn't tell them anything. This was something between Madison and God, and it wasn't Casey's place to tell anyone anything.

Her heart felt heavy with worry for the path Madison was taking, but she knew better than to judge anyone. After all, instead of a plank in her eye, she had the whole darn tree. Even Peter said, *Love covers a multitude of sins.*

As she sat in the stillness of her kitchen listening to Nora Jones sing "Everybody Needs a Best Friend," she decided to write a response to reassure Madison that nothing would ever stop her from loving her daughter.

> Dear Madison,
>
> Thank you for your letter and your honesty. It encourages me to know you trust me enough to tell me something so personal.
>
> Like your mom, there's nothing you can do to make me stop loving you. I've loved you since the day you left my arms, and always will. I'll admit, your revelation worries me because I know how judgmental people can be. It sounds like your pastor is a good one.
>
> I need to get myself straightened out and sin-free before I begin to tell others how to live.
>
> I pray that you know Jesus and have a personal relationship with him. As your pastor said, He is the only one who can take care of our sin problem.
>
> I can't believe you found a copy of that old magazine. The photo shoot was my big break. Mom and I were shopping in Nashville for a prom dress when we noticed a long line of girls. A cosmetics company partnered with a department store to sponsor the talent search. We stood in line for over three hours. It was a lark, just something we stumbled upon. Imagine my surprise when I received a call. I'd been selected to be in a photo shoot in New York. Many things in my life might have been altered had I shopped for my prom dress the previous weekend. I might have had a different life, and you would not exist. I can never regret that, regardless of the mistakes I made.

> A friend of mine, someone I love, has been ill. During these days of waiting at the hospital, God has given me the gift of solitude. I've come to realize I keep going back to that one significant moment when everything changed—the moment I decided to keep your birth a secret. I built a chain of lies that has weighed me down all these years. Pretending to be something I wasn't has been my burden. I'm glad you realize it's important to be yourself.
>
> You asked about your biological father. I hope you will trust me and my instincts, but I feel it's in your best interest not to share his name. I'm sorry.
>
> You and your parents are in my prayers. May God bless you and keep you in his loving care.
>
> Love,
>
> Casey

After writing, the words "Love, Casey," she started to crumple the paper. Maybe she didn't deserve Madison's love, but wasn't that what grace was all about? Without looking at the letter again, she sealed it inside an envelope.

The kitchen clock displayed seven o'clock, and her stomach growled. An examination of the fridge revealed two strawberry yogurts only one day past their shelf life. With a shrug, she opened a container and started eating.

Her fingers itched to dial Daniel. When she'd eaten the last bite of yogurt, she gave into her impulse and hit the speed dial on her phone. He answered after six rings.

"It's Casey."

"The brain surgery didn't make me forget the sound of your voice."

Why is he acting like such a jerk? Maybe the surgery changed his personality? "How are you feeling?"

"Okay."

"Did Wynonna deliver supper?"

"Yes. She and Sparky brought over enough meatloaf for a football team."

Casey chewed her nail. His voice sounded cold. "I'm glad you had a nice evening."

"The visit wore me out."

"You should get some rest."

"That's the plan. I'm about to turn in."

"I love you."

He remained silent.

Casey pulled her hair and resisted beating the phone against the wall. "I just wanted to hear from you."

"I appreciate your concern, but it's time to return to your normal routine. I'm sure your business is suffering without you."

"You're more important to me than the shop."

After hearing nothing for several seconds, she looked at the display on the phone to ensure she hadn't been disconnected. "I'll stop by to see you tomorrow morning."

"I'm going to physical therapy at nine."

"I'll drive you."

"I live four blocks from downtown. It will be good to walk."

"Are you sure?"

"I'm an adult. I know my abilities."

"You're right. Anyway, I need to get back to work."

"That sounds like a good idea."

She paused and waited for him to say something, but after listening to his quiet breathing, she said, "Good night."

After staring into space for a long time, she dialed Emma.

"I've been dying to talk to you," Emma said.

"I took a nap this afternoon, and the day seems to have evaporated."

"I assumed you were with Daniel."

"No, Wynona and Sparky dropped dinner off for him. Daniel told me to take a break."

"Sounds like a good idea to me."

"I guess."

"Have you eaten? We just finished a pizza. I had a coupon for buy one, get one free. We still have a whole pie on the table. Pepperoni and mushrooms. Come over; I want you to meet Kelsey."

"How's she settling in?"

"It's been interesting. I think the house is a little much for her, but as usual, Pepper has helped comfort her."

"For such a temperamental dog, she has a talent for soothing troubled children."

"I know. But not without suffering. Pepper keeps walking from room to room, looking out the window, and every time a car door slams, she runs to the back door barking."

"Poor girl, and you may be putting on a brave face, but you can't fool me."

She heard Emma sigh. "You're right. But if I'm going to take in foster kids, I have to toughen up. Why don't you come over? You can eat and catch me up on things with Daniel and Madison."

"If you're sure."

"I've only got one best friend. I'm not giving you up."

"Thanks, Em. I needed to hear that. I'll be right over."

Casey's heart softened when Emma introduced her to Kelsey. Poor little thing. The child wouldn't look up as she whispered, "Nice to meet you."

Kelsey was much too thin and small for an eight-year-old. Her prominent cheekbones reminded Casey of some of the street children in Africa. Surely, a child wouldn't go hungry in Weldon. Casey lifted a prayer for Kelsey. *Lord, have mercy. Please bless and protect this sweet child.*

CHAPTER FORTY—DANIEL

The following day, Daniel was just slipping into a pair of sweatpants when the doorbell chimed. He'd hardly slept, and he yearned to ignore it. It was likely Casey, and he wasn't ready to face her.

When he finally opened the door, Casey rushed in, rubbing her hands. "I was getting worried. I started to dig out my key."

"I was just getting up."

Casey placed her hand on Daniel's unshaved jaw. "You have dark circles under your eyes. How do you feel?"

He pushed her hand away. "I'm fine, but I need a cup of coffee."

"I can make a pot for you."

Daniel just stared at her, unmoving.

Casey rolled her eyes. "Fine then, you make the coffee."

Daniel ambled to the kitchen. "Have a seat."

He struggled to open the sealed coffee container, and his cheeks warmed.

"How did you sleep last night?" Casey drummed her fingers on the table.

"Okay. It was good to be in my own bed." It had felt good to be in his own bed, in his home.

"That's great."

"Best of all, it was quiet."

Casey laced her fingers together and rested her elbows on the arms of the chair. Outside the window, a pair of cardinals pecked at the ground. "Looks like the birds are glad you're home too."

A feeling of remorse washed over Daniel. "Poor things. I can't believe I forgot to arrange for someone to feed them."

"You had a lot on your mind."

The coffeemaker beeped, and he pulled two mugs from the cabinet, filled one, placed it on the table in front of her, and returned to the second cup.

"Thanks, I love your coffee." Casey took a sip and cradled her mug. "I'm sorry I left angry yesterday." She reached across the table and squeezed his hand when he sat down.

"Have you changed your mind about filing a report?" Daniel lifted his chin.

"I'm focusing on forgiveness and digging up the old memories won't help."

He set his cup down hard, and coffee stained the tablecloth. "I never thought to say this, but you're being a coward and acting selfishly."

Casey's face turned scarlet, and she gripped the cup's handle. "You have no idea what you're asking of me."

Daniel scratched his chin. "It might help if you meet the other women."

She shook her head. "No." Her voice had a steely edge.

"It's not healthy to bury everything like it didn't happen. Can't you see how doing that screwed up your life to start with?"

Casey moved from the table, hugged herself, and looked out the window. She squared her shoulders. "I'm leaving."

Daniel walked to the counter, picked up a piece of paper, and extended it to her. "This is another email from the detective. Call him."

"You can't make me."

He unfolded the paper and held it up for her to see. The row of pictures drew Casey's attention. The similar features of each woman left her holding her breath, and she felt physically ill. With a gulp, she squeezed her eyes shut.

"There might be more victims if you don't speak up." Daniel snagged her bag and crammed the paper into it.

Casey gulped. "If you continue to pursue this, it's over. You and I are over."

Daniel steeled himself. This was not the time to be weak. "Unlike you, I can't look at myself in the mirror and know that women are being victimized by this creep. I'll not have a peaceful moment until he's locked behind bars."

"You can't do this."

"I'm doing it." His voice sounded cold to his ears.

Casey's eyes filled with tears, and he resisted the urge to pull her to him.

"Then it's over. I love you, but I won't be with a man who betrays me."

Casey walked stiffly to the door, looked over her shoulder, and gave him a long sorrowful look. "Goodbye, Daniel."

Daniel dropped into the chair. He'd get the creep behind bars, thus untethering Casey from his life. This was for the best. He couldn't take care of himself, much less a wife.

His gut ached. The phone rang, and he started to ignore it, then he noticed a Nashville area code. He guessed it was the doc checking up on him, and he answered.

"May I speak to Daniel Sheppard?"

"Speaking."

"This is Amanda Jennings with the YMCA of Nashville. Kevin Reynolds listed you as a reference on his job application. Do you have time to talk?"

Daniel rolled his shoulders and sighed. At least he could help his buddy Kevin.

"Yes, ma'am. I've been expecting your call." Daniel moved to the computer and opened a file where he'd prepared a list of Kevin's accomplishments and attributes. After a few minutes of conversation, he closed the file.

"Sounds like he's great at his job." Ms. Jennings's voice was upbeat.

"He's the best. We'll miss him if he leaves Weldon, but if this is what he wants, we want it for him."

When he disconnected, Daniel felt a tightening in his chest. Jealousy of his friend's good fortune left him feeling like a slimeball. His character was going from bad to worse with each passing minute. The stack of mail was piled on the desk, and his medical bills hadn't even started coming in. He could sell his house, but then what? Where would he go?

For the umpteenth time, he attempted to twitch his finger, yet nothing happened, and his gut twisted. *What am I going to do?*

His thoughts turned to Jansen. The guy had to be locked up. Maybe he should contact one of the victims and ask her to attempt to persuade Casey to file charges. The memory of the hurt on her face this morning gnawed at him.

Roaming the house, aching, he traced his finger on the inside of his closet doorframe where his mom had recorded his height through the years. The walls seemed to close in on him as he paced the hallway.

He returned to the kitchen and stared at the Weldon Police Force mug on the counter. Fury bubbled up from a place he didn't realize existed. It seemed an evil force took over his body as he hurled the mug at the wall. Veins of black liquid streamed down the rows of lemons on the vintage wallpaper. He strode to the bedroom in measured steps, yanked his uniforms from the closet, and dumped them onto the bedspread. After he gathered the corners, he flung it over his back, stomped outside to the center of the yard and dropped the load. It took him a few minutes to find the lighter fluid in the garage, and when he lit the pile, acrid smoke filled his lungs and his nostrils flared as the tattered remnants of his life disappeared. When only a scorched circle remained, he turned and braced himself against a cold gust of wind. His legs quivered and it took his last ounce of strength to climb the porch steps. Inside the house, he leaned against the kitchen wall and slid to the floor. *What am I going to do?*

CHAPTER FORTY-ONE—CASEY

Two weeks passed without a word from Daniel. With each new day, the urge to call him intensified. Several times she drove by his house, but she didn't catch a glimpse of him. Last night, around midnight, she drove to his home and parked in the street. Just as she was about to go to the door to knock, the light from the living room turned off.

Early the following day, Casey sat in her kitchen with her Bible open and yearned for the peace she'd discovered in Africa when she'd forgiven Jansen of everything. She had to do the same for Daniel. If only he hadn't put Madison at risk. If only she could trust him. Casey sighed. She'd never trust him again.

A deep sadness welled up. Trust might not come, but she would forgive him. As she said the words aloud, her heart softened.

Later that morning, she turned on her the computer in her office. She needed new clothes. As Casey's fingers clicked from one store's site to the next, nothing seemed to please her. Almost everything Casey sold in her boutique was for Cassandra. She needed something for Casey. No more hiding. Cassandra was history, and Casey vowed she'd never return.

What do I really want to wear? She loved cashmere sweaters, but nothing tight or binding. After selecting several loose and flowing cotton tops and jeans with Lycra, she added several shades of her favorite leggings. For dressier occasions, she ordered tailored slacks and silk blouses. She didn't want jaw-dropping outfits. She just wanted to blend in. She just wanted to be herself.

An idea started to form in her mind. If her life needed a makeover, maybe her business needed an adjustment too. Emma might be right. The blues playing in the background of her life was depressing. Had listening to sad songs added to her mental darkness?

The images from her modeling days covered the wall of her salon. Wasilla's face came to mind, and Casey remembered her raw beauty. She'd take down the photos of Cassandra and replace them with pictures of women of all ages, races, and body sizes to display their true beauty. The idea appealed to her.

A hundred thoughts and ideas swirled through her mind, and she started listing ideas on a notepad. It was time for a fresh start. Casey wanted a real relationship with Madison, and she wanted Madison to get to know the real Casey. It was time for the world to meet the real Casey Bledsoe.

It would be easy to change the shop's atmosphere—the real challenge would be to be rid of Cassandra forever. Casey squared her shoulders. She could, and she would.

Casey threw herself into the makeover of the boutique. In a matter of days, the store was almost empty because Casey had slashed prices. An interior designer had started making plans to transform her hip, glitzy shop into a place of peace and tranquility. Her new strategy included swapping the blues with uplifting music. As she searched for just the right songs to lift the spirits of the customers and employees, she discovered many new contemporary Christian music artists. The new atmosphere of the boutique filled her with hope. Perhaps Emma had been right.

On Friday, just at noon, Casey was studying sketches from the interior designer when Tricia popped her blond head in the door. "Alma Lee from the drugstore is on line one and said it's a heart emergency."

Casey snatched the phone. "Alma Lee. It's Casey. What's wrong?"

"If you know what's good for you, you'll get over here before your sandwich gets soggy."

With her hand placed over her pounding heart, Casey wanted to fuss at her for scaring her, but she knew better than to mess with Alma Lee. Few people could be more cantankerous and intimidating than the local drugstore matron.

In her most pleasant, sugar-sweet tone, she said, "Alma Lee, I think there's been a mistake. I didn't order a sandwich. What's this about a heart emergency?"

"Get yourself over here, and you'll see for yourself!" And she hung up.

Casey huffed. Alma Lee's chicken salad sandwich was one of her favorite foods, but she hadn't ordered one. And what was this about a heart emergency?

Casey's stomach growled. With a shrug, Casey grabbed her black leather jacket and headed for the door.

When she walked into the drugstore, she immediately realized why she'd been summoned. *Why, that old meddler.* There sat Daniel at the counter, eating a club sandwich.

"It's about time you got here," Alma Lee placed a plate bearing a croissant filled with chicken salad on the counter next to Daniel.

Daniel turned around and gave her a cool look.

Dave called out to her from the pharmacy. “Casey!” He pushed through the swinging door. “This is great timing. I just received my albums from Shutterfly.

Dave looped his arm through hers and pulled her toward Daniel. “I designed a picture book from my Africa photos and had one printed for each team member.”

Casey stiffened. *Dave’s in on this too.*

When they reached Daniel, Dave extended an album to him and gave one to her.

Casey’s pulse hammered when her eyes met Daniel’s blue ones, but he had his cop mask in place.

“Open it,” Dave said.

Tearing her eyes away from Daniel, she looked at the cover. The entire Africa team stood together in front of Hama’s bush taxi wearing their purple T-shirts. Raymond must have taken the shot when they’d arrived at the mission house.

Casey forced a smile. At the time of this picture, she’d thought her heaviest burden was her secret about Madison. Thank goodness she’d had no idea of the trials she’d face in the coming days. As she flipped through the pages, a tumult of emotions washed over her. It had only been a few weeks, but since then, she’d been on a roller-coaster ride, and she wasn’t the same person, *thank God.*

Sniffing, she grabbed a napkin and dabbed at her eyes, and hugged Dave. “Thank you. I’ll treasure it, always.”

Daniel cleared his throat. “Thanks, man. I haven’t even had time to think about getting my pictures printed.”

Dave clapped him on the back. “You’ve endured a terrible ordeal. I wanted to do something to remind each of us that we’re blessed.”

“You’re right.” Casey gulped.

“Your sandwich is getting soggy.” Alma Lee wiped the counter with a rag.

"Do you mind putting it in a to-go bag?" Casey said.

Alma Lee dropped her chin, gave her a stern look, then turned her broad backside to Casey and muttered something under her breath.

While Dave and Daniel talked, Casey kept a smile plastered on her face. At last, Alma Lee handed her a bag, and Casey dug through her purse for her wallet.

Dave squeezed her shoulder. "It's on the house." Then he looked at Daniel. "Your money's no good here, either."

Outside the plate glass window, Casey noticed Sally Reynolds rush by. "There goes one of my most demanding customers." She turned to leave the cafe. "Thanks again, Dave." She hugged him, turned on her heel, and walked away slowly, with her hips slightly swaying. *Eat your heart out, Daniel Sheppard.* The temptation to turn and see his reaction could not be resisted, but instead of seeing the hoped-for longing on his face, she witnessed a deep sadness in his eyes. *I guess it's really over.*

Another week passed, and Daniel still didn't phone, but she held firm to her resolution to avoid him. Her bruised heart would not stop yearning for him. Every morning she spent time in prayer asking God to help her forgive him. Her heart was softening, but she didn't think she could ever trust him again. Forgiveness would come ... but trust? She shook her head. It was over.

Casey pretended all was right with the world, put a smile on her face, and dressed in her new comfortable jeans or leggings with flowing tops. Instead of stilettos, she sported flats made of butter-soft Italian leather. Her beaded bracelets from Wasilla were a constant reminder to be thankful. The gold bracelet from Daniel was hidden at the bottom of her jewelry box.

The ambiance surrounding her workers and her customers seemed to be shifting. Throughout each step of the makeover, she felt the shedding of her old life.

Nightmares continued to taunt Casey, but instead of reliving the rape, she experienced being a helpless bystander while someone else endured an assault. One night, she broke from her constraints in the dream, and when she reached Jansen, she awakened screaming, "No!" Panting, she ran her forearm across her face. *I need to call my counselor. Stop procrastinating.*

A few minutes later, as she waited for the coffee to brew, she sat down at the kitchen island, opened Madison's most recent letter, and reread it.

> Dear Casey,
>
> You may not hear from me for a few weeks, because I'm busy with basketball. Coach scheduled extra practices because the Sunbelt Conference tournament is upon us. Also, I have to bring my grades up, so I don't have time to focus on anything except basketball and school. It's a busy season.
>
> Usually, I can concentrate without a problem, but I can't stop thinking about my biological father. It surprised me you didn't share anything about him, and this worries me. My curious nature keeps questions whirling in my brain. Is he a serial killer? Mom says, with my imagination, I should be a writer. Ha! I'd never be able to sit still long enough.
>
> Seriously, it's better to know the truth, no matter how terrible, than not to know. I've been taught from an early age that God is my father, and I'm responsible for my own choices.
>
> I'm glad you didn't freak out to learn I'm gay. Thanks for that. You're right about some people being judgmental, but most of my friends accept me the way I am.

I can accept the truth about my father. Trust me.

There's a stack of books waiting for me, so I'll close. Write back soon.

Love,

Madison

Casey stared at the words, *Love Madison,* and realized she was doing something she'd thought impossible a few minutes earlier—smiling from ear to ear. As terrible as Jansen was, she supposed there were worse people. But wasn't Madison better off not knowing the truth? She might start suffering nightmares too. Or maybe she already was because of her curiosity.

The music playing in the background soothed her nerves, and the words "God's ways are higher" caught her attention. As the song ended, Casey pondered the last words, "I love you." The silence seemed palpable as her heart seemed to say, "God loves Jansen too." *What? Where did that come from? Surely, God could not love someone as evil as Jansen.*

The stool almost turned over when she pushed away, shaking her head. No one could love a man like Jansen. But her mind wouldn't stop hearing the lyrics. "His ways are higher." *What kind of God could love someone like Jansen?*

On Saturday evening, the doorbell rang, and her hopes lifted as she stood. *Maybe it's Daniel. Who else could it be?* Then her stomach twisted in a knot. What would she say to him? It had been three weeks, and he'd not reached out to her once. The bell rang again. "Coming!" she called out.

When she peered out the peephole, her jaw dropped. The woman standing on the front porch might pass for her sister if she had one. Casey opened the door, and the leggy redhead began pulling off a leather glove. Her emerald swing coat looked expensive, and her black leather hobo bag displayed a Michael Kors emblem.

"Ms. Bledsoe, I'm Valerie Kingston." She extended her hand. The scent of gardenias filled the foyer.

Oh, my goodness. She's one of the other victims. Casey's hand trembled as she shook Valerie's. "Call me Casey."

"May I come in?"

Casey stepped back and opened the door wide. "Of course."

She ushered her into the living room. Valerie removed her coat to reveal a cream cashmere sweater over jeans with a green silk scarf tied loosely around her shoulders.

"Would you like a cup of coffee or tea? I have chamomile." Casey's voice sounded tenuous.

"No. Thank you." Valerie sat down in the gray suede armchair, crossed her legs, and smiled without showing her teeth.

Casey sat on the edge of the sofa and straightened the magazines on the coffee table. "I recognize you from the photos the detective emailed to me. I suppose he gave you my address."

Valerie lifted her chin. "No. Your friend, Daniel Sheppard, contacted me."

Casey's nails bit into her palms. "I see."

"Nice guy. He offered to pay my travel expenses."

Guilt lapped at the corners of her mind and flowed down. Casey cleared her throat. "He is a nice guy, but we've parted ways."

"One doesn't need to be Einstein's cousin to figure out why the two of you are at odds, nor why I'm here."

Casey let out a long breath. "You're right."

"Jansen Moore must be stopped. The detective keeps discovering more victims. Now we're up to fourteen."

Casey shook her head. "Fourteen. The email I received listed ten, which is bad enough."

"You are the only one who might stop him."

"I'm not going to sacrifice—"

"The detective's discovered a witness with your case."

"What?"

"The PI Mr. Sheppard hired interviewed several people who worked for Jansen over the years. That's when he discovered Agatha Swanson, his housekeeper and cook."

"I remember her."

Vanessa leaned forward. "She returned to the loft to make sure she'd turned off the oven and heard you screaming."

A fire burned in the pit of Casey's stomach. Her voice was just above a whisper. "How could anyone hear such a thing and do nothing?"

Valerie's face softened. "With three children to feed, she couldn't just up and quit."

"She kept working for him?"

"It took her six months to find another job, and by then, she couldn't find you. She didn't know anything except your first name, plus she didn't think anyone would believe her."

"Why now, after all these years?"

"Because someone finally asked her."

Valerie moved to the sofa and sat next to Casey. "We were all targets from the very beginning. He discovered me in a talent search in Oklahoma City. My hometown of Hennessey has a population of two thousand. Another victim hailed from Mulberry, Florida, a population of four thousand, close to Tampa. We're all small-town girls with similar features. That's why it's been easy to find women he sexually assaulted. Find the winner of one of his talent searches, and you discover a victim. The investigator claims the pattern of the crimes is like a fingerprint."

A heaviness settled over Casey. "I should have spoken up."

Valerie shook her head. "We were all naïve innocents, but we're no longer fledglings. You went on to make a name for yourself. People will believe you. You're Cassandra, for crying out loud. There's no reason for you to lie."

Casey blew out a long breath. *Will I ever be free of Cassandra?* "Do you have nightmares?"

Valerie nodded. "I used to, and I didn't think I'd ever be able to marry or have an intimate relationship with a man."

"I'm sorry."

"I married two years ago, and I have a little girl."

"Wow. That's my dream, too, but this whole sorry mess has created a chasm between Daniel and me."

"He's a cop."

Casey grabbed a tissue and blew her nose.

Valerie gripped Casey's hand. "Jansen is sick. There's something in his psyche that's broken."

"I hadn't thought about him like that. Like, it's an illness."

Valerie's face looked sympathetic. "I began to heal when I started praying for him and for God to help me stop him."

"Pray for Jansen?"

"That's right. I call it spiritual warfare."

"It makes sense, because I've thought on more than one occasion he must be demon-possessed."

Valerie squeezed Casey's hand hard. "Please file a police report. With a witness, the prosecuting attorney might charge him with sexual assault."

Casey looked out the dark window and remembered promising Madison's mother she'd never do anything to hurt their daughter. She closed her eyes and visualized Madison's face—the face with Jansen's eyes. She cleared her throat. "There's someone I need to speak with first. I'm not making a commitment, but I'll contact you and let you know if I'm able to file a police report or do what needs to be done."

"Thank you for considering it." Valerie squeezed Casey's knee. "I know you'll do the right thing." Valerie stood, put on her coat, and slung her black bag over her shoulder. Casey followed her to the front door.

Valerie gave her a business card. "Call me if you want to talk and pray for Jansen. Prayer is our best secret weapon." Then she turned and disappeared into the dark night.

For a long time, Casey sat at the kitchen desk staring at the laptop screen featuring Madison's Facebook Friends page. With trembling hands, she typed a private Facebook message to Madison's mother: "We need to meet. There's something important I must ask you. Name the time and place, and I'll be there. Thank you for considering this request."

After shutting down the computer, she picked up the phone and dialed Daniel. He didn't answer. "And you called me a coward," she said as she disconnected.

Later that night, she lay in bed with Fats cuddled close, and she considered Valerie's words. *Pray for Jansen.* In the silence of her home, she listened with her heart and felt a yielding. "I forgive him," she stuttered. And for a brief instant, she felt warmth, but then she imagined the other women and the coldness returned. *Lord, tell me what to do. How can I stop him and shield Madison?*

On Sunday morning, Casey turned on the computer first thing. A reply from Madison's mother asked, "Can you meet me Wednesday noon, at the President's Kitchen in the Jacksonian Hotel? It's a quiet restaurant in Nashville."

Casey sent a reply. "I'll be there."

Now what? What can I say to her? What will she think of me? I've been such a coward. She gulped. All that mattered was protecting Madison and stopping Jansen. They'd have to figure out a way to do both. At least she'd have someone with whom to share the burden. Someone who probably loved Madison as much as she did. Somehow, together, they'd figure out what to do.

On Wednesday morning, she stared at her closet, wishing she had a fabulous outfit to shield her. *Those days are over. Stop hiding.* At last, she sighed and snatched a pair of black slacks and an emerald cashmere sweater. After adding Wasilla's bracelets, she lifted a prayer for her. Rubbing the tiny beads had become a new habit of comforting. God had rescued her from the desert once, and he'd help her figure this out.

When she stepped into the Jacksonian Hotel, the doorman greeted her with a smile. The Beaux Arts style lobby seemed to be frozen in the Victorian era. Intricate plaster decorated the columns, and the painted glass ceiling caused her to stop and stare at the hotel's beauty. The tall arched entryways suggested grandeur. As she followed the signs downstairs to the President's Kitchen, the heels of her boots were muted by the plush carpet.

The maître d' greeted her. "Welcome. Will you be dining alone today?"

"No. I'm meeting someone."

"A Mrs. Warren, perhaps?"

"Yes."

"This way, please."

He led her to a discreet corner table, and a short, plump woman stood. "Finally, we meet," she said, and she opened her arms and reached out to hug Casey.

Casey stooped down to accept the embrace.

"You feel just like Madison."

They sat across from each other, and the waiter appeared. Casey ordered a Diet Dr. Pepper, and Mrs. Warren ordered an unsweet tea. Casey couldn't help but notice her white hair, which was cut short and spiked. Her dining companion's eyes sparkled as she spoke to the waiter, then she turned her attention to Casey.

"We're going to be great friends. Let's agree to call each other by our first names. I'm Jennifer."

"Of course, and I'm Casey."

They discussed the hotel and the weather until the waiter returned with their drinks, and he stood ready to take their order.

Casey picked up her menu. "What do you recommend?"

The waiter spoke softly. "I suggest the meatloaf. It's our Wednesday special."

Casey lay the menu aside and sighed. "I'm too nervous to eat."

"I'm the opposite. When I'm tense, I eat everything in sight." Jennifer giggled like a schoolgirl. "I'll have the onion bisque and a Caesar salad.

"That sounds good," Casey said. "I'll have the same."

When he left, Jennifer sat up straight. "Now tell me, hon, what's on your mind?"

Casey gave a sigh. "It's a long story."

"Take all the time you need."

Casey relayed her life story to Jennifer. Neither paid any attention to the waiter when he placed their food in front of them. When she could think of nothing else to say, Casey removed a folded piece of paper from her bag. "This is the email from the detective in New York."

Jennifer removed reading glasses from her bag and read with her mouth open. Her face drained of color as she stared at the pictures, then she dabbed her eyes with the corner of her napkin. "What can I do to help?"

"If I testify against Jansen Moore, it will likely make headlines, and Madison may learn the truth about her biological father."

Jennifer looked at the paper on the table again. "Their faces remind me of Madison. Each one is someone's daughter."

"But what about our daughter? Isn't our first responsibility to protect her?"

"When Bill and I adopted Madison, we had no idea of her parentage or the reason you gave her up. We feared drug abuse, incest, and yes ... even rape. No mother gives up a child without a compelling reason."

A weight seemed to shift from Casey's shoulders. "So, you understand?"

She gave Casey a sympathetic stare. "Who could unless they've lived it? We taught Madison from an early age that she has a heavenly Father who loves her unconditionally, just as we do. She knows she's not responsible for anyone's actions or decisions, except her own. Don't use Madison as an excuse to avoid a difficult thing."

Casey inhaled sharply, and Jennifer reached across the table. "I can't tell you what to do, but if Madison's picture were on this email, I'd want you to do everything in your power to stop this man."

"Will you explain this to her?"

Jennifer shook her head. "It's not my place. But you can't write something like this in a letter. You must tell her in person. I'll be by your side if you choose to do so."

"But she's not decided yet if she wants to meet me."

"Oh, she does, but not now. The only thing she can focus on today is getting to the NCAA tournament. Her ability to focus is a strength and a weakness. I call it tunnel vision. It amazes me how she can block out everything and concentrate on a certain task. It's one of the reasons she's successful at the foul line. Others let the pressure get to them, but not my girl."

Casey stared up at the ornate ceiling and thought of all the years she'd blocked thoughts of Jansen, and how Madison's first letter broke the secret vault. "I need to think about what to say to her."

"Of course you do. Thank you for speaking with me first. I'm sure Madison will be shocked to learn the truth, but she has character and strength. This won't break her."

They ignored their cold soup but picked at their salads in silence.

Casey paid the bill, and they walked to the lobby, arm in arm.

"After basketball season is over, we'll all get together for a meeting," Jennifer adjusted her purse strap.

"Thank you." Casey hugged her.

"And thank you—for the most precious gift in the world." Jennifer squeezed her hard. "Knowing that I have another prayer warrior lifting petitions for Madison's salvation increases my confidence she'll eventually turn to Jesus. We're in a battle for her soul, but we are not fighting against flesh and blood, but against spiritual forces of evil."

The two hugged again and they both wiped tears away.

As she watched Jennifer walk away, Casey wondered how to find the words to tell Madison her father was a monster.

When Casey returned to Weldon, she stopped by Daniel's home and rang the doorbell, but no one answered. After digging through her purse for a pen, she wrote a note: "I'm going to New York. Let me know if you want to join me." She attempted to slide the paper under the door, but it wouldn't fit. After a moment's hesitation, she removed his door key. When she crossed the threshold, sorrow filled her, and she scurried to the kitchen table, leaving the missive with his house key on top of it. Then she ran from his home, wiping the tears from her face. The dream to build a life together had been shattered, and the fault belonged to her.

CHAPTER FORTY-TWO—CASEY

Three days later, Casey and her dad boarded a plane for New York. *Daniel should be with us. This was what he'd wanted.* When Casey slid into the limousine, a sense of déjà vu made her head spin. Memories of her first trip to New York with her parents filled her thoughts. The towering skyscrapers loomed overhead as they inched their way to Midtown.

They checked into the hotel and waited for the appointment with the private detective Daniel had hired and the police detective. Rather than meet at the precinct, the PI suggested they convene at the hotel. Since the thought of walking into a police station made her shudder, Casey had booked a suite at the hotel.

Daniel's promise to be with her during the interview left her feeling hollow. *Who is the real Daniel Sheppard?* She wondered. *The one who cares for the birds or the bully who shared my worst secret?*

A drizzle fell over Lexington Avenue, and brightly colored umbrellas appeared to be floating down the sidewalk. Had she really called this home for sixteen years? At first, it had seemed like a dream until it turned into a nightmare. Her fingers grazed the picture of Madison in her pocket, and she removed it. The gray eyes of Jansen stared back at her, and her heart overflowed with love. As terrible as the crime was, the reward of Madison made the sacrifice of her innocence and the resulting turmoil worth it. Peace filled her being, and the calmness surprised her.

A knock sounded, and when Frank opened the door, Daniel stood with two burly men next to him. Casey held her breath and stared. Short brown hair covered his head, and his cheeks were flushed. Her dad slapped him on the back, and Casey narrowed her eyes as she realized her dad didn't seem to be surprised to see him.

Daniel removed his black parka and rubbed his hand over his head. "Frank, this is Buster Kessler, the private investigator I hired."

The bald man gripped Frank's hand and turned to Casey. His eyes held hers. "It's nice to meet you." He shook her hand. "And this is my friend, Adam Maloney. Detective Maloney is with the NYPD and is very interested in hearing what you have to say."

Detective Maloney could pass for a linebacker on the New York Giants football team. His height matched Daniel's, but his heft made Daniel appear slight. Detective Maloney shook her hand. "The mysterious Cassandra Bledsoe. It's nice to meet you."

"It's Casey Bledsoe."

"Please sit down." The detective waved toward the sofa and pulled two chairs from the breakfast table.

The spacious room seemed to shrink with the presence of four men. Detective Maloney placed his briefcase on the coffee table and opened it. "Do I have permission to record our conversation?"

"Yes." She sat up straight and clutched her knees while her heart raced.

He turned on the device, repeated his name, the date, and then faced Casey. "Please state your name, date of birth, and the reason for this interview."

Casey answered.

"You are aware I am recording this conversation?"

"Yes."

She removed an old diary from her bag and handed it over to the detective. "This is my journal from nineteen years ago. You'll notice it ends abruptly. It includes the date I met Jansen Moore on the *Teen Town* photoshoot and my feelings of distaste toward him."

"I'd like to keep this as evidence."

Casey's face flamed as she considered her juvenile mooning over Arnold Alexander from home. *Strangers will be reading my secret thoughts. How embarrassing.* "I understand." She gulped.

When she'd scheduled the meeting, the private detective suggested she write down everything. She read her prepared statement in a monotone voice and blocked all thoughts of the men in the room listening to the graphic details of her attack.

When she finished, it seemed she'd exited from a trance. That's when she noticed her dad's wet cheeks. Daniel sat still, his face white and hard as marble.

"Now, I have a few questions for you," Detective Maloney said.

"Okay."

"Did Jansen Moore offer you money for sex?"

She blanched. "No. I'd heard rumors and been warned to be careful around him, but I only agreed to have dinner with him."

"Did Jansen Moore offer you a modeling contract in exchange for sex?"

"No. After Jansen raped me, he offered me a contract."

"Where is that contract?"

"I tore it up in front of my agent, Alexis Stone. I mentioned her in my statement because she's the one who arranged the dinner with Jansen."

"Why didn't you report this crime nineteen years ago?"

"I didn't think anyone would believe me, and an accusation against Jansen would have killed my modeling career. Plus, the shame and humiliation made me want to hide."

"Where did you go when you left New York?"

Casey wiped her palms on her slacks. "Why is that important?" The thundering in her ears made it difficult to concentrate. *We can't go there. He'll know. He'll figure out about Madison.*

"Answer the question. Believe me, if you're on a witness stand, his attorney will paint you as trash. Did you travel with the jet set, were you a party girl?"

"I'm not the one who will be on trial."

"Before this is over, you'll feel like you are."

Is it worth it? She pictured the faces of all the women who'd been assaulted. *Yes. If it takes having my name dragged through the sewer, I'll pay the price. I didn't do anything wrong other than have a dream. I said no.*

With her heart pounding, she lifted her chin. "I went to the Eagle's Nest. A women's shelter in the mountains of Tennessee."

The detective's face showed sympathy for an instant, then his face displayed no emotion. "Did you have a baby?"

Tears filled her eyes. "Yes. I gave her up for adoption."

"Is Jansen Moore the father of the child?"

She nodded.

"Please speak into the microphone."

"Yes. Being raped by Jansen Moore resulted in a pregnancy, and I gave birth to a daughter at the Eagle's Nest."

The detective rubbed his jaw and said something incoherent under his breath. His voice trailed off, then he lifted a brow. "Do you know how to contact her?"

Daniel reached across the table and squeezed her hand. His eyes looked imploring.

She should have known it would be impossible to keep Madison out of this. Casey clutched her throat. "She contacted me a few months ago, but I'm not going to give you her name. I made a promise to myself years ago that the stain of Jansen's sin will never touch her."

The detective gave her a hard look. "Your daughter's DNA might be the tiny dot of glue that puts him behind bars."

Casey bit her lip and tasted blood.

"But I've been told you have a witness."

"Yes, but the DNA will help prove your statement."

She sat and stared out the window. *Lord, tell me what to do.* After a minute, it came to her. "It will be her decision whether or not to provide a sample of her DNA."

"Will you speak with your daughter?"

"Yes."

"When?"

It seemed no one in the room breathed. At last, she said, "Soon."

The detective made a few closing comments then turned off the recorder. He packed the equipment away with the diary and her written statement. "Thank you. It will be up to the district attorney to decide whether there's enough evidence to arrest Jansen Moore."

Casey tucked her hair behind her ear and gulped.

"If the charges stick, the prosecuting attorney might call you, and the other women who've filed charges might be called to be witnesses to demonstrate the pattern of the sexual assaults."

"Okay."

"We need a sample of your daughter's DNA."

"I know."

"In the meantime, I'll file the report, and we'll see if the district attorney arrests Jansen Moore."

Casey felt empty, numb, and Daniel gave her a weak smile. "Thank you."

There were a thousand things she wanted to say to him. What had happened to the man who claimed to care about her? What had she done to deserve this cool indifference? Maybe he didn't want to be with her now that he knew everything. His dark eyes looked sad. He was hurting too. Whether he'd admit it or not, she knew he had feelings for her, but she guessed all her lies had ruined everything.

A week passed, and Casey continued to exchange letters with Madison, and she prayed each day for the moment they would meet in person.

Daniel returned to church, but he sat in the balcony at Loving Chapel instead of with her family. Still, Casey could always sense his nearness. For such a small town, their paths rarely crossed, which indicated he must be staying in. None of her customers nor her family mentioned him. She yearned to learn if there had been any improvement in his condition. It had been impossible to miss the Bennett Brothers Realty sign in his yard. *Is he leaving town?* Her heart skipped a beat.

Emma told her that he'd picked up his old habit of coaching boys' basketball at the Y. Other than that tidbit, she knew nothing about him, his health, or his plans.

Spending time with Emma and six-year-old Kelsey and Harley helped, as her best friend often invited her to dinner. It appalled Casey when Emma discovered a hoard of food stashed in Kelsey's closet. The child would over-eat to the point of throwing up unless someone intervened because she feared hunger pangs.

Everyone missed Callie and Hallie. The private detective Emma's mother hired reported they were living in a rundown house in Bowling Green. His notes included a snapshot of the girls waiting for the school bus. Their stained clothes and tangled hair caused Casey to cringe.

It thrilled her when one day she received an email from Raymond and Katie in Niger.

> Dear Casey,
>
> I hope you and the others are well. It's hard to believe it's been weeks since you left. Even though the pace is much slower here than in America, the days pass quickly.
>
> It's with much excitement we tell you that Wasilla accepted Christ as her savior today. Her uncle, Ibrahim, started a small church in his compound.
>
> We felt terrible when we left you behind in the village and still can't believe such a thing happened. But now we wonder if God's hand instigated the entire situation. If you had not been left, we would not have met her uncle, and he would not have been the bold witness he is today. A small group meets in his home weekly, and marvelous things are happening. We offer discipleship training as often as we can get to Ibrahim. He is well respected in the village, and many come to listen to us.
>
> A few villagers refuse to buy from his stall at the market. Still, he smiles and says to them he loves them anyway,

> and he speaks to all about the woman with "fire hair" who came all the way from America to tell him about Jesus.
>
> Uncle Bob is organizing another mission team to visit next year, and we hope you will be among the team members. He also tells us that Daniel's surgery went well. Praise God. Perhaps the two of you will both be able to visit in January.
>
> Until we meet again, may God bless you and keep you in his care.
>
> Your brother and sister in Christ,
>
> Raymond and Katie

Casey sighed as she read the email, closed her eyes and tried to imagine being in Africa again. Had she really spent the night alone in the desert? Had she really traveled in the back of a truck with strangers trying to get back to Niamey? As she remembered the laughter of Wasilla, Miriama, and Helima, and the tea and rice they shared, she smiled. When she opened her eyes, she looked around her nest, and said aloud, "Thank you, Jesus, for everything." She started typing a reply to the email.

> Dear Raymond and Katie,
>
> We are all well. Daniel is still recovering from his surgery. Please keep him in your prayers.
>
> Thank you for writing. You cannot imagine my joy at hearing the news of Wasilla accepting Christ. I could be the poster child of missionaries. The headline on the poster could read, 'If Casey can do it, anyone can.' My reluctance to travel to Africa almost made me miss one of God's best blessings. My time in Africa began a time of healing for me, and now I cannot wait to return. I will speak to Pastor Bob immediately and tell him I'm willing to join another team.

Also, I have an idea for a business I'd like to discuss with you. I'm looking into setting up a nonprofit business featuring Sakina's clothing designs. All profits will be funneled back to the people of Niger. My business manager is laying the groundwork. I believe there's a market for Sakina's African designs. I'm anxious to hear what you think about my idea.

Pastor Bob might have mentioned that Daniel and I have parted ways. The fault is mine. I withheld something very important from him. I'll tell you the whole story when I see you again. To sum it up, I am a sinner saved by grace, and I have found forgiveness. And to say it again, if God can use me, he can use anyone.

Blessings to you both. Until I see you again, much love. You are faithfully in my prayers. Please tell Wasilla, Helima, and Miriama that I pray for them daily.

Thank you for the invitation to visit again. The hope of returning to Africa fills me with joy.

Much love,

Casey

CHAPTER FORTY-THREE—DANIEL

Daniel sat in the recliner with a rubber ball and willed his fingers to move, then he inhaled sharply as one finger twitched. *Did that happen? No. Yes, it did. My index finger trembled*—a bead of sweat formed on his upper lip. After weeks of failed attempts, he'd almost given up. Again, he urged his finger to move, it responded, and a surge of adrenaline pumped through him.

"Yes!" he shouted. The urge to call Casey made him lift the phone, but he stopped and shook his head. *Why call now?* When he'd sat next to her in New York, she'd barely looked at him. It took every ounce of his resolve not to grab her and hold her to him. Instead, he'd gripped the arm of the chair with his good hand and stared out the window as she told her horror story.

With slumped shoulders, he picked up the newspaper and reviewed the Boys and Girls Club's advertisement for a new director. Maybe this was something he could do. He closed his eyes and attempted to quell the ache in his gut. He'd talked to his boss last week and learned that in one week, his short-term disability checks would end. It was time to face the truth. Unless he received a miracle, returning to the force would be impossible.

He leaned his good elbow on the table and rested his chin in his palm and tried to pray. With a sigh, he turned the paper over. The picture of Casey, surrounded by her staff, made him wince. She looked happy in the half-page color ad promoting the grand opening of *Casey and Friends*. Posed leaning against an antique rusted truck filled with baskets of wildflowers, they looked as if they were enjoying a day in the country. He wondered what she'd done with her fancy clothes. He guessed they were in the past, just like their relationship.

He couldn't blame her for never speaking to him again. After she'd shared her most vulnerable secret, he'd betrayed her. But he hadn't had a choice. He held his breath. No, he was lying to himself. He'd chosen to hunt down a criminal rather than to trust her to do the right thing, and now he had to live with the consequences. The woman he loved couldn't stand to look at him.

The ringing doorbell broke through his thoughts. When he opened it, Mrs. Dot and Mayor Willoughby, Emma's mother, stood on his front porch. Both of their backs stood ramrod straight. *This can't be good.*

He forced a smile on his face. "Ladies. What a surprise. Please come in," he stuttered.

Virginia Willoughby stepped inside first. "Forgive us for not calling."

"Speak for yourself." Dot fixed Daniel with a stern stare that meant business. The Queen Bee of the Triple D was about to sting him. "I am plum worn out worrying about you."

The two ladies walked into the den and sat down as if it was a regular event for them to visit.

"How are you feeling?" Mayor Willoughby asked.

"Great," he said and immediately felt remorse for lying.

"Are you ready to get back to work?" The mayor sounded like she was on the campaign trail.

"Umm. You know I can't pass the physical."

"But there are other jobs." Mayor Willoughby arched her brow.

"Not in Weldon," Daniel said.

"Get to it, Virginia, I ain't got all day." Dot gave her a fierce look. "It'll be time for the lunch crowd soon."

"It's amazing you have any customers, the way you talk to people," Virginia frowned.

Daniel cleared his throat.

"Why are you sellin' your house?" Dot looked over her vintage cat-eye glasses.

"It's too big for me." Heat traveled up his neck.

"You've got to live somewhere. What's the plan?" Dot narrowed her eyes.

"I haven't decided."

Virginia nudged Dot. "Let me handle this." She beamed her politician's smile at him. "I'm on the board for the Boys and Girls Club. Have you considered applying for the open position?"

An inkling of hope bubbled up. "Yes, ma'am." His voice was barely audible.

"Good. I can think of no one better. Of course, we'll have to see who applies, but I feel better already, knowing you're interested." Virginia looked pretty pleased herself, but Dot continued to frown.

"Get on with it," Dot said.

Virginia rolled her eyes. "Dot wants to do something to thank you for the years you've served Weldon."

"I received a paycheck every week," Daniel drummed his fingers on his thigh.

"Well, we're gonna do it anyway." Dot crossed her arms.

"Do what?" He had a bad feeling in his gut.

"I'm hosting a fish fry fundraiser. Try saying that three times in a row."

"Fundraiser for what?"

"To help pay your medical bills," Dot rolled her eyes.

"I have health insurance."

"But it didn't take care of everything, did it?" Mayor Willoughby looked sympathetic.

Daniel stood up and rubbed his jaw. "I'm not taking charity."

"Please sit down," Virginia said. "Your father helped many people in this community."

"Yes, ma'am. He served on the force for forty years."

"And he also provided supplies and free labor for more than fifteen Habitat homes," Virginia said.

"I think you've confused him with someone else. He wasn't handy around the house."

Virginia crossed her arms. "He learned on the job sites after he retired. Your parents also donated building supplies. The only reason I'm privy to their generosity is that I chaired the Habitat board."

"Dad never mentioned Habitat." *And I thought medical bills drained their savings account.*

"And your sweet mama volunteered for years with the hospital auxiliary," Dot said.

"Yes, ma'am. It gave her great pleasure."

"We are not going to let you lose your home because of your pride," Dot scowled at him.

"But—"

"Don't talk back to me, young man," Dot said.

"Weldon has its problems, and Lord knows, you know that from your time on the force," Virginia said.

Dot stood. "But we take care of people around here."

Daniel tugged on his ear, swallowed the lump in his throat, and turned away from them.

"The fish fry is scheduled for next Saturday, and I expect you to be there."

"Yes, ma'am."

"Now, I've got to go," Dot said. "Give me a hug, you big knucklehead."

He bent down and hugged her with his good arm. "Thank you," he whispered.

"You can thank me by showing up at the restaurant again. I don't like it when my regulars go missin'."

"Yes, ma'am."

The two matriarchs of Weldon left side by side, and Daniel couldn't keep from smiling as he listened to their conversation.

"Goodness gracious, Virginia. How do you get anything done? The grass grew three inches while you lollygagged around small talk."

"One doesn't have to run over people like a bulldozer to get things accomplished." Virginia hit the key fob to unlock the doors of her black Cadillac.

"Well, it works for me," Dot said, and she jerked open the passenger door.

Daniel stared at the "For Sale" sign under his Dogwood tree. Maybe things would work out after all. Then he shook his head. *It's too much to expect Casey to forgive me ... or is it?*

CHAPTER FORTY-FOUR—CASEY

As Casey sorted through her mail, Madison's loopy script made her smile. Last week she'd added a bulletin board in her kitchen to display the pictures printed from Madison's Facebook posts. The collage of her daughter's images made her chest swell with pride. No matter the other things going wrong in her life, the knowledge of Madison's health and well-being caused her to say frequent prayers of thanksgiving.

Casey tore open the envelope and read standing up.

Dear Casey,

Next week, my team will be playing in the Sunbelt Conference Tournament. I sprained my ankle, and I'm out for the season. Major bummer. I can't believe it. Enough about that. I've promised Mom to stop having pity parties. My parents came down and had dinner with me last night to cheer me up, and Mom suggested I write you and invite you to the tournament. The thought of meeting you gives me something to think of other than my injury.

Enclosed are four tickets to our first Sunbelt Conference Game. Mom and Dad have the seats next to these. They're looking forward to meeting you.

I hope you can come.

Love,

Madison

Casey sat down on the stool, dazed. She dropped her face into her hands and repeated the prayer, *Thank you, Jesus*. At last, she rubbed her sleeve across her face and snatched the phone from her pocket. Without missing a beat, she dialed her dad's cell.

"What's up, baby doll?"

"I'm holding four tickets to the women's Sunbelt Conference Tournament in Bowling Green. Madison sent them to me."

"Yahoo!"

Casey held the phone away from her ear. "I'll take that as a yes to the unasked question whether or not you'd like to go."

"Honey, I already planned to go."

"At least you won't have to be incognito. She wants to meet me after the game."

"Hallelujah!"

"I'll let you tell Mom," Casey said.

"Will do. My granddaughter is a college ballplayer. Woo-wee, ain't that something."

"It is that, but she sprained her ankle, so she won't be playing."

"Oh, no. Is it serious?"

"No. just bad timing, and of course, she's in a funk about it."

"The great thing about basketball is there's always another season."

"I guess."

"I'm calling your mama."

"Bye, Daddy." Casey blew her nose and savored the moment. Then she started to worry. Might her parents say something insensitive if they caught on at the game that their granddaughter was gay? No matter what her parents' reaction might be, she was just going to love her daughter. The world might judge Madison, but she wouldn't.

On the day of the Sunbelt Conference, Casey stopped by her parent's house to pick them up for the big game. As she paced around the kitchen table, she looked at the clock. "We need to go. Emma's waiting too."

"Your mom will be right down," Frank said. "We have plenty of time."

After dropping her purse on the counter, she started searching for her keys. "I'm going to start carrying a smaller bag. I can never find my keys."

"I'm driving," Frank said.

"I invited you to go with me."

"You're as nervous as a hypochondriac surrounded by snotty-nosed kids. If we're going to get there in one piece, I'll be the one to drive."

Jolene walked into the room brandishing a folded newspaper. "Did you see the article in the sports section of the *Murfreesboro Post*?

"Since when do you subscribe to the *Murfreesboro Post*?" Casey said.

"Since we found out we have a granddaughter who plays college ball in Murfreesboro," Frank said.

"The article said that the Blue Raider women are expected to win the Sunbelt Conference. That means we'll get to go to the NCCA Tournament." Jolene beamed a smile.

"Nothing is a given," Frank said. "Anything can happen during a ballgame. They have four games to fight through before they can start thinking about the NCAA tournament. One game at a time."

"If that happens, you won't have a voice left," Casey said.

"Let's hope her ankle heals quickly, and if they make it to the NCAA tournament, she'll get to play," Frank said. "I'll be black and blue from pinching myself to see if I'm dreaming."

A wave of remorse made Casey ache. She'd been the one to separate her parents from their grandchild. Even though she kept handing that burden over to God, she continued to hurt—and to lift her hurt up again.

"Let's hurry," Jolene said. "We don't want to be late."

Sitting in the back seat of her father's SUV, Casey wondered whether Madison was nervous too. Emma flew down her porch steps, and Virginia, Harley, and Kelsey waved to them.

As they exited the parkway, Jolene said, "Oh, no! My camera batteries are almost out."

"There's an extra two in the case," Frank said.

"No, I exchanged them at Olivia's birthday party. We've got to stop and buy batteries." Jolene pointed her finger. "There's the Walmart. Pull in."

Frank followed his wife's instructions.

Jolene turned and looked at Casey. "I'll be right back. Do you want me to get you anything while I'm inside? Are you thirsty?"

"No, thanks. I'll just sit here."

"I'm going to visit the restroom," Frank said.

"Me too," Emma said.

Good gracious, are we ever going to get there? Casey silently fumed. As she waited, she opened her phone and scrolled through Madison's Facebook pictures. *Thank you, Jesus.*

Someone yelling drew her from her reverie. A woman stood screaming at someone in the back of a beat-up car.

The crazed woman spat out curse words, not fit for anyone to hear. Casey's jaw dropped. Two little redheads sat in the backseat. *Oh, my Lord, it's Callie and Hallie.*

Casey jumped out of the SUV and ran to the vehicle.

"Callie, Hallie! Are you okay?" Casey shouted.

The furious woman turned, staggered, and glared at her. "Get away from my kids."

The woman's breath reeked of beer.

"You're drunk."

"Get out of my way!"

The twins sat frozen, with open mouths and eyes wide.

"If you get behind the wheel, I'm calling 911," Casey removed her phone from her pocket and planted herself in front of the driver's door. She'd not allow this woman to get in the car.

The woman hit a button on her key fob, the trunk opened, and she staggered to it. "Ain't nobody takin' my kids, again." The woman swung around brandishing a tire iron. Casey couldn't react fast enough to get out of the way. Pain flashed through her skull and a rainbow of colors filled her vision. On the ground, dazed, struggling to stand, she heard the woman scream. "That's what you get for meddlin'!"

Casey reached for her cell phone that she'd dropped on the asphalt. Dizzy, she had to squint to make out the numbers on the keypad. Blood dripped onto her hand. The car backed out and almost ran over her. The voice of the dispatcher answered, "This is 911. What is your emergency?" The car sped away.

Her head swam as she staggered to her feet. Tires squealed. The beat-up car was headed toward the exit, then it turned and was bearing down at her. "Help!" A searing pain flashed through her body as she rolled across the hood of a car, and darkness swallowed her.

CHAPTER FORTY-FIVE—DANIEL

Daniel waited in Johnson Insurance Company's reception area and concentrated on controlling his breathing. Walter Johnson, owner of the agency, was also the president of the YMCA's board of directors. Last week, the entire board had interviewed candidates in their search for the new YMCA director. Daniel had been called back for a second interview today. This must be a good sign. He wiped his damp palms on his navy slacks.

Daniel's phone vibrated in his pocket. He started to ignore it, but he couldn't resist a quick glance. It was Emma.

Daniel accepted the call and spoke in a hushed voice. "Emma, I can't—"

"Casey's hurt." Her voice sounded frantic.

Daniel's gut twisted. "What happened?"

I don't know exactly. It's crazy ..." She talked so fast Daniel couldn't understand her.

"Slow down. Breathe," He said in his cop voice. "Where are you?"

"I'm at the Walmart parking lot in Bowling Green. We were on the way to the Sunbelt Conference. I have Callie and Hallie. The police arrested their mother. I'm waiting for the social worker."

"But what about Casey? You said Casey is hurt."

"The twins' mother. She attacked her ..." Emma wailed.

"How bad is Casey hurt?"

"It's bad. She ran over her with her car."

"Oh, my Lord." Daniel's whispered. His mouth went dry.

"The ambulance is taking Casey to the Medical Center."

"I'm on my way." Daniel strode to the gray-haired receptionist. "I've got an emergency. I need to go."

The chubby receptionist opened her mouth, but Daniel turned on his heel and ran to the door.

Thirty minutes later, Daniel ran into the emergency room and made a beeline for the receptionist. "I'm here to check on Casey Bledsoe. Cassandra Bledsoe."

The woman in pink scrubs pecked on a keyboard and looked at him over her black-framed glasses. "Are you a family member?"

"No. But ..."

Two double doors opened, and Frank and Jolene exited. Red stains that looked like blood covered Jolene's sweatshirt. Daniel could hardly breathe and his knees almost buckled.

Jolene rushed to him. "Casey's just leaving."

Daniel breathed out a sigh of relief. "Thank God. I thought ... Emma said it was bad." His voice broke.

Frank's green eyes, the same shade as Casey's, filled with tears. "A Life Flight chopper is flying her to a trauma center in Nashville for an emergency surgery. Can you drive us there?" Frank's hands shook as he ran his head over his bald head. "I'm not in a fit state to be behind the wheel."

"Let's go." Daniel looped his arm through Jolene's elbow. "You can tell me what happened on the way."

Daniel's hand trembled at he started the truck. He inhaled deeply. *Calm yourself.* The whirl of the helicopter made him look up. He shielded his eyes against the setting sun as the helicopter lifted in the air. He just stared at it until he could no longer see it. The most important person on this earth was slipping away. He'd been such a fool. *I'm sorry. Father, save her.*

CHAPTER FORTY-SIX—CASEY

Casey drifted through warm waters. The whirling noise confused her until she considered perhaps it was the sound of angels' wings. Blinking, she stared into the dark eyes of a stranger. "Hang on!" he shouted over the roar. "We'll land in two minutes. A surgical team is waiting."

The floating sensation filled her with peace, and she knew she was in a place between life and death. The smell of engine fumes pulled her back to earth and reminded her of the ferry in Africa.

The helicopter landed with a thud, causing pain to course through her body, and she felt the fog of darkness close in around her. She pictured Madison's sweet face. Oh, how she wanted desperately to look into her daughter's gray eyes. Jansen's eyes. *I forgive him for everything.* Then she closed her eyes and let go.

Casey's skin burned, and her vision blurred as heat waves shimmered across the sand. As she lay on the ground, she recognized the leaves of the familiar scenery. But instead of the expected thorn tree, it was an enormous baobab tree. The backpack under her head felt like rocks.

In the distance, someone was walking toward her, and she lifted her hand to her brow to shield the harsh sunlight. The stranger wore a brilliant white tunic, but she couldn't make out his face. The air stilled and grew cooler. Her eyelids grew heavy, and she lay back down on the backpack. Her head ached the worst, but every cell in her body throbbed. *Oh no. This must be hell.*

Casey awoke to the smell of wood smoke, and she squinted. Crouched in front of her, the man in the tunic tended a fire. His gentle voice soothed her. "Well done, daughter."

When she struggled to sit up, he said, "Rest."

Peace filled her being, and she closed her eyes. "You've faced difficult choices. Not one sacrifice, not one tear, not one prayer went unnoticed."

A cocoon of love enveloped her. *Who is this man? Where am I?*

He lifted her hand and rubbed her thumb on his wrists.

"Feel the place where they pierced my skin."

Her finger touched the hole at his wrist, and she gasped. "It can't be."

Pain flowed from her body as a breeze wafted over her. The leaves of the baobob tree rustled overhead. In the light of the campfire, his face was filled with tenderness.

"Which do you think is more painful? To witness your child being tortured or to watch your child brutalize someone?" Tears stained his cheeks. "I suffered much for you and for him."

Casey gasped. "You were there."

He touched her cheek. "He lives in darkness and has never known love, but you can lead him to the light if you choose."

"You know how evil he is?"

"I turned his wicked deed to good."

"How so?"

"She has his eyes, but your heart."

Casey visualized Madison's beautiful smile and eyes, and he placed his palm on her cheek. "Rest." Then it felt like a blanket of love covered her, and every muscle in her body relaxed, and she slept.

Voices floated in and out of Casey's dreams. At one point, she thought she heard Daniel's voice. "I love you. Don't leave me."

Her dad shouted, "Don't you dare give up!"

"Frank, you're scaring me," her mother cried.

Sometimes she could hear a stranger's voice with an accent, and it reminded her of Isaaca's dialect. *How did I get to Africa again?*

Emma's soft voice whispered in her ear. "Callie and Hallie are safe. Open your eyes, Casey."

Then a girl's soft voice with a strong southern accent spoke in her ear. "Don't give up. I'm here. I've waited all my life to meet you. Please wake up."

Thoughts ran through Casey's head. The dilapidated car, the screech of tires, the screaming, her mom and dad standing over her. And she opened her eyes to see the gray tear-filled eyes that used to give her night terrors but lately filled her dreams, Casey tried to smile and started to speak, but her voice came out scratchy, and her throat hurt like the dickens.

She croaked, "Water."

Madison hit the call button. "She's awake. She's asking for water."

Within seconds, a nurse stood over her with a cup and straw. "I'm Jenny. How do you feel?"

Casey sipped the cool water. "I hurt all over." She winced.

Casey's parents and Madison hovered above her.

"That's understandable." Jenny held out the straw again. "Your body took a hard hit." She placed the cup on the narrow table over the bed. "I'll give the family five minutes, and then all but two need to clear the room."

Casey attempted to gather her thoughts as she stared at Madison. "I'm sorry." Her voice sounded rusty.

"Don't be," Madison's face softened.

"We sent Daniel to her school. He tracked down the coach and found Madison." Frank tilted his head toward Madison.

Casey drank in the sight of her. "I let you down again."

"No. You're a hero." Madison squeezed Casey's hand.

She remembered seeing Hallie and Callie in the car, and she whispered, "Hallie and Callie, are they okay?"

"Emma's been told they're in a safe place." Jolene placed her palm on Casey's cheek.

"Who would have imagined someone running you down like that?" Frank shook his head. "I stood there frozen, not believing what I was seeing."

"Her eyes were wild," Casey said. "She must have been on drugs or some sort of hallucinogen."

"The police pulled into the parking lot within seconds after she hit you," Frank gulped.

"Poor Hallie and Callie are probably traumatized." Casey tried to sit up, but pain shot through her side. "What's broken?"

"Three ribs, plus your right shoulder's rotator cuff is torn and still needs surgery." Frank gulped. "The windshield cut an artery in your arm, and you have a concussion."

Jolene stroked Casey's cheek. "You almost bled to death. One of the policemen used my scarf to make a tourniquet."

The nurse smiled. "I've called Dr. Mwagi. He's on his way."

"I need an aspirin." Casey touched her throbbing temple.

"The attending physician will prescribe something to help manage the pain." The nurse held the door open.

Casey chewed her lip, as she studied Madison. *Is this real? It seems like a dream.*

Jolene stood on the opposite side of the bed from Madison and smoothed Casey's hair. "Everyone is praying for you."

"Did I hear Daniel talking?" Casey asked.

"He's in the waiting room."

She tried to sit up again but couldn't. "Please, go get him."

"I'll be right back," Frank turned.

A tall black man walked in. "I've been looking forward to meeting my beautiful patient. I'm Dr. Mwagi."

The nurse spoke. "Let's give the attending physician a few minutes with his patient." She held her hand out and beckoned them.

Casey didn't want to let go of Madison's hand, and she tightened her grip.

"I'll be in the waiting room," Madison pulled her hand away. "I won't leave." Then she brushed her lips on Casey's forehead.

Tears rolled down Casey's cheeks.

"Are you in pain?" The doctor's face held concern.

"Somewhat, but—"

"On a scale of one to ten?"

"About a six, but that's not why I'm crying," Casey whispered.

"You've been through a trauma, but you're going to heal."

"I remember hearing you speak in my dreams and thought I'd returned to Africa."

"My home country is Kenya, but I attended medical school in the US."

"That explains some of my crazy dreams."

"Dreams are a good sign. The brain is working."

Casey yawned. "May I have something to eat?"

"I'll have the nurse call Dietary Services, but first, I'd like to ask you a few questions."

After he asked her what seemed like a thousand questions, she closed her eyes.

"Ms. Bledsoe, your food is here," Nurse Jenny said.

The doctor's voice drifted over her. "She needs her rest more than the nourishment."

Casey fell into dreams of Madison and Daniel. *If he really waited for me to wake up, maybe there's hope.*

CHAPTER FORTY-SEVEN—DANIEL

The next day, Daniel stood and watched Casey's chest rise and fall while she slept. Frank had convinced Jolene to let him take her home for a shower and fresh clothes. Daniel had promised to remain by Casey's side.

Casey's face was swollen and bruised. A large bandage, very similar to the one he'd sported after brain surgery, covered her head. When her emerald eyes opened and stared at him, his relief was so great his head swam.

Daniel brushed his lips to her forehead. *Thank you, Jesus. Thank you. Thank you.*

When he could finally speak, he said. "I've been a fool. Please forgive me."

"I already did." Casey's voice was scratchy. "I hope you'll forgive me too."

"We both made mistakes, but I betrayed you. I should have waited. I should have trusted you."

Casey gave him a sad smile.

"I love you with all my heart." His voice sounded husky. "I've loved you from that first night in the diner."

Casey's eyes filled with tears. "But is love enough?"

Daniel stared at her while his heartbeat slowed. "No. There has to be trust." He swallowed the lump in his throat. "I'll never be worthy of your love, but maybe someday, with enough time, you'll be able trust me again." He kissed her cheek as her eyes closed.

A week later, Daniel sat across the desk from Walter Johnson at the Johnson Insurance Agency. Mr. Johnson's tweed suit with elbow patches reminded Daniel of his dad. The paneled wall behind his desk was covered with plaques of recognition for sales awards, and volunteerism. Mr. Johnson's gray hair was styled in a fashion like Johnny Cash. He clasped his hands together and leaned forward. "I've been on the YMCA board for four years, and I've noticed how many volunteer hours you put in at the Y."

Daniel smiled. "I like working with the kids."

"I was beginning to think we'd have to offer the director of the YMCA position to our second favorite candidate."

Daniel's pulse rate increased. He sat ramrod straight in his chair. "Yes, sir. I'm surprised you didn't."

Mr. Johnson smiled kindly. "We knew something terrible must have happened for you to leave."

"Someone I love needed me." Daniel's gulped at the memory of receiving the call from Emma.

Mr. Johnson removed gold wire-rimmed glasses. "I understand Ms. Bledsoe should make a complete recovery."

"Yes, sir. She's scheduled to be released from the hospital today."

"That's good news." Mr. Johnson leaned back in his chair. "We have a few details to go over."

"Yes, sir."

As Mr. Johnson reviewed the benefits package that went along with the job offer, Daniel's thoughts wandered. He glanced at his watch. Casey would be home soon.

When Mr. Johnson stopped talking, Daniel stared at him. "Do you need more time to think about it?"

Daniel smiled. "No, sir. I'd like to accept the position."

Mr. Johnson stood and extended his hand. "Congratulations."

"Thank you. I'll do my best."

"That's good to hear. I think you'll be a great director."

Daniel loosened his tie as he exited the building. He couldn't wait to share this news with Casey. He hoped she'd give him a second chance to prove to her how much he loved her. He was willing to do whatever it took, wait as long as she needed, if she would just give him a second chance.

CHAPTER FORTY-EIGHT—CASEY

Jolene fussed as she drove Casey home. "But I think it will be better for you to come to my house."

"I'm going home." Casey smiled as they passed the *Welcome to Weldon* sign.

"But I have four empty bedrooms. I can take care of you."

"It's going to take weeks for me to recuperate, and I'll feel more comfortable in my own bed."

"How are you going to do that with your arm in a sling?"

"With practice. If Daniel can do it, I can too."

"But you don't have to."

"I know. But I'm beginning to understand a little bit about Daniel's stubbornness. What if my shoulder doesn't heal? I can't have you hovering over me taking care of me for the rest of my life."

"But the doctors think you'll heal just fine with therapy."

"What if it doesn't?"

"You're making me worry."

She stared at her white bungalow. "I'm home." Casey had thought Daniel would be here. Her shoulders dropped. He'd been by the hospital every day. Where could he be?

An hour later, she was settled, with pillows fluffed behind her on the sofa and Fats cuddled in her lap.

Jolene sat across from her and stared. "I'm going to sit with you for a while."

"Mom, you look worn out."

"I can rest here. Few things give me more pleasure than watching you sleep."

She smiled. Since spending time with Madison last week, she realized she could stare at her daughter forever too and never tire of it. Recalling the tortuous task of telling Madison about Jansen made her heart crumble. But Jennifer and Bill Warren had sat beside their daughter while Casey shared everything. Madison's face had lost its color under the fluorescent hospital room light, and she hyperventilated, just like her grandmother Jolene. Of all the things to inherit. But later, she gently hugged Casey and thanked her for telling her the truth. "Now I don't have to imagine the worst, and I can deal with it."

Casey marveled at the strength of her daughter. Where had that come from? Maybe from Granny. She was the one who lost a child to influenza and watched her home burn to the ground. *In everything give thanks*, she'd say.

On that thought, Casey drifted to sleep on the sofa. Hours later, Casey awoke to find Daniel watching her. He leaned forward and rested his elbows on his knees. His green long-sleeved thermal shirt stretched across his muscled biceps. "Sleeping beauty is awake."

Casey yawned and touched her butchered hair. "Some beauty. When did you get here?"

"A long time ago. I convinced your mom to go home and take a nap."

"That's good. I tried to get her to leave before I went to sleep." Casey struggled to sit up.

"Let me help you." Daniel stood and reached for her good arm. "Where are we going?"

Casey giggled. "I was just shifting to make room for you to sit next to me."

"Oh." Daniel moved a pillow. "That sounds nice." He wrapped his arm around her shoulder and Casey snuggled into his chest.

"Dot's delivering supper in a bit, and your parents will be by to eat with us." Daniel rested his chin on her head.

"That's sweet. Do you think there will be fried peach pies?"

"Highly likely, and if not, I'll figure out a way to get some for you."

"That's not necessary. It's a blessing to be here with you. To be home."

"It is." Daniel sighed. "I'm sorry I wasn't here when you got here, but the interview took longer than I anticipated."

Casey lifted her head. "What interview?"

Daniel gulped. "When Emma called me about your accident, I was waiting for my second interview to be the new YMCA director."

"Oh, no. Talk about bad timing."

He shrugged. "It doesn't matter. I figured they'd moved on to the other candidates, but I was wrong. Virginia Willoughby called me a couple of days ago and set up the second interview with Mr. Johnson."

"How did it go?"

He smiled. "I got the job."

"That's wonderful. Congratulations."

"Thanks, but I'd already decided that if they didn't offer me the job, things would work out."

Casey studied him. "That doesn't sound like the Daniel I know and love."

Daniel bit his lip. "I'm not really the same guy."

"What's changed?" Casey shifted and stared into his dark eyes drinking him in and her heartbeat increased.

Daniels eyes filled with tears. "Sitting in my truck, watching the helicopter carrying you away made me realize that nothing in my life mattered without you in it. I was a fool. I prayed and bargained with God for days while you slept in the hospital.

"Oh, Daniel." Casey touched his cheek.

"I'm ashamed to admit it took almost losing you for me to completely surrender to God." Daniel swallowed hard. "My body was damaged by the tumor and the surgery, but my spirit was wounded by pride, anger, jealousy, and ..."

Daniel sat up straight and looked her in the eye. "I felt unworthy of you. I still do. You're rich, and I have a mountain of debt, but I know that's not important. My brain knows that, but my heart is still trying to catch up."

"Money has never been important to me other than it allows me to bless others."

"I know, but I've struggled financially for a long time. I'm trying to deal with my pride." Daniel kissed her hand. "Whatever happens, I'm going to try to trust God and hope and pray that someday, you'll learn to trust me as well as love me."

Casey's brows furrowed. "We both kept secrets. I want us to make a fresh start, but I need time to ..." Her voice faded.

Daniel stared at the floor. "I understand."

Casey snuggled into his shoulder. "Let's start with enjoying this night, and just appreciate being together."

"You got it darlin'." Daniel kissed the top of her head again.

CHAPTER FORTY-NINE—CASEY

Casey sat at her kitchen island and read the headline: "Jansen Moore Arrested." As she expected, the paparazzi were camped out in front of her home, but they would eventually tire of her silence. She had nothing to say until the trial.

Of course, Jansen had made bail, and months would go by before he faced a jury, but a weight rolled from her shoulders. Below his picture, a row of seventeen faces filled the page including her own. *Lord, help us.*

As she looked at his cold gray eyes, she felt pity. *Why would I feel sorry for him?* Fragments of her dream floated around the corners of her memory. She felt like there was something she was supposed to do, but what? What else was there to do? *He lives in darkness and has never known love, but you can lead him to the light if you choose.* Casey chewed her nail as she remembered the dream. It seemed real. How was she supposed to lead Jansen to the light?

On Easter Sunday morning, Casey stood with Daniel and her parents in the churchyard. The first rays of pink hues lit the sky. Luke stood in front of his new congregation and read the story of the empty tomb from the book of John, Chapter 20. "Early on the first day of the week, while it was still dark, Mary Magdalene went to the tomb and saw that the stone had been removed from the entrance ..."

After reading the entire chapter, Luke closed the brief service with a thanksgiving prayer.

More than one stomach rumbled in the quiet, chilly morning, and mere seconds after Luke said, "Amen," the small gathering of people broke up. Most headed off for breakfast at the Waffle House.

"Let's go." Casey tugged on Daniel's arm. "I'm cold, and I need to help Mama with breakfast before everyone gets there.

"Can you walk with me for a minute?" Daniel asked her. "After all we've been through these past months, just being able to stand with you and hold your hand while a new day is being born is special. It reminds me of our first morning in Africa together."

"Of course, I'll walk with you. The blinding sunlight reminded me of a dream I had when I was unconscious. You're going to think I'm crazy, but I dreamed Jesus visited me."

"When I consider how close we came to losing you, it doesn't sound strange at all."

"It seemed real."

"While you dreamed, we endured a nightmare."

She squeezed his hand. "I'm sorry. I remember being overwhelmed by fear during your surgery."

Daniel wrapped his arm around her. "Tell me about your dream."

"I was alone again, in the desert, hurt and broken, and I wanted to give up."

"I'm glad you didn't."

"I remember seeing a man in a brilliant white robe walking toward me, and I felt loved and a sense of peace."

"He's always with us."

"You're right. He told me he suffered much for me and for Jansen."

Daniel nodded.

"I began to feel pity for Jansen."

Daniel opened the gate to a small, enclosed area. "That must have been some dream."

"Thanks for not laughing at me."

"I'd never do that."

Red tulips waved a welcome in the breeze.

"I had no idea the flowers were blooming back here." Casey wiped her nose with a tissue.

"Let's sit here and enjoy them," Daniel said.

"There's room for two." She lowered herself onto the petite bench and scooted to the side.

In one swift motion, Daniel bent down on one knee and reached for her left hand. The heat from his breath warmed her cold fingertips.

Afraid to breathe, she sat motionless, anxious something might make this moment dissipate. The birds serenaded them, and the morning breeze ruffled her hair.

Daniel's eyes watered. "Will you marry me?"

Her eyes brimmed with tears. "I will love and cherish you for the rest of my life, and then for eternity."

"Is that a yes?"

"It's a maybe."

"What?"

"We're not ready for marriage."

"But I thought we were ready."

"Will you agree to go to couple's counseling first?"

"Why?"

"I believe you'll love me, forever, in sickness and in health, for richer or poorer, but I want to be sure you trust me to do the same."

"I'm working on my pride."

"That's not good enough. I want to be able to trust you, with everything."

Daniel looked away. "Are you saying you don't trust me?"

She touched his chin with her fingers and turned his face back to her. "Like you, I'm working on it."

"Okay, but how long do we go to counseling?"

"I don't know. As long as it takes." She slid from the bench onto her knees and felt the dew soak through her slacks as she fell into Daniel's embrace.

He cupped her chin up and kissed her, causing her to lose all ability to think clearly. Daniel dug into his pocket and pulled out a faded blue velvet box. "In the meantime, will you wear my ring?"

Casey nodded.

"May I see your left hand?"

After she held up her hand, he slid the diamond ring onto her fourth finger.

"I love you, Casey Bledsoe."

"I love you back."

Daniel wrapped his arms around her again and leaned in for another kiss. The heat from his body warmed her as she relaxed and experienced a floating sensation. *Is this real, or a dream?*

Happy but chilled to the bone, the couple walked into

the back door of Casey's parents' home as Jolene removed a breakfast casserole from the oven. When she saw them, she dropped the hot dish onto the counter. "Let me see!"

Frank slapped Daniel on the back. "Welcome to the family."

"It's beautiful," Jolene said. "Let's have a celebration breakfast and get back to the church for the eleven o'clock Easter service. I can't wait for everyone to see your ring."

Casey hugged her mom. "We're going to take this slow."

Jolene planted her hands on her hips. "A pair of snails could outpace you two."

"Maybe," Casey said, "But we're going to enjoy each slow step together."

Casey wasn't surprised to see all her brothers and their families show up for the Easter service. She hardly listened to the church's sound system playing "Glorious Day" by Casting Crowns because the sparkling ring on her left hand mesmerized her. The diamond created miniature rainbows as she shifted her hand in the light. The vintage marquis and baguette diamond engagement ring had been his mother's and fit perfectly on her long finger.

Then Jolene elbowed her, and she pointed to the end of the pew, toward the aisle. Jennifer and Bill Warren stood at the end of the pew. The beams of sunlight through the frosted glass seemed to create a halo around Madison's bright russet hair.

Casey gasped, "Madison," and her daughter stepped into her embrace as if it was the most natural thing in the world, and they clung to each other.

"Finally, someone I don't have to stoop down to hug,"

Madison spoke into Casey's ear. Casey closed her eyes and savored this one perfect moment in her life, with those she loved most surrounding her. With a sniff, she inhaled and smelled the familiar scent of the Gold Treatment.

Madison whispered, "Grannie Jo thought it would be fun to surprise you."

Jennifer and Bill Warren stood behind Madison, and Jennifer gave Casey a wink and said, "Surprise!" in a sing-song voice.

Tears rolled down her cheeks as she listened to the final notes of "Glorious Day." It really was a glorious day and a glorious life. *Thank you, Jesus.*

EPILOGUE—ONE YEAR LATER

Casey inhaled the scent of bleach as she stared through the glass security window. The concrete-block walls were painted the same shade as Jansen's dull gray eyes. Casey shuddered.

Jansen's dark hair was streaked with gray and needed a trim. "I suppose you came to gloat," he sneered. His orange jumpsuit seemed to glow under the fluorescent lighting.

"No." Casey lifted her chin and spoke into the microphone.

Jansen glared. "You had no right to keep my daughter from me."

"Monsters don't have rights." Her voice sounded stronger than she felt.

"I wish I'd killed you."

"Then you'd have no hope."

"What kind of hope can you offer?"

"The only kind that can save."

Jansen frowned. "You're crazy, you stupid—"

"I came to tell you I forgive you." Casey fingered her African bracelet.

"I don't need your forgiveness."

"But I need to offer it."

"Forget this." He stood. "I don't know why I came."

She met his cold stare. "God loves you."

His face blanched.

"The guard will deliver a package to you," Casey arched her brow. "It's a Bible."

Jansen's lip curled into a snarl. "Why would you give me a Bible?"

"To give you hope for a better future."

"I have no future, thanks to you."

"We all have a future. It's not too late to make a decision that will determine where you'll spend eternity." Casey stood and met his steely gaze. "Even here, every day can be filled with hope."

Jansen's mouth hung open and his shoulders slumped. "There is no hope in this place."

"You're wrong. Read the Bible. Go to the chapel here. Pray for yourself ... and your daughter."

Jansen stared at her, and then his face seemed to soften. "She has my eyes."

Casey did something she thought she'd never do. She gave him a genuine smile. "But she has my heart." Casey's eyes brimmed with tears. "Goodbye, Jansen. I'll remember you in my prayers." She turned on her heel.

Feeling nothing but pity for the evil man behind bars, she marveled at the lightness of her spirit. *I've done what Jesus asked me to do*. "God, help him," she whispered, then started humming "Glorious Day" as she returned to the reception area where Daniel waited. Casey walked into his open arms and leaned into his strength. It was a glorious day filled with hope.

The End

ABOUT THE AUTHOR

Shelia Stovall is the director of a small-town library in southern Kentucky, where only strangers mention her last name, and the children call her Miss Shelia.

It tickles her to see shocked expressions when folks learn she's traveling to Africa—again. She's the worst missionary ever, but God continues to send her to the ends of the earth as He attempts to mold her into something useful.

Shelia and her husband Michael live on a farm, and she enjoys taking daily rambles to the creek with their two dogs. Spending time with family, especially her grandchildren, is her all-time favorite thing. The only hobby Shelia loves more than reading uplifting stories of hope is writing them.

If you enjoyed *Every Day Filled with Hope*, you will want to read the novel that began the series, *Every Window Filled with Light. https://amzn.to/3tDSfVw*

If you will write a short review and post on Amazon and your social media, Shelia will be most grateful.

Made in the USA
Monee, IL
26 September 2022

14397553R10216